EARTH 2

In the Beginning

The End

Anthony Dugmore

EARTH 2

In The Beginning. The End

Anthony Dugmore

Published by 1st World Library
P.O. Box 2211 Fairfield, Iowa 52556
tel: 641-209-5000 • fax: 866-440 5234
web: www.1stworldpublishing.com

First Edition

LCCN: 2009934645
SoftCover ISBN: 978-1-4218-9109-5
HardCover ISBN: 978-1-4218-9108-8
eBook ISBN: 978-1-4218-9110-1

CONTENTS

Prologue.	Life on Earth	7
Chapter 1.	Selected by Fate?	13
Chapter 2.	The Journey	61
Chapter 3.	The Gathering	91
Chapter 4.	Life Goes On	129
Chapter 5.	Damage Control	163
Chapter 6.	Total Shutdown	191
Chapter 7.	A Surprising Discovery	255
Chapter 8.	Unforeseen Problems	305
Chapter 9.	Journey to Jumla Junction	353
Chapter 10.	Is There Anyone Out There	399

PROLOGUE
LIFE ON EARTH

Imagine earth teeming with a population of over thirty billion—a world where nobody lives on the surface any more.

The year is 2546; the population on earth has grown so vast, civilisation totters on the brink of collapse. With no wars, famine, disease, or birth control, the population has grown quickly and is expected to exceed sixty billion within the next thirty-five years.

A world treaty signed in 2254 joined all the countries on earth together as a single nation and created "Mother Earth". The planet was divided into three supercontinents: Eurasia, the Americas, and Africa. The treaty removed all borders, turning countries into provinces, and removed restrictions on the movement of populations. This allowed people to migrate, and new cities were built wherever space could be found.

Over the past three hundred years these continents have developed peacefully, sharing resources and technology, and evolving into highly technological societies. A new universal language has developed, mainly by consensus with the general population and by some media intervention. Now only one language is spoken by all, the "Mother Tongue", or "Mummer", as most people call it.

With all emphasis centred on improving living standards for everyone on earth, there has been no investment in space research. No one has looked to the stars for over two hundred years, and space exploration ceased when no material benefit could be gained. All resources were needed for the ever-increasing population.

As the population increased the need for food became a major issue. Land for food and land for occupation came into conflict. Cities were built in unsuitable locations not fit for farming, and this, coupled with the lack of planning control, gave cause for concern, especially when disasters started to occur.

In an effort to overcome the problem a few cities were designed and built completely underground. People were invited to live in these new cities, and with many benefits on offer, filling them proved easy. Developers gained valuable knowledge from these prototype cities and further cities soon followed.

By 2350 underground city building was in full swing, and by 2457 no one lived on the surface. It was not all by choice; the last to be housed underground were moved by force, with much bloodshed and many years of unrest following.

Today, in 2546, the main transportation system uses an underground network of pipes and tubes. Pipes provide local transportation and tubes intercontinental connections. These were developed to move resources to new locations when the cities first moved underground. Shuttles operate in this network using magnetic levitation (maglev) for propulsion, and the whole system is fully automated.

The main role of the system is for food supply, with resource and personnel transportation as secondary functions. The latter is restricted to transportation of essential personnel, as space is limited and costs prohibitively high.

It has been almost a hundred years since the last surface city was vacated, and as the cities moved underground vast farms replaced them. Now, the only buildings on the surface are Food Processing Delivery Stations and city tower blocks. Beneath each tower is a city capable of housing and employing up to ten million people. The cities are almost self-contained; food, which comes directly from the Food Processing Stations, is the one exception.

Although the towers are far apart, most cities are within a few metres of each other underground—a fact unknown to most inhabitants. No two cities can see each other, as the land is sculptured to prevent it happening.

The Food Processing Plants are the hubs of all farming, and every aspect of farming is controlled from these surface stations.

All children are provided with a personal communicator as soon as they are old enough to venture outside the home unsupervised. It allows communications with the children and acts as a locator so the parents know exactly where they are. If a child takes his or her communicator off, security rushes to the location to investigate and deal with the situation as necessary. By the time children become adults, wearing the personal communicator is natural and they feel naked without it, which conveniently provides security with every person's location. That fact, plus their DNA profile from birth, makes crime solving very easy.

Children are given a digital companion at the age of eleven to help them through schooling. It also acts as a best friend and surrogate guardian. This companion stays with the children for the rest of their lives, growing as they grow. This companion can be every parent's nightmare, as they sometimes give conflicting advice to the child, while at the same time act as a guardian and offer restraint. The companion must advise a course of action pertaining to the child's vocation, irrespective of the parent's upbringing or grade.

Students are awarded grades according to their academic achievement on completion of college. Personal and practical attributes are also taken into consideration when grading, but not background or upbringing. From this point in their lives, it's not what they do, but what grade they are that matters. The highest is grade one, "The President of Earth", and the lowest is grade thirty.

Society is democratic to a certain point; representatives are elected to speak for citizens at all grades and these representatives are called councillors. The many levels of councillors form a pyramid hierarchy, topped by a city mayor. Councillors have their grades increased and enjoy a better standard of life. Security can remove a councillor from office if there is a breach of the peace or if a crime is committed. Councillors have very little real power, but they do have access to city operations for forwarding complaints and retrieving replies or reasons for grievances. When things do go wrong, councillors have to get things sorted out quickly. The citizens' tolerance is low when things go badly wrong, and councillors have been killed by rioting mobs on more than one occasion.

Small shuttles are the main mode of transport for the masses and operate on all levels except in the tower. Elevators move people from one level to the next, but restrictions on movement due to grade can be an issue. Anyone caught in an out-of-bounds area is punished in some way or other. Elevators go from the very deepest level to the top of the city tower block.

Triron, a man-made element which is one thousand times stronger than iron, was developed using a method called Molecular Reconstruction. Molecular Reconstruction is the name given to a process discovered many years ago, where complex machines were created to alter the atomic structure of elements and change their properties. The first metal was Triron, then came Quadron, almost ten thousand times stronger than iron. The making of the latter was banned decades ago; it required too much energy to produce. Tritanium is the strongest metal, but again is only permitted when necessary due to energy restrictions.

Research and development are carried out at various locations all over the planet. They are usually deep within the highest mountain ranges for safety and security. The main research centre is in the Himalayan Mountains and oversees all other research centres. In the Himalayan Research Centre, scientists and engineers have developed new farming methods employing genetically modified animals and crops, while other centres have concentrated on reducing energy consumption. These centres are home to the best brains on earth, and as these experts are so engrossed in their work, it usually means the birth rate is very low. Children are not drafted unless it's for research, but can accompany their parents to the centres. Personnel are drafted in to perform specific tasks determined by each individual project, though some staff move from one project directly to another and never leave the centre.

Each research centre has immense power-generating capabilities to enable it to perform any task required, which means there is usually an excess to supply the Global Grid. Likewise, if extra power is needed for developing specific products the centre draws on all the cities' power units during quiet periods. The research centres are more technologically advanced than the cities for one reason only; there's not enough power to implement all new developments and discoveries. All new developments are implemented using small-scale production and equip research centres only. For the past two hundred years obsolete equipment has been stored in the Himalayan and other research centres collecting dust. They are only scrapped if their resources are required for new products. Newly-appointed scientists enjoy going through the archives to see what's been stored, just for fun. They also relieve boredom during quiet periods by upgrading the archived equipment operating systems to meet current standards.

At this moment in time the research centres are looking for young recruits to join specific projects. Colleges have finished for some, and the invitations have already been sent out.

CHAPTER 1
SELECTED BY FATE?

John was excited as it was Friday, July 22, his exam results day, and the day that would determine how the rest of his life would progress. At eighteen his education was complete, and he hoped to make the grade to secure a good job. He didn't know if he had done enough to get what he wanted, though he'd certainly tried hard enough, and would soon find out.

Just for the moment he didn't have a care in the world. It was lunchtime and he was sitting on a sun bed looking out from the balcony on the tenth floor of the Bagman City Tower. His chin rested on his arms, which were folded flat on the cold metal parapet, steadying his gaze. And what a view; lush, green fields of grass swayed in a gentle breeze as far as the eye could see in all directions. The sky was clear blue, broken only by small, thin, wispy clouds, and the sun was warming him through. Far off to one side he could make out the sea. It was just visible through a slight haze, the sun glistening on its surface, sending shards of rainbow-coloured light darting in all directions. He thought it was the most beautiful sight he'd ever seen.

There was just one low building in sight, and its colour almost blended into the landscape. He assumed it was a food processing plant, poised on the horizon, with flying vehicles of all shapes and sizes buzzing like flies to and from it. His eyes drifted downward as he caught some movement out of the corner of his eye. He could see motorised farm hands rounding up cows on a nearby hillside. A mobile corral came floating over from the direction of the far-off building and hovered for a moment before closing in on the herd. In total silence it landed near the animals and both ends of the corral opened simultaneously. The fully-grown cattle were ushered towards the far side and began climbing the ramp into the corral, while young stock emerged from the near end. As soon as the tiny animals reached the bottom of the ramp they began feeding as they spread out in a line.

A "Roll-On, Roll-Off, Mobile Corral". He'd heard of them and seen videos of them in training, but had never actually seen one before today, and it amused him. He smiled and continued to watch the flawless process. It didn't take long to herd the cows into the corral and the ramps at both ends to rise and shut, before it lifted and shot off towards the processing plant. The motorised farm hands quickly moved from one task to the next, herding the youngsters into a feeding line, where they would remain for the rest of their short lives.

The whole thing was over in under an hour and soon there was nothing to watch but a line of slow-moving calves and the grass gently swaying in the light breeze in front of them. The grass, he knew, had been developed to grow fast; it needed to be, as it was grazed both day and night. The cattle were genetically modified to eat continuously; even if they slept, they walked and slept eating.

From his education he knew a little of just about everything, which is why he understood most of what was happening out there on the plain below.

He looked directly down the side of the tower and marvelled at how smooth it was. The reddish colour of the Triron tower looked out of place surrounded by all the greenery, and its surface was as shiny as glass. It glistened in the sunshine, and the reflected light gave everything around him a slight reddish tinge. As he looked up, the top seemed to blend with the sky and made it look as if it went on forever. For a brief moment he wondered what it was like at the top and made a mental note to find out more information about it. His chances of reaching the top were just about zero, as his grade wouldn't be high enough to get permission, not by a long shot. He looked from left to right to see what else could be seen, and was disappointed. The building curved back in both directions, making it difficult to judge how wide it really was, and the balcony was too small to make a difference to the view. His gaze soon drifted back to the plains below, and it wasn't long before he was his happy, smiling self once again.

As he watched the young cows finding their feet, a security guard came over to check his authority to be on the balcony. If his authority didn't allow him access to the surface, he'd be arrested on the spot and escorted to the security centre far below. Luckily for him his education involved coming to the surface from time to time, and his request for one last visit had been granted. He offered his personal communicator to the officer to be scanned and watched as her face softened. His authority was in order and the guard wished him a good day before departing. This was his last day at college and he had to hand his communicator in before 4:00 p.m. to be reprogrammed. This could also be the last time he might see the surface, so he was making the most of what little time he had left.

Almost ten million people lived below his feet, just under the surface, not visible from above. Outside the tower it looked deserted (except for the cattle and farm hands), but where he lived in the lower levels it was cramped and overcrowded. It was so crowded it was often difficult to move about, and if everyone came onto the streets at the same time, nobody could move or breathe even. And there was the strange smell that got stronger the lower down in the city you ventured. Antibacterial agents were circulated by the air conditioning system to counteract the stench, which had built up over many years. Still, after some time living with it, you got used to the odour. He thought about how much he would miss the fresh air, but the thing he would miss most when he returned below was the quietness. Where he was at that moment he believed he could hear the grass as it moved back and forth with the gentle breeze blowing over the land. Down in the city, there was the constant drum of machinery coming from deep within, twenty-four hours a day. And then there was the noise of all those people to contend with, day and night.

Soon it was time for him to leave the surface and return to the college, and as things stood at that moment, both seemed to be for the last time. Picking up the few belongings he had from his sun bed, he took one last look at the outside world, then headed towards the balcony doors to find an elevator. As he walked to the end of the balcony, he couldn't remember where the doors actually were. He kept walking right to the end, until what looked like a solid wall opened before him, revealing the doorway and he quickly entered the building. Walking briskly over to the nearest elevator, he stood before its entrance and waited for a few seconds for it to ascend from below. As soon as it arrived, the doors opened and he stepped inside. The elevator was quite small, only meant for ten people at a time, and he stood at the rear, leaning against the wall. Lower down in the city the elevators were much bigger, large enough to hold hundreds of people. Speaking clearly, but quietly, he requested his stop and waited a moment for it to descend. He was going down to level seventeen, ten floors above where he lived, and it would be really quick getting there in this express lift.

Just as the doors were closing, a young woman rushed in and stood beside him.

'Level ten please,' she requested, just as clearly as he'd done, only she was a lot quieter.

John's eyes were closed; he was still thinking about the beautiful landscape view he had just left behind and at first paid no attention to the girl. Then the woman sharing the elevator caught his attention with a soft, enquiring voice.

'Did you enjoy the view?' she asked him.

'Yes,' he replied, giving her a beaming smile. 'Beautiful. So beautiful.'

He turned his head away, still smiling, shut his eyes for a moment, and remembered the warm sun he'd felt on his face.

Not long after, the elevator stopped at level ten and the woman left. He watched her leave, and feeling a little puzzled, wondered why she looked so familiar. As she walked away, she looked back at him with a cute smile and blew him a kiss. He smiled back and gave her a little wave, just before she disappeared into the crowd.

'She was one sexy girl,' he said to himself as the doors closed. 'Not long now.'

As he waited for the elevator to start moving again, he looked at a mirror on the side. The image staring back at him took him by surprise, and he remarked, 'Wow! I've caught the sun this time. Hope it doesn't get any redder.'

The level indicator moved quickly to seventeen, and the doors opened. He instantly noticed the change of smell and the din of the city as he left the elevator, and sighed. He turned onto the main thoroughfare, and as quickly as he could, made his way to the college entrance, dodging the many people moving quickly in all directions and bumping into a few of them as well.

As he entered the college foyer, he began looking around to see if he recognised anyone. It was so crowded he couldn't see very much at all and realised he needed a vantage point. Looking around he noticed the perfect spot and headed straight for it. He'd decided to climb the stairs leading to the great hall, where he could scan the lobby below with ease. It wasn't as easy as it looked and he found it difficult to push past the many other students who had also thought it a good idea. With so many doing the same thing, it took him some time to reach the top, but once above the crowd he soon noticed a few familiar faces and shouted down to tell them to stay put till he got there. He made his way as quickly as he could to meet up with his colleagues; they too had come for this last chance to get together. They were soon chatting, spending some time wishing each other good luck, and hoping they could keep in touch somehow. But that would depend on what they would all be doing from that moment on.

He handed his communicator over with some reluctance. The official took it, looked at it, and placed it in a slot to be reprogrammed. When it was handed back, his authority to visit the surface had been cancelled. There were to be no more surface trips, as now he was restricted to levels ten and below. He watched as his mates had their authority changed and after wishing them good luck for the last time, walked away.

As he walked slowly out of the college, he received a message on his personal communicator. It read, *'Check your college results. They are now available. Love May.'* May was John's personal companion and closest friend. They had formed a good relationship over the many years they had been together.

John walked briskly down the main street, not noticing anything along the way. As he got closer to his parents' home, the streets became narrower and more crowded and his progress slowed considerably. It was gone six in the afternoon when he reached his parents' home. He opened the main door, ran straight in, and had a quick look around to see if he was alone. Thinking he was alone, he headed directly for the communications terminal and sat down. He switched on the console, spoke to confirm his name, and was immediately identity scanned. Once the formalities were complete the screen burst into life.

The image of a beautiful-looking female with a soft voice greeted him, 'Hi John, do you want your exam results?' It was May, his digital companion for the past nine years.

'Shush! Be quiet. Yes, my results please?' he whispered.

Not quiet enough though; his parents and sister Petal were in the next room and soon gathered round to share his news. John turned an even darker shade of pink as the screen displayed his results and grading, and May spoke to congratulate him before he had time to take it all in.

He'd been trained as a non-specialist labourer, with a managerial diploma as an extra subject. John hoped to have a good enough exam score to get a good grade. Grades mattered more than anything, even more than what you specialised in. He read the information a few times, as it took awhile to take it all in. When he'd finished reading the results, he spun, leapt into the air, and let out a loud 'YIPPEE!'

His parents were taken aback by his outburst as this was quite out of character. Then he grabbed them, gave them all a hug, and said with excitement in his voice, 'I have achieved the labour managerial diploma and, not only that, it's the highest diploma awarded in the region, maybe the highest in the whole world.'

There was much hugging, jumping, and shouting over the next fifteen minutes. Then John's father suggested they tell everyone the good news and celebrate the occasion.

And as they went to walk away to tell the neighbours May spoke loudly, *'You have an urgent message which I think you should read before you celebrate.'*

When John heard this, he felt puzzled and slowly returned to the terminal. 'Show me the message,' he demanded.

May displayed the message. It was from the Himalayan Research Centre and read:

> Dear John,
>
> Congratulations on achieving a high grading and excellent exam results.
>
> As part of our commitment to improve living standards for everyone on earth, we need to employ the best possible staff. Your

results show that you have achieved the highest ever grade for your vocation. You are the youngest labour manager on record. With this in mind, we would like to offer you a position in a lifelong farming project here at the Himalayan Research Centre.

If you accept this invitation the following will apply:

1st: This project will provide employment for you, your partner, your parents, your partner's parents and her siblings for your whole life.

Only you and your partner may take up this offer if you so wish.

2nd: By accepting this offer your grade will be advanced. You will be granted grade seven labour manager status.

3rd: This offer is only open until midday tomorrow and you will be expected to take up employment within seven days of accepting. Precise details will be forwarded once accepted.

Note. This offer is only applicable it you have a partner before the take-up deadline expires.

Please reply to the Himalayan Research Centre as soon as possible.

Yours faithfully,

Frank Powel

Administration Manager

Himalayan Research Centre

John sat there for a little while before his sister asked, 'Well, what was the message?'

Stuttering, John told them what the message said. They all went silent, as if something dreadful had happened.

The silence was broken when John's father smiled and said, 'This is an offer too good for you to refuse. I've heard tales that life is bliss in that place. There are jobs for life for everyone. I've never had a steady job, and Mum, you may never have to work again, if you don't want to that is.'

John said out loud, 'We will all be together, and with my grading we'll be better off than ever before.' Then came a cheeky remark: 'That's five grades higher than you Dad.'

His dad gave him a gentle slap on the back of his head for that remark and they had a laugh together. Then he gave John a big hug. 'Well done lad. I'm really proud of you.' Then he looked at Petal and said, 'You should get a better education too.'

Without thinking she blurted out, 'Will there be boys there too?' then blushed as she realised what she'd said.

They all laughed and Petal ran to her room embarrassed.

Then what else the message had said hit John, and he sat down quickly. His partner! He had never thought about that before, and it hit him like a ton of bricks. A partner was a business venture for life, more than that, it could also involve reproduction, which meant intimacy. How was he to get a partner in seven days?

Too embarrassed to ask his parents, he ushered everyone out of the room and turned to May.

'May,' he said, 'how can I get a partner in seven days?'

May went quiet, then slowly replied, *'Get one from the job pool in the morning. Go between six and eight, see a job pool manager, state that you need a partner urgently, and see what happens. It usually works out fine, but if it doesn't then the computer will choose one for you. Choice is usually by grading, vocation, and who is available at the time, whichever way it's done.'*

John was a bit startled to think that his life partner could be chosen by a computer, so he called his father back into the room and told him what May had said.

John's father chuckled and said that was how he'd met John's mum. 'So don't worry son, let's have a party to celebrate your achievement and our new life,' he said. 'See about that in the morning.'

John smiled, relaxed, and forgot about the partner problem for the moment.

It was a good party with all the neighbours and close friends joining in. Everyone had a lot of fun, especially John. It lasted well into the night, and after it, he slept like a log.

His father woke him at five in the morning and John thought he'd only just gone to sleep, which wasn't far from the truth. He felt awful; his head was thumping and his mouth tasted foul. He jumped out of bed and dived into the cleansing cubicle to liven himself up. It failed to do much to bring him round, and after gulping down some breakfast, which made him feel a little better, he set off in a hurry.

He travelled quite quickly, it being so early in the morning, and arrived at the job pool at 6:00 a.m. precisely. John spent the next thirty minutes checking himself in a mirror, thinking about what he had to do, and trying to pluck up enough courage to go inside. With heart pounding, he took a deep breath, straightened himself up, and marched confidently into the main hall where hundreds of people were looking for work. If you couldn't get the job you wanted in the first week on the books, you had to take what you were offered, no questions asked.

All around were terminals, each with a queue of people waiting to register as unemployed and hoping for a suitable vacancy to go for.

John said quietly to himself, 'This is what I would've been doing on Monday if the job offer hadn't arrived.'

He looked around, found a job pool manager, and explained what was needed for him to accept the job on offer. The pool manager gave him a sideways smile and said, 'Well done young lad, you have a job already. Follow me please. You may be lucky finding a partner amongst this lot. There are plenty of new job seekers today, and you have come just as the rush is starting. There's always a rush after college results come through. The only trouble is, those who have grades they're not happy with are usually here first trying to improve their lot. So let's have your CV and job description.'

John gave him the information and followed him into an extremely large room to one side of the main hall. The manager spoke quietly into his communicator then turned to John and told him to wait, as he would be back shortly. After scanning John's information into a nearby terminal, he uttered a 'Wow!' before moving off. With a quick, almost floating gait, the man left the room via another door and John was left quite alone.

He was left standing on a platform overlooking a very large, totally empty room. The manager had disappeared, so John shouted, 'HELLO!' He shouted so loudly, it echoed around the room, and the sound startled him. Looking about he noticed how drab all official buildings seemed. Dull maroon and grey patterned walls, black shiny floors, off-white ceilings that could glow white (if the brightness was turned up), and no decoration whatsoever.

There was just one seat on the platform and he flopped down to wait for whatever was going to happen next. Then, over the loudspeakers came the echoing sound of the manager's voice, 'Females aged eighteen to twenty, grade five to fifteen, who have never been employed, please go to Partnering Room Three on level eleven. Thank you.'

That was where he was, and within thirty minutes over 250 females had filed into the room. They were all given John's job offer and CV to ponder over. Some left the room a little while after that, and those that were left came to see what John looked like, then even more made for the exit. Within twenty minutes, the number had been reduced to just twenty-five and John was a little worried that so few wished to continue.

They stood in a line some distance in front of him, each looking him up and down and wondering what would happen next. The young ladies had decided they would like to partner John, and he had to choose one of them. He was petrified; he'd never really thought about what would happen when the time came to have a partner. So he was relieved when the pool manager came forward to advise him on how to choose a partner from those left.

'Ask them their grade and vocation. Keep in mind that you are a labour manager with a high grade, as some of these may be a very low grade, which could cause problems with standards required of you in the future.' He said, 'On the other hand, there may be a higher-grade girl looking for a partner herself.'

John thanked him and slowly walked towards the line. He stood before each girl in turn, asking her questions as he went and listening to her replies. He decided on the spot who to keep, and by the time he'd reached the end of the line there were only ten left, three of whom caught his eye and one of whom had a higher grade than him. He asked the pool manager if it was prudent to hold each one in his arms to find her reaction to him.

The pool manager said, 'That's novel, but if it will help make your mind up, try it.'

The pool manager explained what John had requested and three girls ran from the room instantly, leaving just seven out of the original 250, all giggling at the sudden departures.

John walked to the start of the line and put his arms around the first girl. She was one of the three he liked: blonde, stunningly beautiful, and a higher grade. But her response was extremely cold, and he continued along the line. The second girl was a lot shorter than him and very plump. His arms seemed to sink into her body and that didn't please him. Next he came to the second one he liked, who took him by surprise. She bumped herself gently into his arms with a glint in her eye and it felt quite pleasing. Smiling, she placed her hands on his arms and pulled them in a little tighter around her waist. He smiled warmly back at her and gave her a gentle squeeze. She was wearing a loose-fitting, knee-length, pale pink stripy dress and it suited her complexion well. They didn't speak much; as their eyes made contact he began to stutter and they both went quiet.

He continued along the line to the next one, who held him so tightly he couldn't breathe; he kept looking back at the one in pink. She was bent slightly forward, looking at him with a wishful look on her face, and biting her bottom lip. He came to the third one he'd liked, but paid her no attention at all. He'd made up his mind; that wishful look had done it.

John went to the pool manager and told him which one he'd like to offer the partnership to. The manager smiled and dismissed the others for him.

Still smiling and without being asked, the young lass skipped over with her hand held out, and as she came close, slipped on the shiny surface of the floor. Down she went, ending up flat on her back with her skirt lifted, revealing a shapely pair of legs. John walked quickly over and stood directly over her. He bent down, offered his hand to help her up, and before he could ask if she was all right, she spoke.

'Hi, my name's Juliette Harper; thank you for choosing me as your prospective partner,' she said in a soft, pleasant tone.

He lifted her up and replied with a smile on his face, 'Hi, I'm John Blight, Grade Seven Labour Manager.'

'I know,' said Juliette. 'I read your CV; quite impressive too. As I told you earlier, I'm a grade twelve waste technician. I, and I hope my family, would love to join you.'

Her eyes glistened as they filled with tears of joy, and John only then realised how lovely she looked. She was just over a head shorter than him, with a clear, pale, almost milky white complexion, with dark brown eyes. Her poker-straight, shiny black hair flowed over her shoulders down to the middle of her slender back.

'Pink suits you,' John said, stuttering slightly.

'Goes with your face,' she replied with a hint of laughter.

They were staring at each other and failed to hear the pool manager asking them to sign a preliminary document of intent. He said, 'EXCUSE ME,' rather loudly, then quieter, 'sign here please. The final contract documentation will be through in a few days. I advise you not to live together before completion of contracts. You may withdraw anytime before then. Do you understand?'

Both John and Juliette came over shyly and said in lowered voices together, 'Yes sir.'

The manager laughed loudly, and said to John, 'Sir! I should be calling you sir. You are two grades higher than me.'

He held out an electronic notepad and indicated for them to touch it.

Both touched the document screen as a signature, and laughed nervously. Then they decided to go their separate ways.

'You CAN meet and call each other,' the manager shouted after them as they left.

On hearing that, John and Juliette gave each other a little wave and a smile. John blew her a kiss, and Juliette caught it with passion and placed it on her heart, just before they disappeared out of the building through different exits.

John was extremely excited; never before had a girl caused such an effect, and he was shaking.

He ran home to tell his parents as fast as he could, and Juliette ran to find her friends to tell them the news before she went home to her parents.

John ran into his home and immediately told May what had happened. He also asked her to send a message to the Himalayan Research Centre accepting the job offer.

Almost immediately he received a reply, acknowledging his acceptance and thanking him for his quick response. May told him she already knew what had happened, but thanked him for the extra information regarding his feelings towards Juliette.

Full job details quickly followed and he read them slowly not to miss any point. Travel arrangements had been made for 5:00 p.m., Tuesday, July 26.

Then he let out another 'YIPPEE!' Not only would he be visiting the surface again, he would be travelling all over the place as well. He couldn't believe his luck; and his partner could accompany him too. He stopped reading and closed the message down. There was a lot to be done.

The next two days were hectic for John and Juliette; there was so much to be done and so little time in which to do it. Both families met for the first time (which was always stressful). John and Juliette got to know a little about each other, and contracts had to be made ready for signing. Family and friends got together for final farewells, and John and Juliette and their families had to start packing.

Juliette's father was a grade eight regeneration physiotherapist. He knew the standard of living his daughter would have from now on would be slightly better than before, and was pleased for her. John was introduced to Fred, Juliette's nine-year-old brother, who was four years younger than Petal, much to Petal's dismay.

John had accepted the job and the work conditions had to be taken into account in the contract. This was to be a partnership for life; if one pulled out, the contract would be broken, and the job would end for Juliette and her family. They would have to leave the project.

Both families made ready for the trip to the Himalayan Centre, and as soon as John and Juliette signed the contract they would be whisked off to a new start. Each family would have a smart new house with all new gadgets and devices. But more than that, John and Juliette would have a place of their own.

The next couple of days flew by, and soon it was the morning of Tuesday, July 26. The day had come for the partnership to be finalised, and both families had travelled to the City Hall for the contract to be completed. It was a big day for them, and everyone tried to keep calm and not get too excited. John and Juliette were nervous as they stood outside City Hall, waiting to sign the documentation that would bind them together as partners, and their nervousness showed.

John turned to Juliette and remarked, 'You look absolutely stunning.'

Juliette went a little red in the face and replied in a quiet and shy voice, 'I'm glad you like what you see; it's all that I am.'

'I'm sure there's more to you than just good looks; I know, trust me!' he said, looking her straight in the eye.

She just stared back at him with a beaming smile on her face and said nothing.

Suddenly it was time, and they went inside to report to the security staff, just inside the entrance. After what seemed ages, though it was only a few minutes, the signing official came out to greet them. 'If you will all follow me please,' she said slowly, with an extremely deep voice.

John whispered in Juliette's ear, 'Is it a man, or what?'

They looked at each other and nearly burst out laughing at the thought. Juliette couldn't hold it all back, and her snigger made the official turn around with a disgusted look on her face. (She must have heard what was said.) Juliette bit her bottom lip and John thought she looked cute when she did that. He gave her a wink to reassure her, and off they went.

John, Juliette, and both families followed close behind the official as they entered the signing room and walked over to the one and only table. The room was empty except for them and the table. No floor or wall coverings, no pictures, just the usual dull maroon and grey walls and black shiny floor.

As they reached the table, they both placed their hands on the electronic document laid out on the tabletop and started to read.

Without them realising, the device scanned their hands and took this as a signature before they had time to finish the first line. Quite quickly the document was replaced with a blank screen, and was followed by the announcement: 'We take this opportunity to congratulate the couple on completing their partnership. May your joining be prosperous! Good day.'

And that was it, all over and done with. In shock at the suddenness of it all, John and Juliette turned to their families and he said, 'It's done. Finalised!'

It was just as well they'd agreed and read the document before they went in, otherwise they could have been signing anything.

There was no time to celebrate. They all had to get home to continue preparing for the move to their new life. There was still a lot of packing to be done.

Juliette went bright red when Petal sniggered, 'You can keep each other warm tonight, can't you?'

John looked at Juliette and wondered what she was thinking. He noticed her reaction to what Petal said. Goose bumps had appeared on her, and the tiny, silky hairs on her arms were standing on end.

There was no reply, except for a smile from John, who promptly gave Juliette a wink and whispered in her ear, 'Are you going to be wearing the shocking pink knickers I saw when we first met?'

She went even redder, screwed up her nose, and gave him a dig in the ribs. 'I like pink. It's my favourite colour,' she replied shyly in a cute sort of way.

Petal looked at her funny, not knowing what she was on about, but didn't follow with the usual thousand questions like she normally did.

By the time they got back to their homes, removal personnel had already started taking away the items they couldn't take with them, which were most things, as only personal items capable of fitting into small cases could be taken. The rest would be recycled to the element banks. Someone else would be living in their apartments quite soon, as there was a high demand for places to live.

John managed to stop a removals man from taking the last seat, a small stool, and placed it firmly on the floor with a bang. Smiling to himself, he sat in front of the communications terminal and retrieved their travel information. It was only then he noticed there was a big problem with their travel arrangements. A pod containing one double and two single berth sleeping compartments had been booked on the overnight shuttle to the Himalayan Centre, and it was due to leave at 5:00 p.m. that evening. A second pod had been ordered for the same time tomorrow. It looked as if arrangements had been made for both families to travel separately.

John called Juliette and as soon as she appeared on the communications terminal made her aware of the situation. She looked very upset and asked if he could sort it out, making it quite clear to him that travelling separately was out of the question from now on.

John placed her on hold and asked May for help.

May tried to sort the problem, but no changes could be made at such a late stage, and the travel arrangements would have to remain unchanged.

The removal personnel weren't scheduled to complete their task until the following morning, so John asked his parents not to travel that evening. After a short discussion, it was decided that John, Juliette, Petal, and Fred would travel that evening, and the parents would travel tomorrow when the removals were complete.

Juliette had been kept waiting for an answer for half an hour before John told her the news. She quickly spoke to her parents and they agreed to the suggested arrangements. She seemed relieved now that she would be travelling with John, and more so knowing that her new friend Petal would be with them.

Soon it was time for them to leave. Juliette, her parents, and Fred turned up at John's home and everyone said their farewells. It was only till tomorrow, so there weren't tears and all took it well. John, Juliette, Petal, and Fred stood by the door, waiting for a spitter to arrive and held hands. Juliette's excitement threatened to boil over as she clung tightly to John's arm. He could feel her shaking and placed his arm around her shoulders. Petal and Fred couldn't stop talking about what it would be like at their journeys end; most of what they said was total fiction.

The four of them had packed overnight bags, had said goodbye to their parents, and were now starting the journey to the shuttle terminal and a new life. They would share a single pod, which, with other pods, would form the shuttle. It would be a twenty-three-hour overnight trip, with no breaks and very little (if anything) to see. Only John and Juliette were to share a compartment. Petal and Fred had singles, and they would share the day room for food and relaxation throughout the journey. This sharing could prove a little embarrassing for the couple, knowing Petal. Their parents were to take a bit longer to arrive at the research centre, as their shuttle was twenty-four hours later, leaving at the same time the next evening.

The spitter arrived and stopped just outside the entrance. As they climbed aboard, the spitter scanned John and welcomed him and his companions. Before they could say another word to their parents, they shot forward and headed for the nearest maglev lift. After travelling a hundred metres, it stopped near an uncluttered street wall and started to rise above the crowds. As it topped the roofs, the maglev track could be seen just a few metres away. It trundled over and sat for a moment before lifting to float above the track. It started moving, slowly at first, then picking up speed as it glided along. They were on the way to the shuttle terminal, shooting past familiar places on the maglev track, thoroughly excited, and smiling happily at each other. But soon they were passing unfamiliar places, heading down to the terminal, down to the lowest parts of the city, and the gravity of what was happening hit home. Juliette squeezed John's hand tightly and he put his arm around her shoulders. Petal and Fred sat closely together, yet not touching, scanning the route from side to side as they shot along. No one said a word.

The journey was quite quick, as it usually was by spitter, and they were soon entering the shuttle terminal. As the doors in front of them opened, they were taken aback by the immense size of the place. John was expecting a single platform connecting to a single pipe. What he saw was more complex than he could ever have imagined. There were many pipes entering the side of the domed terminal, and many levels of different machinery moving pod after pod from one place to another. Vehicles of all shapes and sizes sped to and from rows of large pods, offloading the cargo. And the noise was louder than he'd expected, with much clanging of metal on metal and deeper-sounding bangs as pipe doors opened and slammed shut.

The spitter entered another elevator and started to descend. Its walls were clear and they all watched as it dropped to the lowest level. They sped past pod after pod, turning corners and shooting past what looked like many other platforms. John realised that if the spitter made a mistake and dropped them off in the wrong place they would be totally lost, and that thought worried him a little. As it was, the small craft knew exactly where it was going and soon turned onto a platform full of pods with their doors open. It came to a halt as soon as it ventured onto the platform and they stepped off, not knowing what to do next. John, Juliette, Petal, and Fred had finally arrived at the platform, thanks mainly to the spitter being automated. Though the journey was quick, it seemed to have taken quite some time, and they were glad to have arrived.

A floating flatbed platform, driven by a smartly dressed porter, arrived to take them to their pod. They all jumped on at the same time and the platform bounced up and down a few times before stabilising itself. Then it was off down the platform, slowly making its way past pod after pod. When they stopped, John could see what he assumed was their pod, and the shape reminded him of a flat bottomed sausage; only this one was extremely large. At sixteen metres long and five in diameter, it looked impressive.

Petal was amazed at the size of the terminal and the number of shuttles coming and going through the many pipes. She asked the porter, 'Why are there so many shuttles?'

'Food supplies, raw materials arriving, and empty pods leaving,' came the emotionless reply, as if he'd been asked the same question just one too many times.

'And why so many different colours?'

The porter gave her a stern look, then replied, 'That information, and anything else you want to know, can be found by accessing the console aboard your pod.'

Petal didn't like his attitude and retorted loudly, 'I've a good mind to report you for being so rude.'

John heard what she'd said and turned to the porter, 'No she won't. Leave us now please.'

The porter turned his vehicle about and sped away at high speed. John turned and looked cross with Petal. 'He's obviously not happy answering questions, and probably gets asked that every time he picks someone up. Must be a boring job, so leave it be. OK?'

Petal looked at him, knowing she'd just been told off, and started to sulk. 'OK,' she replied quietly. She was thankful that Juliette and Fred hadn't heard anything.

All of them turned, looked the platform up and down, and assuming the nearest pod to them was theirs, they boarded.

Petal ran inside first, made a beeline for the lounge controls, switched on the entertainment console, and sat back to wait for the journey to start.

She was looking for information on the terminal and shuttle units. When John, Juliette, and Fred entered, they had no idea what it would be like inside, and jumped as the door closed in a flash; with just a slight click it was locked and sealed shut. It left Juliette a little startled, and Fred whispered, 'Wow,' quietly to himself, after a sharp intake of breath.

They all took a quick glance around the relaxation area, home for the next twenty-three hours, before settling down at the brightly coloured table.

John made sure everyone was seated and comfortably settled before the pod was loaded onto the shuttle unit. They looked at each other across the table, each wondering what would happen next, when they felt a slight wobble, which indicated the pod was being lifted off the platform.

'Well this *must* be our pod,' said John, and squeezed Juliette's hand reassuringly. 'It won't be long now.'

'Don't let us keep you two up,' said Petal, looking straight at John and Juliette with a mischievous smile on her face.

A hail of cushions rained down on Petal, and everyone was so distracted nobody felt the pod wobble again as it lifted and moved off.

Pauline had the day off, just as she did every week, and set about her normal routine. Only the day wasn't going to be quite as normal as usual. Things were definitely set to change and she knew nothing about what was to happen later on.

It was eleven o'clock on Friday morning, July 22. That afternoon she would be going back to the Technical College to pick up her diploma. She'd passed all assignments and exams to qualify as a grade six dental technician. This gave her access to all levels and floors when working, which meant she could visit the balcony from time to time. And that pleased her.

As for now, she was a guest of Grade Four Consultant Doctor Brian James, who lived on floor eleven of the Bagman City Tower. This wasn't the first time she'd paid him a visit; she paid him regular visits, almost every week in fact, and never for business.

She made for the balcony on the tenth floor, just below the apartment window. Getting up late and sunbathing during lunch was her normal routine on her days off, and this day was to be no different.

Still half-asleep, she left Brian's apartment and headed for the elevator to take her down one floor. When she arrived, the doors opened and she made her way out onto the balcony. Without looking to see who was also there, she headed straight for the relaxation section. After selecting a suitable place to settle, she stripped to her panties, laid back on a sun bed, and waited for a beauty technician to cover her with sun lotion.

The technician had just started to massage her with oil when Pauline noticed a man looking out over the balcony. Being only a few metres away, she could see how young and fit he looked. He was staring at the land below, and she wondered who he could be. It was unusual to see anyone else there at this time of day on a Friday, even if it was lunch time. He wasn't even looking at her and she was annoyed about that.

In an effort to get him removed, she called a nearby security guard over, asked her to check to see if he was allowed to be there and remove him if he wasn't. Once she'd checked him out, she was to report back to Pauline.

The guard crossed to where he was sitting, checked his authority, and came straight back. 'Excuse me young lady,' she said, 'that man's name is John Blight, a final year student. He has permission to be here, so there's nothing I can do. He can stay.'

On hearing this, Pauline shrugged her shoulders, lay back, and before she closed her eyes, gave him one last look. He still wasn't looking at her and she frowned.

Brian was in his apartment and looked down at Pauline, lying almost naked on a sun bed one floor below. He thought how beautiful she was: twenty years old, very tall, slim, with long blond hair past the middle of her back. The beauty technician had just finished covering her with oil and her body glistened with a slightly reddish, golden sheen in the midday sun. He wished he could be with her, but even with his status he couldn't just leave work without good reason, and she wasn't reason enough.

They'd spent the night together and he'd enjoyed every moment of it. She was a tigress and he'd tamed her. He wasn't sure if they would meet again, that would depend on her work placement, but he hoped they would. Over the past few weeks he'd started to really enjoy her company and would miss her very much.

Just then his communicator chirped up with a message calling him away.

Pauline was thinking of the night she had with Brian. She smiled to herself and thought of nothing else. This was someone she could settle down with; he was confident, strong, tall, and very handsome. He was also grade four, which helped, as this gave him access to almost all levels. And he was rich. Just perfect.

She'd asked the beauty technician to wake her at two in the afternoon so she would have time to get back to college, and it was a gentle shake that woke her. She stepped into a nearby cleansing cubicle to remove the oil, and after a few minutes got dressed. Walking off the balcony, she entered the building and made for the elevator just across the entrance hall.

That man was there too, though he paid her no attention at all, and it annoyed her. She was used to men staring at her, thrived on it even, and was puzzled by his actions.

She asked him with a sexy, soft voice, 'Did you enjoy the view?'

He turned, looked at her, and replied, 'Beautiful, so beautiful.' And as he looked away he smiled.

'Sly dog, he must have been looking at me when I was asleep,' she thought to herself.

Now she was smiling, enjoying what he had said. He was slightly taller than her, and as she watched him, he turned away, closed his eyes, and kept on smiling.

'Nice shade of pink. He can't be used to being out in the open,' she thought.

She also thought he was a weirdo. She'd been waiting for a chat-up line, but nothing came; that wasn't what she was expecting, being all alone with him. She shrugged her shoulders, and watched the level indicator as the numbers increased. The elevator reached level ten and the doors opened, changing the smell inside the small compartment and allowing the cacophony of noise to flood in.

The man winked, and looked her up and down as she left, which made her happy. She made a point of wiggling her backside, knowing he was watching. Just before the doors closed, she turned and blew him a kiss, but didn't have time to see if he'd caught it; too many people obscured her view.

Now she was back in the crowded city and jostling for room to move. It was amazing how many men made a point of bumping into her, but she didn't mind, especially when they apologised and asked for a date. She loved turning them down.

She made her way to the college and entered the hall where she was to receive her diploma. Pauline never went looking for her friends, they always came to her; it wasn't long before she was surrounded by her friends and of course the "hangers on". After all, she was an extremely popular young lady, possessing three main qualities: elegance, beauty, and charm.

It was time for the diploma ceremony to begin, but for her there was no excitement; it was just another dull routine she had to go through. As she made her way to the podium to collect her diploma, there was a chorus of cheering and whooping which made her feel really good inside. Everyone got the same greeting, only she thought it personal and began to walk even taller. She felt serene and great and loved every minute of it. She climbed the steps to the top of the podium and listened as the audience cheered and clapped even louder. She was smiling and giggling as she held out her hand to be greeted by the faculty's head lecturer. She took hold of her diploma and was suddenly overwhelmed with emotion. She faced the crowd, raised her diploma aloft, and screamed out loud. The whole audience seemed to whistle, cheer, and clap, and she loved it. She had a tingling feeling down her spine that made goose bumps appear all over her body. Her legs went weak and she began to shake. She was laughing and crying at the same time; the tears ran freely down her face.

The excitement reminded her of Brian, and as she left the podium, she sent him a message. Moving as quickly as the crowd would allow, she made a beeline for the exit and left the building. She just wanted to get home and prepare for the party later that evening. She hoped Brian would be able to accept the invitation. She'd just sent him a reminder and was still waiting for a reply. She'd told him about the faculty dance earlier that day and he said he would let her know if he could make it or not. Shame he hadn't given her an answer yet, but there was still time. 'Plenty of time,' she thought.

On her way home men stared at her and she enjoyed every bit of it. Pauline put on her usual act, making sure their eyes followed her every movement, everywhere she went. She lost count of how many asked for a date and thoroughly enjoyed turning them all down.

Then she was home, and entered her apartment, slamming the door with a bang behind her. As soon as she was inside, she started to strip, leaving a line of clothes from the front door to her bedroom. She entered her cleansing cubicle and lay back on the soft topped table ready to be massaged. She stayed there for half an hour while the complex mechanism invigorated her whole body, leaving her completely relaxed and refreshed.

Pauline lived in a rented apartment on level eleven which was paid for by her mother, a grade three chief scientist working on a secret project, or something, somewhere. Pauline wasn't bothered where her mother was as long as the rent was paid each month. The apartment was in the not-so-crowded mid levels, inhabited mostly by lower-grade professional workers like herself. Now that she was grade six and qualified, she could move up to level ten, have her own salary, and start fending for herself. She could cut herself off completely from her mother, whom she hated and wanted nothing more to do with.

Her communications terminal was flashing, indicating she had a message; she ran over to see if it was from Brian. It wasn't; it was from someone at the Himalayan Research Centre, and that could wait. She had more important things on her mind just now, like why Brian wasn't getting in touch with her.

Brian was a busy man during the day, and it was his turn to be on call for emergencies for the evening. Twice that afternoon he'd been called to assess a patient for limb regeneration, and he was tired, having had no sleep the previous night. He thought of Pauline as he relaxed, exhausted on the bed, and smiled. Soon he was fast asleep. His personal communicator was set to silent for all but emergency calls, which made him miss the messages Pauline had sent to him.

Pauline was upset; Brian hadn't answered her calls or messages and it was time to leave for the party. She really wasn't in the mood and she didn't want to be there if he wasn't. So instead, she went and sat in front of the communications terminal and was promptly scanned.

The terminal burst into life, and Michael's face appeared, smiling. *'Hello Pauline, what can I do for you?'* he asked.

'Are there any messages for me please, Michael?' she asked in a voice that mirrored her disappointment.

Michael had been her digital companion since she was eleven years old. He replied, *'There is only one message. It's from the Himalayan Research Centre.'*

'OK, let's see it,' she said sadly.

The message appeared on the screen; it read:

Dear Pauline,

As part of our commitment to improving living conditions for everyone on earth, we have a duty to employ staff that will ensure high standards are achieved and maintained.

As a dental technician, your services are required to maintain a healthy work force here at our centre.

This is a compulsory appointment, so the following conditions apply.

1st. You have been assigned to a life-long farming project.

2nd. You have been advanced to a grade five dental technician.

3rd. Employment will be for you and your partner, if you have one.

4th. Travel arrangements have been made for Tuesday, July 26.

There is no need to acknowledge this message.

Your travel arrangements are attached; please read them carefully.

Failure to take up this offer will not be tolerated.

Pauline's arms dropped to her sides; she slumped in the chair and just stared at the screen, numb from shock. Her mouth gaped open, and for once in her life she was totally speechless. She wasn't expecting anything as devastating as this.

All of a sudden her communicator chirped into life as she received a message from Brian.

It read, 'Hi Pauline, sorry for not getting in touch earlier; I've been on call and fell asleep. I'd love to meet up with you. Have you left for the party yet? Call me back. Love, Brian.'

Tears were running down her face as she called him, 'Hi Brian.'

Brian could tell by the sound of her voice that something was up. 'Is there something wrong? Is it because I didn't call?' he asked, curious as to why she was so quiet. 'I'll put you on the main monitor.'

As she appeared on the screen, he could see the state she was in.

There was a long silence, broken now and again by the sound of sniffling. Then she looked at him and spoke. 'Brian, something terrible has happened. I've been drafted to the Himalayan Research Centre. I'm totally devastated.'

Brian paused for a few seconds, which seemed like hours to Pauline, and then said, 'So... It's a great life there, and you'll be able to travel as well. What are your employment conditions?'

He knew one condition of a draft meant she would probably need to have a partner. 'That'll do nicely,' he thought, smiling to himself as he looked at her.

She told him the conditions being imposed on her, and added, 'What could be great about living underground all the time? And on a farm of all places!'

Brian went on to explain what life would be like out there. Just as he finished he said, 'So… You can go with a partner, can you?'

She sat there listening to all he said, feeling better with each word. She'd have more freedom, more surface time during holidays, more money to spend, and a higher living standard. Then she realised the change in his voice as he said, 'So you can go with a partner, can you?'

She went quiet for a minute, not knowing what to say. She wanted to ask him if he'd like to be her partner, but was afraid in case he rejected her. Then she said, 'I don't know if I can find a partner by Tuesday, so it looks like I'll be going alone. You wouldn't be interested in going with me, would you?' The silence that followed made her heart drop.

Brian listened to what she'd just asked him, and was silent. He was expecting her to ask him and he really wanted it. It was just the shock of it being said so quickly that took him by surprise.

Then he heard her voice again; this time she was quiet and inquiring. 'Do you want to?' It was almost in a whisper.

'Sorry, just a bit shocked that's all. Damn, my communicator has gone off. I have to run. I will call you. No, don't worry; I'll be with you as soon as I can.' And he switched the monitor off.

Pauline felt awful. He hadn't given her an answer. What did he mean when he said 'Be with you as soon as I can'? She walked away from the terminal, back to her bed, and collapsed. She felt totally shattered.

A few minutes passed before her personal communicator chirped into life. She sat bolt upright, staring at it as if it were going to do a flip or something. She looked at the message she had just received. It was from Brian and said, 'Yes my love, I will partner you with pleasure.'

As it sank in, she fell back onto her bed. Her arms and legs went flying in all directions with sheer excitement, and she screamed her head off with joy.

When she calmed down, she felt exhausted from all that had happened in the past few hours and was soon fast asleep.

It was one o'clock in the morning and the doorbell was ringing non-stop. Pauline slowly lifted herself off the bed, ran her fingers roughly through her hair, and went to answer it. She had no idea what time it was and, being half asleep, didn't really care. She opened the door without thinking who might be there and peered out through half-shut eyes. Still dazed and in her short nightdress, she stood there and called out. Without replying, Brian appeared and grabbed her, lifting her off her feet. He pushed his way inside and slammed the door behind him. She was instantly awake, aware of who it was and responded warmly to his embrace. She wrapped her arms and legs tightly around him, making sure he didn't—and couldn't—go anywhere. They undressed quickly, got into bed, and held each other tightly.

It was eleven thirty the next morning before she woke. Pauline was thinking it was all a dream, until she turned over and saw Brian lying beside her. All of a sudden it hit her again and she woke him by jumping up and down on the bed.

'Steady on,' he said. 'OK, I'm awake, I'm awake.'

He grabbed her, and she stared straight into his eyes. 'We have to get busy,' she said, 'we have to arrange a formal Partnering Contract. Come on, get dressed.'

He smiled and said quietly under his breath, 'It's going to be one heck of a life with you around.' And he loved the thought of it, as he pulled her back down on the bed.

Later, Pauline went to the communications terminal and asked Michael to arrange everything for her. Michael started the process, and was soon calling her back to see the information he had ready for her.

A ceremony had been organised for Monday morning at eleven, and she crossed the room to tell Brian the news.

'Good,' he said, 'you might as well pack right now and move up with me. How does that sound to you?'

Pauline was ecstatic and ran to get her suitcase. It took her just twenty minutes to pack, leaving most of her things for the removals personnel to fight over once she'd gone; she didn't want or need those items now. Before she left, she asked Michael to contact her mother. He was to inform her of the news and of the fact that Pauline would be staying with Brian, so her mother could stop paying for the apartment.

Michael said, *'I will let you know when I have made contact with her.'*

'Thanks,' she replied. And after taking one last look around her apartment, she slammed the door behind her. Smiling, she held on to Brian's arm, and they walked away.

Brian and Pauline walked to the nearest elevator, just a few minutes away, and ascended to the eleventh floor of the Bagman City Tower. Neither of them said a word for the whole journey, which was over quite quickly. Pauline rested her head on Brian's shoulder and smiled to herself as they stepped out of the elevator and strolled along the corridor to his apartment.

As soon as they arrived he said to her, 'Make yourself at home. I have to get in touch with my office. I have to resign my post as soon as possible and get packing myself.'

'OK, I'll be down on the balcony sunbathing if you want me,' she said, and gave him a kiss when she left.

As she relaxed on the balcony, she thought about all that had happened in the past twenty-four hours. She was only here yesterday, and life seemed so normal then. Now she didn't know what was to happen. The only thing she knew for certain was that Brian was to be her partner, and that was more than enough to keep her mind off what lay ahead.

Brian called his office to let them know all that had happened in the past twelve hours. They were not too happy, but knew they couldn't do anything to prevent his move. The Himalayan Research Centre had priority over everything, and they had to comply. After offering to make arrangements for his medical and personal effects to be moved from his office to the centre, they offered him the weekend off if he wanted it. He did.

He smiled and said quietly to himself, 'That was easy.'

He grabbed his swimming trunks, left the apartment, and went to join Pauline on the balcony below.

Monday had arrived. Pauline was a bit concerned that Brian wasn't getting ready for the ceremony, and time seemed to be passing too quickly. Walking over to him, she indicated that she needed help closing the back of her dress and pressed herself heavily against his partly dressed body.

'Aren't you getting dressed for the occasion?' she asked.

Brian looked at her and said, 'I took the trouble to cancel the venue at the Town Hall. I thought you would like to have it up the tower, in the conference room on the thirtieth floor. I invited some of your friends and a few of mine. Is that OK with you?'

It was meant to be a surprise, and judging by the look on Pauline's face, it was. She looked up at his smiling face, launched herself into his arms, and gave him a hug and a kiss. 'You know it's OK. Thank you so much. I love you.'

Brian went to the conference room early, leaving Pauline to get herself there as soon as she was ready. He had to make sure all was in order, which included finding out if the caterers had supplied enough food or not. Food was always a problem at any function due to shortages, and there hadn't been enough notice for the caterers. This time was no exception;

the caterers hadn't done well and had no food for the venue. So the expected party was off, reduced to just a quick drink with the guests, and that wasn't too bad. Apart from that little glitch, all was in order, and he was a little relieved knowing the event would be over quickly: He didn't really like parties.

The partnering registrar turned up early with the contract and soon all the guests had arrived. So Brian had a few minutes to relax before Pauline arrived.

Pauline walked towards the door of the conference room with butterflies in her stomach, not knowing who was on the other side. To her relief, Brian came out to meet her, and they entered the room together. She looked and felt like a fairy princess as she walked past their friends towards the partnering registrar who held a flat pad in front of him. They knew what was written on the pad and only had to touch it to complete the contract. They stood, looked at each other for a brief moment, and turned with their hands outstretched. One touch of the pad later, the partnership contract had been finalised and the congratulation message was announced.

A kiss and hug followed before they mingled with the guests. Most of Pauline's friends had gone to look out of the windows; they had never seen the surface before and were in awe. One or two even ventured out onto the small balcony and were frightened stiff by the vast, open space before them.

Pauline and Brian made a point of talking with everyone they knew, as this was probably the last time they would see them. Their friends wished them good luck and soon everyone was leaving the party, as there was no food to eat.

It was just the way they wanted, no fuss, no long speeches, just short farewells.

Brian turned to Pauline and said, 'Come, I have another surprise for you. Come with me.'

Although puzzled to think where they could be going, she obeyed without question, and they headed for the elevator. They were making their way back down to the eleventh floor.

When they reached Brian's apartment, he opened the door and said, 'pack your bag; we're leaving.'

Pauline looked totally puzzled as she picked up her bag and threw it on the bed.

Both of them quickly packed the few items they possessed and left the room. After leaving the apartment, Brian walked Pauline towards an elevator closer to the centre of the tower complex. Pauline was shocked as the doors opened, and she slowly entered, looking at and touching the walls. It was much smaller and a lot classier than anything she'd ever seen before. Brian pressed the button for the top floor, and Pauline just stared at him with her mouth open.

Looking at her, he placed his finger under her chin and lifted it up, closing her mouth. 'No catching flies here,' he remarked.

Pauline was delighted, as she had never been so high before, and wondered if Brian had pressed the wrong button. The elevator stopped, the doors opened, and Pauline was blinded by bright sunlight for a brief moment. When her eyes adjusted, she realised she was on the roof, in the Mayoral Garden of all places, and it was beautiful.

Brian said, 'The whole roof is ours until we leave.'

Pauline wondered how the mayor's apartment and garden area could have been reserved for them, and how they could remain there until their shuttle departed tomorrow evening. Mystified, she asked Brian how he had managed to acquire the suite.

'It wasn't me,' he said. 'It was your mother.'

Pauline stood aghast, once again speechless. Brian was wondering if he'd done the right thing when her voice came back.

She shouted, 'She doesn't do anything for nothing. What favour does she want for this?'

Brian had to think fast; he wasn't expecting that reaction. He explained that her mother had spoken to him the previous day and organised it as a partnering present. And that's all he said, trying not to ruin what was, so far, a perfect day.

Pauline smiled and looked at him. 'At least we will be away from here before she can interfere with my life again,' she said a little quieter.

Later that evening Brian took Pauline out into the garden. The lights were on and the whole place looked enchanting.

Brian spoke loudly, 'Lights off.'

All the lights were immediately switched off and the garden was in total darkness. Well almost total darkness. Moonlight flooded the rooftop, something neither of them had seen before. And thousands of stars glinted in the almost totally black sky. Both of them just stared in amazement at the wonderful scene.

Pauline made sure they enjoyed themselves that night. They made love under the moon and the stars for the first time ever.

Tuesday arrived too soon. Pauline really enjoyed being on the roof and didn't want to leave; she'd never been so relaxed. Brian strolled into the garden and headed to where Pauline was sunbathing, which was her usual hobby when she had nothing to do, and found her fast asleep. She was lying on her belly and completely naked. Brian took one look at her bottom and said, 'Ouch, that's going to hurt.' It was bright red.

As he said it, Pauline woke up and tried to turn over. She grimaced as she rolled over onto her back. 'Ouch, that stings. Got anything for it?' she asked, almost pleading.

Brian returned to the apartment and came back a few minutes later with a small tube of cream. 'Turn over. This is going to please me, and kill you,' he said smiling.

Pauline wasn't smiling, she just did as she was told, clenched her teeth, and waited for even more pain. Brian put some cream on his hands and placed them firmly on her butt. He rubbed the cream slowly to start with and then vigorously.

Pauline felt his hands touch her inflamed skin and they felt freezing. Instead of causing more pain, it actually had a cooling effect, and the more Brian rubbed, the better she felt. Then came a painful, sharp sting. Brian had finished applying the cream and slapped her bottom really hard.

Pauline looked at him a little shocked. 'What was that for?'

'Next time you burn it, I'll slap it even harder.'

She turned and looked at her rear end; the only red she could see was the impression of his hand on one of her cheeks. 'Got anything for that?' she asked sarcastically.

Brian bent down and kissed her where it hurt. 'There is that better?' He replied.

Pauline grabbed her glass of water and threw it over him. He shook his head and walked off. She got up off the bed and turned to walk away. Without warning, the sprinkler system turned on and freezing cold water soaked her instantly. She ran as fast as she could back to the apartment and saw Brian standing by the door. As she entered, she turned to him and said, 'Trust the water to come on just now.'

Just after she'd finished speaking, Brian smiled before saying, 'Sprinklers off.' The water stopped flowing immediately.

Pauline glared at him before uttering an ear piercing scream. 'I'll get you for this!'

Brian was expecting her to attack him, so he was ready when she did. He grabbed her arms, and, giving her a bear hug, carried her to the bedroom. He entered the room, kicked the door closed behind him, and not long after Pauline was silent.

It was time to leave the rooftop and start the journey. Pauline had become a little excited, so she packed her belongings quickly, and also packed Brian's, just to keep herself busy.

When they were ready, Brian ordered a spitter to take them to the shuttle terminal, and it arrived quite quickly. They stepped into the vehicle, and it left the roof almost as quickly as it came. The journey didn't last long, as the shuttle terminal was at the bottom of the elevator they had entered on the roof. It was a direct route. As the doors opened and the spitter shot forward, Brian let out a gasp; he'd never seen so much heavy-lifting machinery at work, and everything was being done with precision. The rest of their journey to the platform took them via clear-walled elevators down past many levels of track and shuttle sections to the bottom of the terminal. Looking up he was amazed that nothing seemed to stand still for very long, and so much was moving continuously, it looked like an arcade dodgem game, except here, nothing collided. The terminal was huge, with many tracks joined to the pipes leading out of the city. Shuttles with pods of all sizes and colours were coming and going, making the whole place look very busy, which it was, 24/7.

Many years had passed since Pauline had seen this place, and some of the old memories came flooding back to her. They were happy memories of her mother and father when they were still together and travelled a lot. She took great delight in watching the look on Brian's face and how his mouth only closed for him to gulp now and again. He only looked at her when the final elevator came to a halt and the spitter moved forward.

'This is going to be some adventure,' he said, smiling at her.

They were making their way along a platform to their allotted pod, which would be home to both of them for the next twenty-three hours. They passed row after row of more pods, all waiting to be used at some time or other. The spitter stopped, and Pauline and Brian looked to see where they were. Next to them a pod was resting on the platform with its door wide open, ready for someone to enter.

'I hope this one's ours,' Pauline whispered in Brian's ear. She looked up and down the platform and noticed all the pod doors were wide open, waiting patiently for their occupants to arrive.

'We're a little early by the look of it. There's nobody about,' she stated, noticing a distinct lack of human activity.

Brian noticed there were platforms just below theirs with slightly smaller pods lined up along them, and some passengers were entering them. They were also shaped differently, but he didn't notice that at the time. As they looked around, they saw the shuttle units moving into position, ready to be loaded with the pods and wondered how many there were. Brian was starting a mental count when his thoughts were cut short; the spitter reminded them of the time and asked them to alight.

Pauline stepped off the spitter, walked towards the doorway of the pod the spitter had stopped next to, and Brian followed just behind.

'This one must be ours,' she said, looking back over her shoulder and smiling at him. Then she disappeared inside.

Brian hesitated for a moment before he entered, and didn't say a word. He saw Pauline looking around the interior and calling out the names of each item as if reading from a check list. She walked over to a bedroom, opened the door, and went inside.

She came out smiling and said, 'That's ours; it's huge and really nice.'

She walked over to another bedroom, opposite the one she'd claimed, turned the door handle, and tried to enter; it was locked.

'What's in here?' she asked him. The look on her face gave the impression that she'd thought he might have a nice surprise for her.

'There're only the two of us, so it's probably locked as it's not required,' he quickly replied.

Pauline's smile turned into a frown and she sat down at the table. Brian joined her, sat opposite, and reached across to hold her hands.

Pauline noticed the slight change in air pressure as the door closed quietly, and squeezing his hands tightly, she smiled.

They felt a slight rocking movement as the pod was lifted onto the shuttle section, and as soon as they had settled again, Pauline made a request, 'Clear roof.'

All except the centre of the pod roof became crystal clear, and they peered out. They could see the shuttle terminal again, and Brian watched as the remaining pods were loaded onto shuttle sections. He was sitting, staring, with his mouth open once again and Pauline was amused. She pointed at him and laughed, but it didn't stop him from looking so ridiculous.

The shuttle wobbled slightly and lifted as the maglev came into operation. The shuttle sections seemed to be bobbing up and down independently of each other. As the shuttle units began to move slowly forward, they quickly lined up, and were now moving in unison. They were on their way and could see they were moving away from the platform as the speed increased. Brian noticed the shuttle moving from side to side as it weaved its way through the maze of platforms. The motion reminded him of a slithering snake he'd seen in a movie a long time ago. It wasn't long after leaving the platform and going through the terminal that they reached the perimeter and entered a pipe.

Once in the pipe, Pauline could only see the blur of the ground rushing past, and that made the inside of the pod too dark. Pauline made another request, 'Solid roof and lights on.'

Now they were all alone, the lights were on, and they smiled at each other.

'We're on our way,' Pauline shouted excitedly.

Danni Mitchell leant back against a pillar with her arms crossed. She was looking out over the North Sea, and was thinking.

Just over two weeks ago she'd been the chief scientist in charge of a farming program at the Himalayan Research Centre. Now, having been relieved of her duties, she had time to think about what had transpired and plan her next move.

It had been a month since being told she was to be investigated for financial irregularities with the project, and that it had gone way over budget. Because of that, she'd been summoned and appeared before a tribunal on trumped-up charges, judged on false evidence, and was waiting for the verdict. Three ambitious administrators had carried out her interrogation, and they were determined to remove her from the program, no matter what the cost. Once she was removed from office, they would be able to take over and take the credit for the program, and she would get nothing except a slap in the face and/or a rehabilitation sentence.

Two months earlier her office was engulfed by a fire which destroyed everything. The fire started mysteriously one night when no one was about, and it just so happened all the fire detectors and all the security cameras in the vicinity were faulty at that time. That was really strange; it was the first time in over two hundred years that electronic equipment had failed, and that in itself was very suspicious. The fire destroyed all her electronic documentation relating to the charges set against her, and with no way of proving her innocence, she seemed doomed. Even the copies held on the main computer had been mysteriously destroyed, and the fire couldn't have done that.

However, Danni was not without friends, some of whom were in high places. Where she was staying belonged to the mayor of Aberdeen, her first partner from when she left college many years ago, and the father of her only child, Pauline, who was now living in Bagman City. Her second, and even more powerful, friend was her present partner, Grade Two Ambassador Simon Tallsworth, Chairman of the Himalayan Research Council. Had he not been away on business when this incident happened, the outcome could have been very different. She'd been in close contact with him since her departure from the centre, and he was using his influence to find certain documents, copies of which would not only prove her innocence, they would also bring down her accusers. Electronic documentation had a knack of showing up even after its destruction, and Simon was working on it. She was biding her time, waiting for him to call with an update on the situation and was too restless to sit down.

Having nothing to keep her mind occupied, she started to think about her daughter, who was due to complete her training and take up a position somewhere. Perhaps she could get in touch and talk about old times; that brought a smile to her face. But that wouldn't be an easy thing to do, as she'd only seen her daughter twice since she was thirteen, and they seldom spoke to each other. It was not what you might call a healthy relationship. Giving her a private apartment at such a young age made her grow up too quickly, and that caused a lot of friction between them.

Danni was about to go to bed when the communications console indicated an incoming call. Boris, her personal companion of forty-four years, had been blocked after the tribunal hearing, so she knew it was a direct person-to-person video call, and not many people knew where she was. Her face brightened up at the sound, and she ran over to answer it instantly.

It was Simon. 'Hi Danni, I have some wonderful news for you. I haven't found any of your missing documents, but I have recovered some other documents. They show how those three lowlifes helped themselves to the missing funds and gained enormous wealth from your project. They've siphoned funds from the account over the past decade and I have full details of who has received payment and everyone implicated. A lot of heads will roll when this is made public, which it will be,' he said smiling.

Danni frowned, obviously disturbed by the news, and quietly replied, 'How are we going to play this? We have to expose them very carefully, so they won't have time to destroy that evidence.'

'I'll present the information to the full council when they assemble next Wednesday morning. I'll also tender my resignation if the three are not removed from office immediately.'

'Resign!' said Danni, sounding startled. 'No one at your level has ever done that before. It will make headlines worldwide!'

Simon looked up, catching her gaze. A broad smile spread across his face. 'That's right. If I don't, the council may try to cover it up. It's as simple as that.'

Danni was excited and told him, 'I'd love to be there just after the council make their decision. That would be fun. But I've been suspended from shuttle travel, so how can I obtain a travel permit and be back there by then?'

'The council are due to leave just after they make their decision. If you give those three any indication that you are coming back, it may make them wary. So don't even try; let me organise it. OK. OK!' he insisted, with a serious tone, indicating his annoyance that she could ruin his plans.

'OK. Thank you Simon. Let me know my travel arrangements as soon as you can. I hope to see you soon. Right now I'm off to bed, so good night.'

'Bye. Call you soon, and don't do anything till you hear from me,' were his last words before the screen went blank.

Simon was thinking hard. How could he arrange for a travel permit for Danni at such short notice, and in secret? Then he thought of her daughter, Pauline, who should be completing her college course soon, and he wondered if she could help. He turned to his communications console and asked for all information regarding Pauline Mitchell. A few minutes later he had all the information he required, and started to hatch a plan.

Pauline was to collect her diploma from the college in the afternoon of Friday, July 22. She had acquired a grade six dental technician certificate. She also possessed a strong personality like her mother and was very beautiful.

'Would be nice to have her around, very nice indeed,' he thought, and a smile spread across his face. He also noted that she was seeing a grade four consultant and his eyes lit up. A plan started forming in his head, and the thought that a grade four consultant could be on the way convinced him he was about to do the right thing.

He contacted the Himalayan Centre's administration manager and told him to enlist the services of a certain dental technician who had been brought to his attention. It meant calling in a favour owed him, but it was a small price to pay in order to get what he wanted. When the administration manager was told that a grade four consultant regeneration doctor could be coming with her, it clinched the deal. Pauline was to be drafted to the Himalayan Research Centre and should arrive next Wednesday, shortly after the council meeting had concluded.

It was seven in the morning when the communications console indicated an incoming video call. Danni was having breakfast on the apartment's balcony, enjoying the warm morning sun, and ran inside quickly to answer it. It was Simon.

'Hi Danni, do you want the good news?' He was smiling as he greeted her.

'If there's good news, there must be some bad news as well. So out with it!' Danni said.

'The good news is that you will be on a shuttle leaving Bagman City next Tuesday evening,' he said. 'The bad news is you'll be travelling with your daughter, Pauline.'

Simon went on to explain how he had drafted her daughter just to get a shuttle pod for her to travel in. He also told Danni about Pauline's prospective partner.

'You'll have to contact Grade Four Consultant Doctor Brian James, who resides in Bagman City, and let him in on the secret.' He continued, 'He must agree to partner Pauline for this to work, and he must book a shuttle pod for the three of you.'

'I'm on bad enough terms with my daughter already,' said Danni. 'Oh what the heck, it can't get any worse. OK, leave it with me; I'll sort something out. I'll call you when I've arranged everything. Bye for now, and thanks again Simon.'

'Don't forget, you must insist on complete secrecy,' Simon reminded her.

'OK. Don't worry,' she quickly replied, sounding cross with him.

He said goodbye and the screen went blank, and she decided to leave contacting the doctor until after Pauline had received the draft order.

At midday on Saturday, July 23, Danni received a message from Simon. Michael, Pauline's digital companion, had contacted him as Danni could not be found. The message from Michael stated that her daughter had attained grade six dental technician status, had collected her diploma, been drafted to the Himalayan Research Centre, and Consultant Doctor Brian James was to be her partner. Danni was also informed that her daughter's apartment had been vacated, and rental payment could cease forthwith.

Danni smiled to herself and said out loud, 'This is going to be easier than I ever thought possible. My daughter has actually managed to get a decent man without my assistance.'

For a brief moment she felt proud of Pauline, then she started hatching the next part of her plan.

Danni went back to the communications console and asked for the city hopper to be made available. It was the quickest way to get to Bagman City, and could be done in secrecy as long as she stated it was for the mayor's partner. Her request was accepted and arrangements were made for her to travel the next morning.

She also asked if there were any rooftop apartments vacant in Bagman City and was told the roof was totally unoccupied. When she heard this, she booked the whole roof until Tuesday, the day of her departure.

Sunday morning came and Danni made her way across the rooftop landing pad, where the city hopper was waiting to take her to Bagman City. The hopper buzzed and looked like a bee hovering over a flower. It was the best way of travelling. It was comfortable and luxurious, and as only those of grade three status and above could summon it, there were not many of them in a city.

It was a beautiful day; the sky was clear blue, and the air was hot and very dry.

'Summer is always a nice time,' she said to the pilot as she boarded. 'Shame I work underground and am always too busy to get out to enjoy it.'

The pilot said nothing, just nodded his head to acknowledge her words before holding her hand as she boarded the craft.

The takeoff went without incident, and as the hopper picked up speed, Danni sank back into the soft leather seat. They were flying inland, over lush, grassy plains dotted with grazing animals, and as the hopper turned and headed south, the sun shone brightly into her eyes. When her sight returned to normal, she noticed other city towers, a number of which could be seen from the height they were travelling. The sun glinted brightly off their forty-story, maroon-coloured, mirror-like exteriors, each poised over an underground city of millions. The hopper changed course slightly and passed close to the sea. She saw a fish-farming station just offshore. It was surrounded by fleets of trawlers with white water in their wakes, and it looked so tranquil. Yet she knew that it was working hard, trying to keep up with the ever-increasing demands placed on it. The whole surface of the planet was covered with farms, land, and sea, all working flat-out trying to feed the ever-increasing population, a population that was growing faster than food could be produced. And that's what she'd been working on. For the past decade she'd been developing new farming methods using genetically modified crops and animals to improve the situation. The project was extremely important, as it would affect everyone on earth. It promised great rewards on completion, and that's what all the fuss was about.

The hopper sped along the coast for awhile. The coast disappeared into the distant haze as a completely straight line for hundreds of kilometres; it was made that way during land reclamation many years ago. The pilot changed course and started to veer inland. The green grass gave way to wonderful fields of potatoes in full bloom, brilliant white and vivid yellow flowers in neat rows that looked like long stripes across the landscape.

Suddenly they came to a stop, the pilot adjusted a control, and the sides of the hopper became crystal clear. The pilot told Danni to look straight down and pointed to a city just below.

'That's the remains of Steinforth City. It went meltdown eighty-odd years ago and just over eight million people died. It's now a memorial and mass grave. That's why it's been covered with the clear dome; it keeps the radiation in and people out,' he commented.

That city's demise was the reason nuclear power had finally been abandoned. Now all cities were powered by the earth's thermal energy, and that was judged to be at maximum capacity.

'Power production, my next project!' said Danni to herself, and she smiled.

The hopper continued on its way. Before long they were passing over rolling hills covered in grass that seemed greener than before, and there were cows grazing everywhere.

'Almost there now,' said the pilot as he swept round the Bagman City Tower, waiting for permission to land.

Soon the hopper was resting on the roof landing pad and Danni alighted. She made her way across the roof, through the flower-filled, heavily scented garden, and entered the luxurious mayoral suite. All the roof and rooms had been reserved, just for her pleasure. Her journey of five hundred miles had taken just fifty-five minutes, which included the stop over the dead city.

Danni made straight for the communications console. 'Give me a list of all personnel grade four and above in the city at this time,' she demanded.

The console scanned her, and she waited for a reply. After a few seconds it burst into life.

'Here is the information you requested Chief Mitchell.'

Danni looked over the information displayed on the screen in front of her, only stopping when she recognised a name, and smiled.

'Security Chief Dave Lincoln and Chief Engineer Berty Beam!' The latter name she said with a hint of disgust. They'd all been to college at the same time and formed a close friendship. It was Berty Beam that made her feel uneasy though. For a short time they had been very close, until he wanted to act out his weird fantasies, and started chasing after other girls.

She decided to contact Dave Lincoln straight away. 'Get me the Security Chief,' she commanded.

Soon after Dave Lincoln was welcoming her to Bagman City, 'Hi Danni, nice to see you again after so many years. How are you?'

'Fine. You look good for your age, you old rascal,' said Danni, remembering how he made out with as many girls as he could when in college. 'Have you settled down yet?'

'Yes, been with the same partner for forty years now, a grandfather to thirty-two,' he said, with a note of glee in his voice.

'Wow! It is nice to hear that. I suppose you've heard what happened to me,' she said, sounding a little despondent.

'Aye, it's not like you though; must be a conspiracy or something. Anything I can do for you?' he said, hoping there wasn't.

'As a matter of fact there is,' she said. 'I wonder if you could keep my visit here under wraps, at least until next Thursday. If you don't mind, that is.'

'I won't ask why. But OK, if that's what you want, so be it. Must be something serious going down,' he replied.

'Yes there is, but you'll know all about it Wednesday evening if you keep your ear to the ground. Got to go now, see you sometime, OK?'

'OK. Bye. Take care, and mind the sharks don't bite,' he said just before the console went blank.

Danni smiled at that remark and instantly asked to speak to Chief Engineer Berty Beam. It was quite some time before the console came back to life, and she instantly recognised the face; it was Berty.

'Hi Danni, I haven't seen you for awhile. Fifteen years isn't it? How are you?' he spluttered, quite out of breath.

Danni noticed how flustered he was and saw a young woman moving hurriedly out of view. She remembered that he'd always been fat, and it looked like his waist had grown in proportion with his years.

'It's been some time. I'm fine, and by the looks of it so are you, lardy boy,' she replied.

'Still remember my name then. Sorry to hear about all that bad business over there,' he said sarcastically. 'What can I do for you, *OLD flame?*

Danni and Berty had been an item in their young teens. Her first true love, or so she thought at the time. She shivered with disgust and immediately put the thought out of her mind.

'I would like to meet up with you as soon as possible, if it's convenient,' she said.

'Sure. No problem. I'm in the waste control centre. I'll be here all night by the look of it. A major recovery has just started, some idiot got his arm trapped in machinery and it has to be removed. Jump on a spitter; it can bring you all the way down,' said Berty.

The spitter is the easiest mode of transport in an unfamiliar city. If you can get access, it will take you anywhere you want to go. Not cheap, but the alternative could mean hours walking, following complex maps and asking directions at every turn.

Danni requested a spitter, and one was waiting outside for her within minutes. She picked up her cloak and headed for the door. Once outside she jumped onto the spitter and waited while it scanned her.

'Good evening Chief Mitchell,' came the news that all was in order.

'Waste control centre,' she commanded.

'One moment please,' said the spitter, and it checked her authority before continuing. *'Approved, hold tight please.'*

Off it sped, wheels rumbling as it trundled over the path to the nearest spitter lift. Soon she'd been raised to the track and the maglev immediately kicked in. Danni felt the floating motion just before it picked up speed and headed for the main elevator near the north side of the tower, which was the most direct route into the lowest depths of the city. It entered the top section of the elevator and Danni watched as it selected level twenty-seven, deep in the bowels of the city. Down it went, deeper and deeper, the throbbing background noise increasing as it went. And the smells changed with every floor they passed.

'How can people live with this noise?' she said quietly to herself. 'And the smell,' she said as she pinched her nose.

The spitter reached level twenty-seven and shot off down one narrow alley after another. She was totally lost, but had faith in the little craft as it came to another elevator and headed down once again, this time to level thirty-nine. The noise was now deafeningly loud to her.

When the elevator stopped, the doors opened and a foul smell caught in the back of her throat; it was like something dead and decaying. Only then did she think the waste control centre must be near. The spitter shot out of the elevator into a very dirty corridor, turned another two corners, lowered to ground level, and halted outside an extremely clean door that looked totally out of place.

Danni stepped off the spitter and the door in front of her opened immediately. Berty was just inside ready to greet her with outstretched arms, sweating like a pig and smelling like one too. She took his hands and squeezed them; they were oily and very slippery to the touch, and it was the only contact she wanted with him. She held back the nauseous feeling building up in her stomach and smiled.

He held her hand and whisked her into the control room, where a young woman was cleaning an area of floor covered with what looked like oil.

Berty said a little flustered 'Excuse the mess, spilled my body lotion.'

Danni gave him an odd glance, dispelled a disgusting thought from her mind, and noticed the woman's tunic was partly undone. She shuddered at the though of what they'd been up to before she turned up.

Before Berty could say a word, Danni asked about the emergency he had mentioned earlier. Berty was quite amused to think that she had some interest in what went on in his domain but was also annoyed that she'd paid him no attention.

She walked across the room, looked out the window, and viewed the waste recycling area just below. Thousands of personnel worked in there, sorting everything by hand. It could be automated, except that work had to be found for all the people of the city, and this was the most labour-intensive type of work in the city.

Berty came up behind her and squeezed her left buttock. 'Nice butt! Just as firm as I remember. You're fifty-two going on twenty, and still looking good.'

Danni jumped back, not wanting any more contact.

Then Berty popped the one question that was bugging him. 'What are you here for?'

'You told me you have a serious problem down here. I believe a man has his arm trapped in a machine, and you need to get him out,' she said enquiringly.

'No, no, you silly woman. His arm is in the machine; he's in sickbay waiting for the on call doctor to be found,' Berty retorted. 'I don't really care about him. His arm is in the machine that recycles compost material, and no human waste must go in there *ever*.'

Danni looked at him with even more disgust. 'Show me where sickbay is. I want to help if I can.'

Berty looked really surprised. He thought, 'Danni help a stranger! What is she up to?'

Danni arrived at the sickbay and looked at a man who lay unconscious on a trolley. His arm was severed just above the elbow, and a dirty rope was tied tightly around it to stop the bleeding.

'Just right for regeneration,' she said to Berty.

'It'll take months to get a doctor's appointment for that,' he replied sarcastically.

Danni gave him a nasty look and asked him to contact Consultant Doctor Brian James at once.

He did so, but was still puzzled as to her motives and didn't dare ask why. He knew Danni from old and didn't want to antagonise her.

They waited together, reminiscing over old times and telling life's tales. It wasn't very pleasant for Danni, as Berty's exploits would shock most people.

Doctor Brian James arrived forty-five minutes later with a small pad under his right arm and an air of importance. He entered the room without knocking. After a quick glance around the room, he approached Berty. Berty just pointed at the patient, and Doctor James asked him for some information. Berty explained what happened while the unfortunate chap was being examined.

'I shouldn't have been called here for this. He should have been taken to the hospital for analysis first. Who authorised this?' he demanded, and looked really annoyed.

Danni took him to one side. 'I'm paying for this operation personally, so let's get on with it,' she said.

Doctor James liked hearing the words, 'I'm paying for this'. He smiled, called for a medical team to take the patient to the regeneration hospital on level four, and turned his attention back to Danni.

'I don't know who you are or why you are doing this for, as far as I can see, a complete stranger to you!' he said, with a perplexed look on his face.

Danni silenced him with a finger to her lips, bade Berty farewell, and asked him to say nothing about her visit to anyone. He agreed, so long as she said nothing about the accident, which meant it probably wasn't an accident after all.

Danni waited until they were at the hospital before speaking to Brian, and came straight to the point. 'I'm Pauline's mother, Grade Three Chief Scientist, Danni Mitchell,' she told him. 'I've acquired the roof apartments and garden for the rest of my stay in Bagman City. You are both welcome to join me after the partnering ceremony, if you wish.'

Brian was taken aback, stunned even. He'd never considered that a parent might turn up, let alone someone a grade higher than him.

'Thanks a lot, we would love to join you. I hope I can repay you some day,' he said, stuttering slightly, which was totally out of character for him.

'You can,' said Danni, before he could recover properly. 'You can book an extra single berth for your pod when you travel to the Himalayan Research Centre. And please don't ask why, or tell anyone about it, especially Pauline. OK?'

Brian looked uneasy at the last part of her request, but agreed to do it.

Danni spoke. 'I'll make sure you have clearance for the roof by Monday, and don't tell Pauline that I'm here. We will meet at the pod on Tuesday.'

She turned to leave, but spun around to say, 'Oh yes! Do fix that unfortunate man's arm quickly. Before Monday would be best.' Then she left.

It was Monday. Pauline's partnering ceremony was over, and Danni waited impatiently for her daughter to arrive at the roof garden. It had been a long time since she had seen her last, and was taken aback when she saw her. She was so young, graceful, and beautiful, with an air of confidence that reminded Danni of how she used to be. It seemed a long time had passed before she stopped looking through the one-way window, but it was only a few minutes and she had enjoyed every moment. She touched and stroked the wall that Pauline had stopped to rest against, as gently as if she were actually touching her, then left them in peace.

Danni hurried away and headed for the nearest communications console to call Simon.

Soon after, she was talking. 'Hi Simon, how are you?'

'Fine, and you?'

'Couldn't be any better. I just saw my daughter for the first time in ages and she looks terrific.'

'That's wonderful. How are your travel plans working out?' asked Simon

'I'll be arriving on Wednesday, and travelling on the Tuesday shuttle with Pauline and Brian as planned. So I'll see you then. OK?'

'That's brilliant news; I'll meet you at the shuttle. If there's any unexpected news, I'll keep you informed, though all should go as we expect. See you soon. Bye.'

She just had time to say bye before the screen went blank.

'Must tell him not to sign off so quickly in future,' she said to herself.

Tuesday arrived, and Danni made her way to the shuttle terminal early.

A spitter had been ordered and she was soon on her way. It was imperative that she was settled in the pod before Pauline and Brian arrived. Once settled she would wait until the shuttle started to move, then make her way to the pod's relaxation lounge to see Pauline.

The spitter descended through the floors quite quickly. Danni noticed the change in the atmosphere just as she did when she visited Berty Beam and placed her hand over her nose. She wasn't used to stale, smelly air and couldn't wait to get to the terminal.

The spitter alighted from the lift and dashed down a large corridor filled with the hustle and bustle of people going about their business. After a short journey, it entered another lift and descended even further, till it reached the terminal level. As the spitter alighted, she noticed the change of air and lowered her hand from her face. She looked at the vast expanse of the shuttle terminal and wondered where her pod was situated. She didn't need to worry though, as the little craft took her directly to the pod door, where she embarked quickly, entered, and scanned the layout.

After a few moments she found her berth, went inside, locked the door behind her, and made herself comfortable on the bed. She would have to wait for Pauline and Brian to come onboard and the shuttle to start moving before she could make her entrance.

CHAPTER 2
THE JOURNEY

After what seemed like ages, John, Juliette, Petal, and Fred felt a slight movement.

Fred and Petal glanced at each other apprehensively and said in unison, 'Here we go!'

They giggled to each other as their voices harmonised, and it reduced the tension slightly.

'The pod is being lifted onto the shuttle, by the feel of it,' John said, trying to ease the tension even more. 'We should be on our way soon.'

There was a slight relaxing of shoulders and a hint of smiles from everyone, which pleased him, and shortly after he'd finished talking, they felt the pod move again. This time it wobbled for a brief moment as the shuttle lifted on the maglev track. Then slight acceleration was felt and they slipped a little on the shiny seat surfaces before they braced themselves.

When Brian arrived at the shuttle terminal, he was relieved that Danni Mitchell was nowhere to be seen. He was a little apprehensive at what would happen when she did show her face, as he remembered how Pauline had reacted at just the mention of her mother.

Pauline had entered the pod before him, and as she was quiet, he assumed Danni had been delayed or something. After entering, he looked around and relaxed; Danni was nowhere to be seen. When Pauline asked him why the spare bedroom door was locked, he said nothing and hoped her mother wasn't inside.

The pod accommodating them was very large, a luxury class. Pauline remembered the pods she'd travelled in when she was a young girl, and she smiled. It seemed a lot smaller now that she was all grown up. Even so, it was still a big one.

'This is large for just the two of us!' Pauline remarked enquiringly to Brian. 'How come we have such a large pod?' She was still hoping he had a special treat for her.

Brian had to think quickly and blurted out, 'Perhaps it was the only one they had available. After all, I am grade four.'

She smiled, rose from the chair, and tried the door to the extra berth once again. Returning to the table, she ran her finger along its surface and felt its marble-like texture—cold and smooth. She was just about to head for their berth when there was a slight movement. She sat down at the table and looked at Brian, who was looking a little tense.

'Don't look so worried, it's just the shuttle moving into the main pipe,' she said, smiling at his reaction.

Brian sat down next to Pauline. It wasn't the movement that made him tense. What bothered him was the thought that, if she were onboard, Danni could walk in on them at any moment.

Quite a number of pods had been lifted onto units, and coupled together, they formed a long shuttle. Once the units were all in place, the shuttle lifted and started to move away from the platform area. It was beginning its journey, picking up speed on the Bagman City Branch Pipe, heading for the nearest junction to join the Main Intercontinental Shuttle Tube.

A pleasant female voice made an announcement. *'We will shortly be leaving Bagman City; a slight bump may be felt when coupling with the main train. Do not be alarmed, as this is normal. Have a pleasant journey and good evening.'*

Pauline and Brian's, and John and Juliette's pods were heading for the Himalayan Research Centre, taking the tube route from Finland to Siberia via France, Turkey, and India. The final part of their journey to the research centre was via the Himalayan Branch Pipe. It would take an estimated twenty-three hours to complete the journey. The nearest

Intercontinental Junction was at Verdun in France, just a mere two hours and forty-five minutes away.

John felt the movement, rushed to a window, selected clear view, and looked through the small aperture in the side of the pod. He saw the loading platform, followed by more platforms and tracks, slip by as the speed increased. Then, suddenly there was only the blur of ground rushing past with no features. He shut the window view off and settled down in the relaxation lounge with Juliette, Petal, and Fred.

John and Juliette were embarrassed as they sat at the table in silence, not wanting to go to their double berth and to bed while the other two were there.

Petal spoke first. 'I think we should go to our rooms for awhile. Want a look at mine?' she whispered to Fred, nudging him with her elbow.

Then they left, leaving John and Juliette alone in the lounge.

It wasn't long before Juliette broke the silence with a smile, 'Come on, let's see what our room looks like.'

'You wearing those pink panties?' he asked her.

She smiled, and her cheeks changed to bright pink as she replied coyly, 'You'll have to see for yourself.'

Holding his hand, she walked backwards, not taking her eyes off him even for a moment, and led him to their berth. As they entered the room, Juliette was looking very nervous. Shaking slightly, she whispered, 'Lock the door behind you.'

This was their first night alone together and they had a lot to learn, especially about each other, as neither had done anything like this before.

Fred waited in Petal's room for the next thirty minutes, then poked his nose out to see if the coast was clear. There was no sign of life, so he called Petal to follow, and they entered the lounge to sit at the table. It wasn't long before they were busy scanning the entertainment console for something to keep them occupied. They were chatting to each other as if they were old buddies and had known each other for a long time. There was no entertainment they liked, so they tried to listen at the door of John's berth. All was quiet there too, so they decided to retired to their own compartments for the night, even though it was still early.

Pauline and Brian selected the clear roof and watched the loading area and the rest of the shuttle terminal slip past. It wasn't long before they were staring at the blur of ground rushing past. Pauline requested a solid white roof, to change the clear roof into a white ceiling. It changed instantly but was too bright. So Brian asked for it to be dimmed, and the emitted light changed to a more relaxing glow. It felt soothing, making Pauline snuggle into Brian's arms and think of going straight to bed.

Just then, the door to the attached compartment clicked open. Pauline turned and was startled to see her mother standing in the doorway.

'What the heck are you doing here?' Pauline said with anger in her voice and a look on her face that could kill.

Danni explained that she needed to get to the Himalayan Research Centre secretly and knew of no other way to do it. She also explained how Brian had helped her out.

When Pauline heard that Brian knew about it, she turned red in the face and shouted, 'You bastard, you could have warned me!'

Pauline stormed into her berth, slamming the door behind her.

Brian rushed after her and tried the door; it was locked.

He stood there trying to talk to her through the door. 'Pauline, I am truly sorry. I didn't know things were as bad as that between you and your mother. I would never have done it if I'd known.'

All was in vain. The door was totally soundproof, and she heard none of his attempt at an apology.

Danni turned and disappeared into her berth. She locked the door behind her and decided to keep to herself for the remainder of the journey.

Brian tried to catch her before she withdrew from the lounge, but he was too late. He wanted to find out why Pauline hated her so much, and it now looked like he would have to wait for some time before that would be possible.

He settled on the couch and pulled a travel blanket over him. 'Looks like a cold, lonely night,' he said to himself before dimming the light to off.

Soon after that he was fast asleep.

John and Juliette lay in each other's arms, fast asleep and breathing gently. Suddenly, a vibration woke them up and John looked at the time; it was just after five in the morning. The vibration wasn't violent, but lasted a good few seconds, and it felt strange. They got dressed quickly, made for the lounge, and were greeted by Petal and Fred in their dressing gowns. They too had been woken by the vibration and were slightly scared. They'd not been told that something like this might happen during the journey and wondered if they were joining the main train.

John opened the window viewer to see if there was anything wrong and had quite a shock. He wasn't expecting the train to be in midair, but that's how it seemed. In the early morning light he could see the valley below, very far below. They were passing through the Dolomites, a mountainous region just north of Italy. He called Juliette over to see the view; she'd never seen the surface before.

'Come and see this view Juliette; I think you'll be thrilled. We're above ground,' he said.

Juliette came to the window hesitantly, wondering what it looked like. She had never seen the surface before, and as she looked out of the window, she fell backwards in shock.

'Sorry. I've never seen so much space, and so high up. It made me feel dizzy for a moment,' she said, feeling the effects of vertigo.

John smiled and said calmly, 'Come on! Come and have another look, only more slowly this time. OK!'

Juliette looked at him in horror. 'Sorry, I don't want to see that sight again, if you don't mind.'

John was taken aback. He didn't know what to say and blurted out rather stupidly, 'Chicken.'

Juliette ran crying to the sleeping berth, pushing Petal aside as she went.

John, realising his stupidity, quickly followed her. 'Sorry Juliette, that was a bit insensitive of me,' he apologised, and then closed the door behind him.

Petal and Fred were stunned, wondering what she had seen that had made her so upset. Slowly the two of them came to the window and peered out. There was nothing, just the earth flashing past, so fast, it was just a blur. They looked at each other, moved over to the table, and slumped down on the seats to eat some food. Suddenly light came through the window again and they rushed over to look at what was outside. They were passing over another valley, far below. The sight shocked them too, and they quickly slunk down below the window for protection. Staring at each other with shocked and surprised looks on their faces, they slowly raised their heads again. Only this time they knew what to expect and stayed at the window to peer out at the green, grassy slopes and snow-covered mountains.

They thought it was an amazing sight—so much space, and colourful as well. Fred put his arm around Petal to get better support and, in the excitement of the moment, Petal gave him a kiss on the lips.

Realising her mistake, she jumped back. Fred put his arm to his mouth, wiped his lips with his sleeve, and started spitting.

'Yuk!' he said. 'That was disgusting.'

'Sorry Fred, I forgot myself for a moment. It was all this excitement. It won't happen again,' Petal replied, her cheeks glowing bright pink.

'Too right!' he replied, still wiping his mouth with the back of his hand.

They decided to keep their distance from then on.

Danni was sitting on her bed reading a book. Earlier events had made sure she couldn't sleep, and she kept thinking of Pauline. Danni felt proud at how well Pauline had turned out; she was so beautiful. She wished she had spent more time with her daughter, but it was too late for that.

She felt the shuttle come to a stop and looked out to see where they were. The shuttle had arrived at Verdun. She knew it was going to be stationary for a few hours as it waited for the normal tube traffic to subside. It was always busy at night; food had to be shipped constantly. After an hour she decided to try and get some sleep, as there was still a long trip ahead.

She was woken by what she thought was the shuttle coupling with the train, but then realised she felt the train vibrate. It made her jump off the bed, put on a dressing gown, and head for the lounge. She turned up the lighting in the relaxation lounge and woke Brian.

'Oh! It's you. What's up Danni, you look a little perplexed,' he said, still half asleep.

'The train vibrated a moment ago, and that just doesn't happen in a tube. There must be something wrong,' she told him.

'Was it the shuttle coupling with the train?' he asked sleepily, then noticed what time it was. It was just after five in the morning.

Brian was now a bit worried by Danni's remark. Pauline was locked in their berth, and he had no way of letting her know that something might be wrong. 'Can you find out what it was?' he asked Danni.

'I'll contact my partner, Simon, he's at the Himalayan Research Centre. He should know if there's a problem. Select a clear roof and have a look outside if you can,' she told him and sat at the table.

Danni called Simon on a secure line from the entertainment console. 'Simon. Hi, you look awful, and a bit edgy. Is everything OK over there?'

Simon gave her a chilling look, horror in his eyes, and then started to speak in a shaky voice. 'A large meteor has hit Ukraine and surrounding areas. Damage reports are coming in, but it will be awhile before we have a complete picture of how much destruction has been caused.'

Now Danni looked shocked. 'There was some vibration felt on the train a little while back. Can you find out if it's still safe for us to travel?'

'Sure, wait a moment. I'll just bring the network online . . . looks fine from here. Let's hope there are no more strikes. I've got to go now, too much information coming in.'

'Keep me informed of the situation please?' she quickly asked.

'OK, will do. See you soon?' And he was gone.

The question in his voice made her feel uneasy. What wasn't he telling her? How much destruction had there really been? There was no way of getting him to talk; she'd just have to sit and ride it out.

Brian had been listening to what was said. 'That sounds really serious to me,' he said, and his face drained of all colour.

Just then, a loud bang made them both jump and spin round, their faces as white as snow. Pauline stood in the doorway of her berth, looking sleepy and rubbing her eyes. 'Sorry, didn't mean to open the door so quickly; it slipped.'

She took one look at the expressions on the faces of Brian and Danni and instantly jumped to the wrong conclusion. 'What have you been up to with my mother?' she shouted at Brian. 'I can't leave her alone with a man for one second before she tries it on with him.'

She went towards her mother with a fight in her eyes. Brian jumped up and stepped between them just in time. Pauline let fly her hand and caught him on the side of his face before he could grab her arms. He held her tightly in his grasp and blood trickled down his face where her nails had caught him. The scratch was starting to sting.

Danni shouted at Pauline, 'Stop being a stupid brat and listen to what we have to say; it's deadly serious.'

Pauline cooled slightly, just enough for Brian to loosen his grip and tend to his face with a refresher wipe. She was still not calm enough for him to sit down though.

He stood firmly between them as Danni spoke.

'Earth has been struck by a meteor. It hit Ukraine a short time ago. My partner, Simon, confirmed it a few moments ago. We don't know the extent of the damage it has done, so we'll have to wait for more news. At this moment our journey is safe.'

Pauline looked at her with a shocked expression, then at Brian holding the towel to his face. 'Did I do that to you?' she asked him calmly, now looking slightly bemused.

Brian nodded and wondered quietly, 'Was she so enraged that she didn't know what she was doing? What would have happened if she had had a knife in her hand?' He shuddered at the thought. It must have been quite something for her to see total red so quickly. And it only happened when she realised he was alone with her mother.

Pauline moved towards Brian, touched his hand that was tending his wound, and slowly removed the wipe from his face.

'Ouch,' she said. 'Sorry, I bet that hurts. Come; let me treat it for you.'

She led Brian into their berth, closed the door quietly, and put her arms around him tightly.

'Sorry, I thought for a moment she'd seduced you. It wouldn't be the first time she's done that. She's done it twice before, with boys I liked very much, and it's not nice seeing your mother making out with your boyfriend.'

Brian looked at her and felt a deep disgust for her mother.

'What do you take me for?' he said with a hint of comedy in his voice. 'Your mother may look young for her age, but she's an old prune and a first-class bitch with it. She has too many years under her belt to be attractive to me.'

Pauline smiled. 'I love you,' she said as she kissed him and pushed him back onto the bed.

Then it dawned on her what her mother had said about the meteor, and she started to shake with shock. Tears welled up in her eyes as she uttered, 'All those poor people.' She whimpered and collapsed into his arms.

Brian held her close, stroking her hair for comfort, and kissed her softly.

Danni was worried. This had never happened before. A meteor, no matter how big, would have catastrophic repercussions for the whole planet. Ukraine was a vast, wheat-growing region, and many cities depended on its produce.

It had been over two hours since feeling the vibrations and, as nothing else had happened, Danni relaxed a little. She sat quietly in the lounge, looking out through the clear roof and watching the ground slip by. A junction came in sight, with shuttle units leaving and joining the train just like normal, and the sight distracted her for a little while. Then the ground began flashing by as the terminal disappeared far behind and the train started picking up speed once again. She was about to shut off the view when the pod shot out of the ground and began travelling over water. Startled by the suddenness of the change, she turned and glanced in the direction where she believed Ukraine was. A look of horror appeared on her face, and she was fixed to the spot for a few moments. Once she'd gathered her thoughts, she ran to Pauline's berth, and was lucky to find the door unlocked. Opening it, she quickly burst in and caught them in an embrace, which took them all by surprise.

'Come and see this,' she said. 'We are over the Black Sea.'

They covered themselves quickly and made their way to the lounge. 'This had better be good,' said Pauline, her teeth clenched tightly together in anger.

They entered the lounge to see Danni pointing north, where a black cloud filled the sky. It seemed to be boiling, rolling over on itself, and appeared to be getting closer. They looked down at the water below; huge waves were crashing against the tube support columns, threatening to bring them tumbling down. Danni knew they were strong, but how much they could take was unknown. A fishing vessel had broken in half and was sinking close to a support column; it sank very quickly. The tops of the waves were blown into long plumes of spray by the strong winds, whipped up by the approaching maelstrom. A second tube, running from east to west and parallel to theirs, looked electrified, glowing bright white in places. Both tubes were magnets for lightning, which was bursting from the cloud and constantly striking, causing the tubes to glow eerily in the dimming light.

Danni thought out loud, 'I hope we'll be back underground before that cloud hits us. Who knows how destructive it is.'

Brian held Pauline tightly in his arms, the intrusion by her mother forgotten, for the moment anyway.

Danni shut off the clear roof. She'd seen enough, and if something bad was about to happen she'd rather not know about it. All three sat down together, and for the first time since she was a child, Pauline held her mother's hand. They all held hands and waited. It would be another ten minutes before the train submerged again, ten terrifying, long minutes just spent staring at each other.

Danni begged them to stay with her. It was the first time she'd felt fear. She was really frightened now, and showed it.

Petal and Fred remained in the relaxation lounge, hoping to see more of the surface. They played games on the entertainment console but continued to look at the windows, waiting to see light again.

Light came again. It was over two hours since they'd seen it last, and the train was now above ground again.

Fred saw it first, and rushed over to the window. 'Petal, it's above ground again. Wow! Come and see this Pet.'

'Don't call me pet. I'm not your pet, my name is Petal,' she shouted, scolding him.

'Just come and see this storm,' he said.

She made her way quickly over to the window, and carefully keeping her distance from him, looked out. Just a quick glance made her stare in wonder. 'That looks like a stormy sea. I'd hate to be out in that. Look at that black cloud in the distance. It's coming towards us by the look of it, and it's going to be quite dark soon judging by the colour of it.'

Just then John came into the lounge. Petal smirked at him and said, 'Kicked you out of bed did she!'

John picked up a cushion and hurled it at her. 'That's enough of that, my little Pet,' he said, knowing she hated being called that.

Petal looked at Fred and gave him an angry glance. He was pointing at her and sniggering. He whispered, 'Pet. He he!'

'John, come and see this storm,' Fred shouted excitedly.

John looked out of the window and stared. He'd never, in all his time on the surface, seen anything like this. He'd seen twisters, but never anything of this magnitude. He crossed to the entertainment console and tried to find some news about the storm. The news just stated that a storm was raging over Ukraine and everyone was to remain calm until it blew over.

'Some storm,' he thought.

Returning to the window, he saw the lightning and was fascinated by the colours it produced when it struck the tubes.

He pointed it out to Petal and Fred, 'Look at the lightning striking the tubes. You can make out little sprites jumping from pillar to pillar . . . See you later; I'm off back to bed.'

Petal and Fred pressed their faces against the window to see the sprites, and their imaginations took over.

Petal was annoyed at Fred for poking fun when John called her Pet, and moved closer to him. 'Think it's funny to laugh at me, do you?' she said, and pinched his arm hard.

Fred flinched, but said nothing; he just carried on looking out the window. Petal was bored, and retired to her berth. She was soon back, feeling very hungry, and made for the larder.

Fifteen minutes passed, then twenty, and nothing had happened. Danni smiled and was just about to speak when vibrations hit the train once more, only this time they were a little stronger. 'Not another hit,' she told herself, and crossed to the console to contact Simon once again.

'Hi again, glad to see you are still with us,' he remarked before she could say a word.

'How bad is it?' she asked, as the lines on her face began to show her age.

'The storm surge has just taken out the tubes over the Black Sea. You were lucky to have just passed through that area. It really is bad. But at least we've had no more meteor strikes,' said Simon, with an even more worried look on his face than before.

She could tell from the look on his face that things weren't good. He was ashen and looked totally drained.

'What are our chances of survival?' she asked with a slight croakiness.

'If you get here at all it'll be a miracle. You may have to take refuge somewhere along the way, as the disruption could last for weeks or at least until repairs can be made to the tubes. We'll just have to hope the tube you are in remains intact, as there are earthquakes cropping up all over the planet and we don't know where the next one will occur.'

That bit of news shocked her, and she sat in silence.

Simon broke the last bit of bad news as she sat there with her mouth agape. 'You are travelling through a region known for big quakes, and it won't end until you reach the middle of India. I have my fingers crossed for you.'

'Thanks for the truth. I've never been so scared in all my life as I am now,' she spoke with a dry mouth.

Simon noticed that they were all holding hands round the console. 'Try to put your past behind you and make the most of the time you have together from now on. Who knows how long that will be,' he said with a smile.

Pauline looked at her mother and smiled thinly. 'We'll see.'

'Brian, you're a lucky man. Pauline seems to be a good woman to have by your side. If you can get through this, we may just have enough work to keep you both busy for the rest of your lives. It's bad in the surrounding areas, and although we have all the equipment we have no staff to operate it. We . . .'

The screen went blank. Simon was gone. Danni just stared at it, hoping it would spring back into life, but to no avail. All attempts to contact Simon again came back with the notice 'Destination out of contact, please try again later.' Then there were more vibrations, not big ones, just long and regular.

John didn't say a word to Juliette about what he had seen out the window. The lightning had been so bright, it was still imprinted on the back of his eyes as he entered the bedroom. He crept quietly back into bed, not quietly enough though, and woke her up.

'I'm sure I felt the Pod move that time,' she said.

'Must be back underground again,' he said. 'It seems to vibrate every time we go in or out.'

Juliette giggled when he said that, and gave him a dig in the ribs. The pillow fight that followed left them covered in small pieces of foam.

'What a mess!' she said. 'Hope we don't have to clean it up.'

They stopped when they heard a loud rumbling noise, then looked at each other and laughed. It was John's stomach making the noise. Juliette looked at him for a moment, smiled, and got up to get dressed. John did likewise, and soon they were making food in the larder; they were starving.

As Juliette entered, Petal said, 'Hope we are going to eat something. I'm starving.'

John looked at her pitiful expression and replied, 'You don't have to wait for us. Help yourself next time, OK?'

Juliette opened the larder door and threw a small tea cake at John, hitting him in the groin. He doubled up with the pain that welled up inside him.

'Ouch! That hurt. Was it a rock cake or something?' he said, shuffling over to the table.

They all laughed, sat down for some breakfast, and apart from the sound of munching, were extremely quiet.

As they were eating, the vibrations started again and everyone froze. The vibrations were not strong but they were coming regularly and some plates in the cupboard started rattling.

Juliette went over to make sure they were secure and closed the cupboard door firmly.

'Someone must be jumping around in the pod next-door by the feel of it,' Petal said jokingly.

'It's more like a fairground ride,' John uttered, not wishing to alarm anyone.

'Come to bed when you've finished,' said Juliette, as she ran back to the berth.

Danni was getting even more worried. She knew a lot more than anyone about what could happen. Once an earthquake shook a tube and a number of pods were dislodged from a train. They came to an abrupt stop, and all the passengers were killed, though the pods were recovered intact. Humans do not like going from the speed of sound to a dead stop in less than two seconds. 'It does something to their minds. Well, that's how the news reporter put it,' Danni muttered to herself, remembering the incident.

Then another wave of vibrations hit the train, only this time they were more violent and tossed some loose items around the lounge.

'Better make everything safe. I don't want to arrive dead, killed by a flying saucer,' said Danni with a chuckle.

Pauline and Brian smiled and cleared the lounge of anything that could cause injuries.

Danni tried the communications console again, but it was still dead.

John was holding Juliette when the first violent vibration hit and caused the bed to collapse under them. Luckily it was only a foldaway, which was light, and could be erected again quite quickly. Juliette was a little shocked and, after picking herself up off the floor, picked up the bedding. John took hold of the frame and set about putting it back into place.

John cursed and told her, 'The idiots didn't lock the hinges.'

Juliette got dressed again, ran to the lounge, and, still suffering from the shock, blurted out, 'Something made the bed collapse under us.'

Then she noticed Petal standing over Fred, her face white, and mouth agape.

'What's happened?' Juliette screamed, as she ran to her brother. Fred was lying quite still on the floor, and she noticed a small amount of blood trickling from the side of his head.

'What happened?' she said again, shaking Petal into life.

'The . . . the plate flew from the shelf and hit him on the head,' Petal said, and shaking with shock, started to sob.

John entered the room, saw what was going on, and rushed for the first aid kit. Without saying a word, he set to work on the wound and soon the blood flow had stopped.

'He'll be OK. Must get him seen by a doctor as soon as we arrive at the centre,' John said calmly. 'Let's put everything away just in case there are anymore big shakes.'

Petal looked at Juliette, 'Didn't you close the cupboard door properly?' It was more of an accusation than a question.

Juliette looked at John and the expression on her face told him she had done so. He crossed to the cupboard and examined the door closely.

'The lock is faulty. I'll secure it with my dressing gown tie.' And he shot off to get it.

As soon as he'd completed the makeshift repair, he sat next to Juliette and held her hand as she sat with Fred's head on her lap. Petal was cleaning up, putting everything safely away, and wiped away the small pool of blood. That last task made her feel slightly queasy and she had to run to the toilet.

It wasn't long before Fred was sitting up, wide-awake, and drinking hot and sweet milk. Between sips he complained about his head hurting and Juliette tried to comfort him by stroking his hair.

When Petal reappeared she looked awful. Her eyes were red and she was quite pale.

Danni activated the clear roof, wondering why there were so many new vibrations. Once again they were above ground and there was a strange glow in the sky. Instead of daylight, which she expected, there was boiling blackness all around them with the tube glowing red and blue as lightning struck it. She saw what looked like a rock hit the tube, felt the vibration, and heard the ringing clang.

'There must be many rocks hitting the tube, judging by all the vibrations we're feeling,' Pauline said with a shaky voice.

It was the first time she had spoken for quite some time, and her voice wasn't only shaky, it was also hoarse with fright. Danni noticed the state she was in, and squeezed her hand tightly.

This section was going to take at least forty-five minutes to clear. They were over the Caspian Sea and had slowed down a bit, though they had no way of knowing that at that moment.

'Can the tube withstand what is being thrown at it?' thought Danni. 'I don't have enough information.'

They sat and watched the stormy, black sky, with rocks and dust hitting the tube, fascinated, too scared to do anything else. It was a spectacular sight, like fireworks, only they hoped never to see these ones ever again.

'This is something to tell my grandchildren,' Danni remarked and looked over to Pauline and Brian with a smile on her face.

They smiled back and looked at each other, but said nothing.

Meanwhile, the vibrations continued. Some were violent, but most were gentle. Then the tube plunged underground once more and the vibrations soon petered out.

'That was the last over-sea section,' Brian stated, more as a remark than a question, as he remembered some of his geography lessons.

'Are there any more aboveground sections left?' he asked Danni.

'Yes, just one. As we make a descent from the mountains of Pakistan, we will plunge down to the plains of India,' she told him.

'Pakistan!' he replied, a little shocked. He'd forgotten about that region. They looked at each other knowing what lay ahead, hoping, against all hope, the tube would remain intact.

Brian took Pauline by the hand and led her to their berth. 'Let's try and get some rest,' he said, just wanting to be alone with her, hoping to take his mind off what was happening.

Danni remained in the lounge, hoping communications could be restored. She was continually fiddling with the communications console.

John and Juliette were playing games on the entertainment console when it went blank. 'That's just what we need,' John muttered. 'What are we going to do now?' The look on Juliette's face made him finish his sentence with, 'Don't say it, just don't. OK!' Then he started flicking small food balls at her.

When they started to wrestle, Petal said sarcastically, 'Take a cold shower, you two!'

'OK,' Juliette giggled, as she pulled John towards their berth. 'See if you can get the console working, Pet,' she said, just before the door slammed shut behind her.

She didn't hear Petal shout angrily, 'I AM NOT YOUR PET!'

For Danni, time was passing too slowly, but as it did, she became calmer. There had been no vibrations for fifteen minutes, and judging by the motion of the train, shuttles were coming and going again. She requested a clear roof, looked out, and saw they were passing through a junction. Everything seemed to be running like clockwork and appeared to be working normally, just like nothing had happened. Or so it seemed.

'Good, back to normal,' she said, smiled to herself, and retired to her berth to get some rest.

Thirty minutes later she was thrown from her bed, ending up on the floor after bouncing off the wall. She untangled herself from the bedding and ran to the lounge where Pauline and Brian were already standing.

The three of them looked out of the window. They were still underground and could see patches of dull, red rock flashing past, some of it glowing slightly. They could feel heat coming through the clear wall as they passed, and Danni guessed they were in Pakistan. Crouching down to avoid the radiated heat, they huddled together as the shuttle shot through a brightly glowing patch of rock, too bright to look at and too hot for comfort. The ventilation system went into overdrive to compensate and the sound of rushing air made them shout to be heard.

Danni shouted, 'Close window!'

The roof of the pod went instantly white, the ventilation quickly brought the lounge temperature back to normal, and the three of them rose to sit at the table.

Ten minutes later Danni opened the roof to see if the danger had passed. It looked like solid rock was flashing past once again, and there was a sigh of relief as the temperature in the lounge remained constant. They all crossed their fingers, hoping for no more hot spots, and sat silently looking at each other.

Danni was glad the walls of the tube were so thick and strong. She'd always thought how much energy could have been saved if they'd been made thinner. Now she praised the engineers who designed them all those many, many years ago.

The train shot out of a steep cliff face and slowly descended a mountainside to the plain below. It passed through a river of lava, which was cascading into the valley below like a waterfall, and they all felt the heat. The tube and its support glowed dull red as they passed. The lava was only visible as the train banked in a steep turn. Danni thought she saw the tube wobble for a moment before it disappeared behind a boiling black and red cloud. They were descending to the plains ahead of them, and had to get past the next air lock before something bad happened.

'Melting. Must be ready to collapse at anytime,' Danni whispered, so quietly, no one could hear what she'd said.

The sky was almost pitch-black, even though it wasn't yet four in the afternoon, local time.

'At least there are no rocks hitting the tube now. Hopefully the rest of the journey should go without any more problems,' Brian said, in a more upbeat tone of voice, hoping he was right.

He hadn't seen what Danni had just seen, and Danni said nothing to alarm either of them.

Danni agreed with just a nod of her head. She noticed Pauline was starting to relax a little and smiled at her. 'We still have at least three hours before we reach the Himalayan Branch Pipe,' Danni pointed out. 'So let's get some rest.'

John and Juliette were in bed, and Petal and Fred were in the lounge chatting, when all of a sudden the pod was thrown to one side and back again. John and Juliette picked themselves up off the floor and jumped out of the way as the bed came crashing back down from the wall. Juliette was terrified, paralysed to the spot, as the bed came to rest at her feet.

John spoke with a worried look on his face, 'Quick, let's go to see how those two are, they must be petrified.'

Juliette quickly regained her composure and put her dressing gown on. They entered the lounge to see Petal and Fred hugging each other and crying. They had a look of sheer terror in their eyes and Petal was as white as a sheet.

John saw their faces and tried to make out there was nothing wrong.

'Wow,' he said, 'just like a virtual-reality roller coaster ride. They never told me the journey would be this exciting.'

Petal looked at him with total surprise, 'THIS IS NORMAL?' she shouted, almost screaming at him.

'Yes. And if the console had been working we'd have been informed to watch out for it,' said John jovially, while giving Juliette a glance, as if to say, 'Please agree with me.'

Juliette saw the look on John's face and nodded her head in agreement. Petal ran to John and hugged him tightly, and Fred clutched Juliette just as tightly.

There was an extremely loud bang and violent shaking that seemed to come from the rear of their pod. It was followed by more violent jerks and shakes, and the console burst back to life. John ran over to it, hoping to find out what had happened.

'Juliette, take Petal and Fred to see the mess in our room, will you please?'

Juliette detected the authority in his voice and obeyed instantly. She ushered them both into the bedroom and closed the door quietly behind her as she went.

'Damage report. Now.' John demanded.

John sat and watched the report slowly scroll down the screen, tapping his finger on the table, showing his impatience. He kept looking back over his shoulder at the bedroom door, hoping it would stay closed for a little while longer.

The console displayed a routine checklist, and started to tick off items as it went.

Integrity of Pod: Correct.

Integrity of Shuttle unit: Compromised.

Twenty-five Shuttle units ahead.

Zero Shuttle units behind.

Train proceeding on schedule.

Due to arrive at destination in 4 hours and 35 minutes.

There is no further information available at this time. Please try again later.

'What on earth happened?' John said to himself, shaking with the shock of the report. He asked for any news or information on the situation.

The only reply was, *'Train proceeding on schedule. Due to arrive at destination in 4 hours and 31 minutes.'*

Just then Juliette, Petal, and Fred came back into the lounge and John quickly changed the console to the entertainment section.

'I suppose we'll have to wait till we arrive at the centre before we can find out what's happened,' John said. 'It just told me we are still on time and only a few more hours to go, so it won't be long now.'

John tried to look as if everything was OK, but Juliette knew something was up. He said quietly to her, 'I tried to get some news from the entertainment console but there was nothing available, and that's odd. There was no news whatsoever from anywhere!'

They all sat at the table and tied spare clothing around themselves and the chairs. Anything to stop them from being thrown around if the shaking happened again. No one wanted to risk being thrown around the bedroom again, so that was a "no go" area.

Danni decided to try the console one more time and was surprised that it was fully functional again. She called Simon immediately.

'Hi Danni. You're still with us?' he said with a thin smile.

'I'm a tough old bird, can't get rid of me that easily. What's the situation?'

'We've taken control of all the remaining trains and redirected them here. There are only ten left on the system.' There was a short silence before he continued, 'No, make that nine, we've just lost another. The tube is still intact ahead of you, but a collapse in the tube behind destroyed forty-five shuttle units at the rear. Luckily you went through an air lock before it closed; it may have been the lock closing that cut the shuttle sections off. Anyway, there are only twenty-five units left now. The twenty-fifth pod asked for a damage check, so someone is still alive back there. Whoever they are, they must be scared stiff.'

'Aren't we all? I wondered what caused the violent shaking a short while ago. How much damage has been reported so far?' she asked.

'That's the trouble. We've had no reports, and it makes me think there is too much damage. The tubes are collapsing everywhere, and without them we can't communicate with anyone.'

'That does sound bad!' Danni remarked. She could see the strain Simon was under. It showed on his face, and his voice was a little shaky.

'I have to go now. The Northern Development Dome has collapsed in an earthquake. Call me later, OK?' Then Simon was gone.

Danni looked at her daughter, 'There's nothing we can do except sit it out I'm afraid.'

They sat in the lounge chairs and activated game mode from the entertainment console. The chairs changed shape as their padded areas expanded. Belts wrapped themselves around Danni, Pauline, and Brian's legs and bodies, holding them tightly so they couldn't be thrown about again.

Danni smiled and said, 'If there are any more shocks, at least we'll be prepared.'

She looked across at the larder with its door open wide. What a mess; the food inside looked as if it had been in a blender. She instantly lost her appetite. Releasing the chair straps, she stood up, crossed to lounge, and closed the larder door.

John untied himself from the seat to take a look out of the window. He wasn't expecting to see anything, but was quite surprised. They were passing through a junction, and a number of shuttle units were trying to match the speed of the train, ready to couple. Suddenly they became a blur and disappeared behind. He realised that those shuttle units had come to an abrupt stop. Something must have been in their way, and he shuddered to think what could've happened to the travellers in the shuttle pods. He walked back to the table, strapped himself in, and said nothing.

'Anything out there?' asked Petal.

'No, just ground rushing past as usual,' He replied, not wanting to upset them more than they already were.

There was a change in the pod's motion, so Danni selected the clear roof to see what was happening. They were at a junction and she noticed shuttle units picking up speed along side them. The units were attempting to join the train as it passed through the terminal, and had to match their train's speed to couple at the end. The number of shuttle units made the train look quite long. Soon the units were almost up to speed.

'I hope they can couple,' Pauline said, biting her bottom lip.

As they continued, the shuttle units moved slowly closer, until they were right alongside. They saw clear-roofed pods on the top of shuttle units with many smiling people waving to them. They waved back. The people were just a few metres away.

Then they disappeared from view. The shuttle units became a blur and disappeared behind, and for a moment the junction was obscured by a cloud of dust or smoke. Danni felt a small vibration and quickly realised those shuttles had crashed into something. She went white in the face and shivered, thinking the same thing could happen to the train they were on, just as suddenly.

'At least it was quick,' she said to Pauline, who was staring out at nothing, her mouth wide open.

'They were smiling and waving,' said Pauline with a broken voice. Then she broke down and cried.

Tears came to all their eyes.

'Not long now,' Danni thought, but the tension was beginning to show. It was to be a terrifying time, not knowing what might happen. And they were so close to safety, if there was safety to get to.

Danni contacted Simon once again, mainly for some reassurance and comfort. 'Hi, I think another train has gone. What's the situation with the collapsed dome?' she asked him.

Simon looked tired. 'Hi Danni, I think we'll be OK. It's not as bad as first reported, just a slight buckling of a support and that's been made secure for now. As for your situation, your tube is still intact. As a matter of fact, just about the only one that is. That train you mentioned was one of the surviving ones. Pity, just five left now. It's bad all over. If the impact hasn't caused enough damage, the damage to the food supply system will be felt by everyone, now most of the tubes are out of action.'

'There isn't anything we can do about it; nature must take its course,' she said, trying to ease the pressure he was feeling.

She knew he would be blaming himself for this disaster, and it was no one's fault; there was nothing anyone could've done.

Simon continued with a worried look on his face, 'You'll be passing through Nâgpur City in India soon. We've tried to contact them, but as yet there's been no reply. Can you look out and see what's happening as you pass through it? Most of the research council went there to discuss the issues I presented to them, and I need them back here as soon as possible.'

'I forgot we pass through that city. I've always wondered why the tube goes through, and not around, like normal,' she said enquiringly.

'Long story; another city was needed in the area and that was the only place available. Rather than alter the tube path, they built around it. There are a few others like that too,' he told her quickly.

Danni was concerned about the condition of the tube through the city and wondered if it could it be compromised.

'Are you sure that route is safe, Simon?' she asked.

'As sure as we can be. The tube pressure is constant, and tube communications are fine. Apart from that there's no other information available,' he told her.

'OK, I'll call you when we get to Nâgpur. I hope they're coping OK. Bye,' she accidentally cut Simon off before he could reply.

'Oops . . . a touch of his own medicine,' she thought.

Danni sat back, realising she was very tired. 'I think we should try to have a little nap. Who knows when we'll have another chance,' she said.

Pauline and Brian looked at each other, held hands, and stayed put. 'We don't feel like sleeping just now,' Brian told her.

Danni retired to her berth, not thinking about what might happen if the violent shakes reoccurred. 'Call me when we pass through Nâgpur City, please. The door won't be locked.' As she spoke, she closed the door quietly behind her.

John turned to Juliette and put his arms around her. 'Lets all hug,' he said with a reassuring ring in his voice.

'I'm not hugging her,' Fred said, looking stern faced at Petal.

Juliette put an arm around Fred for comfort. Then Fred said something that made them all extremely worried. 'I hope Mom and Dad are OK.'

Petal burst into a flood of tears and said with a croaky voice, 'John, do you think Mom and Dad are OK?'

John didn't know what to say; he didn't have an answer. Realising the distressed tone of Petal's voice, he quickly replied, 'Yes, they're too far away to be affected by what's happening out here.' He smiled and hid his true feelings well.

Juliette immediately added, 'The storm affecting Ukraine is the other side of the world to our parents, so don't worry about them. They are probably worried about us, and we're OK, aren't we?'

Petal and Fred cheered up slightly when she said that.

'We don't know exactly what's gone wrong, or even if anything is wrong. We may just be imagining things are wrong. This could be something that happens from time to time. We are new to travelling after all,' John said, trying to calm things even more. He knew things had gone badly wrong and Juliette sensed it.

Suddenly Petal and Fred were full of life again.

'I'm off to bed again,' said Petal and disappeared into her room.

Fred said, 'Me too,' and also disappeared.

John looked at Juliette, watched her slump down on her chair, and whispered in her ear, 'Sorry, I don't know exactly what's gone wrong. Something has, and terribly wrong too.'

Juliette looked at him with tears welling in her eyes. 'I thought there might be something; I could feel your tension. What exactly do you know?'

John explained about the news, the damage report, and what he'd seen. He finished with, 'At least we're still alive and heading for the safest place on earth.'

Juliette gave him a little smile and held his hand. 'Can you sit by the window and look to see if there's anything out there?' she said.

John moved to the window and looked out. There was nothing, just ground flashing past. Juliette came and sat next to him, making sure she couldn't see out of the window. He put his arms around her, keeping one eye on the window, and listened to her breathing gently as she fell into a troubled sleep.

John felt himself dozing. Juliette's breathing was sending him to sleep, and he struggled to stay awake. Then he saw a flicker of light in the corner of his eye and was instantly wide-awake, staring out of the window to what was there. He watched, taking care not to wake Juliette, and the sight he was seeing churned his stomach. He wanted to turn away, but a morbid fascination held his gaze. He could see lights glowing with an eerie luminosity through dirty, muddy water, making silhouettes of the many floating objects in the water.

Brian went to the berth and tidied the bedding before returning to Pauline.

'Go and get some sleep,' he said to her. 'I'll wake you if there's any news, OK?'

She nodded her head and Brian helped her into bed with a kiss before returning to the lounge. He selected the clear roof and saw only the ground flashing past. He was about to shut off the view when he noticed a slight change in the motion of the train. He suspected they were slowing down for a junction, and he was right. Wardha Junction slowly came into view. It was deserted and dark, and there were no shuttle units waiting to join. He was expecting the train to pick up speed again, but it didn't, and after a short rush of ground through the window, the glow of dim lights startled him. All around him was the city Danni had talked of, so he hurried over to her room to wake her and opened the bedroom door.

Danni was in her cleansing cubicle and it looked as if she'd fallen asleep. Not knowing how long she'd been in there, he opened the door. She instantly woke up, stood up gaping at him, still half asleep, and rubbed her eyes.

'Sorry, I wasn't sure how long you'd been in there,' he said, handing her the robe hanging on the door. 'We've arrived at the city you mentioned earlier.'

He'd noticed she had a very young body, too young for her age; it was the image of Pauline's.

'Regeneration must have been used for her to be like that,' he thought to himself and wondered, 'Just how advanced are they at the research centre?'

Then he heard Danni speak. 'Sorry, I must've fallen asleep. I've been in there for twenty minutes or so. Luckily I had it on minimum. Thanks for waking me.'

She rushed into the lounge before the robe was properly covering her and it billowed behind her as she went.

Brian followed, and stopped dead in his tracks. He was looking out through the window, as was Danni. What greeted them was enough to shock even those who were used to traumatic scenes. All around were objects floating in water, silhouettes against the dim lights. Danni thought she saw what looked like bodies, floating up from, and down to, the depths of the city. The water was very murky, with only shadows of bodies and other debris blocking the bright city lights. Then, out of the dark, the body of a child came close to the tube, close enough for them to get a fleeting glimpse of a face as it passed swiftly by.

Danni broke the silence, saying with a choked voice, 'It's flooded.'

Brian gasped, 'Don't say anything to Pauline. I don't think she can take much more.'

'She's much stronger than you think, but no, I wouldn't say anything,' she said, crossing to call Simon.

She turned the console towards the window just as he appeared on the screen. 'Hi, Danni, Oh . . . No! It's flooded! Isn't it? No wonder we couldn't contact them. A few dams up here in the mountains ruptured with the earthquakes. That must be the cause,' he said frowning. 'It's odd though, the city should be watertight. Something must be wrong.'

Danni said. 'I wanted you to see it. It's just too much. I can't begin to describe the tragedy down here. I will leave the window view open till we leave the city.'

Simon nodded his head in agreement. 'If you want to; but I have other things to worry about and can't keep watching. It should take you at least forty minutes to pass through the city. Let me know if you see any survivors. We have giant city hoppers on standby and might be able to save some of those poor souls.'

Danni said, 'OK, let's hope there are some souls to save. I'll keep a look out for you.'

'Bye for now. I'll see you approximately one and a half hours after you leave the city,' Simon said, and the screen went blank.

John was in shock. He thought he saw a body flash past as they travelled through the city. He saw the shadows of what seemed like hundreds or thousands of them, but hoped they were just debris floating in the dirty water.

The train was travelling slightly upwards, passing through level after level. He had never thought how big cities were until now. It seemed to be taking an age to pass through. Suddenly, out of his window he saw the surface. The view hit him hard, and he ran to the toilet to be sick. The shock was just too much and he was shaking.

Juliette came to find out what was up with him. She saw his face, and how sombre and gaunt it looked. Putting her arms around him, she helped him to a chair and asked, 'What's the matter with you? You look like you've seen a ghost or something.'

'I have seen ghosts, thousands of them, doomed beyond help, out there now,' he said, pointing to the window.

Juliette made towards the window to have a look, and John rushed to stop her. 'No, don't look. If you thought seeing wide-open spaces was frightening, what's out there is a thousand times worse,' he said.

Before Juliette could peer out, he switched the window view off and held her closely in his arms.

Danni watched the murky waters pass by with an ever-increasing number of shadows blocking out the lights. 'Why don't they switch them off, or something?' she said out loud.

Brian had gone to Pauline. He wanted to make sure she didn't get up and see what was outside. He didn't want to see anymore himself either.

Danni watched as the train slowly climbed through level after level, the water getting lighter and not so murky as it went. Now she could see shapes more distinctly, mostly flotsam and jetsam, but also more gruesome shapes, and lots of them. Suddenly the train was passing through a floating, swirling mass of, well, just about everything imaginable, before it broke through the surface.

Danni couldn't believe her eyes; the city was well lit above the water line too, revealing torrents of water, cascading down through stairwells from above. Everywhere she looked was crammed with people trying to make their way to the top of the city, and they were so tightly packed together they couldn't move.

'If the stairwells were flooding, the emergency exits must be open, and they have nowhere to go,' she thought, and crossed the lounge to call Simon.

Simon must have been dozing; he looked really groggy as he appeared at the console. 'Hi Danni, what's up?' he said, rubbing his eyes.

Once again she'd turned the console to the window for him to see. She said in a voice breaking with sorrow, 'Look at them all, they've nowhere to go. Is there anything we can do for them Simon?'

Simon went quiet for a moment, taking it all in, before replying, 'The water must be coming in through the emergency escape doors on the surface. I don't know why we didn't know about it; there must be something wrong with the sensors or something. The city control room is probably flooded and affecting the instruments. If the city is still running on automatic, then hopefully we can take control from here and shut the escape doors, which should stop the water flowing. The survivors can make their way to the tower and safety. At least till the pumps clear the water away,' he said.

'The tower won't take all those people; there are just too many of them,' Danni said, with a note of alarm in her voice.

'There's nothing else we can do. Any survivors that reach the roof can be lifted off once the storms have subsided. So sorry, that's the best we can do for them, for now anyway.'

Danni was shocked. 'OK, take control and shut the doors, if you can. I'll let you know if it works or not.'

'They should be shut in a minute. My team are accessing the control system as we speak,' he said with a 'look what I can do' air about him.

'Smart ass!' Danni remarked, then waited for something to start happening while the console was still live and in contact with Simon.

It was five minutes before the cascading waters began to show some sign of subsiding, and within fifteen minutes the flooding had just about stopped.

'It's worked by the look of it Simon. Soon all the water will be out of the stairwells, and they can climb to the top,' she said.

'Yes, but it will be everyone for himself or herself I'm afraid. That's human nature for you. I have to go now. See you in an hour or so. Bye.' And Simon was gone before she could reply.

Danni knew that the pumps deep in the city would empty out the water, but it would take quite some time to do it. And there were the dead, probably far too many for the city to deal with, and no food for the survivors either. It didn't look good for them.

Danni had seen enough. She switched off the window view, went to her berth, and slumped onto the bed. Soon she'd fallen into a deep, troubled sleep.

John just sat there, staring straight ahead of him while Juliette stroked his hair. He looked at her and gave her a hug, a really tight hug.

'John, you are hurting me, let go!' she screamed, waking Petal and Fred, whose berth doors were open.

They came rushing in just as John released his grip on Juliette.

'Sorry, I didn't mean to hurt you,' He said, and looked terrible.

Juliette gave him a hug and a kiss, then beckoned to Petal and Fred to come for a group hug. Puzzled, they came over to Juliette, hugged, and held each other tightly. They sat round the table, held hands and stared at one another, brother and sister, sister and brother.

They stayed quiet for quite some time before a strange voice broke the silence.

'Welcome to the Himalayan Research Centre. We hope you enjoyed your journey. Please remain seated while your pod is lowered from the shuttle. Have a nice stay.'

There was a cheer, quickly followed by an outpouring of emotion. They were crying out of control and laughing at the same time. They were totally relieved the journey was over and they were safe.

Shortly after the announcement, there was a slight bump, followed by the pod door seal quietly clicking open. The brightness coming through the door blinded them as they stepped towards the opening. And as the smell of fresh air hit them, they all smiled, held hands, and laughed uncontrollably.

Danni, Brian, and Pauline were fast asleep and didn't hear the announcement.

'Welcome to the Himalayan Research Centre. We hope you enjoyed your journey. Please remain seated while your pod is lowered from the shuttle. Have a nice stay.'

Nor did they feel the slight bump as their pod was lowered to the ground. It was the noise of the pod door seal clicking open and the smell of fresh air that did it.

It took a little while for Danni to realise what was happening before she jumped up, ran through the lounge, and rushed into Pauline's room.

She shouted as she shook them both awake, crying and laughing as she said, 'We've arrived. Get up. Get up. We've arrived. We're safe.'

As soon as Danni left the room, Pauline and Brian jumped out of bed, got dressed quickly, and headed for the lounge. There they saw the pod door wide open. There was a bright, greenish light shining in through the opening, and the wonderful smell of sweet, fresh air entered the pod. They looked at each other, smiled, and hugged.

Danni threw her arms around both of them in the excitement, then thought of Simon. 'Come on, let's go.'

And they all left the pod together.

CHAPTER 3
THE GATHERING

Simon stood on the research centre's control room balcony, looking towards the entrance of a deserted city, and sighed. The city had been built to house the new staff arriving over the next few weeks, and now he didn't know if there would be enough people to fill the one level built so far. Some of the staff who were due to arrive were probably never going to turn up, so the whole issue would have to be redressed sometime in the near future. Upcoming projects were ready to start, and just waiting for the workforce to arrive was chaos.

He turned, walked into the control room, looked at Rose, his second in command, and said with an air of gloom, 'That city would've been alive with well over a hundred thousand personnel in a few weeks from now. How many will actually arrive, I just don't know. What do you think?'

Rose Markham was a grade four senior engineer. She'd been working at the research centre for thirty-four years, ever since leaving college at the age of twenty-two. She lived with her partner Frank Powell, a grade six administration manager working in personnel, and had two children, Otho, aged fourteen, by her first partner and Anne, aged seven, with Frank. Otho had already started his education as a scientist, while Anne hoped to be a doctor someday. Only that wouldn't be decided till she was eleven, but as long as things remained the same, she probably would become one. They all lived, schooled, and worked at the centre, never going to the surface or travelling, and they were content with their lives. Some people were even born at the centre, though that was rarely the case.

Not everyone wanted to go to the surface as most people had never seen or been out in the open, and thus feared it. Even if they were used to the open, there wasn't much to see besides farms on land or on water.

Rose looked across at Simon and said, 'With the number already here, and those we know are on their way, we may be lucky to make four thousand; and that includes the children.'

Simon shook his head in dismay. 'How many trains are still on their way here?'

Rose was about to answer him when he interrupted her.

'Has Danni's train arrived yet?' he quickly followed, with an excited ring in his words.

Rose scanned the shuttle terminal arrivals console for information. 'One train has just arrived; it's the one Danni's on. They are just removing the pods now. And there's another train planned to arrive a little later.'

'A bit of good news at last. I'll go and meet it on my SCAT. It'll get me there quicker,' he said, sounding as excited as a small child getting a new toy.

The SCAT (Small Civilian Airborne Transporter) is a two-seat, scooter-style machine, propelled by miniature Electron Displacement Propulsion (EDP) units, and can fly at great speed anywhere the operator has clearance to go. Being so new and limited in number, only essential personnel have the authority to use them. Simon was in overall command of the centre, so met the requirements to have one available at all times. He kept it close at hand, and had parked it on the balcony, ready for immediate use.

The SCAT was simple to operate; even a novice could fly one immediately by just telling it to go automatic. Manual control could be used by experienced riders. The onboard computer was programmed to make sure the operator caused no harm to themselves or to others, sometimes altering the flight path and speed to ensure a safe and smooth ride.

Simon rushed out of the room, headed directly for his SCAT, and jumped on. The machine instantly started. It lifted to just over head height, shot forward, and then down, over the edge of the balcony towards the dome exit. He rode as fast as the machine would allow, and shortly after leaving the control centre, was entering the shuttle terminal.

Using the onboard computer to find the right platform, he slowly rode along looking for Danni. The SCAT stopped alongside a shuttle section on an upper platform. The pod was being unloaded from the unit, and he waited for it to settle on the ground before dismounting. The pod door opened quickly, and he stood, waiting anxiously for Danni to emerge.

Minutes passed, and there was no sign of life. He became quite agitated, and was about to go inside to see where Danni was, when three figures holding hands ran out, blinking in the bright light. He rushed forward and hugged Danni. She was crying and shaking with relief now that the journey was over.

He turned to Pauline and Brian and smiled. 'I'm Simon. Nice to meet you Pauline.' He held his hand out and touched her. Then he looked at Brian. 'You must be Brian. So glad you came. And so glad you all made it safely.'

Brian took his hand and said, 'Glad I came, judging by what's happened.'

Simon was about to ask Danni some questions, when his communicator signalled an urgent call from the control room.

'I have to take this,' he said, answering the call immediately. 'What's the problem?'

'We've an unscheduled train heading up the tube towards China. And it's out of control,' Rose said quickly, sounding very alarmed.

'OK, I'll be there in a few minutes,' he replied hurriedly.

He turned to Danni. 'There's an emergency to be dealt with. Fancy coming with me? The more brains on this one the better.'

'I'd love to help if I can. But what about these two?' she said, pointing towards Pauline and Brian.

Simon called Brian over and explained, 'Sorry, we've got to rush off. Make your way to the new arrivals centre by the terminal exit, and they'll sort you out. I'll get Danni to pay you a visit later, OK?'

'Thanks. Hope you sort the problem,' Brian managed to say just before Simon walked away.

Simon smiled, clicked his fingers at Danni, crossed to the SCAT, and indicated for her to jump on behind. 'Hold on tight and keep your head down; we'll be travelling fast.'

Danni had never seen a SCAT before. 'These are new!' she remarked and settled down with her arms tight around his waist.

Before she could say another word, they were flying out of the terminal at high speed and she was silenced. She was holding on to Simon as tightly as she could, so tight, it caused him to wince.

'Hey! Not so tight, please,' he remarked and tried to release her grip, which wasn't easy.

Brian watched the SCAT disappear through the terminal exit. 'Wow. I've got to get myself one of those,' he said to Pauline, with a smile on his face. 'Come on, let's get checked in. I'm starving.'

Pauline realised she too was hungry, having eaten nothing all day. She picked up her small bag and, sticking her nose in the air, said, 'Let's go. This is all I possess. Got to go shopping as soon as possible.'

Brian looked at her, speechless, then burst out laughing. Pauline tried to ignore his reaction, but couldn't resist poking her tongue out and strutting off down the platform.

John looked at Juliette, and thought how beautiful she looked in the bright greenish light. Her image seemed to change every time a different light source reflected off her very pale complexion. And he loved it.

'Let's get off this thing before anything else happens,' he said, pulling her behind him.

Once outside they all looked around in amazement. The light was very bright, making everything it touched look peaceful and calm. There was a pleasant smell in the air, and soon they were feeling very relaxed.

Juliette looked up and down the shuttle terminal platform. They were at the end of the shuttle units, and as she turned to look at their pod, she was horrified. Shaking John's arm violently, she made sure he turned to look as well.

They both stood looking at the pod they had just alighted from. It was heavily scratched, with deep, clawlike marks near the rear end. They moved a little to look over at the adjacent pod on the opposite platform. It was still attached to the shuttle unit, and workers were cutting their way into the buckled and holed casing.

'I hope they're OK in there; it's taken quite a battering,' John said, pointing out the obvious.

Next they noticed the damaged coupling at the end of their unit and shook with fright. They realised that it was only by a stroke of luck they'd survived the journey. They cheated death by a whisker. No shuttle unit could couple—theirs was the absolute end of the train. As they continued to look, it became obvious that the supports holding the top pod were missing, along with the pod itself.

John felt a cold ripple run up and down his body, and Juliette went as white as a sheet.

Just then, an announcement brought them back to the land of the living.

'Welcome to the Himalayan Research Centre. Please make your way to the new arrivals information desk, which is situated near the terminal exit. Local time is 21:00. Thank you, we hope you have a nice stay.'

Picking up their small bags, they headed straight towards the exit and stood in a line of people waiting to be checked in. Juliette, Petal, and Fred sat on a bench, waiting patiently for John to reach the front of the queue, which was moving quite slowly.

Juliette noticed a security guard checking the identity of everyone in the line, and when he came to John, he stopped and spoke to him. Shortly after, John stepped out of the line and crossed to them.

'Come on, I've got to go to the front of the line,' he said smiling. 'We're expected.'

When he reached the front of the line, the security guard spoke to the check-in clerk and explained who he was. John was called forward to have his and his companions' identities checked. The check-in clerk was surprised to see Juliette and Fred, as they were not due for another twenty-four hours. She altered the information list to take this into account, and gave them all an information upgrade for their personal communicators. She also gave John a small disc.

'That's the key to use when your SCAT is delivered,' she said.

John looked at her, puzzled. 'What's a SCAT?' he asked inquiringly.

'Don't know exactly. I think they're a new type of transport or something. You'll find out soon enough,' replied the clerk.

'Fred has a head wound. Is there anyone here who can take a look at it please?' John enquired.

'When you get to your apartment, use the communications console to check with the on-call medic,' the clerk replied.

'OK, thanks. Where do we go now?' he asked her.

'There'll be a four-person spitter along shortly. It will take you to your accommodation. You've been assigned to Grade Four Senior Engineer Rose Markham. Please note you'll meet her tomorrow morning in the control centre at ten thirty prompt. Any questions sir?'

John just looked at her, ready with a thousand questions. 'Yes, plenty,' he said.

'Answers to your questions can be found in your new information upgrade,' she said, looking over his shoulder. 'Next please.'

They made their way over to a four-person spitter that had just arrived and was waiting near the exit. Without saying a word, they boarded the craft.

'Please state grade and name,' it requested, as it scanned John.

'Grade seven, John Blight,' he replied.

'Thank you. Please hold tight. You have been assigned apartment number 2130 in Jumla City.

John sat patiently as the spitter elevated three metres to the maglev track, and held on tightly with one hand as it sped towards the shuttle terminal exit. 'Here we go,' he said, holding Juliette's hand tightly with the other.

Danni was petrified; she'd never been on anything like a SCAT in her life, not even on a simulated fairground ride. A city hopper ride was nothing like this; it was totally enclosed, while this was completely open. She closed her eyes tightly, holding back the nauseous feeling in her stomach, and didn't open them again until the SCAT touched down.

'Hope I'll never have to ride one of them again,' she said to Simon.

Simon looked at her and laughed. 'You're as white as a sheet. I've one of these standing by for your use, whenever you need transport,' he said, pointing at the machine she had just alighted from.

'We'll see. I may take awhile to get used to it though,' she said, and followed him into the control room.

'What's the situation?' he asked, as he and Danni entered the room.

'Hi Danni, nice to see you back,' Rose said before answering Simon. 'There's a train travelling towards us at full speed. It's not slowing at junctions and appears to be switched to manual control. We've tried contacting them, but so far there's been no response. We must gain full control before it reaches the tube heading towards China; that tube is blocked,' she said.

Simon looked worried. 'We can't direct it here. If that train hits the shuttle terminal at full speed, there'll be carnage. How many people are onboard?'

'If all the pods are full, there could be over a thousand people onboard. We've no way of telling until it gets nearer to the branch pipe,' Rose said, rechecking the information constantly.

Danni broke in, 'If we can't let it into the branch pipe at that speed, we'll have to slow it down. Any ideas?'

Rose sat with a worried look on her face. She was thinking hard, trying to find a solution. No one had ever needed to stop a runaway train before, and it wasn't going to be an easy thing to do.

With years of engineering experience at the centre, Rose knew the tubes ran close to the walls of the science and engineering testing dome. She asked her console to provide detailed information of the tube system in that particular area, and it soon appeared on her screen.

After looking at the projected image of the complex, she homed in on a small section close to the engineering domes. The tube passed just ten metres from a dome wall, and an access port had been conveniently incorporated to assist with any maintenance. She also noticed the tube made a slight dip to join with the port, and this gave her an idea.

There was silence for a few more minutes before Rose spoke, 'The tube through to China is blocked just past Coqen in Tibet. We must allow the train to continue and send it up there for my plan to work.'

Everyone stopped what they were doing, and looked at her with astonished faces. But she continued speaking, 'There's a dip in the tube just as it passes our testing dome. If we pump water into the tube, it should act as a buffer to slow down the train.'

'The level of water will be critical. Too much, and it will be like hitting a brick wall,' Simon replied, looking very serious.

'Too little, and it'll just pick up speed again,' replied Danni.

Rose looked sternly at both of them, then continued, 'The right amount of water will build up pressure in front of the train and slow it down. Once we do that, we can disconnect the nose section and take control of the shuttle. Failure to slow it down will prevent the nose from releasing.'

'Sounds tricky to me. Even if it is our only option,' Simon said.

Danni agreed, 'Sounds good to me too, but what will happen to the nose section?'

'There's nothing we can do about that. It'll pick up speed again and crash when it hits the blockage. I don't think there's anyone alive in it anyway,' Simon informed her calmly. 'Is there anything else that might go wrong?' he asked. Simon was pointing at a shuttle moving slowly through the tube system and clearly displayed on the system console.

Rose studied the tube system hard, and frantically began making calculations. 'Where did that come from? I wish the systems were working properly. It would tell me if there's going to be a problem or not. As it is, it looks like we've a slow shuttle without a nose section in the main tube, and at its current speed, it'll be in the way of the runaway train long before we can bring it into the branch pipe.'

'What! You're saying there'll be a collision,' Simon shouted.

Now Danni was studying the tube system. 'We passed through Wardha Junction on our way here. Brian told me it looked intact. Put the shuttle in a siding until the rogue train passes, then let it follow on behind. There should be just enough time to do it safely.'

Rose got to work instantly, frantically touching her console screen and entering the required instructions. A few moments later she sat back, and smiled. 'OK. New information accepted by the shuttle. It'll be going to the sidings in about twenty minutes. The rogue train will pass ten minutes or so later.'

'That's great news. Rose, I want you to oversee the pumping of water. Take my SCAT if you want,' Simon requested and placed a hand on her shoulder, giving it a gentle squeeze.

Rose gave Simon a beaming smile, and placing her hand on his, just said, 'Thanks.'

Standing up quickly, her chair tipped over backwards and crashed to the floor with a loud bang. Without looking back, she rushed out of the room as quickly as her legs could move, and was soon standing next to the machine. She loved riding on a SCAT, but didn't have one of her own, so jumped at every opportunity with extreme delight. Rose mounted the machine and tried to start it, but nothing happened.

'Simon, tell it to give me control,' she shouted back into the room.

Simon poked his head out, laughed at her, and ordered the SCAT to accept her commands until further notice. Rose just smiled back, and as she gained control, shot off the balcony like a bullet.

Danni turned to Simon and said quietly, 'We'll just have to wait and hope for a successful outcome.'

Both sat in silence, watching the progress of the high-speed train and the slower shuttle on the tube system console. There were two more trains travelling through the tube system. They were due to arrive just before the high-speed train passed Jumla Junction, but they wouldn't get in the way and therefore didn't represent a problem. Simon looked as if he were biting his nails, though he'd done that so much in past twenty-four hours, there weren't any left.

Pauline was queuing with Brian when a security guard working his way along the line of new arrivals stopped next to her. 'Identity check. Can I see your ID please?'

He quickly scanned Pauline's communicator and then turned to Brian.

As soon as he'd scanned his, he politely made a request, 'Please follow me sir.'

Brian looked at Pauline and, catching her hand, pulled her along with him. They were passing quickly along the line, and everyone stared at them as they went, some with a not-so-friendly look.

The security guard took them straight to the front of the queue and signalled to the clerk to let them through quickly. 'This is Grade Four Consultant Doctor Brian James,' he said to the clerk.

'The clerk stood up, saying, 'Welcome to the Himalayan Research

Centre, Doctor James, sir. Can I have your personal communicator to upgrade your information please?'

Brian thought how polite she was and handed his communicator over. He then explained that Pauline was his partner.

'I'm very sorry,' the clerk said, scanning the information list for Pauline's name, which was further down the page. 'I would like to welcome you as well, ma'am,' she said to Pauline, as soon as she noticed her name. 'Can I have your communicator too, please?'

Pauline handed her communicator over, and waited for the formalities to be complete. Brian turned, put his arm around her, and give her a squeeze. She smiled at him, and took her communicator back from the clerk.

'Thanks,' she said, and watched Brian take his communicator back.

'How come we were allowed to jump the queue?' he asked the girl.

'Most of these people are not supposed to be here. We are processing those who were expected first,' she replied, smiling.

'Aren't we lucky!' he exclaimed, looking at Pauline.

'Thank you for your co-operation. Please select a spitter to take you to your accommodation,' continued the girl almost immediately, more as a command than a request. 'Do you have any questions, sir?'

Brian wanted to know many things. 'What's happening out there?' he enquired.

'All information can be found using your upgraded personal communicator,' the clerk replied, as if reading from a set of well-rehearsed phrases.

Looking a bit annoyed, Brian crossed to a two-person spitter and turned to give Pauline a helping hand as she boarded.

'Please state grade and name,' the spitter requested as it security scanned him.

'Grade four, Brian James,' he said.

'Thank you. Please hold tight. You have been assigned apartment number 14 in Jumla City, suburb number one.'

'That sounds efficient. Here we go,' said Pauline, and held Brian's hand tightly.

The spitter crossed to the maglev track, lifted into the air, and sped off towards the shuttle terminal exit.

John was a little excited as the spitter picked up speed. Soon they were out of the terminal, rising through a steeply angled tunnel. The elevator they were travelling on was climbing at forty-five degrees and appeared to be heading towards a whitish light at a higher level. John looked up and down and judged the elevator to be about a kilometre from end to end.

As they reached the end of the tunnel, the lighting changed to very bright, normal-looking sunlight (which only John had ever seen), and it dazzled them all. By the time their eyes adjusted, they were well inside the main dome, and all around them was lush, green grass.

John had never been so close to it before, and he could smell the sweetness of it. He turned to Juliette and was highly amused by her expression. Her head was pointing straight ahead, but her eyes were darting everywhere and her mouth was wide open.

'What's up love?' he asked.

'I . . . I . . . I've never seen so much open space before. I . . . Is that grass and are those cows and what's that smell and—'

John put his hand over her mouth, preventing her from saying another word. She was in a state of shock, and he put his arm around her shoulders to comfort her. He turned to see if Petal and Fred were OK. They were holding hands, chattering away like mad, and pointing at everything they could see. He smiled at them, then turned back to Juliette.

'How are you feeling?' he asked her.

'How do you think? I'm not used to open spaces. How high is the roof? And how wide is it? And is that grass? It stinks!' As she spoke, she pointed all around.

She hit him with so many questions, at first John couldn't find words to speak. He looked around and tried to guess the size of the dome. 'It's impossible to tell how high it is. It's difficult to judge in this light. It must be at least seven kilometres in diameter though, or maybe more. And yes, that's grass, and that's what you can smell. Oh yes! And the manure from the cattle of course,' he told her, holding his nose.

He asked his communicator for the information and found out he was wrong about the dome's size; it was one kilometre high and fifteen kilometre in diameter, not seven, as he'd estimated. He didn't say anything to Juliette except, 'We should be indoors soon. The city must have many levels to have so many apartments. You should feel better there.'

Pauline's eyes opened wide when the spitter left the shuttle terminal and entered the tunnel; the end of it seemed so far away and very high up. When they reached the top and entered the main dome, she wasn't expecting such a large, open space. Neither was Brian, and they both looked everywhere, with mouths agape, in total awe of the scene.

'Wow! Such a big place. And this is just one of the many domes they have here,' Brian said.

Pauline was crouching behind him. Even though she'd seen wide-open space, she'd never actually been so far out in the open before. She'd only seen it from the balcony of Bagman City. And the smells were so different and powerful, she held her nose tightly closed.

The spitter continued its journey from one dome to the next, all containing farms of some kind, one with cattle, one with sheep, and another with various crops. They passed through three domes before the entrance to yet another dome loomed ahead of them. Only this one was different. Huge columns, thirty metres tall, stood on each side of its entrance. On top of the columns was an elaborately decorated arch with the inscription "Jumla City".

'Welcome to Jumla City,' came from the spitter's speaker.

But they were too busy looking around to notice what it said. As they passed through the opening into the city, they were quite surprised to find it sprawled out and on a single level.

As they travelled along, the echo of a scream could be heard coming from within the city, and they looked at each other, slightly alarmed. The spitter continued on, skirting the edge of the city, and entered yet another dome. This one was named Jumla City suburb number one.

'Welcome to Jumla City suburb number one,' came from the spitter as they entered the dome. The spitter lowered to the ground and began trundling up the completely smooth-surfaced grand avenue and eventually came to a stop alongside a number of large apartments. It then announced, *'Number 14 is to the left. Please alight here.'*

Brian and Pauline stepped off the spitter and it shot off, leaving them standing alone in front of their apartment. They looked up and down the street, as if waiting for someone to greet them with a wave or something. But it was deserted, with not a soul in sight and no sound from anywhere.

'It's like a ghost town you see in the old films,' said Brian, trying to sound spooky.

Pauline looked at him and shivered. 'Let's get inside.'

Brian walked to the front door and was security scanned before it opened; and when it opened, there before them was an extremely luxurious interior.

'Nice. Very nice indeed,' he said, looking around.

Pauline gave the place a good look-over before commenting, 'Much better than your last place. I'm starving. See what's on the menu will you please, love?' With that she walked into the lounge, slumped down on the sofa, and relaxed.

Brian went over to the communication console and was security scanned before it came online.

'Hello Brian, nice to see you again.' It was Lucy, his personal companion. *'Can I be of any assistance to you?'*

'Can you see what's on the menu for Pauline and me please? I'll leave it up to you to decide what we eat,' he instructed her and started to walk away.

What Lucy said next shocked him. *'I'm afraid there is no menu. The larder is stocked with produce ready to cook. I can supply a simple recipe if you wish.'*

'Recipe!' he remarked, quite stunned. 'I've never cooked anything in my life.'

He shouted across the room, 'Pauline, can you cook?'

Pauline came slowly over to him with a puzzled look on her face. 'Me cook! You've got to be joking. Didn't know anyone did that anymore.'

'Well there's food in the larder that needs cooking, and that's all we have,' he said, sounding totally dejected.

Both of them crossed to the larder and opened the door.

'That looks like bread.' She dipped her finger in something yellow, tasted it, and remarked, 'That tastes like . . . butter, and that smells like cheese. Who needs to cook anyway?'

Brian looked at her and couldn't help smiling. He helped take the food to the table, and together they made their first meal of cheese sandwiches, which were washed down with a couple of glasses of ice-cold water, straight from the tap.

'What a feast,' Brian said. 'Must get something sorted soon.'

'Yep, we can't live off cheese sandwiches forever,' Pauline stated, with a mouth half filled with bread. 'We'll find a cook tomorrow. Lets get some sleep now; I'm shattered.'

Brian said, 'Totally agree. Let's go.' And he followed her upstairs to the bedroom.

As they entered the bedroom, he uttered some words that really annoyed Pauline. 'I'd better contact the hospital before we do anything else. They may need my assistance.'

Pauline had reached the bed, and after throwing all the pillows at him, replied, almost screaming, 'No you don't. It's our first night here. Call them in the morning.'

Rose travelled fast, and it wasn't long before she reached the main engineering dome. She hurried over to where Simon had instructed her team to assemble, which was near the tube inspection port. She started to get things organised. There was just over an hour to finish flooding the tube, by which time the train would be passing the dome.

On the way to the site, she'd calculated that half a metre of water would be needed to slow down the rogue train. It would be slowed down just enough to allow the shuttle sections to release the nose cone. She aimed to make use of the tube's low pressure to suck the water in, and if that wasn't going fast enough, she'd requested pumps to be put on standby.

Engineers had turned up and started the work with the aid of a few labourers. But she soon found her engineers had no management skills whatsoever, and was annoyed that she had to oversee the task herself. She found it extremely difficult getting her staff coordinated; even she was out of practice. It was going to be touch and go to get the work completed within the forty-five minutes she'd allotted. Over four kilometres of tube had to be flooded, and the quantity of water required was enormous.

The time seemed to pass quickly, and she was worried when her senior engineer, who was monitoring the tube's water level, walked over with a solemn face and lowered eyes.

'What's the problem?' she asked him, well before he reached her.

He continued to walk right up to her, and only then did he look her in the eyes. 'No problem. Mission accomplished ma'am,' he said with a slight smile.

Rose raised her hand to slap his face, but stopped herself at the last moment. 'I'll find something nice for you to work on next,' she told him angrily.

She called Simon to give him the news. 'Hi Simon, the tube's flooded, and ready for the train. How do things look over there?'

'Another two trains arrived a short time ago. One had only forty-five people onboard; the rest got off when they heard about the meteor strike. The other train, with seventy-five shuttle units, was totally empty. The passengers decided to stay in Australia, as far away from the strike as possible. They left it to the last minute to decide, and by then it was too late to stop the train from running.' He paused, thinking about Rose's plan. 'I hope your plan works,' he said.

Rose was as disappointed as he was about the lack of passengers on the two trains, but soon she was back thinking of the rogue train problem.

'Time will tell if this works, but I'm confident of a good outcome. Can we warn the passengers to expect some sort of impact?'

'Yes we can. As soon as the train passes the branch pipe, we'll program the computer. It should make all announcements and prepare to disengage the nose section as soon as the train slows down,' Simon replied.

'That's great. I'll start making my way back. There's nothing more I can do here,' she told him.

'OK, see you soon,' Simon said, a little more relaxed knowing all had been achieved with time to spare. Now all he could do was sit back and hope it worked.

Danni had fallen asleep on a chair at the back of the room. Simon was watching the tube system console, wondering if there were any trains not accounted for. He started testing all sections of every tube system he could access, redirecting signals anywhere he could, and scrutinising all the information received. Then he found a stationary train. It had halted at a junction in the Philippines, where it was waiting for instructions to continue.

'We have another train to bring in,' he told his staff excitedly, pointing at the tube system.

Soon the train was moving. He'd programmed it not to slow down until it reached the Himalayan Branch Pipe. Once he'd completed all instructions, he smiled, sat back with his feet on a desk, and tilted his chair backwards.

Rose walked in and pushed his feet off the desk. The bang of them hitting the floor woke Danni, making her jump up instinctively.

Rose looked at the tube system and noticed the new inbound train.

'Where did that come from?' she asked, smiling at Simon.

Simon explained how he found it, then added, 'It'll be here in about seven hours.' He looked pleased with himself.

Rose smiled. 'Well done. Any details about it yet?'

'None yet. We'll have to wait,' he replied.

Juliette was starting to look around a little more as they travelled through dome after dome. She'd started to relax a bit, and John sensed it.

'What do you think of our new home?' he asked jovially.

'You call this home! Home has walls and streets and people and noise,' she shouted, shaking her head as she reeled off the list.

'We'll soon be in the city,' he said, pointing to the columns marking the entrance.

He could see many maglev tracks converging near the entrance, and a spitter was just in front of theirs, with two people onboard. 'Look over there. There are other residents here too,' he said, trying to mollify her.

He turned to Petal and asked, 'What do you think about this place?'

Petal replied in a high-pitched voice, 'It's exciting. Isn't it Fred? When do we get to the apartment? I'm hungry.'

Fred nodded in agreement and smiled, but he said nothing.

John assured them they would be there soon, as the spitter had already entered the city.

Juliette shouted, 'They haven't built it yet; there is only one level!' As she spoke, she started to cry. She was used to looking up and seeing a floor above her head, but here it was just open space.

Shortly after entering the city, the spitter stopped. *'Number 2130 is to the right. Please alight here.'*

All four stepped off onto the deserted street. There were no people, no sounds, and the street was totally spotless.

Fred shouted as loud as he could, 'IS THERE ANYONE OUT THERE?' The resounding echo startled them all, especially Juliette, who let out an even louder scream, which bounced back at them from every direction.

John crossed to the door and was security scanned before it opened. They all looked inside and were stunned.

Juliette spoke first, 'Look at the size of this place! Are you sure we have the right apartment John? And look, an upstairs section as well.' The look on her face had changed to utter glee. 'This place is ten times bigger than anywhere I've lived before.'

'It must be ours, otherwise we wouldn't be in here. Petal, look for some food will you?' John asked.

But Petal had disappeared. 'I'M HAVING THIS ROOM!' she shouted from an upstairs bedroom.

Fred ran upstairs to find his room, leaving Juliette and John to find the food.

'Here's the larder,' said Juliette, followed by, 'OH NO! What's this stuff? It hasn't been cooked.' She looked thoroughly disgusted.

John came over and looked in the larder. 'Hmmm,' he said, 'eggs, bread, butter, and cheese. Oh, and tomatoes! This'll do for now. We can sort the cooking out in the morning.'

He looked around to find the cooker, but after five minutes he gave up. He crossed to the communications console, asked for help, and, after being security scanned, heard a familiar voice.

It was May. *'Hello John. Hope you had a pleasant journey. How may I help you?'*

John looked around to see if he was alone (which he was), then turned back to May and whispered, 'Can you find out what's happened to Bagman City, if anything? If there's bad news, tell me when the others are not around, OK?'

May said she'd try to find some news for him and asked if there was anything else she could do.

'Can I have a recipe for the ingredients on the table? Where's the cooker and how do you use it?' he asked, sounding totally frustrated.

May scanned the table and supplied a simple recipe; it was for an omelette to be eaten with bread and butter. She also showed him the cooker and how to use it.

He called Petal and Juliette to watch him make food for the first time ever and, he hoped, the last.

Fred watched as well, but he wasn't expected to cook; he was too young for that. At least, that's what he thought.

The results were less than impressive, but at least they had full stomachs before they went to bed.

John started to follow Juliette upstairs to the bedroom. 'It seems a lifetime since we slept last,' she remarked.

Just then May called him back to the console and he ran back down the stairs.

'I've been trying to find information about Bagman City for you. The last report, received before the tubes started to collapse, seems to be hopeful. Bagman City reported there had been no structural damage and that the city had survived the Tsunami that followed the earthquakes. There's been no communication for the past ten hours,' she said.

'Thanks May. Let me know as soon as you find out more, OK?' he said, then disappeared upstairs to bed.

In the Himalayan Research Centre, and every city on earth, everything ran through the tubes: transport, food, resources, and communications. If a tube failed for some reason, there was usually another route available. The tube system was vast, with many interconnections, just like a spider's web. But at that moment, it was completely broken, or too busy, and the system information being received was very limited.

Danni was very tired, but she wanted to see the rogue train safely stopped in the shuttle terminal. She thought, 'These trains could be carrying the sole survivors on earth. We must try our hardest to keep them all alive, like gathering in a flock of sheep when a storm hits.' And that thought stuck in her mind.

Danni looked at the tube system console and noticed the slow shuttle move to the sidings at Wardha Junction had been successful, and the rogue train was about to pass through. It wouldn't be long before the rogue train would pass the Himalayan Branch Pipe. In less than half an hour or so, it would hit the flooded section. She crossed her fingers for luck, hoping it would work. Nothing like this had been tried before; there had never been a need for it. In that moment, it seemed to Danni that time was passing far slower than usual.

After what seemed like a lifetime, she asked Simon, 'Have we made contact yet?'

'We've just signalled the shuttles and are waiting for a reply,' he said. And almost immediately he followed with, 'We have control. As soon as the speed drops below three hundred kilometres per hour, the shuttle will release and we can bring it in.'

Simon looked relieved, and the whole room erupted with cheering.

'Calm down, don't celebrate yet. We still have to slow it down,' Rose remarked with a shaky, excited voice. She had a worried look on her face, and knew if the plan failed, she'd be responsible for many deaths.

Danni crossed to her, placed a reassuring hand on her shoulder, and said, 'I have faith in your judgement on this one, so don't you fret. If it works, many people will owe you their lives. If it doesn't, then it's not your fault; you did your best.'

Rose just managed a thin smile.

It was starting to get dark, and the artificial lights were dimming everywhere. 'Keep the lights on full till after the shuttle's in the terminal,' Simon demanded.

All the operators looked surprised, but carried out his command.

'That'll confuse the animals,' Danni said quietly, as the lighting came back on.

'How are we going to deal with these people? They aren't booked in, and no provision has been made for them,' said Rose.

'We'll have to set up an emergency reception centre and issue accommodation based on grades. How many staff can we muster for this?' Danni asked.

'The control centre staff are due to be relieved in an hour. We can call their replacements in early,' Simon said.

He looked around and spoke to his staff, 'Produce me a list of personnel available and their vocations as soon as you can. Rose, I'll have to leave you to deal with the arrivals.'

Rose looked at him with a frown, 'Nice one. I'm shattered, but it has to be done I suppose.'

She scanned the list into her communicator and left for the check-in terminal on a spitter.

Simon was watching the tube system console when a voice broke the silence.

'Australian shuttle due to arrive in ten minutes. Number of passengers, 1,230.' It was the shuttle terminal informing them the shuttle had separated from the rogue train's nose cone and would be arriving shortly.

The entire control room erupted with shouting and cheering.

'Well done everyone; a good outcome. Inform Rose of her success and tell her to get a move on. We have a multitude to welcome,' said Simon, with a smile on his face for the first time in hours. He was totally relieved that everything had gone like clockwork.

Rose received the message just as she was nearing the arrivals terminal. A weight seemed to lift from her shoulders. She made for the nearest check-in desk and started organising everyone as quickly as she could.

After scanning the list of available staff, she noticed Grade Seven Labour Manager John Blight had arrived. 'Just what I need,' she said, and called him instantly.

'John.' There was a long silent pause. 'This is Senior Engineer Rose Markham. I'm afraid I need your help at the arrivals terminal right now. Can you come over please? I want you to set up a feeding station as quickly as possible.'

She heard him say in a sleepy voice, 'Yes, sure. How many need feeding?'

'Over a thousand by the look of it, and quickly too,' she replied instantly.

'OK, that's a tall order. I'll be with you as soon as I can,' he said.

'Thanks. See you soon,' she said, and started to contact other personnel on her list.

Staff started coming from the city in a steady stream, and the shuttle was due in less than five minutes. She knew there was enough accommodation for everyone, there was just the problem with food.

'Feed them now and send them to bed for the night. But how do we feed them?' She thought out loud, hoping someone could find the answer to that one.

The Australian shuttle was entering the terminal. Staff positioned along the platform made ready to shepherd the passengers to arrivals. It would take awhile, but it wasn't an impossible task as long as they co-operated.

As soon as the shuttle came to a halt, lifting equipment removed the pods and placed them on the ground. The doors opened and passengers started to alight from the pods on all three platforms. They looked shocked and had bewildered looks on their faces; they were blinking in the bright light. They were all ages, from babies to the elderly, but mostly young adults.

'Young adults. That should please Danni,' Rose thought, as she watched the monitors.

John was fast asleep when his personal communicator sounded. It was a minute before he realised what the noise was, then answered it quickly.

Hearing his name, he paused, shook his head to wake himself up before answering, and quietly said, 'John Blight here. Who is it?'

It was Rose, and he listened to what she had to say before replying, 'OK, that's a tall order, but I'll be with you as soon as I can.'

When she'd finished speaking, he got up, and in doing so, disturbed Juliette.

He whispered into her ear, 'No peace to get some sleep. Got to go to work; my boss just called me.'

She just waved an arm in the air, indicating she wanted to be left alone. He gave her a quick kiss and got dressed.

After a slice of bread and a glass of water, he asked May to call a spitter.

May replied, *'You can have a SCAT if you wish, though it might be better if you had some training first.'*

John decided on the SCAT and asked May for some guidance. He still didn't know what a SCAT was exactly and couldn't wait to see what it was like.

He thought about what Rose had asked him to do, and said quietly to himself, 'It's a tall order! But I'll see what I can do for her.'

Sitting at the communications console, he looked over the list of personnel Rose had sent him, and was pleased with the diversity of staff available. He was also pleased that Juliette's name wasn't on it.

A few minutes later a SCAT had homed in on his apartment, and his communicator informed him of its arrival. He went straight outside to see what it looked like, and to try it out of course.

As he walked towards it, he felt extremely excited. It looked like a two-person scooter he used to ride and race on at the amusement arcade. Only this one was longer, almost three metres long, and so sleek. The sloping windshield indicated it was definitely built for speed. It was a pale, metallic pink colour, with iridescent chrome trim and what looked like a long, totally clear, gel-type, flat seat running almost the full length of the SCAT.

'Juliette's favourite colour. She's going to love this,' he said quietly to himself.

It was floating just above the ground, and to his amazement, spoke just as he reached it. *'I've been instructed to help you fly me, at least until you are competent or until requested otherwise. Please insert the disk you were given when you first arrived.'*

John ran back inside, got the disk, returned, and inserted it into the control panel.

'I am now programmed to accept your commands only. If you would like to mount, we can go wherever you wish,' it stated, and continued to float in total silence.

John mounted the SCAT and felt a weird sensation. The gel seat moulded perfectly to his rear end and was holding him firmly, but comfortably, in place. He looked at the controls, amazed by how few there were, and realised it was going to be really easy to drive this thing.

'Are you ready to go?' it inquired.

He told it to wait for instructions, turned on the small communications console fitted to the SCAT, and asked for a plan of the complex. Almost immediately, a 3-D holographic image appeared above the handlebars just behind the windshield, and as he looked it over, he exclaimed. 'Wow! I had no idea this place was so big.'

'Find me a small dome, as near to the arrivals terminal as possible,' he requested.

The image rotated and zoomed in on a section of the complex. Three domes were highlighted as available for use, and he checked their details. He pointed to a suitable one, close to the size he had in mind. It was Store Dome Number One, which was right next to the arrivals terminal. 'That'll do nicely to set up the feeding station,' he remarked.

The SCAT stated, *'Co-ordinates set. Do you wish to go there now?'*

'Not just yet,' he said.

He remembered from his training that mobile food processing plants, or more commonly called "Mobile All-Terrain Chow Houses" (MATCH or chow house for short), were built to feed city construction workers many, many years ago. He asked if there were any of these units stored at the complex.

The SCAT console stated, *'Accessing archives. Please wait a moment.'* Then, to his surprise, came the reply, *'There is one available in Archive Dome Number One. It has been stored ready for use.'*

'Ready for use! After all this time! How come?' he enquired.

'Engineers updated the technology, ensuring compatibility with current equipment,' replied the SCAT.

He raised his eyebrows in astonishment, and asked for it to be delivered to Store Dome Number One.

He was taken aback when he heard the reply. The SCAT told him, *'You do not have the authority to release it from storage.'*

Annoyed, he contacted Rose immediately, 'Rose, I need authority to move some large equipment needed for the feeding station. Can you help please?'

There was silence for a minute before she replied, 'I'll get Simon to give you complete authority to do what you want. It should make things quicker than having to go through me every time.' And even she sounded annoyed.

'Who's Simon?' he asked.

'Simon is "Number One" here at the centre. The man in charge of us all.'

'Thanks Rose. Maybe I'll meet him some day. I'll call you when I'm ready to set up the feeding station,' John told her.

OK, thanks,' Rose said quickly, and cut him off.

'Take me to the MATCH,' he said to the SCAT. He hadn't the slightest idea what it really looked like or how big it was.

'Hold tight please,' said the SCAT. And off it sped, with John hanging on for dear life.

The journey left him totally exhilarated. He was fully awake by the time he reached Archive Dome Number One. First thing he decided to do was to learn how to operate the MATCH. He thought he could learn to do it as it was being brought out of storage, but soon realised it would take some time to achieve even the basic skills to drive it. May, knowing this, kindly offered to take full automatic control. To move the MATCH, she only required him to provide co-ordinates and instruction of what to do when it arrived. As soon as May had been given the information, and the MATCH was ready to come out of storage, he left for the store dome as fast as he could and left her to it. Now, the only obstacle was the authority to move it.

He still didn't know what the MATCH looked like and definitely didn't know how to drive it; he probably never would drive it. He'd only ever seen a picture of one in his course notes many years ago, and that memory had faded slightly.

It wasn't long before he arrived at Store Dome Number One. It was next to the arrivals terminal. He quickly started calling in staff to help set things up, any staff, it didn't matter what their vocation was, as long as their grade was below his. And of course he didn't call Juliette; she wasn't on his list anyway.

Once all staff had been called, he headed for the arrivals terminal to meet Rose. He had no idea what she looked like, so was a bit apprehensive about the first meeting. When he arrived at the terminal, he was confronted by a multitude of people, all asking questions and looking even more lost than he was. He stood back, asked a security guard where he could find Rose Markham, and was escorted over to a tiny woman with long white hair shouting orders to just about everyone.

'Senior Engineer Markham?' he enquired. 'I'm Labour Manager John Blight.'

Rose turned. 'Hi, that's me, and I'm Rose. First names only please. Full names only if you've done something wrong,' she said smiling at him.

'Pleased to meet you Rose. What do you want me to do?' he said, scanning the area that was filling with even more people.

'Can you organise the staff to set up the feeding station? I want these people fed quickly,' she said.

'I'll see what I can do. Some welcome this turned out to be. Straight in at the deep end,' he replied.

'Sorry about that,' Rose said. 'It's all a bit unexpected.'

'Don't I know it. I'll get started immediately,' John said, sounding sympathetic.

'Keep me informed please. And I don't want to hear any bad news,' she said with an air of authority in her voice.

With that, John turned his SCAT and headed off towards Store Dome Number One to wait for the chow house.

Rose watched him go, wondering how on earth he was going to feed all these people with no equipment to do it. He seemed quite confident, even though she thought he was too young. She hoped he wouldn't let her down.

Simon was watching the shuttle terminal on the control room monitors. Watching the three dimensional image, he could see the shuttle units now had the empty pods replaced, and they'd begun to separate. As each one separated, it was lifted and sent to the holding area in the next dome.

'Soon have that shuttle broken and stored ready for the next shuttle to arrive. We don't have enough platforms for all the shuttles that are coming,' he told his staff. 'How long till the slow shuttle arrives?'

One of his staff quickly replied, 'It'll be here in about thirty minutes.'

He zoomed in to look at the platforms, which were still packed with people, and called Rose. 'Get those people moving. We have another shuttle due in thirty minutes.'

Rose looked astonished. She wasn't expecting it to arrive that soon. 'OK, I'll have to move these people fast. Can you send me two mobile corrals to hold them?'

Simon said, 'They're not cattle you know. How long are you going to hold them?'

'Only until we can process them properly. I just have to clear the platforms quickly. Besides, some of these people may never have seen open space before, and I don't want to cause panic,' she replied.

'OK, good thinking. I understand.' There was a slight pause before he added, 'There are two new corrals on their way over now.'

He turned to Danni and told her, 'Go to meet the corrals. Take some administration staff with you and set up a field check-in post. We have to find out who these people are, and quickly.'

Danni was about to call a spitter when Simon interrupted her; he had other plans. He'd ordered her a SCAT, and one was waiting on the balcony just outside.

'Danni, your transport is waiting on the balcony for you,' Simon remarked without looking at her. 'Just take it easy till you get used to it,' he said while pointing in the direction of it and smirking.

Danni looked out of the window and saw the SCAT.

'Thanks a bunch!' she said sarcastically. 'If I die, I'll come back and haunt you.'

Simon managed a chuckle and smiled. 'I expect you will, just to annoy me. Go on, off you go, and be quick.'

Danni jumped on the SCAT, turned the throttle, and it shot forward. Without lifting, it skidded off the balcony and started to drop straight down. She hadn't been told to tell the SCAT she was a novice, and as it started falling, she panicked and screamed.

Almost a second passed before the computer realised she had no control and took over. It stopped with a jerk and hovered in mid air. *'I will take over if you wish. Where to please?'* it asked her.

Danni looked relieved and said with a shaky, stuttering voice, 'T . . . To the n . . . new corrals landing area that S . . . Simon ordered.'

It stayed stationary for a moment while it checked for information. *'I have found where they are going to land. Please provide better directions in future, it will help speed the journey. Hold tight, and keep your head down.'*

Danni thought it a rather cheeky little thing and managed a thin smile. After all, she hadn't even asked Simon where she was to go. Now she was flying through the air for a second time, her eyes tightly shut. She was gripping the handlebar so tightly, she turned it into a white knuckle ride.

Rose had just finished talking to John when the two corrals arrived at the shuttle terminal. They settled gently on the ground and the doors slowly opened. They had landed end to end, like one long room positioned directly at the terminal exit.

A voice spoke to the people on the platforms. *'Please make your way to the exit. Transport has arrived to take you to the check-in area.'* It repeated this a number of times before most of the people had boarded the corrals.

Rose was relieved. It had been easier than expected, and was not too soon, as she could see the next shuttle was just arriving.

She contacted Simon. 'Simon, the slow shuttle is arriving. Can you keep the pods closed till all those people have left the terminal please?'

'Wouldn't it be easier to move them all together?' he asked.

'Don't want to risk it! We have no idea what state these people are in after their journey,' she replied.

'OK, let me know when you are ready,' he said.

'Just one more thing, can you give John Blight full authority to move equipment and anything else he needs please?' It sounded more like a plea than a request.

'Who's John Blight?' Simon asked.

'He's one of the most important new arrivals we have, a grade seven labour manager. So do it quickly please,' she demanded.

'OK! Keep your hair on. I'll give him complete authority right now.

Speak to you soon.' And he was gone.

Rose watched the monitors as the last of the passengers boarded the corrals and the doors shut behind them. She watched the corrals lift and move to one side, clearing the exit of the shuttle terminal and disappearing up the tunnel towards the main dome.

A short while later she heard a strange buzzing noise coming from the exit. It was quiet at first but was getting louder and louder. It was like nothing she'd ever heard before. First she thought it might be a defective drive on one of the corrals, but she dismissed that as the sound seemed to be coming from a different direction. She made her way to the exit, stared out, and saw something that looked like a dust cloud in the distance. It was getting closer and closer, and the buzzing was becoming a drumming, which vibrated through the ground and up through her body. She looked at the security guard standing beside her, who was also staring, and said, 'What on earth is that?' Then she stood still, waiting to see what was coming and making all the noise.

Rose went through the exit to see what was going on, and was astonished when she saw a huge, square block moving towards a nearby dome. She wondered what on earth it could be. Judging by the markings on its side, it was very old and very dirty. Dust that had settled on it over the years was being disturbed, forming a cloud around it which made it difficult to see. It wasn't flying like the mobile corrals; it just rolled along on many large, ball-like wheels. She counted twelve on each side, and each one was at least ten metres tall. The vehicle approached the maglev tracks that ran from the arrivals terminal and, to her surprise, the track supports lowered to the ground to let it pass.

Rose was amazed. She'd no idea the maglev track did that, and this thing seemed to have the right of way over everything. All spitter traffic had come to a complete standstill, as did everyone who saw it.

'Back to work, you lot,' she shouted when she noticed the workers were idle.

The vehicle was travelling quite fast, and clumps of earth were being thrown high into the air behind it. Then she noticed the ruts it was leaving in the grassy plain by its deeply treaded tyres.

She called Danni, 'Danni, I don't know what just passed the arrivals terminal. Whatever it was left deep ruts in the grass and frightened the cattle. And it's huge.'

There was a pause before Danni replied, 'I can hear something coming towards me. I'm at Store Dome Number One next to you, waiting for the corrals to arrive. I'll see if I can find anything out.'

'Thanks,' Rose told her.

Danni arrived at the dome designated by John for the field feeding station. Because he had chosen this dome, it was also the place the corrals were due to land. She'd started to organise staff, getting them ready to check in the newcomers, but stopped when she heard the noise Rose had mentioned. The noise had increased to a drumming before she turned towards the dome entrance to take a closer look.

What Danni saw next made her jaw drop. A SCAT, carrying a man who was sitting backwards on it, was approaching to the left of the entrance. He was signalling with his arms to this monster of a vehicle, which, to her amazement, followed his every move. Suddenly he raised both his arms in the air and the vehicle stopped in an even bigger dust cloud. Then he dropped his arms to his sides and the vehicle's belly hit the ground with a thump. The wheels disappeared over the top, then ramps, ventilation shafts, doors, and windows appeared in the sides. Cranes, low loaders, elevators, conveyor belts, and small maglev platforms lined up alongside ready for use. The vehicle dwarfed the SCAT many times over, and if it hadn't been for his arms moving, she wouldn't have known the man was there. The dust the vehicle created was settling all around it, making it difficult to see anything for a few moments.

Danni was totally bemused. She'd never seen or heard of a vehicle like this, and she quickly crossed to the man still sitting on the SCAT to get some answers.

John went to meet the MATCH. He didn't realise just how big it was and had quite a shock when he saw it coming towards him at high speed. After telling May to give him semi-automatic control, he told it to follow his arm signals, turned backwards on the SCAT, and looked over his shoulder to ensure he was going in the right direction.

The vehicle was massive. It not only processed food, it was also a canteen capable of seating two thousand people at a time. It only needed raw produce as an input and canteen staff to help with serving. Now it was nearing its destination and he was pleased how easily things were going so far. Then came the first obstacle; a maglev track was in its way and he wondered if the vehicle could climb over it. An announcement from the SCAT console gave him the answer. The processing plant had signalled the track to lower itself. He watched the track as it lowered and the MATCH passed over without any difficulty. He also noticed the noise was spooking the cattle; they were scattering rapidly and he hoped they would settle down when the beast was settled in place.

Once he arrived at the Store Dome Number One, he signalled the MATCH to stop by raising his arms. As soon as it stopped, he dropped his arms and it immediately belly flopped to the ground with quite a bump. Once settled, things starting happening very quickly, as it was getting ready for use.

John asked May, 'What are the strange markings on its sides?'

She replied, *'They are the old disused Chinese language for "Himalayan Region Construction Group". Someone wrote over it "Himalayan Food Destruction Sloop", also in Chinese.'*

John realised that some of symbols looked similar to modern writing from the Mummer language that everyone now used. He smiled as he said, 'They had a sense of humour back then too.'

John looked at the list of staff Rose gave him and frowned. There were plenty of normal staff, but no farmers. He shook his head in disbelief and was about to call Rose, but stopped when he noticed a figure rapidly approaching from behind in one of his SCAT mirrors.

'Hi, can I help you?' he said politely.

Danni was taken by surprise. She was going to bite his head off for frightening the cattle, but instead she just asked, 'What's this thing?'

'A Mobile All-Terrain Chow House. It's capable of feeding two thousand people if I can feed it the raw produce it requires,' he replied, sounding a little annoyed.

His reply took Danni by surprise. 'Who are you?' she asked, quite puzzled.

John realised she had an air of authority about her, and said politely, 'Grade Seven Labour Manager John Blight. You can call me John if you wish.'

Him being so young and having no idea who she was amused her. 'Fine, John it is then. I'm Danni Mitchell, Grade Three Chief Scientist. Call me Danni.'

All of a sudden John was speechless. Danni noticed his silence.

'I saw you shaking your head. Problem?' she enquired.

John looked at his list again and said, 'Yep. There are no farmers on this list Rose gave me. Aren't there any farmers here?'

Danni smiled. Trust Rose to forget them; farming wasn't her strong point. Danni quickly made another list and passed it over to John. 'Good luck, they're not the easiest of people to work with,' she said, smiling.

'I've had some experience with farmers in the past, so I know what to expect,' he said confidently.

John started to call in many types of farmers. Every one of them would be required to stock the processing plant with raw produce as fast as they possibly could.

Simon called Rose. 'Are you ready to release the shuttle passengers yet?'

'Yes. The corrals have cleared the exit,' she replied.

'Thank goodness for that.'

He ordered the pod doors to be opened immediately.

Simon watched in silence as the doors were opened and the occupants started to emerge very slowly. One hundred pods were offloaded and eighty-eight people alighted, all from the luxury pods.

'Not looking too good,' he said to Rose. 'Can you let Danni know how many more to expect?'

'Yes. Will do. When is the next train due?' she asked him

'In about five hours or so. So I'm off to get some sleep. Wake me if you need anything,' he replied.

'Have a good sleep. I'll try not to call you. I'll let Danni know if there are any problems, OK?'

'Thanks Rose, you're a treasure. Night,' he said, and signed off.

The farmers were arriving at the dome and looking at the processing plant in utter amazement. Each was asking what it was and how it worked.

None of them were impressed when John asked for supplies of raw produce to be shipped in as soon as possible. They stood around discussing his request and arguing amongst themselves. Some would comply and some wouldn't. John decided to intervene.

'What's the problem?' he asked a farmer who seemed to be the spokesman for all.

'We cannot provide what you want without disrupting the research program. You have no authority to ask us for anything,' said the man, turning to his colleagues with a smug look on his face.

'And you are?' John asked sharply.

'Bob Griffiths, Grade Six Cattle Manager,' he replied.

John looked him square in the eyes and said, 'Simon Tallsworth has given me complete authority and Danni Mitchell gave me your names. If that isn't good enough, perhaps I should call them over.'

Bob looked at the list John had in his hand and said, 'Right men, you heard him; let's get cracking.' Then he turned, gave John a wink, and said, 'Well done lad. You stood your ground well.'

That did it. Each farmer came to John for a list of produce they had to provide. John shook his head in disbelief; it had been easier than he'd expected. There was only one slight problem: he hadn't thought about what produce would be required. 'One moment please,' he told them.

He casually walked over to his SCAT and on the way, asked May for a list of supplies required by the processing plant. After accessing the archives once more, May provided a full list, furnished with the type and quantity of products required. John provided each farmer with a list of what to bring and exactly where to place it.

Things were going well for him, so he relaxed for the briefest of moments. All of a sudden, he felt tiredness creeping through his body and couldn't fight it. The stresses and strains of the past twenty-seven hours were beginning to take their toll, and he sat on his SCAT to take a short break. Soon his head had drooped to his chest and his breathing became regular; he'd fallen asleep.

Rose arranged to transport the eighty-eight new arrivals to the arrivals terminal. She put six people to each spitter, which was more than regulation permitted, but just possible if they weren't too heavy.

It didn't take long, and once they'd all left the terminal she went to find Danni.

As she approached Store Dome Number One, she noticed the MATCH sited near its entrance. It startled her to see such a large object sitting on the ground like it had always been there. Then she noticed John, head down and looking like he was fast asleep. She smiled as she was passing and let him be.

Not long after she found Danni busy, helping to check people in. 'Hi Danni, what's that thing?'

Danni explained as best she could. She knew what it was, but she had no idea how it worked. 'John's the man to see; he's . . . sleeping on that SCAT over there,' she said, pointing in his direction.

'Yes, he's asleep. I didn't want to wake him as I passed. He came in on the damaged shuttle just over five hours ago, bless him,' Rose said sympathetically.

'I was on that one too,' Danni said, sounding rather cross and giving Rose a stern look. 'He must be under your command?'

'Yes he is under my command, and I think he's really good at his job, considering he's only eighteen,' Rose replied.

'Only eighteen and managed to do all that! I think we should have him on the council; if he can stay awake, that is. What do you think?'

Rose thought for a moment, before replying, 'We need someone young on the council. There's only me, you, Simon and Bob at the moment.'

'Has Simon organised anyone to take a look at Nâgpur City yet?' asked Danni, remembering what she'd seen earlier.

'Not yet, I don't think. Do you want to get things started? I can take over here,' Rose offered.

'Simon is asleep, and I don't want to wake him. I'll organise a search party using a hopper. If they find anyone alive, they can report the situation back to me before I decide what to do,' said Danni as she jumped on her SCAT.

Rose looked at her, 'You're shattered too by the look of you. Get some rest first.'

'No. It has to be done as soon as possible. We must find out if our council members are still alive and get them here quickly. And as for the rest, the biggest hopper only carries a hundred passengers at a time, and time is of the essence,' she said with concern in her voice.

Danni didn't like the thought that they could only take a few people from the city. The Himalayan Centre had room for quite a few thousand, but not the millions of survivors Nâgpur City might hold.

She started her SCAT. 'Take me to the southern observation balcony.'

The SCAT shot off with her holding on tight and with her eyes closed even tighter than before. They were on their way to the top of the largest dome, and she hated heights.

John felt a slight shake on his shoulder as one of the farmers returned with his quota of produce. 'What happens now?' the farmer asked.

John was instantly awake and fell off his SCAT onto the ground just below. It was the first time he'd touched it and its coolness felt nice and refreshing.

'Thanks for getting back so soon,' he said, picking himself up.

He sat back on the SCAT and instructed the chow house to start processing.

All of a sudden things started to move. The recently delivered pallet of produce was taken in and an empty one replaced it. The empty pallet also had a new list attached to it.

'Off you go and get that lot,' John said, sounding just as amazed as the farmer looked.

He knew it would take a lot to satisfy the food processing needs, and soon farmers were coming and going like clockwork, providing all that was needed. Just one hour after supplies started arriving, John received a message from the MATCH. *'Food is now ready for serving in the chow house. There are one thousand places for the first sitting, and the same will be ready for the second sitting in forty-five minutes.'*

He hadn't told it how many to cater for, so it catered for two complete sittings. He sped over to Rose and told her the news. 'Food is ready for serving. I only hope we have enough staff to help out.'

He gave Rose a list of jobs and personnel he'd already organised.

Rose looked at the list. 'We should have enough. I'll start feeding everyone straight away,' she replied. 'There's even enough to feed most of the staff. Thanks.'

Danni was flying through the air, and felt her ears pop as her SCAT rapidly gained height. She opened one eye to take a look, and quickly closed it again when she saw the ground was far below, almost a thousand metres below.

Her SCAT slowed and landed on a platform high on the side of the largest dome. She was just over 1,200 metres above the ground. It was one of four platforms in separate domes, each facing a different point on the compass and close to the top of each dome.

On the platform was a large blast door that led out to an observation balcony with an outer wall made from Quadron, a manmade metal with similar properties to Triron. The view from the balcony looked out over the Himalayan mountain range, which was normally a fantastic sight to see. Only now as she dismounted, she didn't know what to expect.

Crossing to a control panel next to the blast door, she performed a routine test. The test checked to ensure the outer wall was intact and no harmful gasses were present. After a few moments, the results indicated all was in order to open the door, and she pressed her communicator against the panel to be security scanned.

A voice welcomed her, '*Welcome to the southern observation balcony, Chief Mitchell. Enjoy your stay.*'

The door opened within a blink of an eye, revealing a long empty room with its walls, floor, and all fixtures the reddish brown colour of Quadron. Rows of seating faced outwards along the wall, ready for the many people who would normally visit during their leisure time. It was usually a tranquil place to relax or meditate.

Danni walked into the room, moved towards the edge of the balcony, and requested the wall be made clear for viewing so she could look out. As the window cleared, she suddenly realised it was dark. She had totally forgotten it was nighttime. The lights in the dome, and her tiredness, had caused confusion, and she was annoyed with herself.

She called Rose, 'Rose, you could've reminded me it was night out there.'

'Sorry,' said Rose, a little puzzled by the remark. 'I forgot myself till you just mentioned it. Where are you anyway?'

'Doesn't matter. There's nothing I can do till it gets light. In the meantime I may as well get some sleep.'

OK! I'll hold the fort. See you in the morning. Good night,' said Rose despondently. She was extremely tired herself.

'Thanks Rose. Good night,' Danni said, not even thinking about how long Rose had been up.

Rose started to herd the new arrivals into the MATCH where staff greeted them and showed them what to do. She looked over at John and smiled. She was impressed with what he had achieved in such a short time and how he had managed the farmers.

Danni arrived home and smiled to herself. Many weeks had passed since she'd slept in her own bed and she'd really missed it. Now she crept in, trying not to wake Simon, and slid quietly into bed beside him.

'Everything OK?' he asked in a sleepy voice.

'Everything's fine,' she said, and cuddled into him.

Soon they were both fast asleep.

Within an hour, everyone had been fed, and all were ready for bed.

Rose contacted John. 'OK, they're all fed. You can switch it off now.'

'It doesn't work like that. It's been programmed to provide three meals a day for the next week, minimum. I can shut it down, but it will not be ready for use for at least two days if I do that,' he replied.

She was amazed by his remark. 'Why did you tell it to work for a week?' she asked him.

'It's the minimum time it normally operates for. We need to keep stocking it anyway; these people will have to be fed. At least until we sort something else out,' he said.

'Good point! I'll let the farmers know what to expect for the next week,' Rose told him.

'We must let it know what supplies we have. It has to plan a menu for the week,' he said, after May prompted him with a quick message.

'OK, leave it with me. Is there anything else?' she asked him.

'No, that's it. That beast is completely automated. Just do as it asks and feed it.'

'You may as well get some sleep now. There's nothing more to do for the next five and a half hours. See you in the control room at ten sharp,' Rose said, noticing he was having difficulty keeping his eyes open.

John smiled at the thought of going back to bed. 'Thanks. Don't forget to turn the lights off when you go,' he said jokingly to Rose.

Rose laughed as he disappeared on his SCAT, then made her way back to the control room. The check-in personnel were busy trying to house new arrivals, farmers were supplying the chow house with produce, and the last train that Simon found sitting in a junction waiting for instructions wasn't due for some time. It was time for a short break.

Once back in the control room, Rose looked at the progress of the last train moving on the tube system console.

'Any news about that train?' she asked her staff.

The duty senior engineer replied, 'There are people onboard. We've made contact with some, but we're not sure how many there are exactly.'

Rose sat back in her chair, propped herself against a wall, and said, 'Wake me if anything else happens.' Then she remembered what John had said. 'Oh! Yes, turn the lights off slowly. It is nighttime after all.'

She put a cushion between her head and the wall, closed her eyes, and was soon fast asleep. Slowly it became dark outside the control room, just like a normal night should be, except it wouldn't be long before the normal dawn was due.

Rose drifted in and out of sleep during the short night. Her unrest was mostly caused by bad dreams of what it must be like outside the centre. When it was time for her to wake up, a member of her staff gently shook her shoulder. Even that gentle shake was enough to make her jump up, and she looked totally dazed. She was still very tired, and after a fresh cup of tea, went to talk to the duty engineer. While she was sitting next to him, he informed her that the last train was due in shortly, and after watching its progress on the monitor, she decided to call Simon.

'Simon, the last train is due to arrive in about twenty minutes. Are you coming over here or going to the arrivals terminal?' she asked him.

It was a little while before she received a whispered reply. 'Neither. I've just been informed there's a chow house serving food. I will be having breakfast with Danni first. Then I'll be coming over.'

Rose sounded dejected to hear she wasn't to be relieved of her duty yet. 'OK, I'll keep you informed of any further developments.' And she cut him off. She had difficulty keeping her eyes open, and so closed them just for a moment.

It wasn't long before the duty engineer shook her shoulder. 'The train is arriving. What shall we do with the passengers?' he asked.

Rose was instantly awake and asked him to repeat what he'd just said. When she heard what he'd said, she looked around the room and noticed that half the staff were fast asleep with their heads on their desks.

'Wake those required and leave the rest sleeping,' she told him.

She watched as the train entered the shuttle terminal; it was a long one and looked promising. 'Should be a lot of people on this one if all the pods are occupied,' she remarked. 'Get the corrals ready just in case. We may need them again.'

Orders were issued, and she sat down again.

'I hope Simon comes soon,' she said to herself, while looking at the monitors blurring before her eyes as she tried to focus on them.

Her eyes opened wide when she noticed the platforms filling with the new arrivals. 'There must be at least a thousand! Make sure the chow house is ready to feed them. I want these people fed before breakfast time,' she insisted. 'We can process them later.'

The new arrivals, being so disorientated, were easily herded into the corrals, and were quickly on their way to Store Dome Number One, just two minutes travelling time away. It took two journeys to complete the mammoth task, and everything went without a hitch. Within forty-five minutes of leaving the pods, all the new arrivals were queuing for food, though some looked like they were sleeping on their feet.

Rose looked at the time; it was six thirty in the morning. She'd been on duty for almost twenty-four hours, and she felt totally drained.

CHAPTER 4
LIFE GOES ON

Pauline woke early to find Brian still fast asleep in their enormous, comfortable bed. She got up and quietly asked for the bedroom window to open very slowly. As it started to open, she walked towards the crack of light, and as it opened further, the glare of daylight blinded her for a moment. When her eyes adjusted, she couldn't believe what she was seeing; the view was stunning. Lush, green grass covered a sloping field, dotted with orange and lemon trees. Sheep were grazing beneath the trees, and as she looked up, she saw a wonderful, blue sky. It overwhelmed her for a moment. She'd only seen pictures like this in books, and didn't know they actually existed. As she touched the window, it started to open, and taking a deep breath, she sensed the fragrance of the wonderful abundance of blossom covering the trees. It was so intoxicating she totally forgot all that had happened just one day earlier.

She turned to Brian who was now awake. 'Look at the view. And that smell. Mm,' she said, closing her eyes and breathing in deeply once again.

Brian slid off the bed and crossed to the window. He'd never seen anything like it either. 'Wow, this is some place. This fresh air makes me feel hungry. What's for breakfast? I'm starving,' he added.

He'd also forgotten what had happened for a minute. Then he remembered they had to make their own food, and was brought abruptly back to reality.

He made for the communications console downstairs, and asked Lucy, his companion, for an information update. He was told there was no further news, except there was now a chow house, and food was available to all who couldn't cook. He ran back upstairs to tell Pauline and watched as she jumped up and down, yelling, 'Yippee!'

She continued excitedly, 'Let's get ready quickly. Got to get there before the food runs out.'

After sharing the cleansing cubicle to save time, they rushed to get dressed to go and have breakfast.

Brian asked Lucy, his companion, to call a spitter, and was surprised when told one would be along in approximately thirty minutes. Lucy added, *'The chow house is full, and I've booked a time for your breakfast. Please be ready when your transport arrives.'*

He turned to Pauline. 'Must be popular. I can't get any seats.'

'If it's the only place that offers cooked food, then it will be very popular. Nobody cooks!' she replied.

Brian saw what time the table had been booked for; they would have to wait forty-five minutes. The spitter journey would take fifteen, on top of the thirty minute delay. So they sat and waited, looking over the information supplied to them on arrival.

Brian was amazed by the size of the place and all that it contained. Over five hundred square kilometres in twenty-three domes, and it was totally self-contained. There were water and air treatment plants, farms providing all types of produce, and more than enough energy to supply a dozen cities. The hospital facilities were first-class, with regeneration techniques far more advanced than what he was used to, and this made him very excited.

'I'll call the hospital to see if they need my assistance once we've eaten,' he told Pauline.

'I would rather you spent the day with me,' she replied, frowning at the thought of being left alone all day.

Brian just smiled and gave her a hug.

Juliette woke to find John sleeping quietly beside her, and decided to leave him that way. She rose from the bed, crossed to the small window, selected a clear view, and was blinded by the bright light from outside. When her eyes adjusted, she closed the window instantly and shrieked.

Her sudden reaction woke John with a start. 'What's the matter love?' he said, rubbing his eyes to try and wake up properly.

'There is nothing out there. No houses. No streets. No roof. Nothing. Absolutely nothing. Just open space,' she said, with a startled, frightened look on her face.

Looking oddly at her, he got out of bed, crossed the room to take a look, and selected the clear window. The window was quite small for such a large room, though it was big enough if you weren't used to them. Even so, he too was shocked when his eyes adjusted to the bright light. Their window looked out towards the entrance of another dome. Not just any dome though, this one was huge. It was full of water as far as the eye could see. There was no sign of land, and only the shimmering glint of light on the surface broke the emptiness. He was looking out over the surface of Water Dome Two. It was filled with sea water and teeming with life.

Looking down he could see a small, sandy beach at the end of their small garden. A few palm trees were dotted along the shoreline, and small waves crashed gently on the white sand. It wasn't far from their garden fence, and he thought it was perfect.

Smiling, he turned and said, 'I see what you mean. I'll see if I can get another apartment.'

But in reality, he hoped that wouldn't be possible, as it would be great fun for the kids. He also wanted to know what it would be like swimming in open water without the usual crowds of a city. And with that thought, he closed the window.

'Keep the window closed for now. I'll get everyone to pack right now,' he said, leaving the bedroom quickly and heading for the communications console.

Juliette got dressed and followed him downstairs. 'I'm hungry. Any idea what we can have for breakfast?' she asked through a long yawn.

Just then two heads popped up from the sofa, and in harmony Petal and Fred piped up, 'So am I.' This statement was followed by giggling and some friendly shoving and throwing of cushions.

John called for a spitter to take them to breakfast in the chow house. Only he knew it existed, and called them all into the kitchen to explain about it.

'I found an old MATCH last night. It's a mobile chow house. It hasn't been used for two hundred years, but it works. We are going to eat there from now on,' he told them.

'Yuk! Is it safe?' Juliette asked, screwing her face up.

'Perfectly safe. It looked like new once the layers of dust finished settling,' he was trying to make it sound even more terrible; she bit.

'If you think I'm going to eat in a place like that, you must be joking,' she replied angrily.

'Well there's the larder and the cooker. So get cracking; we're starving too,' he said, grinning and content that he had her hooked.

Juliette looked at him with daggers in her eyes. 'You . . . You bastard, you're just winding me up aren't you?'

'Sure am. Now can we get going, the spitter has arrived. Oh! And don't swear in front of the kids,' John said cheekily as he walked slowly towards the door.

Juliette ran after him and jumped on his back. 'I'll get you back,' she said, and wrapped herself around him, piggyback-like.

Little did she know that John wasn't joking. When he told her about the years of dust that had collected on the MATCH, it was actually true.

The spitter scurried off with Juliette hugging John, her eyes closed tightly so she didn't have to see open spaces again, well, not yet anyway. Petal and Fred were chatting away, looking all around and commenting on everything they saw. They had all their belongings with them, and that didn't amount to much, just one little bag each.

Then they saw the chow house, busy like a beehive, with people and vehicles buzzing all around it.

'That must be the place,' said Petal, excitedly pointing at the pale blue block of metal with strange symbols written on it.

Juliette opened one eye to take a peek just as they were arriving at the entrance. She smiled as the aroma of cooked food wafted past. 'That smells nice. Let's go and eat,' she said, and was first into the chow house.

They were all amazed by how efficiently it was running; even John was surprised. The staff had quickly learnt how to perform various tasks (with the help of their personal companions) and there was even a shift system in place.

As soon as everyone was seated, they began looking at a menu and were asked to select meals for the whole week. It seemed like fun to Juliette, Petal, and Fred, but John knew just how complex the whole thing really was and how much work he had to do to keep it running.

'Come on, let's eat. I'm required for work again soon,' John said, tucking into his breakfast.

Juliette reminded him about the problem with their apartment, and John said he would try to sort it out first thing.

Simon woke early and asked his companion what he could have to eat. The look on his face changed to utter glee when he was told about the MATCH.

Simon shook Danni. 'Come on, get dressed. I want to sample the delights being served up at the chow house,' he said.

Danni didn't want to get up; she hadn't had that much sleep. Then she remembered Nâgpur City and shot out of bed. 'Simon, I have to see if we can rescue some of the council from Nâgpur City,' she said, while hurriedly getting dressed and stumbling into just about every object in the room.

'Calm down woman. Breakfast first,' Simon insisted. 'And no buts.'

Simon took her hand and led her outside. They each climbed on their personal SCAT and took off for the chow house.

Simon couldn't believe his eyes when he saw it. He contacted Danni, who was just behind him. 'Who got this thing up and running?' he asked her.

'That labour manager you gave full authority to, John Blight. He did a good job. And he's a nice guy,' she replied smugly.

'Nice to have someone with a bit of experience at last,' he said, not knowing John was only eighteen and straight out of college.

Danni smiled and said, 'You'll have to meet him. I think he would be good to have on the council. Rose thinks so too.'

'He must be good if Rose likes him,' he said as they entered the chow house together.

Soon they were seated, looking over the menu, and deciding what to eat for the rest of the week just like everyone else.

At last a spitter arrived. Brian and Pauline left the apartment, jumped aboard, and made their way to the chow house. As they approached both of them looked openmouthed at it. It was a monster of a block, and buzzing with small crafts, which were coming and going.

'What is that thing?' Pauline asked, still agog.

'Don't know, but the spitter is taking us to it. I guess it must be the chow house,' he said, just as amazed as she was.

The spitter passed the entrance to the Store Dome Number One and made its way to the foyer of the chow house along with many other spitters. Staff ushered them in, welcomed them to the chow house, showed them to a table, and offered up a menu. They looked at what was on offer and ordered breakfast. And as soon as they ordered, they were asked to provide a menu for the week.

They looked at each other and smiled. 'At least we don't have to cook,' said Pauline.

When they'd finished eating, Brian told Pauline to go back to the apartment and find out more information about the place. He was going to the hospital to have a look around. 'See if there's a shopping mall,' he said to her.

'There'd better be,' she replied as she was leaving the table.

Brian saw a SCAT, and wondered who to see about getting one. He decided to wait till he arrived at the hospital to ask if he could have one. Little did he know that he'd already been introduced to the one man who could let him have one, Simon.

Brian and Pauline felt satisfied when they left the chow house. 'I must be off to the hospital now,' Brian told her.

She gave him a kiss and said, 'OK, let me know what time you want to meet up for lunch. I'm off to find some shops, if there are any.'

'You're a dental technician; you should be coming with me, you know.' He was trying to make her feel guilt at not wanting to start work immediately.

'Tomorrow. Not today. Let them know. OK. See you later, love.' And off she went on a spitter, back to the city.

Brian watched her disappear before he jumped on another spitter. 'Hospital please,' he requested.

John, Juliette, Petal, and Fred had finished their breakfast. Petal asked John if he could find out if their parents were OK, and Fred asked too.

'I'll be contacting the control room in a minute. I'll ask then, OK?' They all nodded in response.

'Don't forget the apartment,' Juliette reminded him anxiously.

John called the control room and was put through to Rose. 'Hi Rose, you still up?'

'Yes, but not for much longer I hope. What can I do for you?' she asked.

'Two things: First, could you find out if Bagman City is OK? If it is, could you contact my parents to see if they are well? And can you do the same for my partner, Juliette Harper, please? Second, can we have a different apartment? One with not so much space to look out on. Juliette isn't used to open spaces,' he said, almost pleading for help.

There was silence for a short while before Rose came back to him. 'We still don't have contact with the outside world. As soon as I find out anything, I'll let you know.' There was a long pause before she spoke again. 'And what else did you ask?'

'About a change of apartment. One with not so much open space around it,' John reminded her.

A moment later she replied with some good news. 'I've allotted apartment number twenty-two for you. It's a bit bigger, but it does have other buildings around it. Is that OK?'

'That sounds OK. How come we get a bigger place? The last one was big enough,' he enquired.

'After your performance last night, we have plans for you, lad. So classify it as an upgrading. Go and take a look before we give you more work to get on with. Do you need access to your last place before I lock it down?' she enquired.

'No. We've already packed and have our bags with us,' he replied.

'OK. See you at ten, or there about.' And Rose cut off.

John looked at Juliette, who'd heard everything Rose had said. Her face was one of utter joy. She couldn't wait to see the new apartment. She caught John by the hand and left to head back to the city.

'She has plans for you. Lad!' Juliette said mockingly.

John gave her a squeeze and kissed her cheek before they boarded a spitter. 'Apartment twenty two,' John requested, and off they went.

Danni had finished her breakfast and was rearing to go. She kissed Simon on the cheek and said, 'Bye, see you later.' Then she jumped on her SCAT and disappeared towards the large dome.

Simon decided to relieve Rose in the control room, and left the chow house on his SCAT. A short time later he entered the room, and Rose smiled at him.

'Brilliant, I can get some shut eye now,' she said with a yawn.

'Off you go. I don't want to see you till this evening, OK?' he said.

Rose called for a spitter and was soon on her way home.

Simon looked at the tube system console and noticed a few changes had occurred since he saw it last. He started testing all routes to find out what was happening. He made contact with a tube repair unit in France, and realised some communications would soon be up and running again.

Within minutes of finding the repair team, cities from all parts of the world were starting to come back online. Reports were coming in fast, and most of the cities were reporting various degrees of damage. He read Rose's report and, noting John's request, checked to see if Bagman City was back. It was, and with no damage reported. There was only surrounding land damage caused by a small tsunami, and that was minimal.

He called John to tell him the news. 'John, hi, I'm Simon. Nice to talk to you.'

'Hi Simon. What can I do for you?' enquired John, wondering what he wanted.

'Nothing,' he said. 'I do have some good news for you though. Bagman City reports no damage and no casualties. Quite a few cities are coming back online as we speak, so we should soon know the extent of the damage.'

John said, 'Thanks,' and Simon heard a chorus of cheering in the background, just before he was cut off.

'I've made someone happy. And it's so early in the day,' he said out loud to himself and smiled.

All the staff turned, and looked curiously at him; he didn't normally talk to himself.

Brian told the spitter, 'Take me to the hospital reception.'

Off it sped in a different direction to that of the city. It passed the arrivals terminal, two more small domes, and stopped at the entrance to a building that looked as if it had just been built. It looked so clean, brightly coloured, and a little on the small side, not at all like the one back in Bagman City.

Making his way to the reception desk, he announced, 'Hi, I'm Consultant Doctor Brian James.'

'Yes I know,' said the girl seated at the reception desk. 'You were scanned as you entered the building. It's a security thing. Too many new people arriving, and who knows *who* they are.' She finished her sentence with an aloof tone, indicating she thought herself too good to be doing the job she was doing.

He wasn't impressed with her attitude, but said nothing about it. It could wait for the moment. 'Whom do I report to?' he asked her.

Just then a man wearing a white uniform approached him. 'Doctor James, I'm Doctor Fu Yang. I will be working under you. If you will be so kind as to follow me, I will show you around.'

'Pleased to meet you,' he said, as he followed at quite a fast pace. 'Who's in charge around here?' he asked.

'You are,' came the unexpected reply. 'You are the highest-ranking doctor we've ever had. Normally we have to make do with a scientist in charge. So it's quite a relief to everyone now you are here.'

Brian was stunned for a moment, and then remembered the SCAT. 'Do I get one of those flying machines? I think they call it a SCAT.'

Fu gave him a strange look and replied, 'Don't know, you'll have to ask Simon. He's the number one here, and he'll have to authorise it. He wants to have a meeting with you soon anyway. So ask him then.'

Brian was looking through each doorway as they walked along. Strange appliances filled almost every one of them. 'What are all these rooms for?' he asked.

'Most of them are regeneration units, and we don't have much use for them here at the moment. Some of the higher grades have been making use of them, though,' he explained, sniggering.

Brian frowned. He remembered what Danni's body looked like and understood instantly.

His voice deepened, and he said in a serious tone. 'I might put a stop to that; it doesn't sit well with my conscience.'

'Take care,' said Fu, waving his finger in the air. 'Take great care.'

'Point noted,' said Brian, a little puzzled, and followed him into an office.

'This is your office. There's a spitter lift just across the hall. It'll save you that walk again. If you can get a SCAT, you can use your balcony,' Fu said, showing him around the office.

Brian was impressed, so asked Fu to show him around the rest of the building and introduce him to the staff.

'We don't have many staff at the moment. They were due to arrive in the next few weeks, and now, who knows when. The council decided all staff had to be replaced; morale was extremely low.'

Brian was puzzled and asked, 'Why was morale low?'

'Too many problems with members of the high council, which made life difficult for everyone.'

Brian once again thought of Danni. She must have been part of that.

Soon Fu was showing him round the building, and Brian was excited at what he was seeing. Everything was so advanced compared to what he had been used to. There were a lot of new processes to learn, and he couldn't wait to get started.

Danni was flying high once again, her eyes shut. She was hanging on as tightly as she could.

When her SCAT came to an abrupt halt, she opened her eyes, stepped onto the platform she'd visited a few hours earlier, and, after the ritual security scan, heard the usual greeting, *'Welcome to the southern observation platform, Chief Mitchell'.*

The blast door opened, and she walked inside. 'Clear wall,' she demanded as she walked towards the outer edge.

The wall became crystal clear, and she stood there, fixed to the spot. Full daylight should have been coming through the window, but instead it was a dirty brown colour, discoloured with clouds of brown dust. The snow-covered mountains were also covered with a layer of dust, making it look even darker outside.

Danni called Simon at the control centre and told him what she'd seen.

'Can you get some of the large hoppers to fly out to Nâgpur City please, Simon? We have to see it they're OK out there,' she said.

'No need, they are back online. They're reporting many dead, but can just about manage for the moment. They do want to know about the food situation, as they only have supplies for the next three days or so. What shall we tell them?' Simon asked her.

'We need to find out how many have survived before we can offer support. If there are too many, we may not be able to offer much help,' she said, worried that her farms might not be up to the task, and her project could be jeopardised.

'I'll try and find out how many have survived before offering help,' he told her.

'OK. I'm on my way back to see you now. Find out how many council members survived,' she said quickly, and cut him off.

Danni left the viewing area, jumped on her SCAT, and headed straight for the control room.

Simon was watching the communications console, seeing city after city come back online. 'It's looking a bit better now. Display all continents, and highlight cities already back with us,' he requested.

Soon a picture started to emerge. A large area to the north of the Black Sea was blank. Every city within a thousand kilometres of central Ukraine was offline. The pattern of destruction was becoming more evident as time passed. Many cities were reporting vast numbers of casualties, and were overwhelmed with dead. Nearly all were running low on food, and trying to get the food processing plants running again. Only then did he realise just how bad things really were. The Americas and Africa were the least affected, but even they had food problems to deal with, mainly due to tube malfunctions.

'Contact Nâgpur City. Ask how many survivors they have. Tell them we must know before we can offer to help them. Also find out how many council members survived,' Simon said to the duty senior engineer.

Nâgpur City came back quite quickly with a reply. They had three million survivors. But worse still, they had just over six million dead. A short while later came the report that all council members were in good health, and waiting to be recovered to the research centre as soon as possible.

When Simon heard this news his heart fell. There was no way he could send enough food for three million.

Then came a request from Nâgpur City to send as many pods as the Himalayan Research Centre could spare. They needed them to hold the dead until they could deal with them properly.

Simon contacted the shuttle terminal manager and asked how many pods were in storage. He was told almost two thousand were available, most of them for freight use. He knew at least five to six hundred bodies would fill a freight pod.

'Let them know we're sending enough to hold at least 750,000, more if they store them carefully. That's all we have to offer, I'm afraid. Food is out of the question—too many mouths to feed. We'll roll out the farming project as soon as we have a full picture of where to send the stock,' he told the senior engineer.

Simon contacted the shuttle terminal, and ordered the manager to send all the pods to Nâgpur City immediately.

Then he called Danni and told her the news.

Once he'd told her the bad news, he finished with, 'All the council members are safe. I will send a hopper to pick up them up shortly.'

'No you don't,' she retorted. 'I want to choose who we recover and when. In the meantime, let them stew for awhile.' She wasn't happy with the way the council members had recently treated her, and she wasn't going to forgive, or forget.

A short time later, Danni arrived at the control room and explained to Simon her reasons for delaying the recovery of the council members. 'Payback for the trouble they caused me,' she said vengefully.

Simon decided to change the subject. 'What time is John Blight supposed to come here?' he asked Danni.

'Rose said he was to meet her here at ten,' she replied. 'I'll give him a call.'

A few moments later she was calling him. 'Mm. His console is busy. I'll butt in and see what's happening,' she said, sounding annoyed at finding it busy.

John, Juliette, Petal, and Fred arrived at their new apartment. It was in a spacious, well-groomed suburb with tree-lined streets and neat grass verges each side of the road. Juliette looked happy as they waited for John to be scanned, even though she'd hated the journey from the chow house. The door to their apartment opened, and, as they entered, Petal and Fred rushed upstairs in search of their rooms. Juliette climbed the stairs and made for the cleansing cubicle in the master bedroom. She wanted to freshen up before exploring her new home.

John made for the communications console and tried to contact his parents. To his amazement, his father's face appeared. 'Hi, nice to see you are looking well. Is Petal OK?' John's father asked before John could say anything.

'Yes, we're both fine. Just moved into our new apartment; it's huge,' he replied, then shouted, 'Petal, I've got through to Dad. Come and talk to him.'

Petal ran down the stairs, tripping over and banging her leg on a table edge as she raced across the room. She started to bleed, but kept going till she saw her dad, then suddenly burst into tears. All the anguish she had suffered since leaving home came flooding out, and she was shaking.

John tended to her wound; it wasn't bad, just a small nick, but quite a big bruise started to show around it.

'Hi Dad, nice to see you. When are you coming here?' she asked him.

'Next week I think. The tube system should be fixed by then. If not, it'll be the week after that,' he replied.

Petal stopped crying at the news. 'That's great. How's Mom?'

'Mom's sleeping at the moment; it's only four thirty here. We've been moved into temporary accommodation till we leave, and all our belongings are in storage. I'll get her to call you when she gets up, OK?'

'Thanks Dad. We've got to go now. Juliette wants to contact her parents,' John said with a beaming smile on his face.

'Bye. Love you,' Petal said cheerfully.

'Bye, speak to you again soon. Love you all too.' Then he was gone.

Juliette had come down the stairs as soon as she heard him calling Petal, and now sat by the console and asked to speak to her parents.

'You have no authority to communicate at this time. Please try later,' came the reply.

Juliette got up, looked helplessly at John, and crossed the room to hug Fred.

John looked puzzled; he'd got through straight away. 'Get me the parents of my partner, Mr. and Mrs. Harper,' he demanded.

Within a minute the console burst into life with Juliette's mother staring straight at him, her eyes blinking and sleepy. She rubbed them and looked again at the monitor.

'Hi, how are Juliette and Fred? Are they OK?' she asked him.

'Ask them yourself,' he said, dragging the pair of sobbing blobs of jelly to the console.

Juliette and Fred were overcome with emotion, and it spilled over to Petal. All three started crying and shaking.

'You two look a sight,' their mother said sympathetically. ''What am I going to do with you when we get there? Hey!'

Juliette's father came into view.

Juliette spoke quickly, 'Glad you're OK. Our journey was horrible. We only just made it here. When are you coming?' she asked.

'Next week, the same time as John's parents, if all goes well,' her father replied.

A voice broke the conversation. *'Please terminate this call. There's an urgent call for John Blight.'* It was May.

'Got to go now. Call you again later. Bye,' said Juliette.

'Bye. See you soon,' said Fred. And the screen went blank.

The screen instantly burst back into life. It was Danni, and she found herself looking straight at Juliette. 'Hi, my name's Danni. Danni Mitchell. You must be Juliette?'

'Yes,' Juliette said with a puzzled look on her face. 'Can I help you?'

'I hope so. Can I speak to John please?'

'Yes, I'll go and find him for you. One moment please,' replied Juliette politely.

John came to the console before Juliette had time to say anything to him. 'Hi, Danni, what can I do for you?' he asked, sounding quite cheerful.

'Can you come to the control room? I'd like you to meet Simon.'

'Yes. I'll be there in a little while. Just moved in to our new apartment and I want to make sure everyone is settled first.'

'Ok, see you so—' Danni was cut off before completing the sentence.

Juliette was looking at John with a slightly jealous expression on her face. Then she said in a soft, enquiring voice, 'First name terms already. Who is she?'

John gave her a funny look and replied, 'Danni is second in command here at the centre, and Simon, he's the big boss man. Did you cut her off just then?'

'Oh that. Sorry,' said Juliette in a slightly subdued voice. Then sounding slightly snooty, she said, 'Mixing with the bigwigs now, are we?'

'Yep, sure am. Got to go now, see you later. And don't worry. Bye,' John gave her a big kiss, and left.

Juliette turned to Petal and Fred and said with her nose in the air, pretending she was high-grade, 'I'm off to refresh myself now, darlings. See you later. Ciao.'

Juliette made her way upstairs, entered her bedroom, undressed, and stepped into the refresh cubicle. After ten minutes of intense cleansing and therapy, she stepped out feeling totally relaxed and tingling from head to toe. She felt slightly dopey as well.

'I wonder what's outside our window this time?' she said to herself, and crossed to the closed window.

She stood in front of the window, wondering where the opening was to look out. She said in soft inquiring voice, 'How do you . . .' followed by, in a slightly louder, frustrated voice, 'OPEN THE WINDOW!'

To her amazement the whole bedroom wall became crystal clear. When her eyes adjusted to the bright light, she found herself looking out over her garden, and thought how nice it looked. It had a large patio, potted plants, and a lawn surrounded by a hedge. Beyond she could see a park area with children playing, and assumed the building behind that must be their school. The building was about forty metres from the apartment, had mirrored windows, and she hadn't any idea what it was. Then she noticed a woman waving in her direction. She was waving like mad and signalling by crossing her arms in front of her.

Suddenly Juliette noticed her reflection in the mirrored building, and jumped backwards onto the bed. She grabbed the sheets and pulled them over her. 'Wait till I tell John what I just did, that'll make him laugh,' she said, giggling to herself and shaking with excitement.

The window was full height and she'd been standing in front of it, completely naked, for quite some time before she realised her predicament. That woman had been trying to get her to close the window.

'Close the window,' she said quickly. And it closed immediately.

'Thank goodness they were only small children out there,' she said to herself, still giggling.

John made his way over to the control room and tried to find Danni. He looked around the room, and asked an old man with white hair if he had seen her.

'You want Danni do you? Who shall I say wants her?' he asked.

'John Blight,' he replied, as he continued to look at the electronic equipment around the room, and paid the man no attention what so ever.

The man made a slight noise as he took a sharp intake of breath. 'So you are John Blight. I was expecting someone a lot older, the way she's been talking about you. I thought you had years of experience behind you,' said the man.

John looked at him, puzzled by his remarks. 'Who are you?' he asked.

'Simon Tallsworth, Grade Two Ambassador. Head of this research centre,' he replied.

John looked at him for a moment, and then replied with confidence, 'Pleased to meet you, sir.'

Simon smiled at his politeness. 'No "sir" here if you don't mind, call me Simon, OK?'

'Fine. Is there anything I can do, Simon?'

'The last train arrived some time ago, and everyone's been fed thanks to you. Once the passengers have been processed, can you move the chow house to the centre of Jumla City?'

John just stood there, thinking hard for a moment, then replied, 'Leave it with me. I think I know what needs doing.'

'Don't make it too permanent; it might not be required for much longer. Things are starting to get back to normal out there,' remarked Simon.

'OK, I'll just give it a cosmetic makeover to fit its new surroundings. That OK?'

'That'll do just fine,' said Simon, breaking off the conversation to watch the last of the arrivals being processed in Store Dome Number One. There were just over a thousand in all. Plenty of room for them, but they would have to be repatriated as soon as possible. Most, if not all, of the latest arrivals were not supposed to be at the research centre and were only taken in as refugees when the tubes started to malfunction.

Danni came around the corner and looked straight at John. She smiled and kept talking quietly into her communicator. Placing a hand over her mouth to hide a burst of laughter, she quickly disappeared around the corner again.

A moment later she reappeared with a serious look on her face, and as she came towards John, he could see she was biting her tongue, trying hard not to laugh.

'What's so funny?' John asked as she came nearer to him.

Danni caught John by the arm and led him outside to the balcony. 'I don't know how to say this. So I will just explain it as I heard it,' she said, now smiling.

'I've had a report from a woman in Jumla City. She told me she saw a young female looking out of an apartment window in the city. The young female was facing a park where this woman was supervising a group of young children in a play area. The young woman was completely naked. She signalled to the young female to close the window, but it was awhile before the she understood what she was doing. Quite a few minutes actually. When the female realised what she was doing, she disappeared quickly and closed the window,' Danni said, with a suppressed laugh. She was close to bursting at that moment.

'So, what's that got to do with me?' John asked, smiling back at her.

'That young female was your partner, Juliette,' she replied.

'Oops. No harm done then,' said John, hoping there was no problem.

'On the contrary,' said Danni, 'it *was* next to a school. She was facing the only boys' school here, and just about every boy had a good look at her. She caused such a stir, school had to be suspended for the day.'

John was speechless; he didn't know what to say.

'I've made arrangements for you to move to another apartment. That window is going to be watched intensely from now on,' she said.

John looked at her and smiled. 'I don't think she's realised what's happened, otherwise I'd have been called by now. Let me handle this, I want to see the look on her face when I tell her what she's done.'

Danni smiled and said, 'I think I'm going to like working with you.'

'Shame we have to move again. Still at least she'll be happy to move again, given the circumstances.'

'I've assigned you apartment thirteen in suburb one. It's next to mine. Maybe that number will bring you luck,' she said, as John was leaving.

Simon was looking at the shuttle terminal monitor. He wanted to see how many people had alighted from the last train. There weren't many elderly, maybe a hundred or so. Most were young adults, and there were some unaccompanied children by the look of it. They all needed to be fed, and were waiting to be checked in.

'Danni, get staff over to see to the new arrivals as quickly as you can; they look totally lost.'

Danni took a quick look at the screen and immediately left the room. She mounted her SCAT and shot off. She was riding just as badly as ever and allowing the machine to do most, if not all, the driving for her, though now she was starting to look around just a little bit more.

It wasn't long before she arrived at the shuttle terminal and told the staff to organise everyone into small groups ready for processing. One little boy, who was by himself, was thirsty and asked for a drink. Danni decided to get him one personally, which was totally out of character for her. She usually hated children.

'Shepherd everyone into that,' she said to the group leaders, while pointing at the corral's open door.

The staff started moving the people towards the corral's ramp, and the leading group hesitated as they approached the strange object, floating just a few inches off the ground. The front ones ended up being led by hand, just to get them moving.

When all the people were inside, they were easy to control and it prevented them from running off. As soon as the ramps were raised, the corrals gently lifted and made their way up the tunnel towards the main dome. From there it was just a short trip to the arrivals terminal, where the corral settled and lowered the ramps.

Not long after the people arrived, staff started finding out who they were and where they'd come from. The train had originated in Japan, and with the many earthquakes in that region, cities began collapsing one after another. In order to save their children, some parents had hijacked shuttle pods and sent the youngsters on their way, hoping they would be safe. The task now was to try and return them home as soon as the situation was under control. Danni knew it would be some time before that could happen, and in the meantime, every occupied apartment had to take in some of the young refugees.

Danni walked among them, and noticed two little girls with a slightly older boy huddled together. A member of staff was trying to separate and place them into two different groups: girls and boys. Danni walked over and, with a quickly raised hand, stopped what was taking place.

'Are you related?' she asked the boy.

He nodded to indicate they were, and Danni turned on the staff.

'If brothers and sisters are here together, they stay together,' she shouted, so all could hear.

On hearing her, children started running all over the place, trying to get back together once again. It was quite some time before all was quiet and orderly again. She looked at the three youngsters and decided to take them in; after all, it wasn't as if it was forever. She lowered herself to look at them, took the girls by the hand, and introduced herself.

'Hi, my name is Danni. What are your names?' she spoke in a pleasant, quiet voice.

The boy spoke, 'My name is Miko. I'm five. This is Tina, she's my sister. She's four. And that's Lori, her best friend. Where are we?' he asked.

'You are safe; we will try to get you home as soon as we can, OK? Come with me now,' Danni said reassuringly.

Danni led the three children out of the corral to a nearby processing desk. 'These three are to remain together until we can repatriate them. Make sure they are taken to my apartment, once they have been checked in, and fed,' she told the desk clerk.

Danni left them, and headed straight for the hospital to organise a makeover for herself. She'd also told John to insist that Juliette had a makeover too. She would be known to all the boys by now, and it would be best if her image could be altered in some way.

John rushed home, ran to the front door, and paused for a moment before slowly walking in. He saw Petal sitting on the sofa, playing games on the entertainment console, and asked where Juliette was.

Glancing sideways at John, she said, 'Upstairs, I think.'

He made his way upstairs and entered the bedroom. Juliette was sitting on the bed reading something from a pad, and looked up when he entered. 'Hi, what are you doing home so early?' she said, knowing he must know something to be home at that time.

He crossed to the window and tried to open it. 'Bit dark in here isn't it,' he remarked.

Juliette raised her voice and said, 'Open the window.' And it opened.

John was impressed by the action, and stood looking out at the view. 'Nice view isn't it. A lovely garden, nice park.' Then there was a short pause, followed by, 'And a very nice mirrored building. It's the upper boys' school.

There was silence from behind him, so he continued, 'After they all saw you naked, they had to suspend lessons for the day.'

He turned to look at Juliette just as he finished his sentence, and waited for a reaction.

She was silent, eyes wide and her mouth hanging wide open. Suddenly she screamed as loud as she could and started to cry. Petal and Fred came running to see what was up, just as John crossed and put his arms around her.

'Sorry,' she sobbed. 'I didn't know. I was taken by surprise, and didn't realise what I was doing for a moment.'

'That's OK, but we do have to move again. That window is going to be the most watched place around here from now on,' he said.

'Let's go now,' Juliette said, still sobbing.

Petal and Fred wondered what was wrong. 'What's up?' Petal said with a puzzled expression on her face.

'I just told Juliette we had to move again, that's all,' John said, looking at Juliette.

Suddenly Juliette burst out laughing. 'Silly me, I thought John got promoted. We have to move again. I knew we were in too good an apartment.'

Fred was in a huff. 'I thought you'd been told some bad news or something,' he said, muttering as he went to his room to pack.

Juliette laughed through her tears, kissed John, and started to pack.

Petal looked at John. 'Promoted, yeh! Gave us the wrong apartment didn't they? Thought it was too good to be true.' Then she stormed off to pack her little bag.

It took just five minutes; they didn't have much with them and were quickly out the door. 'Let's walk,' said John.

Petal asked a little worriedly, 'How far is it?'

'It's number thirteen in suburb number one, so can't be far away. Keep your eyes open for it,' he replied.

Little did John know it was just over five kilometres away in another dome. They'd never walked that far before ever! And Juliette would be out in the open.

Juliette shouted at him, 'If you think I am going to walk outdoors for even a second you've got to be joking. Call a spitter now,' she demanded.

John called his SCAT over. 'I think we can all fit on that,' he said, pointing at it.

'Well we haven't got much baggage, have we?' Petal pointed out, shaking her little back sack and smiling.

John sat on the SCAT and Fred jumped on in front of him. Juliette climbed on behind John and clung on tightly, while Petal sat at the back.

'You had better drive slowly,' Juliette whispered threateningly in his ear.

'Don't worry,' John said as he opened the throttle slightly. 'Take us to apartment thirteen in suburb one please,' he requested.

The SCAT shot forward rapidly with Juliette screaming in John's ear, 'Slow it down. NOW.'

He did as he was told, as Juliette gave his ribs a painful pinch, and immediately slowed the machine to a snail's pace.

It was quite awhile before the SCAT arrived at their new apartment. 'Not far,' Petal said sarcastically. 'That would have taken over an hour to walk.'

John just gave her a sheepish smile and walked over to the door to be scanned. There was the same reaction to the standard of décor as in the previous apartment when the door opened. He watched as Petal and Fred raced in to find their rooms once again. 'This is becoming a habit,' he remarked as Juliette entered ahead of him.

Before she had time to look around, John took her aside. He explained that Danni had suggested she have a makeover to change her appearance.

After a short silence and a puzzled looked from Juliette, she remarked, 'If I have to change the way I look, will you still like me?'

John smiled. 'It will still be you, no matter how much you change. Anyway, you only have to change the colour of your hair, if you want. I wouldn't like you to change that gorgeous body of yours.'

When she heard him say that, she brought up her knee, just missing his groin. And as he jumped back, she replied, 'I don't know what I want yet.'

She stood still, sucking her thumb, deep in thought. After a short silence, she asked, 'When do I have to decide by?'

'Right away. Danni is waiting at the hospital for you to arrive. She will explain it all a bit better than I can,' John said a little hesitantly.

'Brilliant! I'll decide on the way over. Let's go,' she said, sounding a little annoyed at the lack of information.

'Petal, you are in charge till we get back. Any problems just give me a call, OK?' he shouted up the stairs.

John heard her say, 'Wow,' followed by, 'OK!' as he was leaving.

Juliette jumped on the SCAT and was already waiting for John to arrive. 'Don't go too fast please,' she told it.

John arrived, jumped on, and drove off at a fast pace.

'I told this thing not to go fast,' she shouted at him.

'It only obeys my commands,' he replied and went even faster.

Juliette just closed her eyes, and clung on as tightly as she could. 'You wait. I'll get you back,' she screamed at him.

He just smiled and said, 'You'll have to get used to going fast. I'm going to try and get you one of these.'

Juliette didn't reply. She just opened one eye, took a quick glimpse, and shut it quickly, wishing they would be there soon.

Danni had just finished talking to Simon when she received another call. This time it was Rose. Danni said, 'Hi, you look a bit annoyed; what's up?'

'A girl has been seen naked by the boys in the upper school, and it's caused a problem. My son's been sent home from school because of her, and the school is closed for the rest of the day. He's seen her and taken pictures of her. All the boys took pictures. She's now the school's pinup.' She spoke quickly, and sounded really annoyed.

Danni thought for a moment before answering. 'I know what happened. Thanks for letting me know about the pictures. I'll have them all erased as soon as I get to a security console. I've taken steps to deal with the situation, and can assure you it won't happen again.'

'I hope not, Otho's hormones are through the roof. He can't stop talking about her,' Rose said.

'I'm not surprised; she's quite good looking, and only a teenager herself. I'll try to persuade her to change her appearance so she won't be recognised; otherwise her life will be a nightmare from now on. I've got to go now, see you tomorrow. Bye.'

'You know who she is don't you?' Rose enquired just before Danni cut off.

'Yes I do, and her name will remain a secret. I think its best to keep it that way,' replied Danni

'If ever I find out, she's in for it,' Rose snapped back, annoyed with Danni for not telling her. 'Bye. Be seeing you,' said Rose sharply, and cut off.

Danni didn't want to tell Rose that "that girl" would be living just across the street to her from now on.

It was time to head for the hospital to see about a makeover for Juliette. Then Danni decided she would have the final part of the makeover Fu promised her. She smiled as she left the room.

Simon was looking closely at the tube system, region by region, watching as more and more of the system came back online. He moved quickly towards the area of Japan, and found it mostly blank.

'Bring up a chart of cities in the area of Japan,' he requested of the terminal console.

Up it came, and Simon frowned. There were supposed to be 252 cities showing; he could only see thirty-two.

'If all those cities are out of action, almost two billion people are unaccounted for,' he told his staff.

Turning to the duty engineer, he asked, 'See if we can make contact with any of them?'

Then after a slight pause, he continued, 'Going on information received from all cities that have reported their situation, give me an estimate of how many casualties we have and can expect over the next month.'

'That will take some time, and will only be a calculated guess, at best,' the duty engineer replied.

'Doesn't matter. Try and break it down into regions as well. We need to offer as much support as we can to the survivors,' he stated and walked to the back of the room for a break.

Pauline made her way back to Jumla City as quickly as she could. Brian had given her permission to use his credit allowance to go shopping and she couldn't wait to get started. She told the spitter to take her home before going to the shops so that she could freshen up before making a start. This was the first time she would have enough credit to shop without worry, and she hoped to get all she wanted. She would have liked a friend to be with her, but she didn't know anyone yet. Even so, she was determined to have a great time.

After spending half an hour getting ready to go out, she had to order another spitter; the last one wouldn't wait that long. The next one arrived quite quickly and off she sped, excited as she travelled the relatively short distance to the shopping mall. As the spitter entered the shopping area, she was astonished by how small it was, and instantly frowned.

'Is this it! Are these all the shops?' she asked, almost crying as the spitter stopped.

'This is the only shopping mall at the Himalayan Research Centre. Have a nice day,' came the unexpected reply from the spitter before it shot off.

She looked around, and noted there were only four shops and a beauty salon. There were two almost-identical shops selling clothes and two identical ones for all other items. The beauty salon looked very classy and out of place amongst them.

The mall was almost deserted. Just one or two other people were window shopping, which made it look eerie. Even those who were there didn't look impressed, judging by the look on their faces.

Her heart sank as she made her way to one of the clothes shops, the one that looked a bit smarter than the other.

After walking through the entrance she was immediately scanned, and greeted. *'Welcome Pauline Mitchell,'* came a very pleasant female voice. *'This is The Jumla City Clothes Boutique. Please follow your personal shopping assistant. We hope you enjoy your experience. If you have any questions or requests please don't hesitate to ask.'*

A pleasant-looking, young female came forward, and beckoned her towards a cubicle at one side of the shop. Pauline followed the girl into the bland room, and was offered a corner sofa to sit on. She was taken by surprise when the assistant walked straight through a coffee table in front of it and invited her to sit down. Pauline walked up to the table and gave it a kick, just to make sure it was there; it was. She walked over and gave the sofa a kick in the same way before she sat down. Once seated Pauline was wondering what would happen next and soon found out.

The assistant spoke pleasantly and quietly, *'We will now present a selection of the latest fashion, taking into account your available credit.'*

'I'm using my partner's credit, Doctor Brian James,' Pauline replied quickly.

'One moment while we check the details,' came the response.

Pauline looked at the assistant and raised an eyebrow; she had frozen on the spot.

After a few moments she started to move again and said, *'Your credit information has been updated. We will now present a selection of the very best fashion available on the planet.'*

Pauline's face beamed with joy when she heard "best on the planet", and was so excited she couldn't sit still. The assistant moved from one side of the cubicle to the other, walking straight through the small table once again, and this action now amused her.

Before the show began, the whole area was instantly transformed into a tropical island setting, obviously using the same imaging techniques used to create the assistant, though that was far from Pauline's mind, and well over her head, technically.

She was even more amused when models, the images of herself, started strutting across the room, all wearing beautiful garments. At first she didn't see the garments; she just stared at herself acting as a model, and started giggling. It wasn't like looking into a mirror though; she thought it was a little spooky. When at last she did start to notice the garments, she asked for the whole thing to start again, just to make sure she missed nothing.

Another assistant came and sat beside her on the sofa, and Pauline paid her little attention; she just watched wonderful outfit after wonderful outfit go by.

She saw a dress she liked, and asked the assistant next to her if she could have a closer look. The model came and stood just in front of Pauline and slowly turned on the spot, showing the drape of the material. As she tried to touch the garment, the model stepped backwards and out of reach, which made Pauline jump slightly. The dress was strapless, had a high, tight-fitting waist that clung to every curve before fanning out to just above the knees.

Pauline's face beamed with pleasure, and she asked what it was made of. The assistant sitting next to her explained, 'It's made of pure silk. Here, have a feel.'

A swathe of cloth appeared on the sofa next to her as if by magic. She placed her hand on it, and liked the soft, cool feel of it. 'I'll have that dress in scarlet please.'

Pauline looked at the assistant sitting next to her and wondered what it would be like to see her hand passing through the image. She brought her arm up quickly and, sticking out a finger, thrust it forward.

The assistant ducked, and said, 'I've been expecting you to do that. Most new shoppers do the same thing.' Smiling, she reached out and took hold of Pauline's hand. 'See, I'm not an image. *They* can't provide samples or refreshments.'

Pauline's mouth dropped, and her cheeks reddened. 'I'm so sorry,' she said.

'That's OK. I'll bring some refreshments before we continue.'

Quite awhile later Pauline left the shop, laden with many bags filled with clothes. Each item of clothing was tailor-made to make her look stunning, for Brian and any other man that wanted to look at her. She had totally forgotten all that had happened in the past few days and was now "back to reality", to life as she wanted it to be.

She called a spitter, made her way back to her apartment, freshened up, got changed into the stunning red dress, and left for the hospital to have lunch with Brian.

Danni was waiting in the hospital foyer for Juliette to arrive, and when John drove straight into the reception area and lowered his machine to the floor, she thought he was quite a cheeky lad. She could see him trying to help Juliette get off the SCAT, and went over to help. She soon realised what the problem was, when Juliette smacked John across the face.

'Bad driving,' she said to herself. To Juliette she said, 'Hi. I'm Danni, Danni Mitchell. No doubt John has told you about me.' As she spoke, she looked straight at John and smiled. She took his hand and gently caressed it.

'Yes, he has mentioned you. And something about a makeover?' Juliette asked. The look on her face was sheer contempt at what Danni was doing to her man.

'Yes. We have to change your appearance so nobody will know it was you who exposed yourself this morning,' Danni told her with a hint of a smirk.

Juliette didn't say a word. She just turned red in the face and lowered her head.

'Come on, we have to get you settled. Have you decided on what you want to do yet?' Danni asked.

'Just change my hair colour, please. Strawberry blonde to pink, I think,' Juliette said, looking at John as if to say, 'You'll be sorry.'

Danni whisked Juliette off, and left John sitting in reception. 'We may be some time,' Danni said as they disappeared round a corner.

Danni went straight to see Fu and introduced Juliette to him.

After Fu had explained the procedure, he asked, 'Do you fully understand what I'm going to do?'

Juliette looked at Danni with a worried look on her face. 'What did he mean when he said I would be completely bald till my hair grows back?'

Danni looked at Fu. 'Don't be so cruel,' she said to him, then turned to Juliette. 'It's normal, but you can wear a wig till it grows back though.'

Danni explained that it was normal to lose every hair on the body, and it would grow back in its new colour. The process had only just been developed, and was in its infancy. 'Don't worry,' Danni told Juliette. 'It's completely safe.'

Fu took Juliette into another room and asked her to strip, climb onto a horizontal cubicle, and lay face down. She waited until he left the room before undressing, and then did it as quickly as she could. Even so, she was surprised to see him return so quickly.

'That was quick,' he said smiling just as Juliette climbed onto the cubicle bed.

He closed the cubicle lid, and altered some settings on the control unit. 'It will be about twenty minutes,' he told her.

Juliette was bathed in a strange greenish light that gently pulsed. It was so pleasant, she quickly fell asleep. It was a type of hypnosis, developed to remove any discomfort that may be felt during the process.

Danni came over to Fu and told him she wanted the last part of the treatment he'd promised her: a full head regeneration to match the rest of her body. He ushered her over to another cubicle where she undressed in front of him and laid down on her back. Fu closed the top and altered the controls. Her process would take a little longer. Soon she too was bathed in the strange green light and sleeping.

Some time later, Brian was looking for Fu. Brian wanted to know exactly who'd been treated at the hospital, as all the records were in a mess. He walked into a treatment room and saw the back of a young woman. She had long blond hair and was wearing a silken robe. She heard him enter, turned, and looked straight at him.

With a surprised and puzzled look on his face, he said, 'Hi Pauline. What are you doing here?'

'I'm not Pauline, Brian; she's my daughter. Don't you know your own partner yet?' said Danni, who looked almost identical to her daughter. He didn't know she was wearing a wig.

Brian was livid. His face went red with anger and he shouted at her. 'When you've finished here, see me in my office. You too, Fu.'

Brian was sitting in his office looking out of the window. He heard someone come in behind him and spun round. He took one look, and shouted, 'You are the most disgusting bitch I've ever met. How dare you do something like that without my approval?'

Suddenly the woman began to shake, sat down immediately, and broke down crying. 'Sorry, I didn't mean to spend that much, I just got carried away with all the nice things on offer,' she sobbed.

Brian just stared at her for a moment, then realised his mistake. 'Damn that mother of yours. Sorry Pauline, I thought it was you in the treatment room a short while ago. She's had a makeover and looks the image of you, the bitch.'

He went to Pauline, and gave her a big hug. 'I'm so sorry.'

Danni entered the room as they embraced, and said, 'Take a cold shower you two. It's not knocking off time yet.'

Brian turned around quickly, ready to rip her head off, but instead was quite shocked to see a totally bald woman standing in front of him.

'Shaving your head won't make me forgive you,' he shouted at her.

'Silly you! I didn't shave my head. My hair fell out when I started the colour change process. I was wearing a wig when you saw me,' she said with a chuckle of laughter.

Pauline looked at her in disgust. 'Why do you have to spoil everything? I thought we were going to get along fine till now.'

'Sorry. If Brian had waited, he wouldn't have seen me looking just like you. From now on my hair will be jet black so he can't mistake me for you again.'

Pauline looked at Brian. 'What do you mean again? Have you touched her?'

'No way. I didn't go near her. I just asked what she was doing here, that's all,' he replied very quickly, with anger in his voice.

'Don't worry, I'll never trifle with any of your men again. I promised and I'm sticking to it,' Danni told her.

'I'll speak with you later, when I've had time to consider what's happened here. In the meantime, I'm shutting all processes down, as of now. Send Fu in now,' Brian demanded, glaring straight at Danni.

As soon as Fu entered his office, Brian laid into him. 'If you ever perform any regeneration without my permission again, you will find yourself drafted to the worst place on the planet. Do you understand?'

Fu nodded his head, indicating he understood, and Brian dismissed him with a wave of his hand. Fu left the office quickly and scurried down the corridor like a scared rat. Suddenly he stopped dead in the corridor, composed himself, and entered the room where Juliette had her treatment. He had caught sight of her out of the corner of his eye as he passed.

She was naked, looking at herself in a mirror, and covered her body as quickly as she could when she noticed him staring at her. Fu had surprised her, and she was extremely annoyed.

Wrapping her gown around herself, she shouted at him, 'How dare you look at me like that? Are you a pervert or something?'

'Sorry. I didn't mean to stare,' he said, and averted his eyes.

'I haven't a hair on my head. Do you have a wig for me to wear?' she demanded furiously.

Fu crossed to a cupboard and showed her a number of wigs. She chose a blonde, shoulder-length, pageboy-style wig and let Fu fit it properly.

'Your hair will start growing immediately. So you shouldn't be bald for long,' he told her.

'OK. Now get out while I get dressed,' she demanded.

Once fully dressed, she left the room and headed for reception to meet John.

John took one look at her and said, 'Blonde? I thought you were going to be a strawberry blonde.'

'It will be. In the meantime I'm completely bald. Not one hair anywhere on my body. I'll show you later, OK?' As she spoke her hand moved up and down indicating her whole body, and she gave him a wink. 'So this will have to do for now.' She was pulling at the wig.

John didn't know what to say. He led her over to the SCAT, and slowly returned home, not wanting a repeat slap after their journey there.

Brian called Fu and told him he was taking Pauline to lunch and wasn't to be disturbed unless it was urgent.

Simon was watching the world city monitor closely. More of the cities were coming back online and reporting their situation. The duty engineer came to him with the report he'd asked for. It took awhile for him to take in the figures, and it was worse than he'd imagined.

A fifth of earth's cities were gone, destroyed or beyond help. A quarter of the remaining cities had reported extreme shortages of food with varying degrees of damage, and of the rest, very few had sustained no damage at all. As things stood at that moment, over eight billion people were presumed dead or missing, and the situation wasn't likely to improve very much. Most damage had occurred to Ukraine, its surrounding regions, and Japan.

'As soon as the atmospheric dust settles, send a long-range hopper out to survey the regions hit,' Simon told his engineer.

Danni entered the control centre, and there was immediate silence.

Simon looked at her and was shocked. He could see by her eyes it was her, but he also saw her daughter. He started to laugh. He'd never seen her looking so young before, and on top of that, bald.

'What happened to you?' he asked.

'Had a face lift and hair colour change. I'm now jet black,' she replied in the same old, croaking voice.

'Nice,' Simon said, winking at her.

Danni came to him, and kissed his cheek. 'What's the situation now?'

'By our estimates, one-fifth of the world's population is unaccounted for. We don't expect much improvement on that.'

'That bad,' Danni remarked, with little compassion in her voice. 'We'll just have to stand by and offer what help we can, where we can.'

'The people that arrived a short time ago have been offered accommodation, so remind John he can now move the chow house for me. I'm off to the shuttle terminal to help organise the pod transfer to Nâgpur. Can you look after things here?' Simon asked her.

'Sure. Off you go. I'll let you know if anything happens,' she said.

John arrived home with Juliette. She was pleased with the fact that he'd gone slowly and gave him a kiss on the cheek. She'd had time to take quick glimpses of the scenery as they went and, little by little, she was getting used to being out in the open. She still felt uneasy with open spaces though, and didn't enjoy the journey.

John entered the apartment and was shocked to see Petal and Fred walking around in their underwear, and soaking wet. 'What's going on?' he asked Petal.

'There's a swimming pool out back; we don't have swimming costumes and we wanted to have a swim, so we just did it,' she replied, grabbing a towel to dry her hair.

Suddenly she realised what she was wearing and was embarrassed at John seeing her bra and knickers. She grabbed another towel, wrapped it round herself quickly, and ran upstairs to her room.

Fred came in and asked if he could have another ride on the SCAT.

'Not till you get dried and dressed,' John told him.

Fred ran upstairs shouting, 'YIPPEE!'

Petal came downstairs fully dressed and asked John how high the SCAT could go. John told her it could reach the top of the highest dome easily.

'Can we go up and look down on the city please?' she begged him.

Juliette was listening and asked if she could also be taken up to look down on where they lived. She wanted to get used to open spaces, starting the hard way.

As there was enough room on the SCAT for the four of them, John decided they would all go up. He wanted some idea of what the city looked like where they lived and how large a plot of land everyone had.

As soon as Petal and Fred were dressed, they went outside and climbed on the SCAT.

Petal was puzzled and asked Juliette, 'What have you done to your hair?'

'Changed the colour to strawberry blonde, and it's staying that way from now on,' She said. 'Tell you all about it later, OK?'

Just as she'd finished talking, she heard John chuckle to himself.

'Hold tight please,' he said, and the machine started to move.

They were slowly going up, straight up, and were soon over the tops of the buildings. 'Let me know when we have gone high enough,' he told them.

CHAPTER 5
DAMAGE CONTROL

Danni was studying a 3-D image of the world map. A few more cities had come back online, not as many as she'd hoped for, but still, it looked slightly better.

The duty engineer called over to her, 'There's been a request from the Northwest Americas. They want as much energy as we can provide to rebuild damaged farming stations in the region.'

'OK, shut down all nonessential equipment and unused domes. Give them as much as we can, at least till someone else asks for help,' she called back.

One by one all unused domes were shut down. Engineering, science, and archive domes as well as workshops, process checking and store domes were shut down. Lastly the isolation dome was taken offline and reduced to a level that could only just support life.

Staff watching the world city map shouted to Danni. She spun round and a look of total horror spread across her face. Like a wave, cities were going down one after another, starting in Alaska and spreading southeast. 'Find out what's happening!' she demanded.

'There's a report coming in,' a member of staff shouted hurriedly across the room.

'On the main screen quickly,' Danni demanded.

'We are suffering quakes at the moment. We have also noticed thousands of meteors hitting the atmosphere. This was also noticed, I don't know if . . . ssssss.' The message went dead.

All of the control centre staff were in shock. It wasn't the sound that shocked them; it was the image. There appeared to be a huge object travelling past earth. It looked as if it was just skimming the edge of the atmosphere, judging by the glow. It was so bright, it lit up the ground beneath as it passed.

Danni called Simon, while keeping one eye on the map. More cities around the world were going offline.

Simon spoke first, 'What's up?'

'We have another problem just starting by the look of it, so get up here now,' she demanded.

'On my way,' he replied. 'Feed me all the information you have,' he said hurriedly, running towards his SCAT.

Without warning, everything around Danni started shuddering. This was quickly followed with the clanging of metal on metal that seemed to be coming from the dome casings.

'What's happening? she asked worriedly.

The duty engineer replied, 'The dome containment doors have slammed shut. We are now isolated and will remain so until we can prove it's safe to open them again.'

'Can we open them quickly?' she asked.

'They can only be opened one at a time. There are air locks fitted at each entrance to allow some access, so we are not totally isolated,' said the duty senior engineer. He continued, 'We have just been informed by the energy control centre that power fluctuations are causing concern and we may lose some power.'

'Just what we need!' Danni yelled, sounding extremely annoyed.

While riding on the SCAT, John was showing Juliette the layout of the suburb below. She was scared stiff and dug her nails into his arm. Every now and again she opened her eyes to take a peak, only to close them again as quickly as she could. Petal and Fred were also holding on tightly and were showing signs of stress at being so high.

'It's only fifty metres up,' he told them.

'That's fifty metres too high for me,' Juliette said with a shaky voice.

Petal and Fred said they'd had enough and wanted to go back down.

John decided not to push Juliette too far this time and told the SCAT to descend slowly.

Just as the SCAT started to descend they heard the clang of metal on metal and it startled them all.

'What's that noise?' Juliette shouted into John's ear.

Before she got an answer, it was followed by a rumbling noise. It increased to a point that would have made them raise their voices to hear one another. Just at the moment when John was going to speak, they were plunged into complete darkness. All the lights went out in the dome and the rumbling noise seemed to ease. As it was easing it sounded as if it was moving away. Then there was deafening silence.

'What's happened May?' John asked his companion.

There was no reply, just silence, broken only by Juliette's rapid breathing.

'Why is there no reply SCAT?' he demanded.

'Communication with the control centre is down. There appears to be a shutdown and this dome has been sealed for safety. It may take some time for normality to be restored. I suggest we return to the ground and wait,' it replied.

Before John could make a decision, the rumbling noise started again, getting louder and louder by the minute. It was much louder than before and they had great difficulty hearing themselves even when shouting. The noise seemed to be coming from all directions.

'Take us down now,' he demanded.

'I cannot tell how high we are at the moment; the ground level is not constant. I believe we are experiencing an earthquake aftershock,' the SCAT told him calmly.

'OK, stay put for now,' John said, holding Juliette closely. 'Are you two OK?' he asked Petal and Fred.

He couldn't be sure if their voices could be heard over the noise, but John's eyes had adjusted to the darkness and he could see them in the illumination provided by the console lights. The SCAT had switched on flashing warning beacons to ensure that other flying vehicles could see them. With the communication console down, there was no interaction possible and everyone would be flying blind. He saw Petal and Fred nodding as they said they were OK; it was still too noisy for him to hear them properly. John looked around and was amazed to see what appeared to be snow; only it wasn't snow, it was dust particles dislodged from the roof slowly falling and reflecting in the light from the SCAT beacons.

A few minutes passed, which seemed like hours, before the noise started to subside, and soon it was just a slight rumble in the distance. The clanging of metal on metal sounded once again and then all became quiet, though they could still hear some rumbling as though the sound was a long way off and moving away from them, like a passing thunderstorm.

A loud bang, followed immediately by the lights coming on, made them all jump, and Juliette screamed with the shock of it.

When John's eyes adjusted to the light he asked for information. 'Are we back in contact with the control centre?'

May answered him, *'Hello John, we are back online. I will check to see what happened.'* May went quiet for a minute then reported, *'There was an aftershock felt all over the planet and, although it shook violently, there's been no reports of damage, and all cities that went offline are back online now.'*

'Thanks May, take us down quickly,' he said.

The SCAT dropped like a stone, which made Juliette feel sick, and as soon as it came to a stop, she jumped straight off. John tried to grab her, but it was too late. Seconds later, Juliette was screaming, three metres below on the ground. The SCAT had stopped in midair to let an empty spitter pass under it.

John settled the SCAT on the floor near to Juliette and told Petal and Fred to go inside. They disappeared inside with Petal crying after she saw Juliette's twisted ankle.

'It looks like you've broken it. Do you hurt anywhere else? he asked her.

Crying with pain she said, 'No it's just my ankle. The pain is unbearable.'

John picked her up, carried her over to the SCAT, and sat her in front of him. 'Hold tight. I'll have you at the hospital as soon as I can.'

He looked back to see Fred looking out of the apartment door.

'It's OK, don't worry, I'm taking her to the hospital. I'll let you know how we get on. Tell Petal not to worry, she'll be fine, OK?'

'OK,' said Fred, and went back inside.

On the way to the hospital, Juliette almost passed out with the pain. The SCAT noted that she was in pain and said, *'Please state the problem.'*

'Juliette has broken her leg and is in pain,' he replied.

'I can assist with pain relief in a medical emergency,' it stated calmly.

'OK, let's see what you can do.'

John watched as a device came out of the dashboard. *'Please place this against the patient's broken leg and press the red button.'*

He followed instructions, placed the device against Juliette's thigh, and watched as Juliette came to. He gave her a kiss before asking, 'How's the pain?'

'What pain!' she said with a strange look in her eyes and a beaming smile on her face. 'Oh, that pain, it's just tingling now.' And she started to giggle.

John gave her an odd glance and smiled back.

They arrived at the hospital and John drove his SCAT right up to the reception desk. The receptionist seemed to be busy and kept him waiting when he asked for help.

'Be with you in a minute. Please wait over there.' She pointed to some seats near the entrance. She hadn't even noticed he was still mounted.

Danni was left speechless as all the domes were plunged into darkness. Then everything started to shake and she had to hold on to the desk. The buildings were designed to absorb most of the shock but they couldn't reduce it to zero with violent quakes. The vibration was violent and she was really impressed by the equipment's performance. The noise was so great she couldn't hear anyone talking, even if they'd wanted to be heard.

It wasn't long before the vibrations and noise started to subside, and almost as soon as it was over, power was fully restored. The domes started opening up with the clanging of metal and soon all was back to normal, at least as normal as it had been half an hour earlier.

'Have we lost any more cities?' she asked, scanning the world monitors.

'None and no further damage is being reported,' the duty engineer said quickly.

'That was either an aftershock or a reaction to that rock that passed over the Northeast Americas.

'Any casualties reported here?' Danni asked, sounding rather concerned.

'Only one so far, John Blight's partner, Juliette. She's broken her ankle and is on her way to the hospital,' came a quick reply.

At that moment Simon walked through the door.

'Ah, Simon, take over will you? Nothing new to report. I'm off to the hospital to meet someone,' Danni told him, and left for the hospital immediately on her SCAT.

When she arrived at the hospital, she saw John and Juliette waiting at the entrance. 'What are you doing here? Why isn't she being treated?' she asked John, looking puzzled.

'We are waiting for the receptionist to call a doctor or someone,' he said.

Danni crossed to the desk and demanded that Brian James be called immediately.

Without showing any sign of urgency, the young girl made the call. Danni was infuriated with her lack of concern. Anger boiled up inside her as she stared at the back of the receptionist, who hadn't even turned around to look at her.

She told her through clenched teeth, 'Collect your belongings and report to the employment office for relocation. You're obviously too good for this job. Perhaps a stint as a waitress in the chow house is desired. Off you go, and tell them to send your replacement over.'

The receptionist spun round with her jaw dropped and asked angrily what authority Danni had to sack her.

'I am Grade Three Chief Scientist Mitchell,' replied Danni.

The young girl immediately picked up her belongings and left in a hurry.

'Come on, let's go and meet Brian. He's in charge here,' Danni said.

John picked up Juliette and carried her to a wheelchair. They went to follow Danni just as Brian came back from lunch.

'That was a long lunch,' Danni said with a smile. 'While you were out, I sacked your receptionist.'

'Saved me the trouble,' he replied.

'What's the problem here?' he said, looking at Juliette.

'Broken ankle,' John said.

Juliette, still under the influence of the painkiller, was barely conscious and unable to speak properly.

'OK, follow me. She'll be fixed up in about twenty minutes, long before the painkiller wears off, by the look of it,' he said, quickly examining her eyes.

John looked at him in amazement. 'Just twenty minutes to fix a broken ankle?'

'Yes, the only trouble is it will be awhile before she can walk properly. We don't have any regeneration physiotherapists working here yet.'

'Juliette's father is one of them. He will be here next week if nothing else goes wrong,' John informed him.

'Excellent,' Brian said as he helped John move Juliette into a regeneration capsule.

Brian closed the lid and adjusted the controls to start the regeneration process. Juliette was soon bathed in strange glowing light and as John watched through a glass panel, he almost fell asleep standing up.

'Don't look at the light. It will send you to sleep,' Brian shouted and caught hold of John's arm to pull him away.

'I felt it,' he said, 'but you just can't help looking at it. It's so pleasant.'

Twenty minutes passed and the lid of the cubicle lifted. Juliette was fast asleep and her ankle looked normal again. Brian suggested she sleep the painkiller off and asked John to follow him to his office for a chat.

John left Juliette with Doctor Fu, Brian's second in command, looking after her.

Danni's communicator started chirping. She had an incoming call from Rose, who was at home. 'Hi Rose, what's up?'

'I've been lumbered with three kids that arrived with the last train. I found them sitting on the doorstep of your apartment. I believe you are supposed to be taking charge of them. They can't stay here; I've too much on my plate. We've just had a bad time with the aftershock and I will have to send them back to the processing station,' she said with a hint of sympathy in her voice.

'I'll find out what's happening and call you back in thirty minutes or so, OK?' replied Danni, hoping that Rose would put up with them for just a little longer.

'Thirty minutes and no longer, otherwise I'll lumber them on Simon,' Rose said as she cut off.

Danni's communicator chirped once more. It was Simon.

'Hi Simon, how are things looking now?' she said before he could speak.

'I've been getting requests from a number of couples asking when the unaccompanied children they are looking after are going home. So I've done some checking. It's been confirmed that most of those children have no homes to return to; they have been completely destroyed. I have a lot of work to get on with. So you will have to sort out permanent foster homes for them,' he told her.

'I'll see what I can do, and let you know what can be done as soon as I can.'

'Fine, Rose will be here in forty-five minutes and she has three staying with her. I don't want her children running around here,' he demanded and cut off.

Danni walked down the corridor to the room where Juliette was sleeping. She saw Fu working on something on one side of the room and walked over to him.

Very quietly she asked, 'Fu, can you wake Juliette up quickly please? Her services are needed urgently.'

Fu understood what she wanted him to do but felt uneasy after his chat with Brian. Even so, he couldn't refuse, and picked up a small injector. He walked over to Juliette and gave her a shot in the arm.

Within a minute Juliette was sitting up and holding her head. 'I feel terrible, and my head hurts,' she said to Fu.

'That will soon pass. This is Danni Mitchell. She wants to have a chat with you,' he told her.

Juliette looked over to Danni, who was leaning against a cupboard. Puzzled, she said, 'So you are Danni. No wonder John was smiling when you contacted him. But I'm sure you looked a lot older when I saw you on the console.' Then she asked, 'What's happening?'

Danni noted a hint of displeasure in her voice and was amused. 'I need you to foster three children for me if you don't mind.'

'I don't know if I'm fit enough to do that. I can't walk on my foot for awhile, and I'll need physiotherapy too. So, sorry, I can't do it at the moment,' she told her.

Danni wasn't happy with what she'd said and retorted, 'It's not a request; it's an order. You *will* do it or things could get really ugly for you and John.'

Juliette just looked at her with her mouth open. She hesitated and felt anger welling up inside her. Suddenly she erupted and screamed at Danni, 'Who do you think you are? I don't care how high you are and what you can do, nobody takes advantage of me. It's not my responsibility to look after children while incapacitated, and don't expect others to do it for you with that attitude.'

Danni looked shocked. She stood in silence, just staring at Juliette. Nobody had ever screamed at her like that before or disobeyed her.

John was sitting in Brian's office waiting for Juliette to wake up. 'How long till she is able to walk properly again?' he asked.

Brian looked at him. 'She'll be able to walk on it in a week's time, but it'll take about six weeks to get back to normal. If we had a regeneration physiotherapist, it could be back to normal in a day or so I think.'

'Juliette's father is one of them. He'll be here next week if all goes well,' John told Brian.

'So you said earlier. That should speed up her recovery,' Brian told him, then changed the subject. 'Are you responsible for that mobile chow house?'

'Yes, I found it the archive dome. There's loads of interesting equipment in there,' John said, feeling quite proud of his achievement.

'I think just about everyone is grateful for that; nobody can cook. I've heard that you may be offered a place on the high council. Did you know that?' Brian told him.

'No, I'm shocked to hear it; I don't know what to say,' John said with a slight stutter.

'A word of warning: watch out for Danni, she's a dangerous woman. So take care; she only thinks about herself.'

'Don't worry; I'm just looking out for my family, but thanks for the warning. I thought there was more to her than met the eye. How come she looks so young all of a sudden?' John whispered, feeling a little uneasy saying it.

'Regeneration. She had access to the equipment with the help of a pathetic doctor, and Doctor Fu is now on a final warning. He must inform me of all treatments before starting, especially after what he did for her,' Brian told him.

John was about to reply when he heard Juliette screaming at someone.

John and Brian looked at each other with puzzled expressions, then ran to find out what was going on. When they entered the treatment room, Juliette was red in the face and full of anger, while Danni was standing speechless in the corner.

'What's going on?' Brian asked.

Fu looked frightened and blurted out, 'Danni made me wake her up with the painkiller antidote then demanded her services as a child minder.'

Danni went red with anger and stormed out of the room. 'I will be in the control centre with Simon,' she shouted angrily as she departed.

'What made you shout at her?' John asked as he put his arm around Juliette.

Juliette shrugged him off and glared into his eyes. 'She's your friend; that's why she thinks she can demand that I do things for her. She said she will make things very difficult for us now.'

Brian cut in, 'She's a really nasty piece of work; John's only looking out for you and your family. I'll report her to Simon immediately. And don't worry; she can't do anything to harm any of you now that we know what she said.'

'I'll speak to you later,' he said to Fu. And with that he returned to his office.

John looked at Juliette. 'How do you feel?' he asked her.

'Like I've been in a fight,' she replied quietly, allowing John to put his arm around her.

Brian entered his office and called Simon on his console. He wanted a face-to-face discussion. 'Simon, I have a complaint about Danni,' he said angrily.

As Simon was about to speak, he saw Danni appear behind him and was cut off.

A minute later Simon contacted Brian. 'Sorry for that. I've sent Danni out of the room. What's the complaint?' he asked him.

'Danni's been throwing her weight around. She made Fu wake Juliette Harper early from regeneration rest and demanded she foster some kids. When Juliette said she wasn't fit, Danni said she could make things very difficult for her and John if she refused,' Brian told him, watching as Simon's face screwed up and turned red.

'Leave it with me. I'll deal with her and I'll make sure she can't cause any problems for John and Juliette. I wanted to have a chat with you, but not like this,' Simon said angrily.

'OK, I'll leave it for you to deal with. She's not welcome at the hospital anymore. I'll have a proper chat with you soon,' Brian said as he cut him off.

Danni was waiting for Simon on the balcony; he'd sent her there after cutting Brian off. She paced up and down, watching him through the window. He was talking and frowning as he listened, and she was boiling inside. After a short time, Simon closed down the communications console and pondered for awhile before heading towards her at a fast pace. He opened the door and stood looking at her.

'Why do you have to do these things? Why do you think so many people hate you?' He spoke to her with a hint of sadness in his voice.

'She has no job here at the centre, so why not give her one? She would make an ideal foster parent and it would keep her out of trouble,' replied Danni.

'I don't care if she is the best foster parent in the whole world, you *don't* demand her services when she's not fit to work, or at any time, come to that. At the moment Juliette is looking after two youngsters herself, and compared to you, she's an angel,' he said, pointing his finger at her. He continued, 'I want you to apologise to John and especially Juliette and maybe to Fu and Brian as well. If not, I'll have to reprimand you, and that will go on record,' he said authoritatively.

'OK, I'll do it later. I have three children to take back for relocation first; Rose can't cope,' she said sarcastically.

'There you go again. You should never have offered to take them on in the first place. You have too much work. Now get out of my sight,' said Simon, holding back the urge to shout at her.

Simon went back into the control centre, sat at a desk, and asked for a cold drink. He sent messages to John, Juliette, Brian, and Fu asking them to let him know when Danni had made her apologies to them. He felt a sadness he had never felt before and was beginning to understand why the councillors had tried to remove her from office. He also wondered if she *was* guilty of the charges brought against her. She'd shown him her nasty side, and he wondered how he could rectify the problem, if there really was a solution, given their current circumstance.

John asked Fu to help him seat Juliette on a wheelchair, then he pushed her to Brian's office. They entered just as Simon disappeared from the communications console screen.

'What physiotherapy equipment do you have here?' Juliette asked Brian.

Brian wondered why she asked and replied, 'Many types, we just don't have the staff to operate any of them.'

'Yes, but what types do you have? I'm familiar with most of the equipment in Bagman City, where I was living,' she told him.

All of a sudden Brian looked interested in what she was saying. 'Do you know how to operate the equipment? Can *you* treat your own foot?'

'Should be easy if I can have access to the operational data format of each piece of equipment,' she told him.

As soon as she asked for that information, he realised she knew how the equipment operated. 'Looks like you've been helping your father a lot,' he said.

'Every moment possible. I hated being trained as a waste technician,' Juliette said.

'Well if you can show me you can do the job, I can get your vocation and grade changed. How does that sound to you?' he asked her.

She smiled, squeezed John's hand, and looked up to see him smiling back at her. 'That will please my Dad,' she told them both. 'Let's get started right now.'

Brian wheeled Juliette along a corridor to a quiet section sealed off by a plastic film screen. He broke through and entered a room containing equipment that was brand-new and unfamiliar to everyone.

Juliette set about finding out what each device did, paying special attention to the one that could help her predicament. She made herself comfortable on a couch and started reading the particular machine's instruction set. After which, she turned on the piece of equipment and placed her foot into one of its openings. After pressing a few keys on a pad, she jumped and was suddenly fully alert. She laid back, looked at John, and said, 'That's a nice feeling.' And her eyes glazed over.

She relaxed fully, and John watched as her face and arms rippled with goose bumps. After a lot of giggling and squirming, the program ended, leaving her totally limp and slumped on the couch. The equipment had shut down automatically after just five minutes.

Juliette sighed, 'It's finished too quickly; that was so nice.'

John gave her a weird look and asked, 'Is that it?'

'Yep, it's all over and I should be able to walk normally again. Shame though, it was so nice,' she said, looking at the machine. And with that she stood up.

After walking carefully across the room, Brian said, 'OK, I'm convinced. You are now my regeneration therapist. I'll try and get you a grade eight status.'

'I'm amazed how quick that process was. That machine is so advanced compared to what we used in Bagman City,' Juliette said to Brian.

'It's the first time it's been used; we only took delivery of it last week,' he told her.

'The side effects worry me. If we do any large-scale therapy on machines like that we will have to sedate the patients. It is *very* pleasing,' she told him.

'Oh, right, got your drift. That's fine. You're the expert in this field now,' he said and gave her a wink.

Brian left Juliette showing John around the room and returned to his office. He called Simon once again.

Simon greeted him with caution. 'Hi Brian, what can I do for you?'

'Hi Simon, some good news this time. I've been treating Juliette Harper and made a remarkable discovery. Her father has trained her as a regeneration physiotherapist. It's a bit unorthodox, but we have a need for her services, so can I have her status changed to a grade eight regeneration physiotherapist? At least till her father arrives next week?'

Simon went quiet for a moment then replied, 'Yes, why not. It will make up for Danni's earlier performance.' Simon was quiet for a moment before replying, 'Looking at the grades for that vocation, I will suggest grade nine till she is fully approved, OK?'

'Thanks Simon; speak with you soon,' Brian said and cut him off.

Brian returned to find John and Juliette hugging each other. And as soon as she realised he'd seen them together, Juliette giggled and quickly hid behind John.

'You've been advanced to grade nine regeneration physiotherapist till your father arrives next week. We'll see what happens after that, OK?'

Juliette was still hiding behind John and managed a squeak. 'Thanks Brian.'

'What happens after that depends on your father,' he continued, a little puzzled by her reaction.

Juliette came from behind John and looked over at Brian. He was smirking and turned his face away from her, trying to hide the laughter that welled up inside him.

'I see you have important work to be getting on with. I'll make a note of the side effects you mentioned earlier,' he spluttered.

John looked at Brian then Juliette, and almost burst out laughing himself. Juliette had quickly buttoned up her top behind him; the only trouble was the buttons didn't match up with the holes and the whole thing was a mess.

Brian left them alone. It was obvious they were up to something and he smiled. 'I'll try not to disturb you,' he said as he left.

As soon as Brian departed, John pointed to her front, and when she looked down, she made the remark, 'Done it again haven't I?' She turned a lovely shade of pink once again.

'Don't worry about it. I love you just the way you are,' he said, smiling at her.

'Let's see about getting me another wig. The other one must be in the bushes back at the apartment. I forgot to pick it up after I fell off the SCAT,' she told him.

'No not *just* yet. Not a hair anywhere is there?' he said, catching hold of her and carrying on where he'd left off earlier.

Danni arrived at Rose's apartment on her SCAT. A spitter had just arrived to collect the children. She gave Rose a nasty look as they were handed over, and not a word was spoken by either. Danni and the children jumped on the spitter, headed for the accommodation centre, and were soon arriving outside the centre: Danni's SCAT had followed the spitter to the centre and was hovering just above it. The SCAT lowered to the ground just as the empty spitter moved off, ready for Danni to use immediately.

Without a word to the three children, Danni handed them over. She just said to the staff, 'They need relocating. Rose didn't have time for them.'

Those few remarks shocked the workers who knew Rose well enough not to think bad things of her. They felt sympathy for the youngsters, and quickly took them away from Danni.

Danni was about to leave when she saw a young man staring at her. She walked over and asked his name, 'Hi, who are you?'

'Po Chak,' he replied rather shyly and with a slight stutter.

She took his communicator signature and told him, 'Expect a call off me later. We could have some fun if you're interested?'

'Ye . . . yes, I'd like that,' he replied, a little embarrassed.

'Good,' she said as she mounted her SCAT and left for the control centre.

Rose walked into the control centre and reported to Simon. 'Hi. Sorry I'm late. Danni took her time taking those children she dumped on me. Do you have anything to report before I take over for the night?'

She looked at the situation around the globe. A few more cities had come back online reporting various degrees of damage and casualties. It fitted the prediction report made for Simon and her heart was heavy.

'So many dead,' she whispered to him.

She looked at the tube situation and was amazed how many were up and running again. Even Nâgpur had starting to get food supplies through again. Things were slowly getting to get back to normal, but she knew it was still very bad for many of the cities out there.

'How much energy are we providing?' she asked the duty engineer.

'All we can spare at the moment. Most of it is going to the least affected cities. By getting them functioning normally, we can use them to help others,' came the reply.

'Has everyone settled into their accommodation now?' she asked.

'Almost. Just a few left,' the senior engineer answered.

'Contact John Blight and tell him its time to relocate the MATCH please,' she told the senior engineer.

John and Juliette left the regeneration section and made their way to reception. On the way they called in to see Brian.

'You leaving?' he asked them.

'Yes, we want to make sure my sister and Juliette's brother are all right,' replied John.

'Come over for a drink and meet my partner Pauline.'

'That'll be nice,' John said, looking at Juliette for approval.

She smiled and gave him a wink.

'See you this evening at about nine o'clock. Ok?' he asked them.

They looked at each other and Juliette smiled. 'OK, we'll see you both then. Bye.'

As they were about to leave, Fu was entering. Brian indicated for him to sit at the other side of his desk before looking back at them both and smiling. 'Thanks, I'm sure Pauline will be over the moon at meeting new friends,' he said, then ushered them out and closed the door to his office.

John and Juliette reached the foyer, jumped on the SCAT, and headed for their apartment at high speed.

'Slow down please,' she told him, digging him in the ribs again.

He eased off, but she still didn't feel easy at being out in the open or travelling at speed.

John and Juliette started getting ready early for their evening with Brian and Pauline.

Juliette suddenly realised she only had a few clothes with her. 'What am I going to wear? I don't have anything except what I'm wearing.'

'Let's shoot over to the shops and buy you a dress quickly,' replied John.

Juliette's eyes opened wide with delight. 'Are they still open?' she asked him.

'May! Are the shops still open?' he asked.

'Yes they are open till eight thirty tonight. I can make an appointment for eight. Is that time OK?' asked May.

John was amazed to find that everything was running normally after so much had happened.

'Fine, that gives us an hour to prepare,' he said smiling. Then he took Juliette by the hand and went to lead her upstairs.

Petal shouted after them, 'We are hungry; we haven't had lunch yet. Can we go now please?'

John turned to Juliette. 'We haven't eaten either. We'd better have something before our date. Will you call a spitter May?' he asked.

Within minutes a spitter was at the door ready to take them for a meal. It wasn't their allotted time, but because it was John, the chow house staff made allowances. He was welcome at anytime.

They arrived at the chow house, chatting about all that had happened during the eventful day, and continued talking as they ate. Their meal was hurriedly eaten and when it was over they left and headed home. Soon they were back at the apartment and John asked the spitter to wait a moment.

John didn't really fancy shopping for girl's clothes. He'd never done it before and the thought of it made him feel uncomfortable.

'Juliette is going shopping for clothes,' he told Petal.

Petal's eyes opened wide. 'Can I come? *Please*,' she asked Juliette.

Juliette saw the look on John's face and realised he would be useless on a shopping trip. 'John, if you don't mind, is it OK if just myself and Petal go shopping?'

He was just about to say something when May interrupted. *'The control centre is calling,'* she stated.

John looked as disappointed as he could and told them to go without him; it looked like he could be busy for awhile.

Juliette and Petal were delighted and made their way to the shops on the spitter with both of them giggling and chatting away like mad.

'Hi, what's up?' John asked as he jovially answered the call.

'You're in a good mood. I was asked to remind you to move the MATCH,' the senior engineer told him.

'Haven't forgotten, just haven't had the time yet. I will see to it right now. Can you get it cleared of all personnel immediately please?' he asked hopefully.

'No problem, I'll do it straight away. Have a nice evening.'

'Hope you have a nice one too,' John replied before cutting off.

Juliette and Petal arrived at the shops not long after leaving the apartment. They were excited and wondering what to expect. It looked a lot different to what they were used to and they were slightly puzzled by the lack of shops and shoppers.

They walked into the same shop as Pauline had been in earlier that day and were scanned. The assistant came to them and asked them to visit the other shop instead. Juliette, not knowing why, did as she was instructed and entered the other shop. She couldn't believe her eyes. There were models that looked exactly like her and Petal wearing many different dresses and walking around. They both giggled and sat to watch the parade. Juliette didn't want to spend too much time and picked a red dress made of a fine polymer material. It appeared quite soft, had a nice sheen, and would cling to her body well. Little did she know it was exactly the same design and colour as Pauline's red dress.

Petal saw a dress and asked, 'Can I have that dress and that bikini please?'

The assistant stated, 'Your credit is exhausted madam. Do you have any other means to pay?'

'My partner is John Blight and this is his sister, so can he pay?' Juliette said, biting her bottom lip. She didn't feel easy at suggesting it.

'One moment please,' said the assistant, who stood completely still for a few seconds, which looked rather spooky. 'That will be fine. You can purchase those items using a credit from Mr. Tallsworth.'

'Who's he?' asked Petal, a little puzzled.

'Mr. Tallsworth is in charge of this research centre and has awarded Mr. Blight a bonus for outstanding service,' came the reply.

Juliette smiled at Petal and said, 'Don't forget to thank big brother for this, OK?'

Petal nodded to her and watched openmouthed as the shop assistant walked out of the room through a solid wall. 'Did you see that?' she asked Juliette.

'See what?'

'The shop assistant walked straight through the wall,' Petal replied, looking a little shocked.

'Don't be silly. You must be tired or something. Come on let's leave; I want to get back home,' Juliette said, looking at her sympathetically.

Taking hold of Petal's hand, she left the shop. She was happy with her purchase and wanted to get ready for the evening. Petal just stared back at the shop.

Danni walked into the control centre, closely followed by Simon, and asked what the situation was.

Simon gave her a strange look and replied, 'Rose will update us in a minute. We will go through everything then.'

'OK, I'll be over there watching the world city map,' she told him.

A moment later Rose had finished compiling the evening report and Simon called Danni over to them.

'We must take stock of everything that has happened since the meteor strike. I would like your expert opinions on all scientific and engineering matters. Spend the next thirty minutes gathering as much information as you can. We can then sit down and have a discussion,' Simon ordered.

Danni looked at the time on her communicator and sighed. 'Is it going to take that long?' she asked him.

Simon looked at her with annoyance. 'Why do you ask that? We have to understand exactly how we have fared in all this chaos. What else do you have to do that could be more important?' he asked her.

'Nothing,' she said quickly.

Simon knew she was up to no good. He could sense it having known her for many years. He knew exactly what she was like when younger and now he'd begun to wonder why she wanted to look so young again.

He spun round, hid his anger from her, and walked over to the security console to make a call. 'Get me the duty security manager please,' he requested.

Within seconds the duty manager was looking at him and said, 'Hi Simon. What can I do for you?'

'I want you to put a tag on Danni Mitchell for the next seven days. I want to know where she goes and whom she sees. And I don't want you to let her know under any circumstance. Ok?'

The duty manager said, 'Will do. Is there anything else?'

'Can you contact all surviving members of the Himalayan Council and find out when they can come back here?' he requested.

'Sure, that should be easy enough.'

'You have thirty minutes to supply me with their replies,' Simon demanded with authority.

'Oh! That's going to be tough. I'll get started right away. Call you back soon.' And the security manager cut off.

Simon looked around the room. All the staff were busily gathering information for him to discuss at the meeting. They were researching to see who was at the centre, what they did, and their grades. They needed to find out how many people were supposed to be there and how many who were supposed to be coming were now missing, presumed dead. Although the research centre had survived, it still had to be populated correctly. Everything had to be re-evaluated and now was a good time to start.

The next thirty minutes seemed to pass slowly for him and he spent his time on the balcony looking down through the entrance of the city below. He was amused when the MATCH trundled past and wondered where it was going to end up.

Rose came and stood next to him.

'That John Blight, he does as he's told, doesn't he? A good man?' Simon asked her.

'Good! He's brilliant. Definitely council material,' she replied.

'I think he's going to put it where apartment twenty-two was. The one where your son saw the naked girl. Any bets?' he asked jovially.

'If I ever find out who that girl was, I'll give her a piece of my mind,' Rose replied sternly.

Simon smiled to himself.

'What's so funny?' she asked.

'Nothing,' he replied, and walked back inside to start the meeting.

John was thinking hard about where to position the MATCH. Then he had a brilliant thought. 'Fred, how would you like to help me move the chow house to the city?' he asked.

Fred's face lit up. 'Love it,' he said and rushed to put his shoes on again.

John and Fred jumped on the SCAT and were soon at the MATCH.

'What does MATCH mean?' Fred asked, pointing at the inscription on its side.

'Mobile All-Terrain Chow House,' John told him. 'Now follow me. You can ride in the cab.'

Fred was ecstatic; he looked down from the cab of the MATCH at all the spitter traffic taking the last of the diners away as quickly as they could.

John was busy. He wanted to place the chow house where apartment number twenty-two was, and so was arranging for it to be removed.

He contacted engineering and asked, 'Can you make a gap for the MATCH please? I want to put it where apartment numbers twenty-one and twenty-two are as soon as possible.'

The duty engineer checked his authority. 'Wow, you have complete authority. OK, on our way now. It will be clear in twenty minutes.'

'Thanks. See you there if I can move the MATCH that fast,' he told him.

'Any bets we are gone by the time you arrive?' the engineer asked.

'Sorry, no bets, I have to make this thing fly. I don't have much time to complete the task,' replied John, and cut him off.

John asked May for help once more. Only she knew how to operate the controls properly, and within a minute the whole thing was vibrating. He felt it lift off the ground as the wheels were engaged and saw the spitter tracks around them lower to the ground. A horn sounded, which caused cattle to run in all directions, and soon their way was clear. A slight jerk indicated they were on the move.

Fred was darting back and forth, looking in every direction. People were waving as they passed them by and he waved back at them. It was moving fast. A cloud of dust followed behind and clumps of earth flew into the air, churned up by the enormous wheels. John looked out of the rear window and saw his SCAT following behind. It was easier than he had hoped for, and they were soon entering Jumla City. The MATCH made its way down the main boulevard and everyone living there came out to watch it pass. They soon ran inside again as more of the two hundred years of dust was displaced, choking and blinding them.

When the dust settled, everyone could see the mess it left in its wake. There were clumps of mud everywhere and flattened trees on both sides of the street.

John looked back and saw the damage. He called the farming control centre. 'Hi, John Blight here. Can you send some help to clear up the mess the chow house has caused in Jumla City? The main boulevard is muddy and trees need replanting.'

He was surprised when his request was accepted without question and settled back to watch May move the MATCH into place. There was no sign to indicate that an apartment had ever been there; it was just a large flat hard surface.

'Wow, that was quick,' he said to Fred.

Fred was also surprised to see the empty area where they had not long ago stayed, even though it was for such a short time.

The MATCH made itself at home in this new location and, within minutes of arriving, was ready for use again. May gave the new location to the farm control centre so produce could be redirected to Jumla City, and engineers set about redirecting spitter tracks to the entrance.

John contacted Rose. 'Hi Rose, the chow house is now located at the end of the main boulevard where apartment number twenty-one and twenty-two used to be.'

'Thanks John; you're a darling,' she replied.

'Don't mention it,' he replied and cut her off. To Fred he said, 'Let's go and see if they are back from shopping yet.'

They jumped on the SCAT, headed home, and found they were alone.

'Still shopping. I'm going to try and contact my mum and dad,' said Fred, and he sat in front of the console.

John made for the cleansing cubicle to freshen up before Juliette came home and, after spending the next ten minutes in there, heard Juliette's voice call from the bedroom. She was home and sounded excited.

After looking at what she had bought, they both got dressed for the evening at Brian's place and went downstairs.

Just before they left, John went to the console to help Fred. Fred was frustrated that he couldn't contact Bagman City. Straight away John made three-way contact with both their parents and said a quick hello. He left Petal and Fred to talk about their new experiences and what they could expect when they arrived.

Simon, Danni, and Rose sat at a table in a quiet side room just as Bob Griffiths and Brian James walked through the door.

'Ah!' Simon said. 'Just Frank Powell to come and we can begin.'

'Who's Frank Powell?' asked Brian.

Rose glanced at him. 'He is my partner. A grade six administration manager in charge of administration here at the centre,' she told him.

A clerk entered with refreshments, followed by Frank.

'Hi everyone, sorry I'm late,' he said and sat beside Rose.

Brian was watching Bob's face; he seemed to be on edge. Danni was smiling at him and Bob didn't know what to do.

'Bob, can we change places? I want to talk to Danni for a minute if you don't mind,' he said.

'Not at all,' said Bob, seemingly relieved at the suggestion.

Everyone looked uneasy with Danni. She looked so young and beautiful, but behind the looks was a deviously clever mind, and that worried them.

Simon started. 'It's nice to see you all together again. Just in case anyone is in any doubt, this is Danni sitting next to me. Shall we begin?'

Just then Mel Tong entered. He was the grade four chief security officer. 'Sorry I'm late everyone; I thought I wouldn't be able to make it in time.'

'Thanks for coming,' Simon said quickly.

Once Mel was settled Simon, asked him to report on security.

He started with a run down on all personnel. 'We have an odd mixture of personnel at the moment. A lot of grade six to eight technicians and supervisors, very few farmers, and even fewer workers. It's the number of orphaned children that concerns me the most though. We must try and farm them out to the cities. We have just over five thousand people in total and only around three thousand of them are meant to be here. So we have a lot of relocating to do as soon as possible.'

'What's the food situation?' Simon asked, looking at Bob.

'If the tube system allows us to roll out the animal breeding program as scheduled at the end of the month, there will be no problem. If not, even with the people we have here at the moment, we will soon be overrun with cattle and sheep. They are breeding and growing faster than we can eat them. The same goes for the crop program. So we don't have a problem with a lack of food; it will soon be the opposite,' replied Bob.

Just as he finished speaking, Simon looked to Rose.

She started, 'The tube system is up and running again. The only problem we have at the moment is a lack of pods to relocate the people we don't need. And we sure don't have any pods to roll out the farming project. I have asked cities needing cattle replacements to send us as many pods as they can spare. So we just have to wait and see what arrives over the next few days.'

'And dome security?' Simon asked.

'I was getting to that!' remarked Rose, indicating she'd been interrupted.

'Dome integrity is 100 percent in all but one dome. Archive Dome Number Two has been buckled slightly and is under repair. It should be back to normal later this evening. There's nothing more to report,' she finished, looking straight at Simon.

'Thank you Rose,' he said. 'Danni, how's the farming project looking?'

'Fine, just as Bob said; if we don't roll it out soon we will be overrun with animals,' she said.

'Is that all you have to say about it?' asked Simon, puzzled by her lack of input.

'What else can I say? The project is ready to roll out. There's nothing more for me to do now. It's not my responsibility anymore and besides I haven't been here for the past month. So I don't know *what's* been happening,' she told him.

Simon wasn't impressed. Although she hadn't been there, he had been providing her with enough information for her to keep on top of it, and she'd given him advice on that information.

She had changed. He wasn't sure if he knew her anymore and he wondered if it was the trial, the facelift, or the tube journey. But he suspected the makeover had done the most damage. He hoped she would be herself again when everything returned to normal. He'd just have to wait and see.

He turned to Brian. 'Hi, pleased to meet you at last,' he said, shaking his hand. 'Anything to report on health matters?'

'Hi everyone, my name is Brian James. I'm a grade four consultant doctor. Pleased to meet you all. We are desperately short of staff at the moment. Juliette Harper has had her vocation changed to a grade nine regeneration therapist till her father arrives next week. Without her, all the equipment is useless; I haven't a clue how it works. Generally, the health of everyone is satisfactory, with only a few minor injuries to date. I hope it stays that way for now. That's all I have to report,' he said, looking around the table. 'Oh, just one more thing; Doctor Fu Yang is on probation for misuse of regeneration equipment. All future use of the equipment must be authorised by me. Is that clear?' he finished, looking straight at Danni.

Everyone nodded in agreement except Simon. 'I'll call in and see you in the morning,' he said to Brian.

Frank Powell spoke next. 'Everyone who came here by appointment has been accommodated as previously arranged. All the others have been placed in temporary accommodation suitable to their grade and family size. Single males and females have been housed separately. The unaccompanied children have been scattered to all families that have children or those who can cope with them. Thanks to John Blight, we now have somewhere to feed everyone.' He paused while everyone clapped to congratulate John.

'I will make sure I pass on your appreciation when I see him this evening,' Brian told them.

'Well, that just about wraps everything up. Tomorrow we start sorting this mess out,' Simon said. 'Anything else?'

'I want John Blight's grade increased to grade five. I also propose he joins the council,' Rose requested.

'His boss is due to arrive next week and he's grade six,' Frank pointed out.

'I've read his CV and I think John is a far better person to have as a senior labour manager, even if he is so young,' she replied.

'If Rose thinks he's worth the grade increase, then I support her. Anyone against? No. OK, his grade is increased as of now. Has anyone any objection to him joining the council?' There was a pause before Simon continued. 'No objection. Good. John is now a council member. Let him know when you see him later please, Brian,' said Simon, looking around the room to see if there was any sign of disapproval.

'With pleasure,' Brian said with a beaming smile on his face.

'That's it, meeting adjourned. Our next one will be tomorrow at the same time, unless anything else crops up.'

Danni left the meeting quickly, jumped on her SCAT, and headed out of the control centre. Once clear she made her way over to the farming control centre in the main dome, and as she travelled she called Po Chak.

'Hi Po, you ready for some fun?' she asked.

There was silence for a moment before he whispered, 'Yes, I'm over near the entrance to domes three and four. I'll call for a spitter. Where do you want to meet?'

'Don't worry about a spitter. I'll be over to pick you up in a minute or two. Just wait for me,' she said.

'OK,' came the slightly shy and puzzled-sounding reply.

Danni was excited as she flew at top speed over to where he was, and it wasn't long before she could see him waiting all alone.

As she pulled up alongside him, he looked worried and asked, 'How did you get one of them? Did you steal or borrow it for a favour? Who are you?'

It amused her knowing he didn't have the slightest idea who she was. She was wearing a long blonde wig and looked the spitting image of Pauline.

'I'm Pauline, Pauline Mitchell. Jump on and we can go somewhere quiet. You OK about travelling fast?' she asked.

'I don't know; only been on a spitter till now, so let's see what it can do,' he told her.

Danni shrieked with delight; she hadn't felt like this for many years and was going to make the most of her newfound youth. She opened the SCAT up and headed to the top of the main dome at high speed.

'Where are we going?' Po asked with excitement and a hint of terror in his voice.

'To the southern observation platform medical centre,' she told him.

Danni landed on the observation platform and opened the door. She made sure Po didn't hear her name and grade when greeted. Once inside she headed for the medical centre and opened up.

'State medical requirement,' came a metallic-sounding voice.

'Two with fatigue, and in need of rest,' she stated.

Po watched as a wide bed lowered from the wall and refreshments were made available. Danni jumped on the bed and indicated with her finger for him to join her. She pulled Po to her and pinned him down.

'Lights low,' she said, and as they dimmed she kissed him hungrily.

Simon arrived home and called out, 'Danni, I'm home.'

He said it in hope, rather than expectation of her being there. He crossed to the communication console and called security.

'Where is Danni Mitchell?' he demanded.

After a short time he received the reply he didn't really want to hear. 'She's in the medical centre on the southern observation platform.'

'Is there anyone with her?' he asked.

'Yes,' came the reply.

His heart sank. That's why she wanted to get away from the meeting so quickly.

'Send me details of who she's with,' he said.

Once he had the details, he retired to the bedroom to rest. A short time later he dozed off and slept uneasily.

CHAPTER 6
TOTAL SHUTDOWN

John walked over to Brian's apartment. The evening was pleasantly warm and there was a smell of citrus blossom in the air. Juliette was on his arm; she too thought it was a lovely evening.

'I'm looking forward to meeting Pauline; I've been told she's quite good-looking. Have you met her yet?' she asked him.

'No. Anyway, who can beat you? You're beautiful; short but beautiful,' he said, hoping to provoke a reaction from her.

It did; she gave him a dig in the ribs and replied smugly, 'Nice things come in small packages.'

'Very nice things,' he told her, and gave her a gentle squeeze.

It only took a few minutes to cross the street to Brian's apartment, and as soon as they arrived, John knocked on the door.

Shortly after, Brian appeared.

'Hi, hope we're not too late?' John asked apologetically.

'Not at all. Come in, nice to see you both. Nice dress,' he said, looking at Juliette.

Juliette felt herself blush slightly. She entered and saw Pauline bending over a table laid out as a buffet. She went straight over and said quite sternly, 'Hi Danni, didn't expect *you* to be here.'

Pauline's face went as red as her dress as anger built up inside her. She turned on Juliette and shouted, 'I am not Danni. I am Pauline!' And as she finished, she burst into tears and ran from the room.

Juliette looked at John, then at Brian. 'I can't seem to do anything right can I?' And also burst into tears. She ran to John and he gave her a hug.

Brian came over and said softly, 'It's not your fault; it's Danni who's messing with nature. She's screwing everything up. Don't worry about Pauline; I'll go and talk to her. OK?'

Juliette gave him a nod. 'Tell her I'm sorry. I didn't mean to upset her,' she said, still sobbing.

Brian went to the bedroom where Pauline had run. He entered, walked over to the bed, and stroked her back. 'Juliette is sorry; it's not her fault. Blame your mother for screwing things up,' he said softly to her.

'I know, but it still hurts,' she replied, sobbing just a little less.

'Juliette is just as upset as you are, so come on, let's start again,' he told her in an upbeat tone.

Pauline crossed to a mirror and looked at herself. 'What a mess. Go and see our guests are settled; I'll be there in a minute,' she said, and gave him a kiss.

'Yuck, that was salty,' he remarked, and got a gentle knee in the groin for saying it.

He returned to the lounge, told them Pauline would join them shortly, and offered them a drink.

Pauline made her entrance; she walked over to Juliette with her arms held out to greet her. Juliette stood up and went to her and they hugged. Both started crying.

'Sorry for my mistake Pauline, I didn't mean to upset you,' Juliette said quietly in her ear.

'I don't blame you; I blame my mother. She's always done things like this.'

Pauline pushed Juliette away, held her hands, and started to laugh. 'I think we are going to get alone just fine. We have the same taste in clothes.'

Juliette looked at Pauline's dress and noticed the silk clinging to every curve. She remarked, 'Not the same material though. That looks stunning on you.'

'Make sure you buy silk next time,' Pauline replied. 'Still, you look stunning yourself. John's a lucky man.'

Juliette looked a little embarrassed at that remark. No woman had said she was stunning before and it sounded weird.

Noticing Juliette's embarrassed look, Pauline changed the subject quickly. 'You have some news for John,' she said, looking over at Brian.

'Yes, I have some very good news indeed. Earlier today Juliette's grade was increased to grade nine. So firstly, congratulations to her.' He paused for a short applause before continuing, 'A short time ago it was decided at a staff meeting that you too, John, should have an upgrade. You are now grade five, and in overall charge of labour from now on,' he said, looking at John with a beaming smile on his face.

'I don't know what to say,' said John, and sat down with the shock of it.

'You can afford silk from now on. We must go shopping together sometime,' Pauline told Juliette as soon as John stopped talking.

Juliette hunched her shoulders with delight and nodded her head in approval. She was speechless and hugged John's arm tightly.

John stood up and shook Brian's hand.

'The council send their appreciation for what you did. Feeding that multitude last night was no easy task. So it was also decided that you should join the council, effective immediately,' Brian told him.

'I feel honoured to be chosen to sit on the council,' he replied proudly.

Juliette hugged him again and kissed him hard. 'I'm proud of you,' she said.

John was still in shock when Pauline came over to him. 'Haven't I seen you somewhere?' she asked him.

'Don't think so,' he said hesitantly.

Juliette was watching his face with interest and a hint of jealousy welled up inside her.

'Michael, have I met John somewhere?' Pauline asked her companion.

'On the Bagman City tower balcony last Friday. You said he watched you sunbathing while you slept and called him a "sly dog".' Michael stated without emotion.

Pauline went red in the face with embarrassment when Michael continued, *'You tried to get him removed from the balcony.'*

Pauline turned away from John, who was standing speechless. Juliette was looking at him with daggers in her eyes.

Brian looked puzzled. 'John ask your companion if you have met her before. Maybe you have but can't remember it.'

John asked his companion to work with Pauline's to search for a link between them.

A few seconds passed before May spoke. *'You were on Bagman City balcony at the same time. I have no record of interacting with her until you entered the lift and descended to level seventeen. Pauline did ask you about the view you'd seen up there and you replied, "Beautiful, so beautiful." But I think you were referring to the scenery and not her.'*

Pauline looked at John. It was her turn to look at him with daggers in her eyes. 'I thought you were talking about my body,' she said, with a hint of disappointment in her voice.

Brian was bemused and stepped in between them. 'Hold on a minute. We are here to have a pleasant drink together, not to fight over past events. It's obvious that there's some sort of misunderstanding. Now let's sit down and start again.'

John took Juliette's hand and said to her, 'It looks like our paths have crossed, but I didn't know her till just a few minutes ago.'

Juliette calmed down and snuggled into him. 'Sorry I got a bit jealous. I love you,' she whispered in his ear.

'I'm sorry, I was only thinking about myself,' said Pauline and hugged Brian.

Brian smiled. 'There. I'm glad we've come to some form of agreement. Maybe we can have a good evening after all. Anyone for a drink?'

All of them said, 'Yes please,' in a chorus of cheerful voices which started them all laughing.

Rose was sitting in the control centre checking the condition of the Himalayan Branch Pipe and Jumla City Junction. A number of cities were sending pods and she was tracking their movements on the tube system. She smiled when she saw a few more cities in Japan come back online, but that smile soon changed to a grim look. Reports were coming in about the cities and as she started to browse through them, she bit her lip. It wasn't as good as she'd hoped; although damage was minimal, the number reported as dead or missing was horrific, and there was an extreme shortage of food for most survivors.

Rose walked away from her desk and entered a side room. Tears filled her eyes and she cried like never before. A senior female member of staff noticed her distressed mood and offered her a hot drink and a shoulder to cry on.

Rose hugged her colleague for a moment before composing herself. She said, 'Thanks, I needed that.'

She sat down and stared into her cup with an expressionless look on her face. When she'd finished the drink, she dried her eyes and re-entered the control room. She sat looking at the world city map, hoping just a few more would come back, but judging by the reports she'd read it wasn't very likely. She placed her head in her hands and stared at the desk. She saw more reports waiting for her to read and pushed them off the desk onto the floor.

She decided to call Simon for support. 'Simon, I need some help here, could you come over please?'

Simon could see her distressed face staring at him. 'Yes. Sure. I'll be with you as soon as I can. You look as if you've had some bad news or something. What is it?'

'You'll see why when you arrive,' she told him.

'OK, I'll be with you soon,' he said and cut off.

'Switch off the city map,' she said to the duty engineer. She retired to the side room to wait for Simon.

Danni and Po moved the bed out onto the viewing platform, selected a clear wall, and lay next to each other, staring up at the stars. It was almost a full moon and it was snowing outside from the odd cloud that passed every so often. The surface of the clear metal was so smooth nothing could stick, not even the frozen snow, which just fell away as soon as it hit.

She looked at Po and smiled. He looked so relaxed, and she tingled all over. They had been together for over an hour and were now resting, quietly breathing, and she wondered if there was to be more. She hoped so. She turned and placed her hand on Po's chest. He opened his eyes, looked upwards, and sat straight up, mouth wide-open.

He lifted his arm and pointed to where he was looking. 'Pauline, what's that?' he shouted and looked at Danni.

Danni looked up to see what he was pointing at. She couldn't believe her eyes and sat silent for a moment. When she spoke it was with a sense of urgency. 'Quick, get dressed. I think things are going to get a bit—' She stopped midsentence. 'Michael, sound the earthquake alarm now,' she ordered.

Po looked at her with surprise. 'Who are you?' he demanded.

'Never mind that, just get dressed quickly so we can get out of here,' she told him. Then she called Rose in the control room.

Rose was resting, waiting for Simon to arrive. Without warning the earthquake alarm sounded and she rushed into the control room. 'Who raised the alarm?' she shouted.

Her communicator sounded. It was Danni. 'Look at the communication console screen quickly!' Danni shouted anxiously.

Rose crossed the room and looked. 'What the! Danni what is that?'

'It looks like a massive lump of rock to me, and it just missed hitting earth, judging by the way it's moving away. It seems to be distorting the atmosphere directly underneath it. Try and find out if it will cause any problems,' Danni demanded.

Rose noticed she wasn't alone. 'Who's that?' she asked.

'Never mind him. Let me know what's going on and call Simon,' she demanded. Then a little quieter she said, 'And don't mention who I'm with. Got it?'

The last bit wasn't a request; it sounded more like a threat and that angered Rose.

'Wait till you get here, I'll give you a piece of my mind. And Simon is already on his way,' she told Danni before cutting her off.

Danni looked up one last time before leaving the platform. She noticed the sky filling with thousands of shooting stars, and they seemed to be increasing in number by the second. As the doors sealed shut behind her, she noticed Po; he was already seated on the SCAT.

'I'll drop you off at the farming control centre,' she told him.

Rose turned to the duty engineer and asked him to switch on the world city map. As it came on she noticed cities going offline, like a wave passing over the screen. There was loud banging and the clanging of metal as dome security doors slammed shut, followed by silence. She was still watching the city map when she heard a faint rumbling in the distance. The rumbling seemed to be getting louder as the leading edge of blacked out cities advanced towards them.

'Oh no, it's starting again,' she said, just as Simon walked through the door.

'What's happening? Has there been another strike?' he asked her.

'No, it looks like a massive rock or small planetoid has just missed hitting us. Danni sent a picture of it from the southern observation platform,' Rose said, and waited for him to ask why she was up there. She was puzzled when he didn't react.

'Play it back,' he demanded with anger in his voice.

Rose was certain he knew who she was with and left it at that.

'Here's the playback now,' she told him.

Simon watched in silence when he saw the object passing. 'It's huge. Calculate how big it is and its trajectory. I want to know everything about it.'

'The scientists are working frantically to reproduce the object's passage past earth,' Rose told him.

Seconds later a 3-D image was displayed at the centre of the room. The object was huge, almost a quarter the size of the moon. He looked at the direction it had come from and froze. The trajectory indicated it had glanced off the side of the moon and probably dislodged an enormous amount of debris, all of it heading for earth.

'If it hadn't glanced off the moon, it would have hit earth, and that would have been the end of us all,' Rose said very quietly.

They noticed it was having some effect on the upper atmosphere and was close enough to disturb the ground at the closest passing point.

Simon looked at the world city map and saw even more cities going offline. It looked grim.

It was a little while before things started happening. First, a noise could be heard, like distant thunder. The rumbling was getting louder by the minute and things were starting to shake.

'Looks like its going to be a big one this time. Let everyone know what to expect. I think its going to get worse, much worse,' Simon said.

Brian was offering a snack to John, and Pauline was chatting and giggling with Juliette.

'Those two are getting on well. I'm glad she's found a friend,' Brian said.

'I'm glad too. Now maybe she won't feel so bad when she screws up, as I expect she will from time to time. At least now she has someone else to talk to,' John said smiling, and gave Juliette a wink.

'Juliette has just told me it was her who appeared naked this morning,' Pauline whispered to John. And the three of them started laughing.

Brian just looked on puzzled by their outburst. 'What's so funny?' he asked.

'Nothing, just a secret between girlfriends,' Pauline told him.

John heard something. 'What's that noise Brian?' he said, looking puzzled.

'That's the earthquake alarm. You had better go home straight away and check on Petal and Fred. They don't sound that alarm unless they know it's going to happen,' he said, with a worried look on his face. 'I'll have to make my way to the hospital just in case I'm needed,' Brian added, and called for a spitter.

Pauline hugged him as John and Juliette left. 'Do you have to go?' she asked.

'Yes I do. If you get a bit worried just pop over to Juliette's and stay with them. I'm sure they wouldn't mind,' he said, and gave her a kiss.

The spitter arrived quickly and he left shortly after, hoping to get to the hospital before the domes closed down.

John and Juliette arrived home to the relief of Petal and Fred.

'There's going to be another quake, isn't there? Will we be all right?' Fred asked.

'As long as we remain indoors we'll be OK. These apartments are designed not to move too much, no matter how violently the ground shakes,' replied John to the relief of everyone.

A little while later Petal heard the dome doors slam shut. 'What was that?' she asked with a frightened squeak, staring at John and looking scared.

'Don't worry. It's the dome security doors slamming shut just like last time, remember. They will stay shut till the quake has passed. I'll see if I can find out any news,' he said, looking at Juliette.

She gave him a worried smile and sat in front of the communications console with him. Petal and Fred came and looked over his shoulder.

'May, try and find out what's going on please,' he requested of his companion.

May went quiet for a short time before announcing, *'A large rock or planetoid has just missed hitting earth. The scientists are trying to find out how much effect it will have on us. Cities are going offline as we speak. No more news. News link has been terminated by security till further notice.'*

'Well that's it! We'll just have to wait it out. I'm sure things will be OK; after all, it didn't hit,' John pointed out.

A little later Juliette said, 'What's that noise?'

'That's the earthquake starting to rumble,' said Fred, and John nodded in agreement.

By the time Danni finished talking to Rose, sending the picture, and waiting for Po to find all his clothes, the earthquake alarm had sounded. She jumped on her SCAT and with Po hanging on behind, headed for the farming control centre to drop him off.

On the way she heard the clang of dome doors slamming shut. When she arrived she heard the rumbling start, and decided it was too dangerous to be outdoors in an earthquake.

She went inside and reported to the duty farm manager, who looked at her and said, 'Who are you?'

She introduced herself and took over. Soon she'd familiarised herself with farm conditions and called the control centre.

Simon answered. 'Danni, I see you're at the farm control centre. What are you doing over there? You should be here.'

'It was closer as I was checking on the condition of stock,' she replied.

Simon knew she was lying, but didn't say anything. He wanted her to dig her own grave. He'd just about had enough of her antics.

Rose muttered under her breath, 'Stock of what? Flying pigs? She was at the top of the dome.'

'What was that?' asked Simon, as he hadn't quite caught what she'd said.

'Nothing,' she replied.

'What's the situation?' asked Danni, distracting him from what Rose had muttered.

'Most of the cities in the Americas, Africa, and Europe have gone offline. And it may get even worse. Predictions indicate the passing object has had a devastating effect on the planet, and its destructive power is only just starting to show itself. This may be bigger than the meteor strike, much bigger,' Simon told her, and he looked worried.

The rumbling was getting louder, much louder, and the farm staff started looking at each other with worried looks on their faces.

'Don't worry; we're quite safe in here. Can't say the same for the cattle out in the fields though,' said Danni, and gave Bob Griffiths, the farm manager, a nasty look.

'If you'd taken the time to check the information properly, you'd have found that we put all the cattle in mobile corrals and they're airborne. So they are quite safe,' he replied, shouting with a hint of anger in his voice. 'You told us to get them ready to fill the pods when they arrived, so we were ready for this.'

She looked around the room and saw all the farm workers staring at her. A number of their wives were also present, shaking their heads in disbelief that she was in charge of such an important project.

Pauline was sitting in her lounge, feet up on the sofa, listening to some music. She had it on quite loud so didn't hear the rumbling start. In a quiet interlude she became aware of the noise outside, switched off the music to listen, and heard the rumble of the earthquake all around her. It was getting louder by the minute, so she switched the music back on and turned up the volume.

Without warning the sofa she was sitting on jerked to one side, nearly throwing her off. It frightened her so much she clung to it with a vicelike grip. The floor seemed to slant down towards the front door and the sofa slid rapidly in that direction. Pauline was petrified; she'd been told if the apartment moved it wouldn't move much and she should just feel small vibrations. This was much more, and as the sofa collided with the door-frame, she was thrown off, hitting the door with a gentle thump. She picked herself up, opened the door to see what was going on outside, and reeled backwards with fright. The ground outside was moving rapidly up and down, like someone shaking a carpet, with dust and debris flying everywhere. She felt like she was looking uphill and that really shocked her. Just a short while ago everything was level, and now she felt as if she were falling off the planet. She looked across the street to John and Juliette's apartment and it looked level, not at the same angle as hers. As she stared, the ground seemed to come back up and tilt the other way. The motion made her feel sick, and she wished she was across the road with company.

The rumbling was getting worse, with banging and grinding noises mixed in with it. Every so often she could hear the sound of clanging metal and hoped it wasn't the dome collapsing around her. Every little sound made her jump and her nerves were close to snapping. Every vibration was felt, like being hit with a hammer over and over again.

All of a sudden the shaking stopped. It wasn't quiet though; the rumbling noise was subsiding, as if moving off. The ground had stopped shaking and the apartment wasn't level. It was tilted, and as she opened the front door, she realised the ground was just over a metre below the step. Within five minutes the dust began to settle and she started to notice the damage. Trees and bushes were uprooted, the ground seemed cracked in many places, and her apartment was definitely at an odd angle to the ground. She could see John's place through a dusty haze and wondered if they were all right over there. At least their place looked level. She was relieved when she saw Juliette looking out of a window and waved frantically to attract her attention. Juliette saw her and waved back with a smile on her face.

Pauline wept with relief, grabbed her shoes and a jacket, and, jumping off the step, ran outside. She'd decided to hurry over to their apartment and be with them.

John was sitting near an upstairs window, looking out at the ground moving, and frowning. At first he noticed gentle vibrations on the ground outside, but they soon turned into violent heaving that shook everything around the apartment. Trees tumbled, bushes were uprooted and thrown around like straw blowing in a breeze, and the angle of the ground was ever changing. At first he could see other apartments levelling automatically as the ground moved beneath them, all except Brian's place that is—it seemed to follow the ground movements and that was odd.

He ran downstairs, crossed to the communications console, and tried to call Pauline; there was no reply.

'I hope she's OK over there,' he said to Juliette, who watched what he was doing.

John was trying to see if he could do anything to help her out. He accessed the engineering system and tried to find out if he could help and was told her apartment was offline.

That worried him and he called Juliette over. 'Can you go upstairs and look across to Pauline's? See if you can see anything,' he said.

Juliette went upstairs, made for a bedroom window, and looked out. As she looked the shaking stopped; now there was only rumbling, and that was diminishing. The dust had started to settle, and she couldn't believe her eyes. The devastation caused was horrific. The only things that looked intact were the apartments. She looked across at Pauline's and could see it wasn't level. A spitter had lodged under one end, preventing it from moving. Then movement caught her eye. Through the dust she could see Pauline waving frantically.

She waved back to her and shouted to John, 'Pauline's OK, she just gave me a wave.'

As she watched she saw Pauline jump off the step and come running across the open ground between them. She was dodging the many obstacles blocking her path.

'John, Pauline's on her way over to us now,' she shouted to him excitedly.

She watched, smiling for a moment, then gave a final wave and rushed downstairs to greet Pauline. Juliette heard a loud rumbling noise. It increased rapidly to banging, much worse than before, and this time even their apartment was shaking. She ran to the front door to let Pauline in but couldn't see any sign of her through the dust. Leaving the door open, she ran back upstairs to take another look outside. She couldn't see anything; the air was full of dust, worse than before, and the ground was heaving violently up and down once again.

'I can't see Pauline,' screamed Juliette.

John ran to the front door, looked out, and screwed his eyes up as the dust hit him. Through half shut eyes he tried to step out but was beaten back by the violent movement just outside the door.

'I can't see anything and it's too dangerous to go out. I'll go as soon as it stops,' he said, just as Juliette ran into him crying.

He slammed the door shut to keep the dust and the noise out and hugged Juliette tightly.

The rumbling was deafening, much louder than he'd heard it before, and their apartment was shaking and heaving a little bit too. The movement was just like a boat ride on a choppy sea.

John made his way back to the console, leaving Juliette looking out through the front door window, more in hope than anything that Pauline would appear, and called the control centre. He didn't want to call Brian until he knew what had happened.

'Simon, what's the situation?' he asked when he saw Simon's face appear.

'We've been cut off from the rest of the world, even worse than before. The branch pipe has collapsed and filled with debris and water. We had to seal the shuttle terminal doors when the pipe gave way during the shock.'

'That sounds really bad and it seems to be getting worse. Is there worse to come?' John asked him.

'I think this is as bad as it will get. Just can't say how long it's going to last though,' replied Simon with a frown.

'How are the rest coping?' John enquired.

'I don't know, 50 percent of the domes are off li—' Communication was lost, cut off in midsentence.

John looked at Juliette. 'No more news for awhile, it's gone dead.' He crossed to Juliette, pulled her away from the door towards the sofa, where they huddled together with Fred and Petal. The girls were crying and Fred looked frightened.

The rumbling was starting to diminish, replaced by heavy banging that made them jump with each thump. 'Sounds like something's hitting the dome,' Petal said through her sobbing.

John didn't have a clue; they were hundreds of metres below the mountaintops, so that shouldn't happen. 'Must be something hitting another dome close by. Some are close to the surface,' he said, trying not to alarm them.

They sat in silence, jumping with each bang, and the apartment was shaking and heaving constantly. A very loud bang rang in their ears and the lights went out, throwing them into complete darkness. The darkness was so complete, it seemed to crush them. The banging seemed to be louder now and was definitely getting more intense. Mixed in with this was the creaking of metal, as if it was under great stress.

John rushed upstairs, bumping into things on the way, and cursed the kids' messy ways. He made for the main bedroom at the rear of the apartment, opened the balcony doors wide, and called his SCAT on his communicator. It had been hovering safely above, waiting for his commands, and came instantly, homing in on his communicator. It switched on its lights, turned sideways to gain access to the bedroom, and once inside, settled on the bedroom floor. John quickly closed the doors behind it.

The light flooded through the apartment like a beacon drawing Juliette, Petal, and Fred to it. They rushed upstairs into the room with smiling faces and huddled on the bed just looking at it.

'Whoever made these couldn't have known just how useful they were going to be,' John remarked, happy now they had light again.

Juliette looked to the window and a tear appeared in her eye.

'Thinking of Pauline?' John said sympathetically.

Juliette nodded her head. 'Yes.'

'Can't be much longer. I'll go and look for her when it stops,' he said.

Her facial expression didn't change; things didn't look good for Pauline out there.

'How long will your power last, SCAT?' he asked, sounding slightly worried.

'I have enough charge to last five years at present consumption. I suggest you charge me from time to time to keep me at full capacity,' came the reply.

'Wow! They pulled out all the stops when they designed you,' he remarked.

The SCAT made no reply and they sat silently amidst all the noise from outside.

Simon watched the world city map even more closely now; it was like watching an advertisement for flashing lights. All over the planet cities were going offline and online. The rumbling was getting louder minute by minute and he was getting worried.

He turned to Rose and said, 'It looks different this time, very different.'

'I've never seen an earthquake behave like this before,' she replied. 'We'll soon have the prediction report, then we'll know exactly what to expect.'

'We have a report coming in from the shuttle terminal,' an engineer said.

'Let me deal with it,' Simon said.

The terminal manager started talking. 'The branch pipe doors have buckled; there's water and mud coming through the seam,' he said, puffing as if out of breath; only it wasn't through fatigue, it was fear.

'What are you doing to rectify the problem?' Simon asked.

'We're welding the door seams closed using an element projection beam. It seems to be working but we're running out of Triron. Any ideas where we can get some quickly?' the manager replied.

'Use the station buildings, anything that you want. Idiot! With the branch pipe blocked there's no need for them. We can worry about that later,' said Simon, annoyed that he had to make the suggestion. 'Don't worry about anything except the integrity of the dome. Use what ever you need, OK?'

'OK. Thanks Simon. I'll call you if we get any further problems.' And he cut off.

Simon looked at Rose, and by the look she knew he wasn't impressed with that manager.

'I'll have him replaced as soon as possible,' she told him.

'Simon, John Blight is calling, do you want to speak to him?' the communications technician asked.

'Yes, put him through,' he said.

John wanted information about the situation and Simon filled him in. The situation was worse than before, and they didn't know how bad it could get or how long it would last.

He was just about to explain the situation with the domes when all communications failed.

'What's happened?' Simon asked the communications technician.

'We've lost power to the main computer and it's shut off all but essential functions,' came the reply.

Before Simon could say another word, the world city map went red and then blank, indicating that all had gone offline. He was going to order a redirection of power when and almighty bang rang in their ears. Before he could say another word, the lights went out and they were thrown into total darkness. The noise had changed to banging, which was so loud it was deafening.

'What's happened?' Simon shouted.

Rose caught hold of his sleeve and shouted in his ear, 'We've lost power throughout the whole centre. We'll have to wait till it's restored before we can sort this mess out.'

'What about the backup lighting?' he asked her.

'Looks like that's failed as well,' she replied.

'It's a total shutdown,' Simon shouted back at her, just as there was a lull in the noise. Everyone in the room heard what he said.

John was wondering how long the banging was going to go on for, when it stopped just as suddenly as before. Once again the rumbling could be heard as if distant but the shaking had stopped and the dust was beginning to settle. He got up, crossed to the balcony doors, and opened them wide.

'Outside SCAT,' he demanded, and it turned sideways to leave the room.

It hovered just off the balcony, and he leapt over the railings onto its seat. Within a minute he was over the top of the apartment and scanning the ground with all the lights turned fully on.

It took him a little while, but his persistence paid off. There, in his lights, was Pauline, half buried under a fallen tree and almost fully covered in dirt and dust. If she hadn't been wearing the red dress, he may never have found her.

He used the SCAT to gently nudge the tree away and jumped to the ground alongside her limp body. Her right arm and leg were completely crushed and she had a nasty gash across her face and chest. Her clothes were in shreds and her body looked as if it had been whipped raw. With a heavy heart, he bent over and checked for a pulse. He picked her up, laid her on the SCAT, jumped astride her limp body, and made for his apartment.

Danni's eyes were darting from one dome monitor to the next; she'd never seen anything like this in her life, and it was frightening. The domes were moving from side to side and tilting, with the ground heaving up and down in all directions sideways. The noise was horrendous, deafening everyone around her, and it was awhile before she realised that Bob, the farm manager, was shouting at her, and then only when he touched her shoulder.

'What's up Bob?' she shouted, trying to be heard above the noise.

'The cattle in mobile corral number eighteen are playing up. This noise is spooking them,' he replied loudly.

'I'll give them some gas; that should keep them quiet for awhile,' she replied, and started to carry out the process as quickly as she could.

'Play them some loud music instead. Using gas can be dangerous,' he suggested. But it was too late, and he watched as the cattle settled down on the floor to sleep.

Without warning, Danni lost control of the farm control console as it went offline and didn't know if the gas had been delivered correctly. She looked up at the video monitors just in time to see something crash through the roof of Farm Dome Six, followed by rock, mud, and water. The dome's video monitor went dead almost immediately after that, followed by a terrific bang that rang in everyone's ears.

'Did you see that? We've lost Dome Six. It's next to the arrivals terminal; they must be having it bad over there,' she screamed at Bob.

'The domes are the weakest here. We moved all the corrals out of there before the quakes started, so no cattle have been lost yet,' Bob told her.

Danni took his arm and held him tight. 'I don't like the look of this,' she said, just as they were thrust into complete darkness.

Bob stood still. Danni was gripping his arm so tightly her fingernails were digging into him. He tried to release her grip and found it almost impossible; her fingers were like steel rods. He placed his free arm around her and she snuggled into him like a little child. Only then did she release her grip and he hugged her tightly, forgetting she was a wolf in lamb's clothing.

One of the farmers produced some emergency lamps, much to the relief of everyone. They were bright after the short time they had spent in complete darkness and everyone blinked while his or her eyes adjusted. The lamps were placed in every room they were using, making it look almost normal.

A short time later the shaking came to an abrupt end and the noise diminished to a distant rumbling. Danni pushed herself away from Bob's arms and looked up at him. Bob looked down at her as she stared into his eyes. He was shocked by the expression on her face. She looked totally blank, ghost-like with no expression at all, and it worried him.

Danni ran to the restroom, pushed the door open, and slammed it against the wall. The bang made her jump sideways and she collided with the wall as she made her way inside. She looked into a mirror and was shocked by what she saw. Staring back at her was a young, sullen, grey face, with sunken, red eyes and a blank look. She ran some cold water, splashing her face rapidly and trying to wash the look away. She grabbed a towel and threw it over her head, paused for a moment, then rubbed her face hard and removed the long blonde wig she was still wearing. Once again she looked into the mirror; now her face looked hard and wizened, her eyes showing her age and not her looks. She composed herself, re-entered the control room, and walked over to Bob.

'What's the situation now?' she asked him sternly.

Bob looked at her, surprised by her baldness and saw the look on her face. 'Nothing has changed. You've only been gone a few minutes,' he said.

Danni looked around the room. This time she could see everyone clearly, unlike before when she had been blinded with fright.

'What are you lot staring at?' she said, scanning the room with hard-looking eyes. 'Haven't you seen a bald woman before?' Then she turned towards Bob once again.

Bob looked at her and saw her left eye twitch. She rubbed them both very hard, which made her eyes even redder, and now she looked really evil.

They were all starting to relax when the rumbling and shaking started again. Power was restored to the main systems and the lighting came back on in the farming control centre where they were standing. Bob looked around the room and could see the relief on everyone's face. The farm control console burst into life once again and Danni set to work asking for information. Danni read out loud the information line by line.

'Farm Domes One to Five are intact with minimal damage to the land. Farm Dome Six has extensive damage and is offline. Farm Dome Seven is offline, damage unknown.' She paused while accessing more information, then continued, 'Water Dome One is intact. Water Dome Two is damaged and offline. The tree dome is intact but there is extensive tree damage with many uprooted,' she finished and looked up at Bob.

'It looks like we have our work cut out when things start getting back to normal,' Bob replied while looking down into her red eyes.

'Farm Dome Six, Farm Dome Seven, and Water Dome Two are built of the same stuff, Triron. Once we are over this we must try and restore them,' Danni said.

Bob watched as the ground started to move as violently as before. He realised things were going to be very different from now on. If Triron domes were collapsing here, what was happening to the cities? They were all made of Triron. He closed his eyes, lowered his head in despair, and thought about his family in Ireland; they had gone ahead to make ready for his retirement, which was just one week away.

Danni took a look at mobile corral number eighteen. The command to release gas had gone through before the power shutoff but there was only one problem, the gas should have been switched off after a few minutes but there was no way to stop it when the power went off. She looked with a heavy heart at the cattle in the corral; they were lifeless on the floor, and nothing could be done for them. Sadly she switched off the lights, lowered the temperature to prevent premature decay, and switched the corral's video monitor off.

Brian was sitting in his office when the main power failed. The emergency power kicked in and he tried to contact the control centre to find out what was happening. Communications were out and Fu had just entered his office with a worried look on his face.

'We've had some casualties come in from the shuttle terminal. Can you come and help?' he said to Brian.

Brian was up and out of his office like a shot, heading for the regeneration section. He entered the triage room and was surprised at finding only three casualties waiting for attention. He turned to Fu.

'Only three? You called me for only three. What's up with you?' he shouted at him.

'You told me to contact you if anyone required the use of the regeneration unit,' Fu replied.

Brian wasn't amused with the way he said that and replied, 'You are supposed to be a professional. Can't you use your own initiative for once?'

'Sorry, I was worried you would suspend me if I used the equipment without your authority,' he said very quietly.

'You'll have to speak up; I can't hear you above this noise. Never mind, just get on with it. I'll help you this time,' Brian shouted as he started to work.

Brian was relieved when the noise and shaking subsided; it allowed him to concentrate on the task at hand.

He looked at Fu and remarked, 'After this, don't call me unless you can't cope. I have to make sure this facility is functioning properly now the main power is out.'

Fu bowed in reply and Brian went back to his office to check on the situation. The main power came on as he entered his office, and the rumbling was starting once again.

Simon held Rose's hand in complete darkness. The noise was deafening and he shouted, 'Does anyone know if we have emergency lamps here?'

A voice could be heard just above the noise with a reply, 'They were removed for upgrading five days ago.'

Rose squeezed Simon's hand and remarked, 'We'll have to wait for the power to be restored.'

Within minutes of her saying that, the shaking ceased and the noise became distant. Now it was worse: silence and darkness. They could hear everyone breathing heavily and the odd whisper between staff. Simon heard a giggle from the back of the room and tried to remember who was over there when the lights went out. 'Someone's making the most of the darkness,' he told Rose.

'Leave them. It's one way of taking their minds off the situation,' she replied.

Simon said nothing, and stood listening to the sounds around him, hoping the lights would come back on.

The lights came on and seemed so bright, everyone was blinded for a moment. Then the rumbling and shaking started once again. This time it was more intense, with loud banging coming from the dome casings.

'I hope the domes can stand up to this punishment,' Rose told Simon.

He looked at her and held his fingers up; they were crossed for luck. 'So do I,' he replied. But he was puzzled; they were hundreds of metres under the mountains.

Minutes after the video monitors came back on, they went blank once again, and Danni screamed, 'What's happened now?'

A voice shouted from the rear of the room, 'The main computer has gone down.'

Danni looked at Bob and shouted through clenched teeth, 'That's all we need. Send someone over to engineering to see how long they will be offline.'

'Only you have the means to travel. Nobody else has a SCAT, so *you* go,' he said sarcastically, knowing she would be petrified at the thought of being out there all alone.

As Danni stepped outside, she asked Po Chak to accompany her, just in case anything was to go wrong. Little did she know that Po had a partner, and she was in the room with them.

The shaking diminished as she walked forward and almost stopped as she mounted her SCAT. Po jumped on behind her and, after a quick appraisal, she decided to head straight for engineering to lend a hand.

'So you are Danni Mitchell, not Pauline like you said?' Po enquired.

'So what? We look like twins now,' she replied, sounding annoyed.

'Who is Pauline then?'

'She's my daughter. Now shut up and let me concentrate,' she shouted at him.

Within minutes she was testing the air lock to the science and engineering control centre. Access was granted and she passed through.

Her ears popped as she entered the dome and she asked Po if he had felt the same reaction. He indicated yes with a nod of his head. Danni headed straight for the central computer complex.

Within minutes she was helping to sort out the mess caused by the violent shaking. The computer only had to be put back together to work again, and it would prove as complex as a jigsaw with all parts the same colour.

'This is going to take some time to fix. Can we get the communications up and running quickly?' she asked the senior engineer.

'We haven't enough staff to do both at the same time. Which one do you want first?' he asked her.

'Comms first, I think!' she said, slightly enquiringly, to him.

Po just looked on in amazement. He'd never seen anything like it before and probably never would again. He froze to the spot, afraid to move in case he touched part of the glowing, pulsing, jumble of spaghetti that surrounded him. It looked menacingly alive with energy, and he felt the static charge it emitted as every hair on his head stood on end.

Brian was back in his office, and the few patients that he had were being dealt with. He was tired and just wanted to rest, so he rubbed his eyes and thought of Pauline, home all alone. With the terrific noise and all that shaking, sleep was impossible, so he sat and had a hot drink to keep himself awake. By the time he had finished the last drop, the shaking and banging had subsided and were now only a distant rumble.

'All over,' he thought, got up, and made his way back to the ward to let Fu have a break.

John shouted to Juliette, whom he could see hanging out the window. 'I've found her. She's barely alive and I'm bringing her in now.'

He looked down and saw Pauline's body starting to swell. She was alive but only just, and in need of urgent medical attention.

'I've changed my mind; I'm going to take her directly to the hospital,' he shouted as he passed the balcony.

He thought hard, then gave the SCAT a command. 'Take the most direct route to the hospital, and make it fast. She's not going to last much longer.'

Without warning, the SCAT started to gently pulse and openings appeared on each side of the front seat. Iridescent blue tubes protruded and began to secrete an opaque, sticky substance. It quickly spread over Pauline's upper body, dissolving any clothing she had left on. Once fully covered, flashes of blue electrical charge shot through pathways that seemed to penetrate the substance and her breathing became more natural.

'Life preservation control has been implemented. Patient can remain in suspension for up to one hour,' the SCAT said clinically.

John was silent, and for a moment looked down at Pauline. Her head and upper body appeared to be covered by a flashing jellyfish, alive and pulsing. It looked disgusting, and smelled of strong antibacterial agents, which made him wretch slightly.

He positioned himself so he wouldn't interfere with the process, and sped off as fast as he dared; his legs astride her limp body. The SCAT passed through a fog-like, dusty atmosphere and soon reached, and checked the status of, the air lock leading to Farm Dome Two. It checked out as being safe, and the air lock opened to allow them access. After a quick dash through the air lock tube, they entered Farm Dome Two and

John immediately noticed the change of smell—definitely farming land. The headlights blazed out towards the centre and reflected off a number of mobile corrals, suspended and tethered together for safety. There seemed to be a little less mist in the air, but it was dust just like before, thrown up by the quake. He made his way between the corrals, being careful not to hit the tethers holding them together as he passed quickly by.

Soon the corrals were far behind and he raced across the dome to find the next air lock. It wasn't long before he arrived and was checking if the main dome could be accessed. All was in order and the SCAT entered the dome. John noticed a drop in air pressure and popped his ears to compensate. Inside he started to pass between mobile corrals once again. They were floating motionless and glowing ever so slightly in the dark, with only the noise of the engines heard, hissing quietly. This time he noticed there was less dust in the air, so he rose above the corrals to travel faster. In the distance he could make out the faint lights of a building; he wasn't going that way and took no more notice.

Simon was relieved when the shaking and noise stopped. He turned to look at the world city map and was dismayed at what he saw. All the cities were blank, indicating they were offline.

'Are communications working yet?' he asked.

Rose checked with the communications engineer before replying, 'It may be another two hours before comms are restored; a vital piece of equipment has been damaged and has to be reconstructed. They are having problems with the main computer too, so that may be why the cities are offline,' she replied hopefully.

'Now that the quakes have stopped, can we open the dome access doors?' Simon asked. 'We may have to use old-fashioned messengers to provide information.'

Rose was busy checking all dome conditions and their integrity. It was extremely difficult. She had to make all decisions based on minimal facts because the main computer was out of action or not fully functioning.

'Sorry, can't allow the domes to open. I don't have enough information from one dome to the next, or of the outside. We don't know how many domes are damaged. And on top of that, we don't even know if this is over yet,' she informed him.

Simon saw anger and frustration showing heavily with the expression on her face, and pointed out, 'We rely too much on technology. When it fails, we suffer.'

Rose didn't even raise her head; she was too busy trying to find out as much information as she could. With the domes closed and communications down, she was trying to organise messengers, starting with the control centre staff.

Thirty minutes after saying farewell to Juliette, John arrived at the hospital dome air lock and performed a status check. Access was granted and the SCAT quickly entered the hospital compound. Once again his ears popped as the pressure returned to normal. John remembered the layout of the building and set down on the balcony of Brian's office. He jumped off the SCAT, opened the balcony doors wide, and guided the machine into the room. Looking around, he found the intercom and immediately called Brian.

Brian rushed in to see what all the fuss was about. He stopped dead in his tracks when he noticed a body on the SCAT.

'What's happened?' he shouted at John. 'Who is it?'

'It's Pauline I'm afraid. Get her seen to quickly,' John said urgently, seeming to take charge of the situation.

Brian looked shocked at hearing the news, but immediately composed himself. He called Fu, telling him to bring a portable life-support table, made a few checks on Pauline's condition and smiled. 'Thanks John, she should recover quite quickly from this. How are your family coping?'

'Going straight back to find out. How long before she is well enough to have physiotherapy?' John asked.

'Tomorrow, if all goes well. Why?' Brian asked enquiringly.

'I'll have to let Juliette know when she will be needed,' he replied with a wink of his eye.

Fu arrived and started to remove the jellyfish from Pauline's upper body. John was surprised how easily and cleanly it came away. She was lifted on top of the floating table and connected to a life-support unit that took over immediately by creating yet another "jellyfish".

Two nurses entered the room and cleaned the SCAT thoroughly before replacing the medical unit under the front seat. John just watched in awe at the speed and efficiency of the staff, and how well they knew their equipment.

'I'll be off home again now. Give my regards to Pauline when she comes to,' John told Brian as he mounted the SCAT and moved quickly out through the balcony doors.

Brian smiled, raised his hand in a farewell gesture, crossed to the balcony door, and closed it quickly. Turning, he left his office and rushed to catch up with Fu. He pushed Pauline along the corridor towards a regeneration ward.

Po looked on as engineering staff rushed from one section to the next, carrying parts and repairing broken conduits. The energy was building around him and he felt a little uncomfortable as his hair was not only standing on end, it was tingling too. He looked around, saw Danni giving orders, and was puzzled at the way everyone obeyed without question. 'Who is she?' he thought. He also thought how good she could be for him. It could mean higher status.

Seeing a member of staff heading his way, he leaned over and caught hold of an arm.

'Hi mate, can you tell me who she is please?' he said while pointing towards Danni.

That's Danni Mitchell, Chief Scientist Grade Three,' came a puzzled reply as the man carried on walking past.

Po couldn't believe his luck and smiled quietly to himself. He now knew she had lots of power and was rich. He couldn't wait to get back and tell his partner. It looked like they were on the way up. 'Not just a farmhand for much longer,' he said quietly and his grin grew.

He was brought back to reality when a static discharge shocked his arm. He saw a gap in the cabling and headed for it as quickly as he dared. Every move caused another discharge to zap him, and by the time he reached the clearing, he could hardly stand. After flopping to the floor, he sat up and looked around at everyone staring at him with open mouths. Then he heard Danni's voice shouting his name.

'Po you stupid idiot! How on earth did you get in there?' he heard her say, just before a huge zap knocked him out.

Danni ran to a computer console, pressed a few buttons, and the pulsing subsided.

'Get that idiot out of there quickly,' she shouted to staff nearest to his limp body.

Once Po was clear he quickly came to, shaking his head to clear the stars he was seeing. 'What happened?' he asked Danni, who was staring him in the eyes.

'You, young man, are lucky to be alive. You were in the computer core, and it was just about to go to full power,' she told him with a mixture of anger and worry in her voice. 'If the computer came on with you inside, who knows what damage could have been caused. You could've killed us all and destroyed it completely. It's my fault,' she told him, 'I shouldn't have brought you here.'

'Sorry, I thought that area was clear of those shocks,' he replied, ashen-faced.

'Come on, we have to run this up again. Stay close to me and you will be fine. You have just put us back by at least an hour,' she told him.

Po couldn't get any closer. Danni felt him brushing against her and she smiled.

As she started to run the computer up, the ground started to wobble and it felt really strange. It wasn't violent, more like a boat riding on the sea swell.

'Stick with it and watch out just in case we have quakes again,' she told everyone.

John was racing home and about to enter the air lock to suburb one. Just as he started the usual pre-entry checks, the dome wall moved up then down. No noise, just moving up and down and gaining momentum with every passing second. He reached out to access the air lock control panel as it passed, only to get just a touch before it was out of reach once again.

'I'll have to wait till this stops,' he said to the SCAT, his only companion at that moment.

'Get some rest. I will wake you when normality is restored,' it replied quietly.

John turned round, leaned back against the control panel, and stretched out along the seat. He shut his eyes and listened to the near silence. He could make out a distant rumbling and the occasional groan from deep within the earth. And now the dome walls were starting to creak and grind.

It seemed as if he'd been asleep for hours when he was woken by a terrific bang, followed quickly by many others. He would have fallen off but he'd place a safety strap around himself before going to sleep.

'What was that?' he shouted into the blackness.

'It appears the domes are being bombarded again,' The SCAT replied.

John wanted to know what was happening out there and tried his communicator once again. Still nothing. He looked at the time; it was two in the morning. He raised his head and noticed lights blazing from a farm building a short distance away.

'Head for that building over there,' he ordered his SCAT.

It turned round to scan; it didn't know what lights he meant, but found them anyway. Picking up speed, the SCAT quickly reached what appeared to be a farmhouse, and set down on the porch.

John jumped off, brushed himself down, and walked inside, knocking the doorframe as he passed.

'Hello, is there anyone home?' he enquired.

The rugged face of a man poked out from behind a curtain. He stood up, called for his partner to come, and walked towards John.

'Hi, my name is John Blight. I can't get home while this is going on. Do you mind if I keep you company for awhile?' he asked his hosts.

'So you are the John Blight everyone has been talking about. Cocky young feller aren't you?' came a hoarse reply. 'Excuse my voice, not used to shouting. Not used to talking either, so let's leave it like that.'

John watched silently, but not in silence, as the man's partner placed some food and drink on the table. Only then did he realise how hungry he was.

'Thanks,' he said, helping himself to just enough to see him through the next hour or two.

Farmers were strange folk; some were very quiet while others were very noisy. The quiet ones had no children while the noisy ones always had very large families—both ends of an extreme and nothing in between. He'd also noticed that only the odd word, and not whole sentences, were spoken by most of them when they got together, which wasn't very often, as most lead very solitary lives.

He was just about to take a morsel of food when his communicator chirped. He looked at it for a few seconds before realising someone was calling him and then answered with glee in his voice. It was Juliette.

'Hi! How are you and the kids?' he asked before she could say anything.

The farmer gave him a strange look when he asked how the kids were. Then he said, more to his partner than to John, 'A family too! And so young!'

John said nothing and listened to Juliette trying to talk through a flood of tears. She was overcome by emotions built up in the past few hours.

'Are you OK?' she asked, quickly followed by, 'We are all fine now that we know you are all right.'

'I'm glad to hear that. As soon as I can access the air lock I will be home. I'm in the next dome having some food with a farmer and his partner,' he replied.

Not wanting to keep her in suspense, he told her about the trip to the hospital and finished with, 'So Brian said you can come and give her physiotherapy tomorrow. If that's OK with you?'

'That's brilliant. I look forward to seeing her well again,' Juliette said, smiling.

'I'll have to go now. I'm going to contact the control centre and see if there's any news about what's happening out there. Hopefully all is well back home. See you soon,' he said, cutting her off with a blown kiss.

Rose and Simon were standing next to each other when they felt a slight movement that started slowly and increased with speed by the second.

'Not unlike sitting in a boat on a pond,' Simon said quietly to himself,

Rose was standing very close to him and overheard what he said. 'Speak for yourself! I've never been on a boat. Makes me feel sick,' she whispered back and sat down quickly.

A few minutes later she was holding her head in her hands and was beginning to feel awful when the banging started again.

'Looks like it's about to start all over again!' Simon said loudly.

He was right, only this time there was no shaking, just the rocking motion.

Minutes later everyone in the control centre was blinded as the lights came back on. Simon's eyes adjusted quickly and he looked around at his staff. They all looked drained, physically and emotionally, and he wished he could send them all home to rest.

Then he caught a glimpse of his own face, older and more withered than he'd ever noticed before. 'I'll definitely be following Danni to improve myself!' he said to himself, trying to cheer up.

Rose looked at him talking to himself and said loudly, 'We have communications back. I'll try and find out when the computer is going to be back online.'

She immediately called the engineering centre to get an update and was surprised to hear Danni's voice. 'What are you doing there? I thought you were at the farming control centre!' she said, a little shocked.

'I decided I would be more use in engineering, seeing as it is chaos over here,' replied Danni. 'Anyway, you have comms back and the computer should be back in about thirty minutes or so,' she finished, sounding a little smug at her achievement.

Simon shouted to Rose, 'Tell Danni to get back here as soon as the computer is up and running.'

Rose told Danni and Danni cut off without a reply. 'Charming! Nice talking to you too!' Rose said in a manner so Simon could register her annoyance.

Simon just closed his eyes and felt a little more frustration at Danni's reaction. 'She's tired too!' he remarked, trying to make an excuse for her.

Rose started calling all senior staff in every dome, asking for information and trying to get some idea of their predicament. It wasn't easy, but slowly she was getting a picture that made her heart sink.

Farm Domes Six and Seven were wrecked, along with Water Dome

Two. The shuttle terminal external doors were welded shut, blocking the way in and out, and thermal energy systems were all offline. They were using an old-style nuclear reactor to provide power and it wasn't very stable, but at least it would last long enough to carry out repairs.

The domes that were damaged were made of Triron and Simon was worried about the condition of the remaining Triron domes. 'Check Store Domes One and Two and also the pod store,' he told Rose.

But Rose was already on to it.

Simon watched the ground outside moving up and down. Then he watched as an earthquake shook the ground and quickly obscured it with a cloud of dust. It lasted just two minutes, then stopped as suddenly as it had started. Now there was no movement and the dust started to settle once again. The banging on the domes was erratic, one occurring every few seconds, and they were so loud, each bang made everyone jump.

'It was better when there were many bangs; at least we expected them,' Rose told him, as she jumped with a bang that sounded extremely close.

'I only wish I knew what that banging was caused by. We are deep inside a mountain range and should be protected from objects hitting the domes,' he told her quietly, so as not to alarm his staff. But he could see they too felt uneasy with it.

Fu pushed Pauline into a side room containing a long regeneration cubicle, and opened the top. Brian helped him slide her onto the cubicle table and asked Fu to leave. As soon as he was alone with her, he removed all her garments and closed the top. At the head of the unit he began setting the controls to give full body regeneration and started the process. As he walked away, he realised that the small scar she had on her left ankle would be gone by the time the regeneration had finished and he smiled. She hated that scar, and now, because of what had happened, it would be history. He made sure no other changes were made. 'Perfection could not be enhanced,' he thought, still smiling. And just to make sure Fu didn't try anything, he'd locked the control panel.

Brian made his way back to his office. He intended to sleep there with the aid of earplugs. Even in the hospital dome the banging could be heard, and now that the shaking had stopped, he hoped things would settle down again.

John finished the snack his hosts had provided and was waiting for the movement to subside just enough for him to access the air lock. When the ground started shaking again, he became really worried and called Juliette. There was no answer and not knowing why left him in a state of shock.

Two minutes later the ground stopped moving and he said farewell to the farmer. 'See you again sometime. Thanks for the meal,' he said with a wave of his arm.

Within minutes he was on his SCAT and heading for the air lock. After a quick check, it opened and he quickly passed through. As soon as he entered, he noticed the thick dust in the air and had to move carefully, using the SCAT's sensors to pick out objects in his path. Soon he was at the door to his apartment and found it open. Dismounting, he ran inside and found the ground floor deserted. A thick layer of dust had settled everywhere. He made for the stairs.

He opened the door and entered the main bedroom to see three dusty, dirty faces staring straight at him. Juliette rushed forward and threw herself at him, clinging tightly and sobbing with joy. The other two were only slightly behind her and their weight made him crumple to his knees. He too sobbed and hugged them all.

'Never mind the banging, let's try and get some sleep,' he said, looking at their shattered, dirty faces, streaked with tears. He closed the bedroom door and they all collapsed on the large bed, John and Fred on one side and Juliette and Petal on the other. They tried to relax but jumped with each bang of the dome.

'I hope this stops soon,' Juliette said hopefully.

John just hugged her and gave her a kiss on the lips. 'Try to relax,' he told her, and within minutes he was fast asleep.

Juliette could hear him breathing lightly against her neck, cuddled in even tighter, and smiled contentedly to herself.

Petal whispered in her ear, 'He must be completely drained to sleep through this lot.'

Rose was surprised when a familiar voice greeted her. It was Pedro, her companion, and it indicated that the computer was back online.

'Simon, the computer is back online. I'll get an analysis of our situation quicker now,' she said with a hint of relief in her voice.

Simon and the whole control room cheered at that news. At least now a glimmer of normality could be brought to bear on their situation.

'Once you have all the information available and can make sense of it, call all senior staff in for an emergency council meeting. And don't take no for an answer,' Simon told Rose, before retiring to the back of the room for some refreshment.

He wasn't sure if Rose had heard what he'd said; she had her head down as she was taking in the overwhelming amount of information being presented to her and her team of engineers. But he knew her and trusted she'd heard him. He smiled as he walked away.

Danni watched as the computer core started to glow with energy and felt the static it emitted.

'Let's get out of here before it gets up to full power,' she shouted above the noise.

Danni watched as all her staff left as quickly as they could. She pushed Po in front of her and headed for the exit. The energy buildup gave her a sharp shock in her right buttock and threw her into the back of Po. He caught her as she fell towards the floor. She was slightly stunned and had to be helped out of the room. Being the last one out, he closed the door, and it shuddered as the locking mechanism sealed it shut behind him. He heard a slight hissing sound, followed by an increasing hum coming from behind the door.

'Good, it's sealed and depressurised. Wouldn't like to be in there now,' Danni whispered in Po's ear before gently biting it. 'Come on let's get back to the farming control centre,' She said while smiling and staring into his eyes.

Po said nothing and followed her towards the SCAT. She was talking into her communicator and looked extremely annoyed at being interrupted.

Danni turned and said, 'They expect me to go straight to the command centre for a meeting. Huh, they've got a hope!' And she carried on as if nothing mattered.

Mounting her SCAT, she indicated to Po with a flick of the wrist. 'Jump on,' she said, and he obeyed without question.

Minutes later she was at the main dome air lock and testing to gain access. It didn't take long before they were flying at speed towards the farming station. She felt Po's hands gripping her waist and liked the feel of his strong hands. Taking the SCAT up fifty metres, she came to a stop and told it to hold station.

Po could just make her out in the dim glow of the console lights. He watched as she turned towards him, placed her arms around his neck, and slid into his arms. He could feel her breath against his cheek and bent forward to kiss her. Within minutes they were in a full embrace and struggling to keep their balance on the motionless machine.

Simon asked Rose who was coming to the meeting.

'Me, you, Brian James, Bob Griffiths, Frank Powell, and Mel Tong,' she replied.

'And what about Danni?' he demanded.

'Don't know, she didn't reply to my request,' Rose said and watched Simon's face glow red with anger.

Simon rushed over to the security console and called Mel Tong. Mel answered immediately.

'Mel, find out where Danni is and if she's with anyone. And be quick,' he demanded as anger welled up inside him.

It wasn't long before he had a reply. 'Her SCAT is stationary in the main dome and she is with Po Chak. There is no indication of anything being wrong as it's in park mode,' Mel said.

Simon cut him off and requested full security access to grade status. After being scanned, a voice requested the reason for accessing the system.

'Please state nature of business and reason for access,' the emotionless computerised voice said.

'Downgrade Chief Scientist Danni Mitchell to Senior Scientist Grade Five. Upgrade Senior Engineer Rose Markham to Chief Engineer Grade Three immediately,' he stated through clenched teeth.

'Please state reason for downgrade,' came a quick response.

'Disobedience and unprofessional behaviour,' he replied.

'Your order has been carried out and will become active within thirty minutes,' the computer said, and Simon shut the console down.

Walking over to Rose, he whispered in her ear, 'Congratulations on becoming chief engineer grade three.'

Rose just looked at him and smiled. 'Thanks!' was all she managed to say, and then rushed off to call her children and tell them the good news.

Minutes later Rose was sitting back at her console, organising damage inspection and repair teams. Simon watched and was smiling at her devotion to duty when his communicator chirped up. It was the farm manager Bob Griffiths.

'Hi Bob, what can I do for you?' he asked calmly, wondering if Danni had found out yet.

'I've had a complaint from a farmer's partner that Danni has run off with her man. Do you know where she is? I can't contact her,' he said, and sounded very annoyed.

'It isn't Po Chak that's missing, is it?' Simon asked, with no sound of surprise in his voice.

'You know about it then?' Bob muttered, even angrier than before.

'Yes, I have had enough of her antics. Wait till she finds out what I've done as punishment,' he said with a hint of pleasure. 'You'll have to wait till she knows before I can comment.'

'OK, as long as you have it in hand, I'll leave it up to you. Though I think Po's partner will have something to say when she sees her next,' Bob remarked before cutting off.

Smiling, Simon turned to Rose. 'Looks like sparks are going to fly at the farm control centre shortly.'

Rose just looked oddly at him and stated, 'I will have to call John Blight. I need his help to organise repair parties. My lot are useless.'

'He's on the council so should have been called anyway,' he reminded her.

Danni was annoyed with Po. He hadn't lived up to what she was expecting. She got dressed quickly. As soon as both of them were ready, she took control of the SCAT and headed for the farm control centre in the main dome.

When she arrived, she entered the room looking arrogant and full of herself. She brushed past a woman, knocking her off her feet, and didn't know or care who the woman was.

Po looked at Danni as she walked over to the farming control console, then down at the woman sitting on the floor. Bending, he offered the woman his hand and helped her to her feet. After giving Po a nasty glance, the woman brushed herself down, strode straight over, and stood next to Danni. Danni didn't even notice her standing there; she didn't even see what was about to happen next.

Without warning, the woman tugged at Danni's arm and swung her round. Just as Danni's eyes made contact with the woman's, a clenched fist struck Danni squarely on the nose.

Danni was in shock. No one had ever hit her before and the pain was unbearable. Her communicator chirped, indicating an incoming call. It was from Simon and, not wanting to antagonise him any more than she had already, she decided to answer it immediately.

'Hi Simon, what can I do for you?' she asked, sounding as if her nose was blocked.

What came next caught her on the hop.

'I have been told you are pestering the farmers. Is that true?' he asked.

'No I haven't. I'm just checking up on the situation here,' she replied, holding back her anger and covering her nose.

'Then why did you sneak off with one of the farmers?' he said, rather annoyed. 'You are supposed to be my partner, not available to everyone who will have you.'

Danni boiled over. 'We will see about me being your partner. I can have just about anyone I want with my looks,' she replied smugly.

'In that case, consider yourself free to do what you want. Oh, and because of your unprofessional behaviour I've dropped your status to senior scientist grade five,' he said with a hint of pleasure.

'I'll get even with you for doing that,' she shouted, and cut him off.

She caught hold of Po's hand and dragged him out of the office. Po's partner quickly followed, caught hold of Danni, and spun her round. Before Danni could protect herself, she found a fist striking her square in the face for a second time. She felt her nose break, and as she sat on the floor, she noticed her two front teeth felt loose as well.

Dazed, she picked herself up off the floor, mounted her SCAT alone, and made her way to the hospital to see Fu. He would be able to repair the damage quickly. She called him.

'Hi Fu, I've fallen. I broke my nose and loosened my front teeth. Can you help me please?' she said, feigning a sob.

Fu went quiet for a minute, then replied sympathetically, 'Yes, come over straight away, I'll sort you out in no time.'

'Thanks Fu, I'll reward you well,' she told him with a soft, sweet-sounding voice.

Fu's job was on the line and he didn't want Danni messing things up even further. He called Brian immediately.

'Brian, Danni has broken her nose and damaged her front teeth. She wants me to see to it straight away and is on her way over right now. Should I proceed or not?'

Brian thought for a moment then said, 'Yes, proceed but sedate her well. I want to be there to program the regeneration capsule. Use a full-body capsule.'

'OK, thanks Brian.' And Fu was gone. He was a little puzzled that Brian wanted a full cubicle to do such a small job, but shrugged it off. He set about preparing for her arrival and thought no more of it.

Brian called Simon. 'Hi Simon, Danni has called in with a broken nose that needs fixing. Fu is dealing with it and keeping her sedated till I get there. I will be performing the operation, is that OK?'

'You don't need my permission to do it! And by the way, she's been demoted to a grade five, so you outrank her. I wish she'd never had regeneration; I think it went to her head. She's no longer my partner, so do what you want,' he said to Brian, with some sadness showing on his face.

'Is that so? I'll see what can be done to reverse the damage done,' Brian said with a hint of glee in his voice.

'You have my full backing whatever you do,' Simon said, now chuckling with pleasure at the image Brian had placed in his head.

'OK, I'll let you know how I get on. Bye for now,' Brian said, and cut him off.

Danni arrived at the hospital, made her way to the ward where Fu had told her to meet him, and was pleased to see him standing next to a cubicle. She was in a hurry, and didn't ask him anything as she entered the room. After stripping, she laid down on the open-topped cubicle bed he'd prepared for her and attempted a smile. Fu's face grimaced when he saw the damage to her nose and teeth; they looked a lot worse than he'd expected. The cubicle top lowered into position, locked, and Fu set the sedation level to deep sleep. Before long she was fully sedated and Fu set the controls ready for Brian to switch on.

Brian made his way to the ward and found Fu standing over the cubicle Danni was in. He walked up and dismissed Fu. 'It's the end of your shift Fu. Off you go.'

Fu reluctantly left and Brian set about altering the controls. 'That should do it. It'll be complete in about two hours,' he said out loud, and retired towards his office to wait.

Fu was just outside the ward, but out of sight of Brian, and sneaked back in as soon as Brian had gone. He looked at the settings Brian had programmed and a look of horror came to his face. Quickly he tried to readjust them, but found himself locked out by a security code. Tears came to his eyes and he lowered his head in despair. He slowly walked out of the room and found Brian leaning against the wall just outside the door, ready to greet him.

'I thought you might try that,' Brian said. 'That's why I locked the controls. I've only added fifteen years to her look. I hope it will bring her back to her senses.'

Brian knew it wouldn't be necessary to discipline him. Fu doted on Danni and what was being done to her would be enough punishment for him. He turned and left to attend the meeting with Simon, whistling a merry tune as he went.

John was woken with a start. His communicator chirped up, indicating an incoming call. Rising, he noticed the rest were still fast asleep, though moving rather restlessly.

He carefully rose from the bed and headed downstairs to answer the call. It was Rose. 'Hi Rose, what's up?'

'We are having an emergency meeting and your presence is required,' she replied, sounding sympathetic as she noticed his red eyes and dirt-streaked face.

'When?' he asked through an enormous yawn.

'Right now. You haven't had much sleep have you? And you could do with a wash; you're covered in dust.'

John looked at the time and realised he'd been asleep for only thirty minutes or so. He turned back to Rose and replied. 'Not long. I'll freshen up and get there as soon as I can. We're all covered in dust from the quake.' Then he cut her off.

He wondered if he should wake Juliette and tell her, then felt a tap on his shoulder. He turned to find Juliette standing, looking like she was sleepwalking. 'What's up?' she asked, scratching her almost-bald head.

'I have to attend a meeting at the control centre. I must freshen up before I go,' he informed her.

'Do you mind if I join you?' she asked sleepily.

'Come on then. But we must be quick.' He was smiling, took her by the hand, and pulled her upstairs to the cubicle.

He took a little longer than he meant to and was late in leaving for the meeting.

Simon stood, watching the senior members of staff arriving and was pleased that everyone who was called could make it.

'So glad you could all make it at such a hectic time. It's been a long night so far and who knows if things are going to settle down. If anyone has a theory about the noise coming from the dome casings, please speak,' he said before sitting down at the table.

Rose yawned and spoke first. 'Sorry about that, I'm so tired,' she said, placing a hand to her mouth. 'I think the domes are being hit by small meteors raining down on us. We've sustained some damage and a number of cattle have been killed. Luckily there haven't been any human casualties, other than Danni Mitchell, and that could be construed as self-inflicted. Oh! And Pauline Mitchell, who is undergoing intensive regeneration. Simon will explain a little more,' she finished, looking straight at Simon.

Simon stood up and walked towards the balcony window. He didn't want the group to see how upset he was at Danni's actions. He explained what Danni had been up to and the total lack of responsibility she had shown, then concluded his speech with, 'I've demoted Danni to grade five senior scientist and lowered her authority. She has to go through one of us to get things done from now on,' he told them.

'That sounds serious. Will it affect your partnership?' Bob asked.

'She is no longer my partner. Oh, and just to put a smile on your face, I've made Rose grade three, effective immediately,' he said quickly, taking them by surprise.

Everyone congratulated her, and Rose thought it all rather embarrassing.

'Has anyone else got any problems that need sorting?' Simon asked.

Everyone went silent.

At that moment John Blight rushed through the door and startled everyone as the door banged against the wall.

'Sorry I'm late. I had to make sure my apartment was secure after the quake,' he said, then sat in a chair behind Brian.

Simon walked back to his seat and sat down. He looked at John and said, 'At least you made the effort. Rose will want to speak with you after the meeting about organising repair parties. There's a lot to be done.'

John looked at Rose and nodded.

Then Brian uttered, 'It's stopped, the banging has stopped.' And a smile spread over his face. He continued, 'Pauline was brought to the hospital by John. If he hadn't acted as quickly as he did, the outcome would be very different. Her condition was extremely critical at the time and now she's on the mend. I hope to be talking to her by this time tomorrow.'

John placed his hand on Brian's shoulder, but said nothing.

Brian continued, 'Danni is in a regeneration cubicle at the moment. I don't think anyone here will be surprised that she had her nose broken by a jealous partner. She will be up and about in around an hour or so.'

There was silence and everyone was looking at Simon, waiting for some reaction. There was none.

Simon looked around the table, and as he did so, said, 'I want full reports from every one of you by our next meeting a few hours from now. Has anyone anything else to add?'

There was complete silence.

Rose took the silence as an indication that the meeting was over and turned to Simon. 'Do you mind if I go home to bed for an hour or so? I'm not much good to you at the moment,' she said, struggling to keep her eyes open.

Simon looked sympathetically towards her and at the rest of the team. 'You can all go to bed for an hour or two if you can find someone fit enough to hold your post for awhile,' he said. 'If it remains quiet until dawn, we can start finding out what's really happened out there. We also have damage that needs seeing to, though none that can't wait a few hours.'

'The duty engineer is fresher than I am, so I'm off. I'll takeover Danni's SCAT if that's OK with you?' Rose asked Simon.

'That's OK. I'm off to the hospital with Brian. Danni's being treated and I want to be there when she wakes up. I think there's going to be some sparks flying if what Brian has just told me transpires.'

Rose was waiting for Danni's SCAT to arrive and managed to catch Simon just as he was about to leave. 'From now on I don't want Danni at our meetings. At least until we can find out what state her mind is in,' she told him.

Simon nodded in agreement. He turned and left, hoping to have a little relaxation before Danni came round.

Rose called John over. 'John, I want you to start organising repair parties first thing in the morning. I'll have the duty engineer send you details of all the recorded damage. If you're not sure where to start, just give me a call, OK?'

'Sure. I'll see you later tomorrow morning if I get a free moment,' he replied with a yawn, and left.

Rose turned to the senior engineer and instructed him to call John at six thirty if nothing else happens. She knew that Simon wouldn't call her unless it was urgent. She needed a few hours sleep and dawn was still some hours away.

Brian mounted the SCAT behind Simon, and asked a question that was burning a hole in his mind. 'Simon, is there any chance of having one of these for myself?'

Simon was silent for a moment before speaking. 'I think there is one available. If there is, I'll get engineering to send it to the hospital. Let's check.'

Simon made the call and came back with the answer Brian wanted to hear. 'They're sending one over to the hospital complex right now,' he said, smiling.

By the time Simon was accessing the air lock to the hospital complex, a SCAT could be seen coming towards them at full speed, all lights blazing brightly with a flashing red beacon that easily caught the eye, even with the dust still lingering in the air.

Brian saw it first and was so excited, like a child waiting to play with a new toy. He pointed it out to Simon immediately.

'We'll wait a moment; it can follow us through the air lock. *Then* you can play with your new toy,' Simon remarked jovially, noting the boyish grin on Brian's face.

A few minutes later they were through the air lock and landing on the balcony of Brian's office. Simon jumped off the SCAT and didn't even wait for Brian to show him where to go. Fu was there to greet them, and scuttled off with his head bent low. He wasn't smiling. Both of them followed quickly behind.

They entered the room where Danni was undergoing treatment, and Simon made directly for the control panel.

'Brian, it's about to finish. Could you make a slight adjustment and keep it going for about another hour or so?' Simon asked.

Fu looked at him in horror.

Simon's communicator signalled an urgent call and he moved aside while Brian made the necessary adjustments.

Everyone stopped dead in their tracks as the rumbling noise started again and slight tremors could be felt. They quickly realised they could be aftershocks.

'Hi, what's the problem?' Simon asked the duty engineer in the control centre.

'I've been asked to inform you of a creaking noise and discolouration in the casing of the pod store,' came the alarming message.

Simon bit his lip; it could be serious. He wanted to be there when Danni came round, and this was not the news he wanted just now.

The tremors subsided quite quickly, and soon all was peaceful once again. Everyone relaxed except Simon.

'Is it serious?' Brian enquired, just as he'd finished making the adjustments.

'Nah, nothing to worry about, it can wait,' Simon blurted out, alarming himself with how flippant he was behaving.

The three of them retired to Brian's office for refreshments while waiting for the process to complete.

'I hope you two realise the implications of your actions!' Fu remarked with anger clearly noticeable in his voice.

The reply was silence, broken only by the occasional bang from a dome casing and the footsteps of staff passing the office door, which remained wide open.

Brian looked at Simon. 'Isn't Danni's treatment a little harsh?'

Simon gave him a nasty look, but said nothing. He just stared at the wall with a worried look on his face.

Once again they were all silent.

John reached the access port to Suburb Number One and requested access. As soon as the air lock opened, he sped to the other end and waited for it to open as well. Looking through the small window, he could clearly see the haze of dust still lingering in the air.

The port opened, a whiff of dust caught his nose, and he sneezed. 'This stuff gets everywhere,' he remarked to himself, and shot forward towards home.

On the way he thought about the chow house, and wondered how it had fared. 'I'll have to check on it first thing,' he thought.

He quickly reached home, landed on the bedroom balcony, and as quietly as he could, opened the doors. Tiptoeing inside, he slipped off his shoes, climbed onto the bed, and put his arm around Juliette.

'Get off me,' shouted Petal, annoyed at being woken. 'Juliette's the other side of me. Now move over.'

John climbed over the top of Petal and pushed his way between Juliette and Fred. Now they were all awake.

'Back already. Wasn't worth going was it?' she said quietly.

'Hush, let's just get back to sleep,' he replied and settled down.

Soon they were all fast asleep.

Simon, Brian, and Fu made their way back to the regeneration cubicle holding Danni. It was starting to open as they entered the room and they hurried over to help her up.

Fu took one look at her and turned away, trying not to show his disgust. Simon and Brian stood on each side of her and helped her to her feet.

'Is my nose repaired?' asked Danni. Then with a puzzled look on her face she asked, 'Why all the attention?'

When she was standing, they walked her over to a full-length mirror and stood her directly in front of it.

Danni screamed. 'WHAT HAVE YOU DONE TO ME?' she shouted with a look of horror on her face, and started to cry pitifully.

'As you abused your position to regain your youth, then took advantage of your situation, we thought it only fitting to punish you in this way,' Simon said, sounding a little guilty.

'I look about ninety! HOW COULD YOU!' she screamed, then started shouting insults and sobbing even more.

Simon and Brian left Fu to comfort her, and as they entered Brian's office, they could still hear her screaming insults in the distance.

'It's not nice! You could've just put her back to her proper age,' Brian remarked, looking at Simon and feeling annoyed that he'd been so petty minded.

'What's done is done,' Simon said with a slight smirk on his face. 'I have to go to the pod dome to see what's happening over there,' Simon told him. 'See you later, when I get back.'

'I'm off to bed for a short nap. It's going to be awhile before Pauline's treatment is complete,' Brian uttered sadly.

Simon put his hand on Brian's shoulder in support, then felt a nudge. Brian had given him a dig in his side.

'Did you feel that?' Brian asked.

'Feel what? That dig?' Simon said, sounding puzzled.

Brian looked puzzled too. 'I felt something.'

'I have to get to the pod store quickly. I need to find out what's going on over there,' Simon said once again, and they both left the room.

Each mounted their SCAT and left as quickly as possible. One behind the other, they raced across the dome heading for the air lock, taking the shortest route possible.

Simon called the control centre. 'Anything happening?' he asked.

'We just felt a few small tremors, that's all,' the duty engineer informed him.

'OK. Keep me informed. I'm on my way to check out the report of damage to the pod store wall. Then I'll be with you. You can wake Rose if you need help, but try and wait till I can get there,' he told the duty engineer. To Brian he said, 'Brian, you can go home and check on the condition of your apartment. It sounds as if some repairs are needed. You may have to sleep at the hospital until they are completed.'

'I'll go home first,' said Brian, noting Simon's eagerness to be off.

'I'll let you know if your services are required. In the meantime I hope you have a quiet day. Give my regards to Pauline when she is up and about,' Simon told him.

Once through the air lock, Simon's SCAT broke off and headed towards the shuttle terminal. Brian headed directly towards Suburb Number One.

'Stops off. Let's see how fast you can go. Take control until I'm familiar with everything,' Brian suggested to his SCAT, and sped off at high speed.

Not long after, he was through the air lock of Suburb Number One. Passing through he also noticed the dust in the air and, like John, sneezed.

Simon arrived at the shuttle terminal dome air lock and made it through quite quickly. He went over to see the damaged external doors and was amazed at the sight. It was a mess, but it was secure, so that mess had to wait as he had more pressing things to deal with. The damage to the pod store wall worried him, really worried him. He was just about to leave, when he heard the unmistakable sound of a spitter trundling across the ground towards him. He turned to find the terminal manager alighting and coming towards him.

'What's the problem in the pod store?' Simon asked.

'About time!' the manager said, trying not to show Simon his annoyance at him being so late.

'I came as fast as I could! Now jump on behind, and we can be off,' Simon told him, trying to make out he was a very busy man—which he was most of the time.

Simon could feel the man clinging tightly to his tunic. He knew the manager was petrified when he failed to respond to the question, 'Are you OK back there?'

Simon wasn't sure if it was the speed or height that did it—maybe both. He smiled as they reached the air lock and prepared to enter.

Once through, he was taken to one side of the pod store entrance and noticed the problem immediately. A huge fissure had opened in the wall. It started at ground level and extended halfway up the side towards the roof.

'And the discoloured casing?' Simon asked.

'It's over there. We need to go over and have a look at the far wall. It shows slight discolouration and may be a potential weak spot,' the manager told him.

Simon sped towards the far wall and stopped just over a hundred yards from the problem. At that distance the extent of the discolouration could be clearly seen. The manager dismounted and started walking towards the wall.

Simon dismounted, followed him, and was soon looking at a crack in the making. There was a jagged line stretching from the ground to at least fifty metres up the wall, pale blue in colour and getting paler as they watched. He touched it and pulled his hand away quickly.

'Yow! That's hot. Too hot for my liking,' Simon stated.

'It wasn't that pale a short while ago!' the manager remarked worriedly.

Simon was trying to remember what was the other side but couldn't. 'Do you know what's on the other side of that wall?' he asked.

'I think its Water Dome Two, the fresh water dome,' the manager told him hesitantly as if making an educated guess.

Without warning there was a loud clang and Simon saw a fissure open before his eyes. Water and steam came rushing in at them at an alarming rate, and bubbling mud suddenly appeared from nowhere. The noise of the steam rushing through the tiny crack deafened them and the high-pitched screech made them covered their ears. Even then they could hear the screech resounding through their sculls.

Simon and the manager rushed back to the SCAT, mounted quickly, and headed for the air lock at high speed.

By the time they arrived at the dome entrance, the lights were starting to dim as clouds of steam filled the air. They could feel the temperature increasing quickly and it felt uncomfortable. The crack must have open even more as the screech turned into a roar.

'It must be wide open now for the temperature to rise this quickly,' stated the manager.

'Quick, there's the air lock!' Simon said, pointing at the small door next to the main entrance.

They moved as fast as they could. Simon tested the air lock access panel and as it turned green, opened the hatch. They entered, only having enough time to slam the door before a wave of steaming hot, muddy water hit the outside. Simon made sure they were sealed in before driving to the other end, and then checked to see if it could be opened. A smile came over his face as the condition indicator turned green and the door opened.

'Come on, let's get out of here as quickly as we can!' he said to the manager, who looked white with fright.

They left, shutting the air lock behind them.

Just as they were leaving the vicinity, they heard a loud rumble from behind. Simon halted, spun his machine around, and stared at the wall next to the air lock. It was changing colour rapidly. Another, much louder clang made both of them jump and was quickly followed by the now-familiar sound of gushing hot water and steam.

Simon had forgotten about the crack in the pod store wall and now another crack had opened in the shuttle terminal wall linking the two. He turned his SCAT, applied full throttle, and headed for the exit air lock as fast as it could travel. He knew there was no way to outrun the steam and water coming into the terminal, but decided to try anyway. He hoped the water level wouldn't reach the air lock too quickly.

He contacted the control centre and the duty engineer answered him.

'Hi Simon, what's happening?' he asked, sounding concerned.

'The pod store and shuttle terminal are flooding. There are cracks in the walls leading to Water Dome Two and hot water and steam are flooding in. I think that I'm trapped. If I don't make it out, tell Rose she is my successor. She is to train John Blight as soon as possible to be second-in-command. Don't let Danni have a say in it, OK,' he demanded.

'OK! Will do. Good luck out there; sounds like you'll need it. Keep me informed of the situation for as long as you can,' the engineer said, his voice shaking with emotion.

Simon could feel the air temperature rising as he neared the air lock leading to the main dome. The water level was lapping at the bottom of the doorframe and he gave a smile and shouted over his shoulder. 'Looks like we've just made it in time,' he said, pointing at the air lock. There was no reply.

Simon reached over to access the door-locking mechanism and frowned. It was red, indicating it wasn't safe to enter, and he was extremely worried. Peering through the inspection window, he saw the tube was half full of staff slowly making their way out of the other end. He looked down, saw the water level just reaching the lip of the door, and watched as the air lock indicator lights went out. They were replaced by the brightly flashing words "LOCKED. ACCESS PROHIBITED".

It didn't look as if they were going to get out, and Simon contacted the control centre to update them. The air temperature had increased significantly and he had difficulty talking. 'We are trapped in the shuttle terminal and cannot survive much longer.' He coughed in the choking heat. 'Can you let everyone know please? And thank them for their friendship and support over the years.' He coughed again and stopped speaking.

He looked down at his hands and saw blisters. The air pressure caused his ears to pop and he went deaf. His sight dimmed and he turned to shake the hand of the terminal manager. He wasn't there. Simon hadn't noticed him disappear and felt very alone. He adjusted the medical controls to supply pain relief and waited to feel the effect.

Strapping himself to his machine, he gave his last order. 'Stay just above the water level and wait for my recovery,' he told his SCAT, and leaned forward to relax as the pain relief kicked in.

Little did he know, the SCAT, noting his predicament, placed a force field around the machine and rider. Simon was out of it, heavily sedated, and slumped over the control panel.

The SCAT informed the control room of the situation. *'Conditions have been stabilised by a force field surrounding machine and rider. Ambassador Tallsworth has enough air for two hours, after which I can administer life support for a further hour only. Further advice is required.'*

Water Dome Two was much higher than the other domes and could flood the two smaller ones easily. Simon didn't stand a chance, and the duty engineer knew it. He contacted Rose immediately.

'Can you come to the control centre as quickly as you can? I have a serious situation that needs addressing,' he told her.

'Yes, sure! What's the problem?' she replied with a croak.

'I'll fill you in on the details when you get here. Be quick,' he replied, before cutting her off.

Rose got out of bed and quickly made her way to the refresh cubicle.

'Where are you off to now? You haven't been home long,' said Otho disappointedly.

'They need me in the control centre; something has happened,' she replied sleepily. 'It must be serious; they've told me to hurry. I don't have time to make you breakfast before I go, so help yourself.'

Rose entered the cubicle and sat down to relax. Its pulsing action soothed away her tiredness. Five minutes later she was disturbed by her communicator chirping loudly, and hurried over to the bed to answer it.

'Hi, what's the problem now?' she said, sounding a little annoyed.

It was the duty engineer again, and he asked, 'When are you due to arrive?'

'I will be there as soon as I am ready! Is it that urgent that it can't wait just a little longer?' she shouted back at him. Then it dawned on her what he'd said when he first called: he had a serious situation. 'Sorry about that! I'll be there in ten minutes or so,' she continued more calmly, now she was fully awake.

Rushing down stairs, she bumped into Otho and told him to get out of the way because she was in a rush. Grabbing a slice of bread and a block of cheese, she dashed out the door before Otho could say a word.

She jumped on her SCAT. 'Control centre as fast as you can,' she commanded, and ate her scant meal on the way.

She arrived at her destination and rushed inside. Looking around she asked, 'Where's Simon? I thought he would be dealing with this.' She walked over to her desk.

The silence in the room made her turn around and look at the duty engineer. 'What's the problem?'

The duty engineer stuttered as he replied in a solemn tone, 'Simon is trapped in the shuttle terminal. We think he has about two and one-half hours to be rescued. He is unconscious and his SCAT is keeping him alive.'

'What happened?' she asked very quietly, tears welling up in her eyes.

'We are not sure just yet. Engineering is trying to find out, but whatever it was, it happened very fast.'

'Let me know as soon as you know anything,' Rose requested and turned away to hide her face.

A few minutes later she called Fu. 'Hi Fu, can you do me a favour please?'

Fu was puzzled as to why Rose wanted a favour of him and replied, 'Yes sure! What can I do for you?'

Rose waited for a few seconds before clearing her throat to speak. 'Can you inform Danni that Simon is trapped in the shuttle terminal and it doesn't look good.'

There was complete silence from Fu, so she continued, 'We are still trying to find out exactly what happened and I'll let you know when we do.'

There was still silence, and the seconds ticked by like hours.

Finally Fu spoke. 'I am sorry to hear that news. I will break it to Danni as soon as she wakes.' He cut her off.

As Fu listened to what Rose had said, his head drooped and tears filled his eyes. He put his hands to his face and, lifting his head up, let out a scream. Uncontrollable crying quickly followed, and he crossed to the wall where he banged his head repeatedly, saying to himself, 'No! No! NO!'

A passing nurse stopped, looked into the room, and asked if there was a problem. She was taken aback by what happened next.

Fu instantly ran from the room, waving his arms about wildly and shouting, 'She's doomed! She's doomed!'

He ran down the corridor and entered the room where Danni was sleeping. She was heavily sedated, and he immediately administered an antidote. Within a minute she was fully awake and trying to sit up.

Fu helped her up, and before she could say anything, he blurted out, 'Simon may be dying!'

Danni looked at him with disbelief, waiting for him to say he was joking or something. As she waited, the expression on his face told her it was true, and she started screaming uncontrollably, just as he'd done. Then she stopped as suddenly as she started, muttered gibberish to herself and started digging her nails into her arms, causing welts to rise up as she scraped the skin.

Fu took one look at the droplets of blood falling to the floor and decided to sedate Danni once again. He worked as quickly as he could, and within seconds of applying sedation, she was fast asleep. Fu began tending to her self-inflicted wounds and sobbed as he did so.

He cleaned the blood off the floor before leaving the room sobbing, with one eye twitching and his hand gently stroking Danni's black wig.

The nurse who saw him earlier bumped into him as he entered the corridor and asked him if everything was all right now.

'No it isn't! It never will be now that Simon is probably dead. How selfish!' Fu shouted with spittle hitting the nurse in the face as he foamed at the mouth. 'He was the only one who could have given her another chance!' he screamed frantically.

The nurse stepped back, trying to give him a wide berth, and allowed him to pass. She rushed over to a cleansing cubicle and immediately cleaned her face. With a disgusted look on her face, she decided to report his outburst to Brian as soon as she could, and find out if what he said about Simon was true.

Rose wondered how Danni would take the news and shook her head with sadness.

'Call John and Brian in for an urgent meeting,' she told the duty engineer.

'What time do you want it for?' he asked.

Rose looked straight at him. 'Now, you idiot. From what you said we don't have long to attempt a rescue.'

She retired to her desk and sat with her head in her hands, trying to hold back the sadness welling up inside her. A member of staff brought her a hot drink and she sipped it, trying to recall the good times she'd had with Simon.

A short while later the duty engineer disturbed her with the report about what had happened to Simon.

Rose looked at the information supplied by the engineering section and shook her head. The tragedy was caused by a series of catastrophes, starting with the rupture of Water Dome Two by the earthquakes. The water flooded the ground surrounding the pod storage, and when that dome ruptured, the water caused the destruction of the energy plant deep beneath it. So much heat and water coming together so suddenly caused a massive explosion of superheated steam that rapidly boiled the water. The pressure was so great, it found the weakness in the terminal wall and cracked it wide open. The pressure and heat build-up was so fast there was no chance of Simon getting out in time. Simon implemented life support for himself, but even that wouldn't last long. The temperature in the pod store had risen to 250 °C and the pressure was 5 bar and rising. The shuttle terminal wasn't much lower and showed signs that it too was increasing in temperature and pressure.

'Where do we begin?' Rose asked, looking at the duty engineer.

He shrugged his shoulders and turned back to his routine tasks.

'Keep me informed of any further developments please,' she told him.

He turned his head, looked over his shoulder at her, smiled sympathetically, and nodded. 'OK.'

John was fast asleep when something woke him, and he wondered what the noise was. He opened one eye and realised it was his communicator chirping. Slowly he rose from the bed and Juliette tried to pull him back. He released her grip and answered the call. It was the duty engineer in the command centre telling him to attend as soon as possible; an emergency had arisen. He looked at the time, and realising he'd only had an hour's sleep, fell back onto the bed. Juliette smiled, and wrapped herself around him. He gently pushed her away, got up, and told her he had to go quickly. As it was an emergency, he just opened the balcony doors, walked out, closed them behind him, and mounted his SCAT.

'Control centre as quickly as you can,' he commanded.

Juliette stood on the balcony and gave him a wave as he disappeared over the roof.

Brian was fast asleep when his communicator chirped. He jumped straight off the bed and fell flat on his back. His senses were still asleep and he couldn't keep his balance. Slowly sitting up, he leant back against the bed, and, once he'd realised it was a call, answered it.

'Hi! What can I do for you?' he croaked, clearing his throat as he spoke.

He listened to the duty engineer telling him about the emergency and requesting his presence at the control centre.

It was unexpected because he hadn't been asleep very long. 'I've only been asleep for an hour and I have to attend another meeting! What's going on?' he shouted, stumbling towards the cleansing cubicle to freshen up. It wasn't easy sleeping in an apartment where everything was at an odd angle.

Soon Brian was ready to leave and walked through his front door. Sensing his approach, the SCAT, parked outside, made ready to leave and greeted him as he climbed on. Within a minute he was on his way.

Rose waited patiently for John to arrive. And when he did, she immediately told him about Simon's predicament.

Last in was Brian, still looking like he'd just gotten out of bed and forgotten to change his crumpled clothes.

'Be seated,' said Rose, indicating a chair with a sweep of her hand.

She continued talking to John, asking if there was anyway of getting the SCAT out of the shuttle terminal quickly.

'There's nothing we can do if we can't get the air lock open. The SCAT can be remotely operated to enter if the door can be unlocked,' he told her.

Rose asked John to explain what was happening to Brian while she contacted engineering to find out if it was possible to open a locked air lock access door.

John made his way over to Brian and sat next to him.

Rose was talking to someone in the engineering section and didn't look happy. When she finished, she crossed to John and Brian to explain what she'd found out. The look on Brian's face brought tears to her eyes.

'I've just spoken with engineering. The only way to unlock an air lock door is to override the system. The only trouble is, when we do that, it opens both ends of the air lock at the same time and has to be closed manually to reset it. So that is out of the question.' She paused for a moment before continuing. 'John. When you were looking through the archived equipment did you see anything there that could be used to recover the SCAT?'

John thought for a moment. 'Nothing that comes to mind. We only have one and one-half hours left. It will take longer than that to get a machine out of storage, that is, assuming we can find something suitable,' he replied.

'Well it looks like there's nothing we can do. Simon is doomed,' Rose said quietly with a wavering voice.

John crossed to a console and accessed the archive information. 'May, help me scan the equipment for anything that can penetrate a dome wall without causing problems.'

Thirty minutes passed before John shouted over to Rose, 'Got it. There's a tube construction unit in Archive Dome Two. It can access the shuttle terminal dome without causing problems. It's touch and go though. The machine will take time to get ready.'

'How long?' Rose enquired, sounding a little excited.

After making calculations, the smile on John's face disappeared and he shouted out, 'Two and one-half hours. That's how long it will take to get it into position. Then thirty minutes to do the task.'

'That's two hours too long,' said Rose quietly, as her face drained of all colour.

'I'll get it out of storage, just in case another situation arises,' John told her.

There was no reply.

They sat in silence, watching the time pass slowly, and waiting for the SCAT to make a final report.

When it did, it was a shock, even though they were expecting it. *'Life support has failed. Force field will remain in place until recovery can take place.'*

Simon was gone.

A few minutes of silence followed the report.

Rose spoke first. 'We'll let everyone know what's happened after our meeting at 9:30 a.m. You can both leave now.'

John stood up, walked over to Rose, and took her hand. 'So sorry,' he said sympathetically. Then he turned and headed for the door.

Brian was right behind John and as soon as John left, he approached Rose. 'I didn't know him for long, but he's a character you don't forget and I'm sure you will have many memories. So don't think of him as gone, think of him on a long vacation or trip.'

Rose managed a smile and Brian moved forward to give her a hug.

She stepped back as he reached out and replied, 'I'll be all right. You go. I need to be alone for a few moments'

'Sure. If you need anything, just let me know. I'm off to the hospital. I'll inform Danni personally.'

Rose looked at him for a moment before uttering, 'I wouldn't want to be the one that has to do that. Simon was the only one who could control her, and look what she did to him. Good luck.'

'Luck has nothing to do with it. Wait till you see Danni. I think her will is broken. She may even have gone a bit gaga.'

Rose gave him a strange look and he left the room quickly.

John mounted his SCAT and headed for home. 'How many times have I made this trip today?' he said quietly to himself.

'At present you have made . . .' the SCAT started to reply to the question.

'Be quiet,' John remarked, as if scolding a bad child. Then he remembered the chow house and changed direction.

As he approached the MATCH, he looked pleased. It was still level and hadn't sunk into the ground. He set the SCAT down near the main entrance and asked May to open it up.

As he walked in he was shocked. He'd been expecting a bit of a mess, but not as much as he now saw. Although the tables and chairs were secured in place, cutlery, plates, cups, and, worse of all, food (cooked and raw) covered everything.

'How on earth are we going to clear this by breakfast?' he remarked.

May heard what he'd said. *'This chow house was designed to operate in unstable regions many years ago. When it was built, this problem was anticipated. There are cleaning robots standing by to clear this mess. Shall I active them?'*

'Take a picture first. If it's clean when people turn up, they'll think nothing happened to it.'

May scanned the room, taking a 3-D image of the mess. When finished, she told John to stand by the door. When he moved back, sections of wall opened and cleaning robots started to appear. Some floated up and started cleaning the ceiling and walls. Others collected the utensils, crockery, and cutlery. The robots were everywhere, washing, cleaning, and tidying up. John was impressed.

'I think we better leave before we are cleared away,' remarked May.

'I agree, let's leave them to it. How long before they're finished?' he asked.

'Approximately one hour,' replied May.

'Start supplying the farmers with lists of produce. This thing needs restocking. And get the engineering section to check and repair the spitter tracks.'

He thought for a moment then continued, 'When it's ready for business, inform the chow house staff. They have to do their part too.'

He jumped on his SCAT and headed for home once again, and not long after, he was opening the balcony doors to enter the bedroom. It was dawn and the dim light filtering in through the window showed an empty bed. He headed for the stairs and heard voices. Smiling, he descended and was amazed to find the three of them cleaning up the mess. They were still dressed in their night clothes and looked almost as dirty as the dust-covered furniture.

'I can see you are all very busy. I've just come from the chow house,' he said loudly, just to make sure they all heard him.

Juliette looked at him and replied, 'Why didn't you take us? We're hungry too.'

John looked around the room and before showing her the images he'd just taken, remarked, 'You think this is dirty, wait till you see what the chow house looks like. I think you'd rather clean this place than that.'

He asked May to project the 3-D image in the centre of the room and smiled when he saw the look on everyone's faces. 'It's all clean now,' he said rather foolishly.

Juliette threw an electron duster at John, hitting him in the face. 'Here, use this. If you can clean that place so quickly, you can help us.'

John didn't have a leg to stand on. He shrugged his shoulders and set to work.

'I have another meeting at 9:30 a.m. So if the chow house is up and running by 8 a.m., we can all go for breakfast. Otherwise we'll have to make our own.'

'I hope it's ready by then. My stomach sounds like an earthquake.' The comment came from Fred who was cleaning under the table.

John started to laugh. 'Have you lot seen what you look like? You're covered in so much dust you need to follow each other to keep the floor clean.'

Petal ran to a mirror and looked at herself. 'Yuck! What a mess. I'm filthy.' Then she rushed upstairs to a refresh cubicle.

'Well done John, now there are only the three of us cleaning,' Juliette said, sounding a little annoyed.

'Make that two,' said Fred, and he too disappeared upstairs.

With that Juliette threw down her mop. 'That's it. It'll have to wait till later.' And she walked away.

John followed her. 'I'll scrub your back,' He said and chased her upstairs.

As they stood in the cubicle, Juliette asked, 'When you go to the meeting can I come with you? You can drop me off at the hospital when it's finished. Is that all right?'

'No problem,' he whispered in her ear, then gave her a hug.

Not long after, John's communicator chirped. It was May, informing him of the progress being made over at the MATCH. *'The chow house has been thoroughly cleaned. Engineers have almost completed repairs to the maglev tracks, farmers are already supplying produce to provide a basic breakfast, and staff are being made aware they are required to man it.'*

'Excellent. Please pass on my thanks to everyone involved. What time is breakfast going to be ready by?' he asked.

'Nine o'clock at the earliest,' May said, giving him the reply he didn't want to hear.

'That's no good to us.' Turning back to Juliette, he said, 'Looks like we have to make our own food this morning.'

Brian left the control centre in a hurry. He'd left Fu alone with Danni for far too long and was a little worried about what Fu might be up to. He parked on his office balcony and rushed inside. Fu was sitting at his desk and Brian immediately asked, 'How's Danni? What state is she in?'

'Don't worry, I haven't undone your handiwork. I think she has gone crazy. She had to be heavily sedated to stop her from harming herself more than she has already,' Fu said without looking at him.

'What's she done to herself?' Brian asked, sounding a bit guilty.

Fu explained, 'She scraped the flesh off her lower arms with her nails, and exposed quite a number of small veins. There was blood everywhere.'

'She can't have more regeneration for at least six months, so the wounds will have to heal naturally' Brian replied. Then he looked puzzlingly at Fu and asked, 'What was she doing awake? She was heavily sedated before I left. Did you bring her around?'

Fu looked up at him. 'I wanted to tell her about Simon's predicament. It's hopeless for her now that he's gone.'

Brian didn't say a word. He caught Fu by his collar and frog-marched him to the door. After throwing him out into the corridor, Brian slammed it shut behind him.

Back at his desk he checked on Pauline's progress and smiled. Her treatment was progressing perfectly. He heard his belly rumble and asked Lucy, his companion, if the chow house was functioning.

Lucy replied, *'The MATCH will be serving breakfast from nine o'clock. Shall I reserve a place for you?'*

'No. That's too late. I have a meeting at nine thirty.'

He called a nurse and asked if he could make him a hot, sweet drink. Soon he was sipping very sweet hot chocolate, and started to walk towards the room where Pauline was being treated; he just wanted to be near her.

Rose stayed in the control centre, reminiscing over the good times she'd had with Simon, and looking at a picture of him. Sometimes she was smiling, but now and again the occasional tear surfaced and her eyes became redder as she rubbed them with her fingers.

Then she realised what time it was. 'I'm going to freshen up before the meeting starts. If you need me, I'll be in the washroom,' she informed her staff and left the room.

John got dressed quickly and told everyone to hurry up. If they had to cook their own breakfast it would take some time.

After asking May for a basic recipe once again, they were soon eating scrambled eggs and sausages. The latter tasted foul; they hadn't been cooked thoroughly and were full of fat. Still the eggs filled their bellies a little, at least till later when they could visit the chow house.

After telling Petal and Fred not to get up to any mischief, John took Juliette by the hand and she followed him upstairs to the bedroom balcony. Petal went too.

'Off again?' she enquired.

'Yep! Juliette is going over to see how Pauline is getting on straight after my meeting at nine thirty. So we'll see you later, OK?'

'Ok. Bye. See you both later,' said Petal, sounding a little bored.

Juliette suggested that she and Fred could continue with the cleaning. Petal didn't reply, she just turned and left the room.

When they were alone, John turned to Juliette and spoke quietly, 'Before we go I'll tell you what happened earlier this morning, so it won't come as a shock later.'

Juliette could see the sad look on John's face and replied, 'It's bad news isn't it? Is it about Bagman City?'

'No, it's Simon. He was caught in a tragic event earlier and died. He was trapped in the shuttle terminal and we couldn't get to him in time.'

Juliette knew how much Simon had done for them and although she'd never met him, she too felt a great sadness for him. Tears welled up in her eyes. 'That's sad news. How is everyone taking it?' she asked.

'Not many people know yet, so keep quiet about it. I think Rose will make a public announcement after the meeting.'

John mounted his SCAT. Juliette jumped on behind, and, placing her arms around his chest, hugged him tightly. Their journey to the control centre was completely silent.

When Rose came back into the room, all the meeting's attendees had arrived and were standing by the balcony doors, chatting quietly amongst themselves.

'Please take a seat,' she indicated to everyone.

They were ready for the meeting to start and sat in complete silence, each not wanting to mention the tragic news of Simon's death.

'It's obvious you all know the bad news. So before we start, let's have a minute's silence in honour of Simon,' Rose said solemnly.

That minute seemed to last forever. Juliette, who was standing against the wall, sighed and it sounded loud in the completely silent room.

'Sorry,' she whispered, just as everyone started to stir.

John looked at her, winked, and turned back towards Rose.

Juliette turned to look out of the window and caught Rose's attention. She rushed over to Juliette, stood directly behind her, and whispered in her ear, 'My dear, your dress is too thin. I can see a perfect silhouette of your body through it. Move away from the light.'

Juliette quickly moved away from the window, went red in the face, and replied quietly, 'Sorry, I didn't realise. Did anyone see me?'

'Just me. I think you got away with it,' Rose said as she turned back to the meeting.

John looked at her, puzzled, and Juliette mouthed, 'I'll tell you about it later.'

'Simon's last instruction was that I should take over as number one. Does anyone have any objections?' Rose asked.

After a short silence, everyone nodded in agreement, and she continued. 'John, you are to be my assistant. I will be training you to be my second-in-command. Has anyone any objection to that?'

John looked at her with his mouth open. 'I've only just arrived at the centre. Are you sure I'm up to doing the job?'

'Don't you think you are?' she asked him.

'I'd like the opportunity to find out,' he replied, smiling.

'Any objection, anyone?'

The response was different this time. Brian stood up and congratulated him for taking on such an enormous task.

Everyone around the table was given a task to perform. Each task involved trying to get things back to normal.

John spoke, 'The last task Simon gave me was to check the integrity of the domes and try to open up the branch pipe to Jumla Junction.'

'That's fine. Only your first priority is to recover Simon from the shuttle terminal. Then you can continue with other tasks. Report what you encounter to me as soon as you find anything untoward,' Rose replied.

After a short break for refreshments, Rose concluded the meeting with a warning.

'Danni Mitchell is not in the loop anymore. She has no authority whatsoever. I will assign her to the scientific dome and desk work as soon as she is well enough.'

She looked around the room at everyone, and noted that only John didn't have a smile on his face. 'Don't you approve of what's been done to her?' she asked him.

'I think as a punishment it was quite severe. And I don't think she will recover from it,' he replied seriously.

'Mm. You may be right. Ah well, it's too late now.' As she spoke, she turned and left the room.

John walked over to Brian and asked, 'You off to the hospital now?'

'Yep! Is Juliette going to be there when Pauline comes out of regeneration?' Brian replied, looking over at her.

'Yes. I'll be dropping her off before I start work.'

'OK. See you there,' Brian said, and quickly left the room.

John walked over and stood next to Juliette, who was looking out of the window and watching Brian leave on his SCAT.

'What did Rose say to you earlier?' he quietly enquired.

Juliette told him what happened and was livid when John doubled up.

'You've done it again,' he just about managed to say through his laughter.

Everyone left in the room started looking at them, and with that, she turned about and walked out onto the balcony.

John followed her quickly. He could see the problem for himself. 'I can see every curve of that beautiful body of yours. Let's go quickly,' he said as he jumped on the SCAT.

Juliette didn't say a word, she just jumped on behind and dug her fist into his side.

John bent over with pain, put the SCAT into forward, and shot off quickly. He knew Juliette still didn't like going fast and waited for her to complain. She didn't, he just felt even more pain as she dug into him again.

He slowed down, felt her arms wrap around his body, and in no time they were passing through the air lock into the hospital complex.

John told her, 'I'll have to leave you here. I have checks to carry out to see if we can access the shuttle terminal.'

'That's OK. I'll be preoccupied. Pauline needs physio for a few hours or so,' she told him.

He set his SCAT down on the balcony next to Brian's machine, entered the office, and saw Brian sitting at his desk talking to a nurse.

As soon as Brian saw them, he ushered the nurse out and greeted them. 'Thanks for coming. Pauline is about to be taken out of the cubicle and moved to the physiotherapy section.'

Brian quickly offered Juliette a white coat and said, 'Put that on and follow me. I'll make sure you have a uniform as soon as possible.'

'I'll have to leave you to it, I'm afraid. I have to start work,' John said, and stayed near the balcony door.

Juliette went to him and gave him a kiss. 'See you later,' she said quietly in his ear, then gently bit it.

She looked back and smiled at him, and John watched her until she was out of sight. He smiled, turned, and quickly left.

Brian entered the ward where Pauline was undergoing treatment and was shocked to see her missing. He rushed out of the room and caught the arm of a passing nurse. 'Where is Pauline?' he asked her quickly.

'Doctor Fu took her to the physio section about fifteen minutes ago,' she replied.

Brian looked shocked. 'Come on, Juliette. I hope he's not up to his old tricks again.' They rushed down the corridor.

As they entered the physiotherapy unit, Juliette shouted, 'Stop! Don't do another thing.' She rushed over and pushed Fu aside. 'What have you done?' she screamed, and stopped the treatment instantly.

Fu looked like a frightened child, cowering in the corner where she'd pushed him. 'I only wanted to speed things up, and get back into Brian's good books,' he replied quietly, sounding like a frightened child.

Juliette opened the lid of the cubicle and saw Pauline looking up at her with glazed eyes. She had a smile on her face, but couldn't talk.

'You didn't even sedate her, did you?' Juliette asked.

Fu just shrugged his shoulders, averted his eyes, and replied, 'I didn't know it was needed.'

'You could have killed her, you idiot!' she shouted. Then a mischievous smile crossed her face as she remembered the effect she'd felt. And quietly she said to herself, 'Though she would've died with a smile on her face.'

She quickly sedated Pauline, and as soon as she was fast sleep, closed the lid. Juliette then adjusted the controls. She said, 'Fu even got the settings all wrong. If she'd survived, she would have looked like an overdone bodybuilder when it finished.'

Brian boiled when he heard that. 'Fu, consider yourself suspended, pending a disciplinary hearing. Now get out of the hospital.'

Fu left quickly, with his head bowed and feet dragging on the ground.

'He was trying to get me back for what I did to Danni. I'm sure of it,' Brian told Juliette.

'It sure looks that way. But I don't think he knew exactly what he was doing. Now she's going to look as good as new when she comes out of this unit, though she will be bald, just like me.' And she chuckled to herself.

Brian walked over to the unit and entered a lock code. 'Just being cautious,' he told her. 'Come on, I'll show you the rest of the equipment we have here. We had a few casualties last night and some will be here later for physio treatment.'

John left the hospital and headed directly to the engineering dome. He had to find out what could be done and what would be difficult to achieve; the word impossible wasn't on his mind. He didn't want to read the information sent by Rose. He wanted to hear what the staff had to say about the situation.

CHAPTER 7
A SURPRISING DISCOVERY

John arrived at the engineering dome, and as he entered the main section, a senior member of staff greeted him. 'Hi John, we've been expecting you. Rose called and asked us to help you all we can.'

'Thanks. I would like to start by looking at what we can do about accessing Water Dome Two,' he said. 'We have to stop the leak. Do you know where it may have occurred?'

'That dome has to be accessed from outside or through the main feed to the water treatment plant here in engineering. And it's the main feed that's cracked,' the staff member informed John.

'Give me all the information on the feed,' John requested, trying not to make it sound like a demand.

As he read the information, his eyes lit up. He noticed the feed pipe was six metres in diameter. Then he asked for all the details regarding the tube construction unit, and after studying the information, he explained what he wanted to do.

'The tube construction unit will fit inside the main feed. Can we use it to carry out a repair? Remember, it will have to work under water, and possibly at high pressure and high temperature,' he reminded him.

After checking over the details, the engineer smiled and said, 'Well done. It may just do the job.' Then a look of amazement spread across his face. 'The machine should be here in about ten minutes. It's already on the move. Who organised that?'

'I did. I thought it may come in handy,' John said in a matter-of-fact manner.

'As soon as it arrives, we'll send it into the feed. It shouldn't take too long to repair the damage,' said the engineer.

'What's your name?' asked John.

'Rajinda Singh, Grade Four Senior Engineer,' he replied.

'Thanks Rajinda. Can you organise a team to carry out the repairs? I want to find out what's happened outside the domes.'

'We can't get out. The shuttle terminal is sealed off, and even if we could, the pipe doors are welded shut,' Rajinda replied quickly.

'Let's have a look at the plans. Rose used an access port to flood the tube passing close to this centre,' came a voice from behind a monitor.

'Thank you,' shouted John. 'Where is it?'

He made his way over to the engineer who had made the suggestion and looked at what he'd managed to find. 'Looks like we can use the access port to send a probe down the tube. What do you think?'

The engineer checked the archive dome for anything that could be used as a probe and found nothing.

John was also busy; he was checking to see how many SCATs were still available. 'There are seven SCATs in stock. We can use one of them to do the job. Send one over to the access port now.'

With that, a number of engineers boarded spitters and followed John over to the port.

'It's large enough for a city hopper to get through!' remarked John when he saw it. 'So we shouldn't have any problem getting in. How long will it take you to get it open?'

'It takes about ten minutes to open it. Do you want to do it now?' asked Rajinda.

'Yes, do it now. Get the SCAT ready to enter the port as soon as it arrives, and program it for reconnaissance,' John told them.

As engineers set about unlocking the access port, John called Juliette to find out how things were going for her. After she told him what Fu had been up to, he shook his head in disbelief and called Rajinda over. 'I hope it isn't catching. Two senior staff members have been disciplined since I arrived. Make sure none of your staff joins them; please ensure they obey orders.'

Rajinda gave him a strange look. 'Danni's been demoted. Who else has been disciplined?'

'Fu. He's on a final warning or something,' replied John

'We thought he had it coming!' Rajinda replied, speaking the last words on the subject.

The access port was ready to be opened, and John watched as a number of engineers put on heavily armoured protection suits. They tethered themselves to rings in the dome wall close to the port entrance, and signalled they were ready. A shield of clear Triron was placed over them and the door, and was given an airtight seal before they slowly opened the access port.

John watched the SCAT move into position, facing the entrance and ready to move forward into the short tunnel separating the dome from the tube. Inside the shield the atmosphere very quickly became hazy, and as the door swung wider, everything inside became obscure. Dirty water could be seen running down the clear wall, but it was running at odd angles, not straight down to the ground as one would expect. It was obvious there was a lot of turbulence inside, and John frowned.

'I think the SCAT's gone in!' came a muted response from an engineer inside the shield. 'I can't see a thing, and the air pressure is causing my suit to leek. The smell is putrid. Like rotting matter.'

John replied quickly with a direct order. 'If it's in, close the door, make sure it's sealed, and we'll get you out of there.'

He watched as the water running down the walls of the shield trickled to the ground, and not long after, could make out the engineers inside. Their pure white suits were now a dirty brown colour, as was everything inside the mini dome. Only the dome wall and the shield remained clean; nothing sticks to Triron.

'Get them decontaminated and debriefed as quickly as possible,' he said and walked over to his SCAT. 'What information has the probe sent back so far?' he asked the engineering centre.

'Very little, I'm afraid. As soon as it entered the tube, it registered wind speeds in excess of a thousand kilometres per hour, and that was it.

Nothing else has been recorded.'

'Did anything go wrong with it?' John asked, puzzled by the reply.

'If the recorded wind speed is correct, the SCAT's engines would be too weak to hold station. It was probably swept away in less than a second.'

John sat quietly, stunned at the response he was given.

The control room spoke again. 'We have taken samples of the sludge deposited inside the shield, and it will be analysed as quickly as possible. Oh! We also know the tube pressure was almost six bar, just above safety limits for the suits our engineers were wearing. We closed the door just in time, by the looks of it.'

Again John sat quietly, mulling over what he'd heard. A few moments passed before he spoke. 'How long till we get the samples analysed?'

'A full analysis takes about five hours, but an initial report will be ready in about thirty minutes.'

Just then the clear shield was removed to allow the engineers to move away from the access port. As the shield moved, the smell made John wretch. It was disgusting; he'd only smelled things that bad when down in the oldest part of the recycling plant in Bagman City.

'OK. Send me the initial report as soon as it's ready, please,' he said, holding his nose. He turned his SCAT towards the dome entrance. 'I'm off back to see Rose. Smell you later,' he said, and left.

Juliette was having a snack with Brian when a nurse entered his office. 'Pauline's cubicle alarm has gone off, sir. Her treatment is complete,' she stated, and left.

Both left the office and hurried to the treatment room. Juliette stood over the cubicle as Brian entered the release code. Slowly the lid lifted towards the ceiling, and Pauline's body was exposed. Juliette couldn't help making a remark at what she was seeing. 'Wow! She is beautiful, isn't she?' And as she looked at Brian, she went bright red in the face.

'Yes, she is,' said Brian as he covered her body with a sheet.

He walked over to a nearby trolley and came back with an injector. 'Now to wake her up,' he said, smiling.

Moments after administering the stimulant, Pauline was wide-awake.

Juliette took her by the shoulders and raised her to a sitting position. Almost immediately Pauline held out her arms towards Brian. The look on her face was one of longing, and tears came to her eyes.

Juliette saw her expression and said quietly, 'I'll leave you two alone. Call me if you need me.' And she left the room.

Brian was amazed. Pauline was in his arms. He could feel her hugging him tightly and looked down into her eyes. 'Nice to have you back,' he said, and kissed her.

'One minute I was crossing the street, the next, I'm in here with Fu standing over me. I couldn't move.' Then her tone changed. 'I'll chop his dirty little hands off when I see him,' she finished, sounding extremely angry.

Brian boiled inside. 'Leave his punishment to me. I know exactly what to do with him. I think he would make an ideal companion for Danni. He's about the same age too. Yes, just perfect!'

Pauline looked puzzled by his remarks, and was just about to speak, when Brian continued, 'I'll explain later when you are feeling more like yourself.'

Pauline still looked a little puzzled, so Brian asked her what was wrong.

'Where's my suntan gone? I can't remember the last time I was this white. And my scar, it's gone too.'

'Regeneration doesn't do finishing touches, but it does repair scar tissue,' he told her. 'Anyway, never mind about the tan. It's you I love, with or without it.'

After helping her put on a robe, he pulled her to her feet, and walked her around the room. Then he offered support until he could see she was steady on her feet, before dancing around the floor with her gracefully. Pauline was laughing at his attempt to sing a song; it was completely out of tune and sounded awful.

He called Juliette in. Pauline wanted to thank her, and when they saw each other, they hugged and cried.

'Thank you so much,' said Pauline.

'Don't thank me. Thank John. He found you and saved your life,' Juliette replied.

Pauline looked at Brian and smiled. Then she said, 'Well I thank both of you then; we both do.'

'Well, now that you are up and about, we must go shopping together sometime,' said Juliette cheerfully, trying to change the subject.

Pauline's face lit up with a beaming smile. 'You read my mind. I was going to ask you that.' They both laughed.

'I have to go and check on the kids. Petal wants to know how you are and sends good wishes. She'd like to meet you. Perhaps we can take her shopping,' Juliette said.

'How old is she?' asked Pauline.

'Thirteen,' she replied.

'Just the right age to teach her how to shop,' laughed Pauline, and they both started giggling.

'Too true. I took her to buy a dress and she was so excited. Let's dress her up on the next trip,' said Juliette, sounding a little mischievous. She turned to leave.

'I'll catch up with you later. Bye,' Pauline replied loudly, as Juliette was already out of the room and on her way.

John arrived at the control centre and looked for Rose. Asking around, he found she'd gone home to freshen up and have lunch. While he waited for her to return, the interim sludge sample analysis arrived. As he scanned the short list, he noticed something that surprised him. There was too much salt, much more than there should be so far inland, and it puzzled him. He put it aside and continued to collect data on the condition of the domes. Time passed quickly.

Rose came into the room and saw him pondering over notes he'd made. They were scattered over her desk, and it looked a bit messy.

'What have you there?' she enquired, looking over his shoulder.

John explained what had happened when the access door was opened and the results from the sample. Rose frowned as she took it all in, and read the reports as he spoke.

She walked to the window and stared out. After a long silence, she turned and spoke. 'It looks like horrendous storms are raging on the outside and the tube is broken at both ends. I wouldn't be surprised if the salt were actually sea water, whipped up and carried inland.'

'We should know for sure when the full analysis comes through in about three hours or so,' John told her.

Both checked the information John had gathered and Rose decided the integrity of the surviving domes must be ensured before carrying out repairs to the tube. The trip to Jumla Junction could wait for now.

John told her about the repairs underway to stop the water leak. Once that was complete, the pressure in the shuttle terminal and pod store should decrease and access could be restored.

Juliette called for a spitter to take her to the main dome air lock and entered it quickly. Running to the other end, she opened the access door and found a spitter waiting for her just outside. It was going to be just like this, passing through every dome, until the main doors could be opened once again. Still it only took thirty-five minutes to complete the journey and she arrived home to the relief of Petal and Fred.

'I'm starving. Can you make me something to eat?' asked Fred.

Petal was upstairs, still cleaning her room and, on hearing Juliette's voice, came running down. 'How's Pauline?' she enquired, sounding a little worried because Juliette was back so soon.

'Pauline's fine. She's up and about and itching to go shopping with us,' Juliette told Petal with a smile.

Juliette walked over to the communications console and requested a sitting at the chow house; after all, it was now lunch time.

'A spitter is on its way. We can have lunch straight away. How's that?' she said, looking at Fred.

Fred only said one word. 'Brilliant.'

A few hours passed and the full sample report was sent directly to Rose. It was quite long and extremely detailed and technical. She started to explain in layman's terms what it all meant and John sat next to her as she reeled off what he already knew.

'I was right. It is sea water,' she stated, then continued, 'Most of the sample is made up of pulverised rock, earth, and decomposing vegetable matter.' Then she stopped, and a worried look crept over her face. 'There are also traces of Triron particles, which is disturbing. It also says there is a significant amount of human and animal DNA mixed in with it. Too much for my liking.'

'That can only mean one thing,' replied John. 'Some cities must have been destroyed.'

'Judging by the amount and range of DNA, there are many millions of dead out there, and a number of cities may well have been destroyed,' Rose told him, showing her sadness with a quiet voice.

By the time they'd finished checking the data, a report came in stating that the leak in Water Dome Two had been repaired, and the tube construction unit was back in the engineering section. The unit had been checked over and was ready for use once again.

'The pressure in the shuttle dome has already started to decrease. They say it's going down very slowly and we'll have to see how far it's dropped tomorrow morning.'

Rose and John continued checking every piece of information they had, and, by the time it had all been processed, it was early evening and time to stop.

'Right, that's enough for today. We should go home and have some rest. The real work begins tomorrow,' Rose told him.

'Thanks. It feels like I've been working for days,' he replied, and headed for his SCAT.

'It sure does,' Rose agreed. 'Wait for me, I'll travel with you.'

And they were gone.

Juliette, Petal, and Fred arrived back at the apartment. With their hunger satisfied, they were ready to finish cleaning up the dust. It was so fine it took a number of washes to get rid of the many streaks left behind.

Juliette's communicator chirped. It was John. 'Hi. Are you coming home?' she asked before he could speak.

'Just popping in to have something to eat. Have you eaten yet?' he asked.

Then they heard an unexpected bang. Not a big one, but the clang on the dome casing made them all jump. 'Is it starting again?' she asked him, sounding a little worried.

'I don't know. It's almost nine hours since the last bang, and if it is meteors hitting us, then we can expect a few more.' The last part of his sentence was almost drummed out by two bangs in rapid succession. They were much louder.

'I'll have a quick bite to eat and be home as soon as I can,' he told her.

'Be quick,' she said with a slightly shaky voice, and cut him off as Fred ran up to her, looking worried.

It started slowly, but soon the bangs coming from the outer casing starting to increase in frequency. The small ones weren't too bad, but the loud ones were a problem. Being irregular, they made everyone jump.

John arrived at the chow house, picked up a plate, filled it with snacks, and made ready to leave. The chow house was busy until the bangs started, then as if someone had said, 'Everyone out', it rapidly emptied and was now almost deserted. Walking back to his machine, he bumped into Rose, who was doing the same, except her plate was larger and she'd really piled it on.

'It's for the family,' she explained, looking a little embarrassed.

'I'm lucky, my lot have already eaten,' he replied, and held her plate until she was comfortably mounted on her SCAT.

After handing her plate back, John watched her shoot away from the foyer and quickly followed. Allowing his SCAT to drive in automatic, he started eating as soon as he could.

On the way home he noticed more white flecks floating down from the dome casings and the banging was increasing minute by minute, probably releasing more of the particles.

He called Rose. 'Looks like its going to be a noisy night again. Let's hope there's no damage this time.'

'I don't like what's happening,' she said with her mouth half full of food. 'As soon as I've dropped the plate off at home, I'm going back to work. I'll stay all night if I have to,' she told him, sounding concerned.

'Do you need me?' John asked.

'No, not at this time. I'll call if you're needed. Go home and look after your family. Oh! And can you look after mine if they get a little scared. Please.'

'No problem. At least *you* said please. Tell them to call me and I'll pop over to collect them,' he replied, sounding happy.

'Thanks. See you in the morning,' she said, and cut off.

John was parking on the balcony of his apartment when a rapid succession of extremely loud bangs resonated from the dome casings. As he entered the bedroom, Petal ran into him. She was crying and put her arms around his waist, hugging him tightly. Juliette and Fred entered the room and joined in. Every bang made them all jump in unison.

'Will this be going on all night?' asked Juliette, shouting to be heard above the noise.

'Possibly. We just don't know at the moment. In the next few days we hope to remake contact with the outside. Then we can find out what's really happening,' he told her.

John made sure he didn't mention the condition of the tube or the results of the sludge sample.

Brian called Fu back to the hospital and waited for him to arrive. While waiting, a nurse entered his office and placed a plate of food in front of him. There was more than enough for Pauline and himself, and he called her in to share. She was in another room choosing a wig to wear that closely resembled her natural colour.

As they ate Fu arrived and rushed into the room. 'You wanted to see me?' he enquired sheepishly.

Brian swallowed what he was chewing and spoke to him. 'I was going to place you in a regeneration unit and make you as old as Danni, but I decided that was a little over the top.'

Fu looked at him, totally shocked, and before he could say anything, Brian continued, 'Danni is going to need mental therapy and some friendly support for awhile, at least till she can be trusted not to cause herself any harm. You have the task of being her personal physician, and it's your one and only responsibility. Do you understand?'

Fu almost managed a smile as he replied, 'Thank you. I'll make sure she causes as little trouble as possible, and try to manage her unstable mental state.'

'You'd better make sure she doesn't cause even the slightest problem, otherwise you'll both be in for it, OK?'

Fu nodded in agreement and stood quietly.

'Off you go, and see to your patient,' Brian finished, with a finger pointing at the open door.

Fu scuttled out and Brian definitely saw a smile on his face.

Pauline looked at Brian and was annoyed. 'You didn't have a go at him for touching me when I was helpless,' she said angrily.

Brian instantly shouted, 'Fu get back here now.'

As Fu entered his office, Brian walked up to him and let fly with a barrage of insults. 'You are nothing but a pervert, a sick little pervert. You will never treat female patients ever again. You disgust me.'

Fu stood there trembling as Brian shouted at him. His head hung low, but he didn't say a word.

Brian continued, 'Pauline told me about what you got up to when she came out of regeneration and that, in my book, is gross misconduct. From now on the only person you will be allowed to treat is Danni. If I find you have been treating anyone else you will spend six months in rehabilitation.'

'I'm sorry,' said Fu, looking round at Pauline. 'You looked so much like your mother, I couldn't help it.'

When Fu said that, Pauline couldn't hold back any longer. Standing up, she rushed over and slapped him as hard as she could across the face. Within a few seconds, his left cheek reddened and more tears came to his eyes.

'Get out of here,' she shouted, and he left quickly.

'Ouch! Now let's get back to our meal,' Brian said with a smile on his face. 'I bet that hurt him.'

'That slap must have really hurt; my palm is still stinging,' she said, blowing cool air onto her hand and smiling back at him.

A little while later they were so preoccupied listening to music that the first bang went unnoticed. So when the second, much louder, bang occurred it came as a shock and both jumped. Brian ran over and switched off the music to make it easier to listen.

'That sounded like something hitting the dome,' he said enquiringly, and called the control centre. 'What's happening?'

The duty engineer answered his question. 'We've had a couple of bangs on the dome casings. I'm about to call Rose for advice.'

As soon as he'd finished talking, a succession of extremely loud bangs rang throughout the hospital, vibrating any object not firmly fixed in place.

Brian turned to Pauline, and seeing the frightened look on her face, said, 'Don't worry. It was like this last night too and little damage occurred. I think we'd better sleep here for tonight. This dome is made of Quadron, and is one of the strongest domes.'

Pauline ran into his arms. 'Thanks, I couldn't sleep at home alone with this going on. How long will it last for?' she asked with a trembling whisper.

'Could be all night. Though I hope not,' he replied as the bangs became more frequent. Some were minor and didn't cause too much concern, but others were extremely loud and those made them jump.

If the bangs came at a steady pace, they could live with it for awhile, but the bangs came in bursts, sometimes many and at times just one or two. They were increasing in number as the minutes ticked by, and even Brian looked a little worried.

Fu ran into the room. 'I'll be just down the passage sitting with Danni. Call me if you need my assistance,' he said to Brian.

Brian just ignored him, and left the room with Pauline. He knew there was a soundproof room with a bed somewhere in the physiotherapy section, and he hoped it would be good enough to blank out the noise for the rest of the night. On the way he passed a frightened-looking nurse and stopped to reassure her; he also informed her of where he'd be if things started to heat up. When she'd made a note of where that was, he was off down the corridor and soon entered a sparsely furnished room. There was a cleansing cubicle in one corner and a small table with one chair in another. Up against the back wall was a low, but wide, single bed.

There were many bangs coming from the dome casings now and as he closed the door, a smile crept over his face. 'There,' he said. 'Total silence. Let's get some sleep, just in case anything happens later.'

'I'm not tired,' said Pauline with a wicked look, and dropped her robe to the floor.

'Neither am I now,' he remarked, and smiled as he looked at her. She'd even removed her wig.

Rose arrived at the control centre just as the banging reached a feverish pitch. It sounded like hail on a tin roof, only a lot louder and occasionally deafening. The loudest bangs rang in her ears and she felt a little disorientated each time. As she crossed the room to speak to the engineer in charge, there was a bang so loud it stunned her for a moment and sent tabletop items crashing to the floor with the vibrations. She stood up, crossed to the window, and looked up at the dome casing. It was only an instinctive glance, but what she saw made her turn white.

'There's a large dent in the casing just above us,' she shouted. 'Get someone from engineering to take a look at it. And make it snappy!' she demanded.

As she looked around the room she noticed the shocked look on every face. 'Keep calm, we're still safe. The dome's still intact,' she said, trying to reassure them though she was petrified and shaking.

'Rajinda Singh wants to have a word with you,' a voice from behind a console just across the room said.

'Put him through to my office,' she said, and quickly left the room.

As soon as Rajinda saw her face, he started speaking. 'I don't like what's happening. Your dome is made of Quadron. If it's dented I think the control centre should be moved to the hospital complex. It must be really bad topside if we are sustaining damage.'

'I agree. Start the move straight away. How long will it take?' she asked.

'It will take awhile; we have to redirect cabling and conduits. So, by Monday morning if all goes well,' he replied.

'Well, let's hope nothing goes wrong till then,' she stated, and cut him off.

Rose was quite for a moment, staring straight ahead, then reached for the comms terminal and called Brian.

But Brian didn't answer, a nurse did. And after a short pause, she said, 'Can I help you ma'am?' She realised who she was speaking to.

'I want to have a word with Dr. James. Is he there?' Rose enquired.

'Yes ma'am, he is here. I will inform him immediately, and get him to call you back,' she replied politely.

'Be quick,' Rose told her sharply and cut off.

Brian was fast asleep with Pauline snuggled next to him. He'd been pushed back against the wall and, without a cover on, felt the cold metal on his back. He thought he heard a voice, but couldn't be sure and tried to cover himself.

Then he heard a deep throated 'Huh hum, excuse me sir.' The voice came from the partially open door.

He got up quickly, put on his trousers, and crossed to see who was there. He opened the door, and shading his eyes from the bright light, saw a nurse standing with her arms folded, leaning against the wall opposite.

'Did you want me?' he asked.

'Yes sir, Chief Engineer Markham wishes to speak with you urgently,' she told him quickly.

For a brief moment he wondered who Chief Engineer Markham was, then he was fully awake. 'Ah! Rose. Yes fine. I'll be there in a minute.'

The nurse turned and walked off down the corridor, while he stood looking back into the almost black room, and wondered if he should wake Pauline.

She was fast asleep and, trying not to wake her, he finished dressing. Just as he was about to leave, she spoke quietly. 'Where are you off to in such a hurry?'

'Rose called. She wants to speak with me urgently,' he replied just as quietly. 'Go back to sleep, I'll be back soon, OK?'

He left before she said another word and hurried to his office. As he walked along the corridor, he could hear the bangs still coming from the dome casings and looking at the time, realised he'd been in that room for two and one-half hours and asleep for only a small part of that. Rubbing his eyes, he entered his office and sat in front of the comms terminal. He glanced in a mirror and saw a tired-looking, unshaven, scruffy face looking back at him. Shrugging his shoulders, he called Rose. As soon as he could see her face, he asked. 'Problems Rose?'

'You look as if you've been sleeping. How can you sleep with all this banging? It's horrendous.'

'There's a soundproof room here,' he replied quickly.

'All right for some. Anyway, I wanted to let you know we are moving the control centre to the hospital complex. Can you let engineering know exactly where they can set it up please?' She made it sound like fait accompli. He had no option but to comply.

'I don't think there's enough room. I'll check and let them know within the next thirty minutes, if that's OK,' he told her.

'There'd better be room. Thirty minutes is fine. I'll let them know you'll contact them. Thanks Brian,' she said then cut him off.

Brian sat quietly, a little stunned. 'What has happened for them to want to move the control centre?' he asked himself. Then he accessed the hospital complex information and asked Lucy, his companion, to assist him. 'We have to find somewhere to site the control centre,' he said.

After a short wait, Lucy replied, *'The isolation dome has never been used. It's a little on the large side, but not in use.'*

Brian looked at the information and raised an eyebrow. 'I'd forgotten about that place. I don't even know what's in there. Let's go and take a look before suggesting it.'

'I will check internal conditions before we enter. It hasn't been opened since being built over two hundred years ago. Most of the information is too technical for my programming to understand.' Lucy sounded disappointed, as if she'd let him down by not knowing more about the place. 'There are a number of files regarded as top secret and I cannot access them,' she informed him.

Brian was puzzled. What was so special about this place that needed that level of secrecy? 'Come on, I'm intrigued. Let's go and see what this place looks like. Carry out the necessary checks and unlock it. We'll enter through an air lock, just to be on the safe side.' Feeling extremely excited, he rushed to the balcony and jumped on his SCAT. 'Yee ha! Let's go,' he shouted. And they were off.

Lucy made a comment that took the smile off his face. *'The access port is communicating with me. I cannot understand the language. My programming does not contain that information.'*

Brian looked puzzled. 'Contact Rose Markham and ask if she knows anything,' he told Lucy.

A few minutes passed before Rose contacted him. Even she looked puzzled. 'I'd forgotten about the isolation dome myself. Your companion contacted me with the information and I'm stunned. I haven't seen or used that language since leaving college. It's ancient Greek, and only taught to engineering and scientific personnel grade five and above. Now I'm puzzled. I'll contact security to get clearance for entry. It is asking for a special code before it can open up. I'll meet you at the access port, by which time I hope to have the code.'

Brian was sitting still, hovering alongside the port. He could see through the inspection window and shone a light to see inside. The tube was long and at the end he could see something he'd never seen before. As the light hit, the exit port door glowed. It looked eerie, and reminded him of looking through a kaleidoscope, with colourful rays bouncing back at him. He was mesmerised, and didn't notice Rose approach.

Rose quietly positioned her SCAT close to the access port control panel and entered a code using the key pad with strange markings on it. She watched as Brian jumped when the port started to slowly open. He turned and looked at her with a surprised look on his face.

'There. It's open. Let's find out what's so special about this place. My companion is reading through the secret files and will give me a report shortly,' she shouted.

The banging had increased again and she looked worried.

'What's the problem?' Brian shouted back as they entered the air lock tube.

As the access door closed behind them, it was like someone was turning down a speaker system; the noise became quieter the more the door closed, and as it clicked shut they could only hear a slight rumble.

'That's better,' said Rose quietly. 'You can hear yourself think now.'

The SCAT headlights lit the tube along its full length, and as they looked to the far end, they were amazed at the sight. They couldn't see the air lock door; there was just a bright glow where it should be. It seemed to change colour as the angle of light hitting it altered as they moved slowly forward. The glow was bright, very bright.

Brian looked at Rose and asked, 'What is it?'

Rose looked back, just as puzzled as he was, and shrugged her shoulders, indicating she had no idea.

As they moved further into the tube, Rose could make out a control panel. It seemed to be suspended in mid-air, floating in the light, and she headed straight for it. As she closed in, her SCAT suddenly stopped dead, and there was a loud clang. She was thrown forward onto the SCAT's instruments, and exclaimed, 'What the heck!' She quickly turned the machine sideways to reach for the panel. 'Whatever that is, it's hard, and we can't even see the surface. My machine can't even detect it. It's like there's nothing there.'

Brian slowly moved his SCAT forward and bumped into something solid, just as she'd done. He turned his machine parallel with it and put out his hand slowly to touch it. To his surprise, he touched what appeared to be a wall, only it couldn't be seen and it felt so smooth his hand couldn't stay in one place. His hand felt and looked like it was floating over the surface, and a mild electric current buzzed gently in his palm, which raised goose bumps all up his arm. He could see rainbow-coloured light reflecting outwards from deep within the wall and it reminded him of something, though he couldn't remember what.

Rose entered the required code and waited for the panel light to turn green, indicating access would be allowed. It didn't. Instead she heard a strange voice coming from just below the light. It was making a statement in Greek.

Her companion, Pedro, translated for her. *'Please wait. The life-support system is being checked. It will take five minutes.'*

Rose looked at Brian and sat silently waiting. The five minutes seemed to last for hours, but eventually the red indicator turned green and a click told them something was happening. A slit appeared in the wall next to the left side of the control panel, and as it grew wider, they could see the surface did have an edge. Only it was the darkness beyond that made it stand out clearly. The access door was slowly opening before them.

As soon as the door was fully open, they moved forward into the dome, and as they did, the lights came on. Their jaws dropped at the sight before them. Looking up, they noticed the roof and dome casing. The roof was glowing, just like the door, only it was bigger, much bigger. There weren't any lights attached to it, so they weren't quite sure how far away it was and it appeared to have infinite depth. Reflected light seemed to come from deep within the dome casing. The light was so colourful, an iridescent, electric blue with millions of rainbows, and it looked wondrously beautiful.

It was awhile before Rose could take her eyes off the colourful display over her head and look down. The first thing she saw was familiar looking buildings, only there were many, and it looked as if there were quite a few levels.

'Let's go down and take a look,' she told Brian, and immediately dropped from the platform they were resting on.

Brian followed but looked back. He wondered how people would get in and out if there was only a platform for access. He didn't see the sloping pathway leading down; it was made of the same substance as the walls and almost invisible to an unfamiliar eye.

Catching up with Rose, he said, 'Looks like we'll have to open the main door to gain access. There's no way down.'

Rose just looked at him and laughed. 'Don't be stupid; there's a pathway down the side of the dome. If you look closely enough you can just make it out.'

Brian felt really silly for asking that question and decided to keep his mouth shut until spoken to. He looked back once again and studied the wall but he still couldn't see the pathway.

There were many levels, twenty in all. There were homes, shops, places for entertainment, full medical facilities, and schools.

'It's a mini city,' Rose said, totally dumbfounded. 'I think it's bigger than the main dome.'

Brian had spent a short time looking at the hospital facilities a little earlier, and frowned. 'The medical equipment is antique. I'd say at least as old as this dome, because I've never seen anything like it. It's really primitive compared to modern standards.'

Rose was quietly thinking to herself and didn't really take in what he'd said. 'Pardon, what did you say?' she asked apologetically.

'I said the medical equipment is ancient.'

Pedro, Rose's companion, started to speak. *'This is a city designed to withstand the worse man can throw at it. The dome is made of Diamondium, a diamond-based, man-made material, and the only one of its kind on earth. It was built during a time of great unrest when there was the possibility of a war to end all wars. It was kept a secret and called the isolation dome. Not to isolate viruses or bacteria, but to isolate the research centre's population from the rest of the world if the need arose. It can house up to twenty-five thousand personnel and has five lower levels for cattle rearing and food production.'*

Brian and Rose listened to every word, their eyes completely transfixed on her communicator.

When Pedro finished speaking, there was complete silence, except for the slight hiss of the SCAT engines as they hovered just off the floor on the uppermost level of the city. Both Rose and Brian looked up at the dome roof then looked at each other.

Brian spoke first. 'Have you noticed how quiet it is?' he whispered.

Rose looked at him and smiled. 'There's no need to whisper. I don't think there's anyone listening to us. Though it is quiet.'

Then Brian said excitedly, 'Now I remember what the dome casing reminds me of—the diamond in the ring I gave to Pauline at our partnering ceremony. Only that ring doesn't look so good, it only sparkles.'

Once again Rose was only half listening and said, 'Uh huh.' She was obviously more interested in what she was reading on her console screen than what he was saying.

'It took nearly all the natural and man-made diamonds on earth to make this dome. I'm afraid the diamond you gave Pauline is probably man-made.'

Brian sighed. 'Don't tell her. She'll be even more disappointed than I am.'

Rose smiled and carried on reading. After a few minutes of sitting quietly and taking in the information, Rose made a statement that took him by surprise.

'How long will it take you to move all the hospital equipment to the medical centre in here?' she asked.

'There isn't that much to move. It's the weight that's the problem. It can't be carried by hand and maglev trolleys won't go through air locks.'

'Leave that problem to my engineers; that's for them to sort out.'

She called engineering, then called again. There was nothing, absolutely no answer, whatsoever.

Pedro spoke. *'There are no communications, and the main computer is offline. The computers haven't been updated since completion. Only the life-support computer is on.'*

'Well that's now top priority. Let's get out of here and get things organised. We'll move everything and everyone into this dome as soon as possible,' Rose said, and sped off towards the air lock, which took a little while to find as it blended well with the walls. Even she had difficulty seeing the platform, and had to rely on the SCAT to retrace their entry point.

Brian headed back to his office and Rose rushed to get back to the control centre. There was still banging on the dome casings, but it wasn't as bad as when they'd gone inside the isolation dome.

Rose landed on the balcony and entered the centre. Everyone looked shattered. The noise had taken its toll, and one or two staff had been taken to hospital as they were suffering from shellshock. After making sure they knew she was back, Rose entered her office and called engineering. After explaining what she'd found and asking for the equipment to be updated immediately, she walked into the control room and spoke to the staff. 'We will be moving to a new dome next to the hospital complex until things settle down. Engineering are making the necessary changes and I expect the task to be complete by tomorrow evening. Oh, and by the way, it's really quiet over there.'

John pushed the four of them onto the bed, and they all grabbed pillows to place around their heads to try and deaden the noise. It wasn't doing much good, and with each big clang they still jumped. Then they heard an almighty clang that resonated through their bodies. Juliette screamed, John's face screwed up with agony as his ears popped, Fred went stiff, and Petal passed out. Even though Petal was out cold, her body still jumped with each loud clang.

'I can't stand this much longer,' Juliette shouted in John's ear, just as there was a slight lull in the noise.

John was almost deaf and could only just make out what she was saying. 'I don't know how long it's going to last,' he shouted back.

Juliette shrugged her shoulders and placed a hand to her ear as if to say 'I can't hear you'.

He waited for another lull to shout it out again and she nodded and frowned. There were tears in her eyes; the noise was painfully loud and almost continuous.

John walked unsteadily over to the balcony, opened the doors, and drove his SCAT inside. He bent forward over the console and spoke into the microphone. 'I want you to sedate the three people on the bed. Will you comply?'

The SCAT positioned itself at the end of the bed and John watched as a long, snakelike arm extended towards Juliette. It gently touched her arm, and as she looked to see what touched her, she settled back down on the pillow and stopped jumping to the noise. A minute later Petal and Fred were also sedated and looking at peace on the bed. He jumped off the SCAT and made sure each one of them was comfortable before lying down beside Juliette.

'Now sedate me for three hours. Only wake me early if I'm called,' he said to the SCAT. And moments later he was sleeping.

Fu ran to Danni to ask if she was all right. The banging was getting much louder and more frequent, and it was making him feel slightly disorientated and sick. As he entered her room, he found her sitting in front of a mirror brushing her black wig on the stand in front of her. It looked like she was singing to herself.

'Danni, how are you feeling? Is this noise getting to you?' he asked as loud as he could. Then he realised she wasn't singing, she was just saying, 'Clang, clang, bang,' in rhythm with the noise.

She was smiling, didn't turn to look at him, and didn't even answer. He was worried and crossed to the medication cabinet. He was going to sedate her.

But Danni had been watching his every move out of the corner of her eye. As he approached and placed the sedation gun against her arm, she spun round taking him by surprise. Whipping the instrument from his hand, she quickly placed it against his forehead and pressed the trigger. He dropped like a stone, ending up a crumpled heap on the floor. Dropping to her knees, she laid him on his side and lay next to him. Then she placed the gun against her head and pulled the trigger. Her arm dropped instantly to the floor beside her.

They would be out for some time. Sedation to the head isn't the recommended practice, as it can leave a person in a comatose state for weeks, though it causes no damage whatsoever.

Rose noticed the frequency of the banging decreasing and judged it wouldn't be long before it stopped altogether. The planet's rotation would shield them during the day, and she hoped earth would have moved away from the meteor storm by the following night.

The banging soon petered out and quiet was restored.

'I want a damage report on my desk as soon as possible. Including a casualty list,' Rose demanded, holding her forehead in an attempt to sooth her headache. Her ears were still ringing. Turning back to her office, she called John Blight. She was surprised when May answered the call.

'John is asleep at the moment, shall I wake him?' she asked.

Rose didn't know what to say. How could anyone have slept through all the noise? 'Yes. Wake him immediately,' she demanded.

'I'll get him to call you when he's fully awake,' May told her politely.

'Thanks,' Rose said, then realised she'd thanked a companion and muttered, 'I must be going nuts!'

Brian went to wake Pauline only to find she wasn't in the room where he'd left her. Stopping a nurse in the corridor, he asked if she'd seen her and was told, 'I think she's gone to see her mother.'

Brian was a little worried and rushed to the room where Danni had been sent to recover. As he opened the door, he saw Pauline dragging her mother over to the bed.

'Here, let me give you a hand. What happened?' he asked, after looking round and seeing Fu was also on the floor.

'I don't know what happened. I found them slumped together on the floor fast asleep.'

Brian helped her lift Danni onto the bed then turned to see to Fu. As he examined him, he noticed a slight discolouration on his temple and the sedation gun lying close by. 'Looks like he's been sedated through the head. Does your mother have a mark on her forehead?'

A moment later Pauline replied, 'There's a slight red blotch on her right temple. What does it mean?'

'They've both been sedated on the head. I'll send in a nursing team to deal with this. They're going to be in a coma for awhile.'

'How long?' Pauline asked.

'Anywhere from a few days to a few months. It all depends on the level of sedation used, and I'll have to do a blood check to find that out.'

'Good. She can't cause any problems for awhile,' Pauline said quietly to herself.

Brian heard what she'd said. 'I totally agree with you.' As he spoke, a smile crept over her face. 'Come on let's get moving. We are going to live in the isolation dome from now on. It's not what it seems.'

Pauline looked at him with a puzzled expression on her face. 'Is it better in there?'

'It's actually a mini city, and bigger than the main dome,' he told her quickly, and rushed out of the room.

Pauline followed. She was making a mental list of questions she wanted answers to, and couldn't wait to see the place. 'When can I see the place?' she shouted after him.

'We have to get all the equipment ready for transporting to the new hospital,' he said excitedly. 'And you should see it. Wow! It's amazingly beautiful inside.'

Now she was itching to see it. 'I want to see it. Take me there now,' she demanded.

Brian just laughed. 'You'll have to wait until engineering have updated the systems before we can go in. Until then I don't think its safe enough.'

Now she looked really puzzled. 'Unsafe! Why?'

'If anything goes wrong inside, we won't be able to alert anyone. The communications are well out of date.'

May instructed the SCAT to give John the sedative antidote and wake him. As he came to, he wondered what was happening and just lay there looking up at the ceiling. As his head cleared, he noticed the banging had stopped and could hear Juliette gently breathing next to him. He sat up and asked May why he'd been woken.

'Rose called. She wants you to call her back as soon as possible,' his companion told him.

He wandered downstairs to the communications console, contacted

Rose, and as soon as her face appeared, asked, 'What's up?'

She looked at him for a moment before replying, 'How come you slept through all the noise?'

'Sedated. All of us were sedated,' he said, sounding a little guilty. 'It was either that or suffer unnecessarily.'

'Well it looks like it worked. You look fresh compared to everyone here. Can you come to the control room? We've a lot to discuss.'

Yep. I'll be there as soon as I've had a bite to eat. Fifteen minutes OK?

'Yes that's fine,' she told him, and cut off.

John ran back upstairs, looked at the three sleeping beauties lying on the bed, and wondered if he should wake them. He thought for a moment before deciding he had to do it. Who knew what time he'd be home next. After instructing the SCAT to administer the antidote, he sat next to Juliette and waited for her to open her eyes. She didn't, she just rolled over and bumped into him. Then she opened her eyes and smiled.

'I was having a lovely dream. I dreamed we were living in a city once again, and felt so safe,' she quietly told him. Then she quickly sat bolt upright, turned, and saw Petal and Fred sitting up, rubbing their eyes. 'The noise has stopped,' she whispered.

'The banging has stopped, and I have to go to work. You'll have to look after these two again,' he said, gently stroking her cheek. 'Sorry.'

Putting her arm around Petal, Juliette asked, 'How do you feel?'

'I've a splitting headache and buzzing in my ears,' she replied, rubbing her forehead and closing her eyes.

'Lay back and rest for now, Pet. I'll ask Brian if you need any treatment,' John told her.

She just glared at him, then shouted, 'My name is Petal, not Pet.' She started crying.

John jumped over next to her and gave her a hug. 'Sorry, I'll try not to call you that again.'

She snuggled into his arms and stopped crying. 'My head really hurts.'

He turned to Juliette. 'I'll take her with me. When Rose has finished with me, I'll drop her off at the hospital.' Then looking back at Petal, he said, 'We'll soon have you well again.'

She managed a thin smile, but he could see the pain behind it.

'When Rose has finished with you? Sounds interesting!' Juliette said, sounding jealous. Then she laughed when she saw the look on John's face. 'I know. It's just another meeting.'

He jumped up and landed on top of her. 'You wait till I get back. You'll be in for it,' he said, smiling, and gave her a big kiss.

Fred looked on and remarked, 'Yuck! Get a room you two. That's disgusting.'

'This is our room,' replied Juliette, and stuck her tongue out at him.

Fred got up and left immediately, muttering to himself as he went. Petal left the room and stood next to the SCAT on the balcony.

'Look at the time. I don't have time for breakfast now. I must dash; Rose is expecting me about now.'

Juliette gave him a hug and another kiss and pushed him away. 'Go, before I get undressed and beg you to stay,' she said quietly in his ear.

'You get undressed and you won't have to beg me to stay,' he replied, and quickly left the room.

He mounted his machine and Petal slowly snuggled into his back, hugging him closely.

Quietly he asked, 'Do you have anything for headaches?' Before he could say another word, the small snakelike arm shot out and hit his leg. 'Not for me, you idiot. It's for Petal.' He felt a warm feeling creeping up his body.

The arm hit him again, then moved to the rear, and he watched as Petal took a jab in her thigh. 'What was that?' she asked, sounding alarmed.

John felt funny. His head swam for a moment before the antidote kicked in. Petal was shaking him and screamed sluggishly, 'What was that?'

He turned and looked at her frightened face. 'It's ok. That was a pain killer. It should be taking effect just about now.' He could see the expression on her face change from anguish to calm.

With slurred speech she replied, 'The pain is going.' She closed her eyes and slumped against his back.

John dismounted and applied a seat belt to make sure she didn't fall off. He jumped back on, pulled her close, and told the SCAT to take them straight to the hospital. Then he called Rose. 'Rose. I'm going to be a bit late. I'm taking Petal to the hospital. That banging has given her a terrific headache and I'm a little worried about her. Do you mind?'

'Not at all. A number of personnel have been taken to hospital for the same problem. So get here as soon as you can. We're going to move. We all are.' And she cut off.

John was puzzled. 'We're all going to move. Where to?' he said to himself.

'May, what did Rose mean by move?' he enquired.

He was at the hospital entrance before May replied, 'I have no information at present. A number of engineering staff have gathered at the entrance to the isolation dome and are awaiting instruction from Chief Markham. That is the only new development.'

John left Petal slumped on the SCAT and crossed the foyer to see the receptionist. Without realising there was a slight queue, he barged past everyone, and didn't even notice the looks they gave him.

'My sister Petal has something wrong with her,' he said out loud, ensuring the girl behind the counter heard him.

The receptionist looked up, saw Petal slumped on the SCAT, and instantly called for help. 'She looks in a terrible state,' she told him.

John looked and said quietly to himself, 'She's only got a headache and been sedated.' Then he noticed the queue looking at him and Petal with unhappy looks and decided to keep very quiet.

Brian shot around the corner and went straight over to see Petal. On the way he looked over and saw John calling him over.

'What's the problem here?' Brian asked, picking her up and carrying her inside.

John gave the queue a quick glance and waited till they'd left reception to speak. 'Last night, during all that banging, she passed out with pain and I sedated her. When she came out of it this morning, she had a terrific headache and couldn't hear properly. I sedated her again and brought her straight here.'

Brian looked a little annoyed. 'You shouldn't use the sedation willy-nilly.

Using it too often is not without danger. Anyway, she probably has concussion and a few checks will determine her treatment.'

'Can I leave her with you? I have a meeting with Rose. Something about moving,' John explained to him.

John was surprised when Brian answered, 'Yes. We're all moving to the isolation dome. It's wonderful in there.' Brian laid Petal on top of a floating stretcher and pushed it through a swing door. Turning, he said, 'Leave her with me. I'll sort her out and let you know when to come and get her.'

Before John could say another word, Brian rushed through the swinging door into the treatment room and he was left alone with so many unanswered questions.

'Right, let's go and see what this is all about,' John said, rushing past a nurse who had to move quickly out of his way, and heading for his SCAT. As he entered reception, the queue was still there, waiting patiently to be seen. And even more people were arriving as he left the building. He did feel a little guilty about jumping the queue but quickly forgot the subject when he looked over towards the isolation dome's entrance. He could see engineers buzzing like bees all around the air lock access. Two were approaching the main dome air lock on a spitter. He was about to enter it, but waited for them to arrive, hoping to gain some more information before meeting up with Rose.

As they entered, he waited until the air lock door clicked shut and rode next to them before speaking. 'So, we're all moving. How much work has to be done before it's ready?' he casually enquired.

'We have to update the comms and computer systems. The city is bigger than the main dome, so there's a lot to do in there. It should be ready by Monday if all goes to plan.'

'Ah! That's good,' said John, trying not to sound too surprised by the information.

As the door opened at the end of the tube, he bade farewell to the engineers and headed straight for the control centre at top speed.

He arrived on the control room balcony, dismounted, and rushed over to Rose's office. 'Hi!' he said quickly.

She put up her hand, signalling him to stop and be quiet. She was talking to Rajinda. 'So it's going to be easier than we expected. That's great news. Keep me informed of all news, good or bad, OK?' Then she looked up at John and smiled.

'What's all this I hear about moving into the city inside the isolation dome?' John asked, and watched Rose's expression change to one of amazement.

'Goodness me. News does travel fast. How did you find out so quickly?'

'A little here, a little there. It soon adds up, and before you know it, a picture emerges.'

'Proper little detective,' she replied, chuckling to herself. Then she went on to explain what she and Brian had found during the night.

'Wow. Can't wait to see it. Diamondium, I've never heard of it.'

'According to the information being translated, Diamondium is effectively pure carbon. Once made, the atoms are so dense and strongly bonded together, there is no way to separate them again. So it can be made, but not unmade. It's classified as indestructible.' She paused for John to take it in, but as he remained silent, she continued, 'Some small Diamondium pieces were made for jewellery. Here, take a look.'

John looked into the small box in front of her and was amazed at what he saw. There were a few rings and a necklace inside, with small gems that seemed to glow as light fell on them.

Rose lifted one out of the box and placed it under a bright light. The room became instantly flooded with rainbow-coloured lights, dancing about as she moved her hand slightly.

'Wow! Juliette would love one of them,' he said, mesmerised by the shine.

Rose took his hand, placed the necklace in it, and closed his fingers around it. 'I'm sure she will,' she said, smiling at him.

'Are you sure? Won't it make some people jealous?' he asked.

'I'm having a ring; Pauline will be getting a ring.' Then, placing her hand back in the box, she said. 'Here, this one's for Petal. Oh! By the way, is she OK?'

'You've given me the one with the biggest gem!'

'And Petal the smallest. So don't worry about it. Sit down and listen to what I want from you this weekend, or what's left of it anyway,' Rose told him.

Rose and John studied the information being translated from Greek for the next thirty minutes. Most of the information had to be translated once again into layman's terms so that John could understand; it was too technical. Rose heard John's stomach rumble, left the room, and ordered some refreshment to be sent over from the chow house. She looked so annoyed when she found it closed, that one of her staff offered to go home and make some cheese on toast for them.

'We'll have a break for refreshments before continuing. One of my staff is going home to make a snack for us; the chow house is closed. We need to discuss how to proceed with repairs and recover Simon's body,' Rose told him, and a tear came quickly to her eye as her emotions welled up.

'Thanks. I'm starving. I'll just give Juliette a call to see how she's faring,' he said, and rushed to a comms terminal in the control room.

Juliette sat quietly with Fred and asked, 'Are you feeling hungry?' He just nodded to indicate he was, so she asked her companion if the chow house was serving food.

'Due to staff shortages, the MATCH is closed until 1:00 p.m. Lunch will be served at that time. Do you want me to book you a table?' he replied, sounding apologetic.

'Yes please. Can you suggest something for me to cook for breakfast?' she asked.

Juliette's companion was called Mister. She'd never treated it as a friend; it was more of a father figure to her. She only spoke to it when she needed advice about something.

Her companion gave her a list of items to cook, and directions on how to cook them.

'Looks like were having scrambled eggs on toast,' she told Fred and rushed downstairs.

The comms terminal projected full instructions just over the kitchen worktop, and she rushed about getting the required items. She checked them off the list before continuing. 'Mixing bowl, frying pan, fork for whisking, knife, bread, eggs, and butter. Right, let's start.' She smiled nervously, and looked at Fred.

He had a worried look on his face and remarked, 'Are you sure you know what you're doing?'

'It's simple. I've only got to break the eggs into the bowl and stir them. Then cook them in the pan with some butter,' she replied confidently. 'Oh! And brown the bread a little and butter it. Simple.'

Fred left her to it and went upstairs. 'Call me when it's ready,' he shouted, and went into his room.

Brian placed Petal's head inside a small regeneration unit and switched the unit on. He watched the information on the display to see if there was anything wrong. As he watched, the regeneration unit seemed to disappear and began to display and image Petal's head. Second by second, layer upon layer of Petal's scalp was peeled back, eventually revealing the brain, which seemed to be translucent and floating in midair. He noticed two sections standing out in red and studied them closely. Then a deep frown spread over his face.

'It looks like she has a burst blood vessel deep inside her brain, and burst an eardrum,' he explained to a nurse standing alongside him. As he finished talking, the unit turned opaque once more, and it started pulsing. Brian read the diagnostic information. It was quite serious; there appeared to be some brain damage. Though it was slight, there would be no way of telling how much she would be affected until the process was complete.

'We'll wait until the process is complete before letting anyone know how she's doing. If asked, just say she's undergoing treatment and to call back later,' he told the nurse, and left the room.

On the way back to his office, he popped into the ward where Danni and Fu had been taken. Both of them were sleeping peacefully in clear-topped recovery chambers and a number of tubes extended into their bodies. After checking the data on each patient, he left with a smile on his face.

'They'll be out for quite some time,' he chuckled to himself.

John called Juliette on the comms terminal. He wanted to see her face when he told her he had a present for her. As her face appeared, he smiled and said, 'Hi, I dropped Petal off at the hospital and Brian is looking after her. How is everything there?'

'How is she?' she asked, sounding sympathetic and frowning.

'I don't know yet. As soon as my meeting with Rose is over, I'll give the hospital a call to find out.'

'Let me know as soon as you have any information, OK?' she said. Then she looked a little puzzled. 'Why are you grinning?'

'I have a very special present for you. It's something that you'll really like and will cherish.'

'What is it?' she enquired excitedly. Her words sounded more like a demand than a request.

'You'll have to wait till I get home before I show you,' he told her tauntingly.

'That's not fair. How long will you be?' she asked, sounding and looking like an extremely disappointed child.

John heard a noise in the background. It sounded like an alarm going off. 'What's that noise? Is that an alarm going off?' he asked, sounding very concerned.

'OH NO! Got to go. Bye,' she shouted, and cut him off.

Fred rushed out of his room wondering what the screeching, pulsing noise was, and ran straight into a wall of acrid black smoke.

'Juliette, what's happening?' he shouted over the noise. He slowly made his way down the stairs, coughing as he got closer to the kitchen.

Juliette jumped up from the console after cutting John off and ran to the kitchen. She was driven back by the thick black, foul-smelling smoke, and instantly panicked.

Then Fred joined her and tugged at her arm. 'Is that our breakfast on fire in there?' he asked, sounding very annoyed.

Before she could reply, the sprinkler system activated and quickly subdued the flames which had been in the kitchen. The kitchen fan turned on full, quickly removing the remaining smoke, to reveal the mess left behind.

Fred looked at Juliette and started to laugh. 'You are dripping wet and covered in black steaks. You look a right mess.'

Feeling really annoyed, she shouted, 'This is John's fault. If he hadn't called, this wouldn't have happened.' Then, looking at Fred, she too burst out laughing. 'Talk about me being a mess, you should see yourself. You're black from head to toe.'

He looked down at himself, screwed up his face, and shrugged his shoulders.

'I think we'd better clean this mess up before John gets home. Please don't say anything to him about it. Please!' Juliette begged.

'Clean it yourself, and I'll say nothing,' he said, and walked off. 'I'm going to clean myself up.'

Juliette looked at the mess and started to cry. She consulted her companion to ask for some advice. 'What do I need to clean this mess up with?' she asked.

'Use the auto cleaners. I can activate them if you wish. They can clean the kitchen while you clean yourself,' he said instantly.

Juliette looked puzzled. 'Don't tell me there are cleaning robots installed in this apartment.' Then she started to look annoyed. 'We could have used them to get rid of that dust yesterday morning.'

'You didn't ask for any assistance,' replied her companion.

Juliette was fuming. 'Activate them now,' she insisted and headed for her bedroom. Being a waste technician, she knew all about auto cleaners.

John was a little worried when Juliette cut him off. He crossed to an engineering console and asked for information on his apartment. He wasn't at all surprised to find the sprinkler system had been activated, and was extremely relieved that no injuries had been reported. He also noted that cleaning robots were at work.

Rose looked over his shoulder. 'What's up?' she asked, puzzled by the look on his face.

'Oh nothing much! I think Juliette almost burnt our apartment down, trying to cook breakfast I expect,' he replied, and didn't sound a bit surprised.

'Everyone OK?'

'No casualties reported and the cleaners are at work. So nothing to worry about,' he told her calmly.

Rose looked at him oddly and smiled. 'Come on let's get back to work.'

Brian watched as the regeneration unit was removed from Petal's head. He looked at her peaceful face and asked a nurse to pass the sedative antidote. After applying a shot to her arm, he watched as she came to. Her eyes were bright and she was smiling up at him.

'How do you feel?' he asked quietly.

'Fine, now my headache has gone,' she replied very slowly.

Brian hid his emotions well. The reply was slurred and far too slow.

'We have to carry out some checks before we can let your brother take you home,' he told her, and turned to speak to the nurse.

'I feel fine now. You can tell John I want to go home. This place gives me the creeps.'

Brian looked at her and smiled. 'That's better. I thought for a moment there could be a problem with your speech. The sedative took a little longer to wear off, that's all it was. I'll call John immediately.'

He turned to the nurse and asked her to go through the brain function test outlined on the regeneration unit's monitor, and winked at Petal as he left the room.

After entering his office, Brian called John. John didn't answer, but Rose did. 'What is it? We are very busy at the moment,' she told him rather abruptly.

'Just pass a message to John will you? Tell him his sister is ready to go home. Her treatment was successful and it looks like she suffered no lasting brain damage.'

'It sounds like she was in a serious condition,' Rose remarked.

'Very serious. She had a bleed deep inside her brain which could have been disastrous for her memory. Luckily John got her here before it became too serious. Full recovery is expected within a few months as long as the tests we are performing show no further problem exists.'

Rose was silent for a moment before replying, 'I'll just tell John she is ready to go home. You can tell him exactly what was wrong. I'll send him over as soon as we've finished our meeting, in an hour or so.'

'OK. That's fine. Bye.' He cut off.

Rose looked at John, told him that Petal was fine and that he could take her home as soon as their meeting was over.

'Thanks Rose. I bet she's itching to get out of that place. She hates the smell of hospitals,' he said joyfully. 'Come, let's crack on.'

After going through the list of damage, they eventually had a work plan. The seriously damaged water dome and pod store were top priority. Second was the recovery of Simon from the shuttle terminal, and finally repairs to Farming Dome Six. The damage to the control centre dome casing could wait. It hadn't been breached, only dented. Once they'd completed that work, they could concentrate on regaining contact with the outside.

As soon as the meeting was over, John bade farewell to Rose and headed for the hospital. It was a quick journey and he was soon putting down on Brian's office balcony. Brian saw him arrive and went to greet him. John spoke first.

'Hi, Brian. How's my little sister?' he asked, and shook Brian's hand.

'She's fine now. Please, come in and I'll tell you what I found.'

John sat quietly, looking a little worried, and waited for Brian to explain.

'Your sister had a brain haemorrhage and a burst eardrum. If you hadn't brought her in as quickly as you did, she could have been permanently brain damaged. We can repair the damage, but we cannot replace the memories or function that would have been destroyed.' He took a short break to let what he was saying sink in.

'Are you saying she's lost her memory?' John asked, sounding extremely worried.

'Goodness, no. The damage was minimal and tests indicate there isn't any significant memory loss. We won't know if she has lost anything until you find something is missing. She appears to be fine medically, and should recover fully over the next few months. Just don't let her do any brain-jolting exercises until I see her next. I've made an appointment for her in six months' time.'

'Can I see her now?' John asked. He was desperate to check his sister still had all her faculties, and wanted to hold her close. He knew she must be itching to get out of there.

'Follow me; she's just down the corridor.'

John got to his feet and quickly followed him down the corridor and into the treatment room where Petal was resting. As he entered the room, she jumped off the bed and ran into his arms, smiling.

'How are you feeling?' he enquired anxiously.

'I'm fine. Just get me out of here. The smell is horrible and this place gives me the creeps,' she shivered, and watched him smile back at her.

'Come on let's jump on my steed, and I'll get you home quickly. I have a wonderful little present for you, and one for Juliette.'

'A present? What is it?' she asked excitedly, and kept tugging at his sleeve the whole length of the corridor.

'You'll have to wait. I'm giving Juliette hers first,' he said, making sure she was sitting correctly on the SCAT. He was happy when she placed her arms around him and stopped talking.

'Here we go,' he said, and sped off the balcony as quickly as he thought safe.

It was a quick journey and before long, he was helping Petal to the ground. As they approached the apartment, John wondered what state it was in inside, and frowned. He hoped the auto cleaners had done their job well, and as he opened the door and looked inside, he was surprised to see everything clean and tidy, with no smell of smoke. Walking into the lounge, he saw Juliette and Fred trying to get the entertainment console working and quietly sneaked up behind them.

'Can I help?' he asked quietly in Juliette's ear.

Surprised, she jumped up and spun round. On seeing him and Petal standing there, she screamed, 'Yippee! You're home.'

After giving him a huge kiss and hug, she turned to Petal and asked, 'How are you feeling? Better?'

Petal didn't say a word to her, she just looked at John and said excitedly, 'Go on, give her the present.' It was obvious Petal couldn't wait to have hers.

'OK, hold on. Let me get my breath back first,' he told her, and taking Juliette by the hand, led her upstairs.

Juliette didn't say a word. She was extremely quiet and looked very coy as he gently pulled her into their bedroom. As he turned she smiled and placed her arms around his neck. 'What do you have for me?' she asked, pushing herself against him and gently rocking from side to side.

John fumbled in his pocket, but had to push her away before he could grip the little box the gift was in. As he pulled it out, the look on her face changed from one of excitement to one of astonishment.

'Is that it? It looks rather small,' she said, sounding a little disappointed.

'You know the saying 'nice things come in small packages'? Look at you for instance,' he replied cheerfully.

She smiled and waited for him to open the lid, biting her bottom lip in anticipation. 'Come on, open it then,' she said impatiently.

'Close your eyes,' he said, and as soon as she did, he opened the box. After taking the necklace out, he placed it around her neck. The clasp was a bit tricky, but he managed to do it up after a bit of fumbling. He was pleased. It looked perfect, just reaching her breastbone. He turned her around to face the mirror then took a white light laser pointer from his pocket and switched it on. 'You can open your eyes now.'

As she opened her eyes and looked at the necklace and the gem, her face lit up. 'It's beautiful,' she said with a whisper.

Then he pointed the laser at it. Even he was taken aback at what happened next. The gem began to shine. It shone so brightly, both of them had to almost close their eyes to look at it. Her breast seemed to have been replaced by a dazzlingly bright light, with many coloured shards of glinting light. John switched off the pointer, but the light coming out of the necklace didn't diminish. They looked around and saw brilliant-coloured rainbows filling every corner of the room.

It looked so wonderful, and, from looking at Juliette's face, John noticed she was mesmerised. She looked absolutely beautiful. The light reflecting from her skin seemed to be just as radiant as the light from the stone, and her expression was one of utter pleasure. He pulled her to him and kissed her passionately.

'I think you'd better close the door. I want to thank you intimately for this,' she whispered in his ear, and pushed him towards the door.

Petal was downstairs waiting patiently for John to return, when a bright light caught her attention. Getting a little excited, she slowly climbed the stairs, wondering what it was, and as she did, the light got brighter and more colourful. As she reached John's bedroom door, she was shaking with excitement at the brilliance coming from the slightly open door. With a huge smile on her face, she stretched out her hand to push it open. But before she could touch the handle, the door slammed shut, the light disappeared, and she suddenly felt really annoyed. Running back downstairs, she slumped onto the sofa then jumped to her feet. 'Yuck! This sofa is soaking wet. What happened?' she shouted at Fred.

'Juliette told me not to tell anyone. She burnt breakfast earlier this morning and the sprinkler system was activated. Please don't say I told you,' he said, sounding ashamed.

'Well, you could have warned me not to sit down. I'll have to change now.' Petal was extremely annoyed, and ran back upstairs to her room. On her way past John's room, she thumped the door in frustration, which was silly as it was totally soundproof.

Rose contacted engineering and asked Rajinda for an update on the pressure in the shuttle terminal. Although she could see the pressure was almost normal, she wanted a second opinion on whether it was safe to enter. 'Hi. I want your opinion. Do you think it's safe to enter the terminal now?' she asked him.

'I'd wait till later this afternoon. The pressure should be almost normal by then. I've initiated the air lock opening procedure; it can be done with one push of a button.'

'Let me have control over that. I want to be there when Simon's body is recovered,' she insisted, and by the look on her face, she wasn't going to allow anyone else to do it.

'Sure. I'll send you the code and direction on how to set up the button on your console. Standby,' he replied, without raising any objection.

Rose watched the monitor as the information appeared on her screen. Reading it quickly, she performed the necessary routine and patched it through to her personal communicator.

'There, all done. I can do it from anywhere now. Thanks, I'll call you later,' she said, and cut him off.

Rose tried to call John, but was told his communicator was offline. Puzzled she contacted security to find out what was happening. 'John Blight's communicator is offline. Why?' she asked, sounding a bit annoyed.

After a slight delay, the security officer replied, 'He contacted us to let us know that he was removing his communicator to relieve some pain in his wrist. He said it will be off for a short time, and will automatically tell us when he's back.'

'Leave a message for him to contact me as soon as he's back online,' she told him, a little relieved that he wasn't offline for a more serious reason.

'Will do,' the officer replied quickly before she cut him off.

Juliette was overwhelmed with her present and insisted John stay for awhile. He couldn't resist, she looked even more beautiful in the bright light, and she was biting her bottom lip which excited him so much.

'I'll contact security and let them know I'm going to be offline for an hour or so,' he whispered, and called them immediately.

After he'd finished talking, he removed his communicator and placed it on top of the dresser.

'I'll do the same,' said Juliette quietly, and copied what he'd said to security word for word. Then, she too removed her communicator, and dropped it off the side of the bed onto the floor.

The security officer sounded a little baffled. Finding two people living together who had the same problem at the same time was unusual, but he didn't ask any questions, and just accepted the excuse.

Since accepting the communicators as children, they were never without them, except for upgrading or medical purposes, and now they felt really strange. It was like being completely naked for the first time. Juliette lay on the bed, and giggled as John stood looking down at her glowing radiantly in the light of the gem.

'Wow! You look deliciously edible,' he remarked, then jumped onto the bed beside her.

They were light-hearted, full of energy, and in an explosive mood. To prevent the light from being blocked, Juliette took the necklace off and hung it on the bed post. The whole setting looked surreal.

Rose entered the control room and looked at all the blank external monitors and information panels. There wasn't enough information coming through to keep her occupied, so she called Brian to see how the casualties were getting on.

'Hi Brian, any problems over there?' she asked, sounding a bit bored.

Brian explained what Danni and Fu had done, and about the amount of time they could be out for.

'It couldn't be better. At least we don't have to worry about Danni messing things up for awhile. Though she will miss Simon's funeral,' Rose said, sounding as if she felt pity for her.

'When is that?' Brian enquired sympathetically.

'If all goes to plan today, we can have the funeral tomorrow afternoon,' she told him.

'That quickly!' Brian said, a little puzzled about the swiftness of it all.

'There aren't enough people here who know him to have a state funeral,' she muttered, sounding a little depressed. 'When we regain contact with the outside, I think they'll have enough to worry about, and his passing will be just another statistic. So it's better this way.'

'OK, keep me informed please. I have to go now,' Brian said.

'Will do,' Rose told him, and cut off.

John walked out of the cleansing cubicle, saw Juliette still lying on the bed with a smile on her face, and sat down beside her. 'Your turn,' he said quietly, and gently stroked her side.

She squirmed as he tickled her and sat up giggling. Looking at the necklace still hanging on the bed, she commented, 'It's dimmed quite a bit. How long has it been glowing?'

John reached for his communicator and placed it on his wrist. Looking at the time, he frowned and said, 'Oops! We've been offline for ninety minutes.'

As he stopped talking, his communicator indicated a waiting message, and he read it immediately. 'It's from Rose. She wants me to contact her as soon as I'm back online.'

'I hope you're not in trouble,' she said, looking a little worried.

'Don't worry about it. I'll sort it.'

Juliette picked her communicator up off the floor and rushed to the cleansing cubicle. 'Got to get ready for lunch,' she said hurriedly.

John got dressed quickly and headed for the door. 'I'll call you later, love,' he said and left the room.

On his way downstairs, he was met by Petal. 'Finished?' she asked, sounding a little disgruntled.

'Sure. Let's go down and I'll give you your present,' he smiled at her.

When they entered the living area, he placed his hand in his pocket and instantly looked shocked, 'It's gone!'

Petal's face dropped like a stone.

'Only joking,' he said, laughing as he showed her the small box.

Petal didn't wait; she just grabbed the box out of his hand and opened it.

'Is that it? It looks so small.'

John took the ring out of the box and placed it on the ring finger on her left hand.

Fred was watching and said, 'Engaged now. Is that allowed?'

Petal just glared at him, then watched, slightly puzzled, as John took out the laser pointer.

'I've got to go now,' he said, and as he turned, pointed the laser at the ring.

As he walked towards the door, he could see the light radiating around the room and heard Petal screech with delight. He opened the door and heard Petal shout, 'Thank you. It's beautiful. What is it?'

'I'll tell you later,' he said, closed the door, and ran towards his SCAT, which he'd ordered down from the bedroom balcony.

After jumping on, he headed straight for the control centre to meet with Rose. When he arrived, he walked quickly into her office and found it empty. Turning back into the control room, he asked where she was.

'She's gone to lunch,' someone said, and he looked disappointed.

'If I'd known that, I'd have gone too,' he said to himself, and left.

He made his way to the chow house, and arrived just as Juliette, Petal, and Fred turned up. 'Hi,' he said, creeping up behind Juliette. As she turned around, Petal took her hand out of her pocket and lit up the chow house foyer with her ring.

'Put it away, everyone is staring at you,' he told her quickly.

But it was too late. Rose came rushing up and took them all aside. 'Try to keep those gems hidden when they're shining like that. They are so rare, they're bound to attract a lot of attention,' she said, covering Petal's hand with hers.

'Hi John. Glad to see you are back. Have lunch, and be at my office by two. We have a lot of work to do.'

John was pleased she didn't sound annoyed and replied, 'Thanks. I'll sit with my lot, if you don't mind.'

'Not at all. Frank, Otho, and Anne are with me, so I won't be alone,' she told him and went inside.

John and his troop followed behind, and were quickly shown where their table was located.

Brian was treating the last of the patients. Luckily for him there weren't any serious conditions to deal with; being the only doctor available could have been a major problem. He was thinking of Pauline. He'd started showing her how to operate the equipment, and hoped she could cope. Part of her dental training involved using certain types of regeneration units, so it wouldn't take too much effort to train her to operate the big stuff. After all, Juliette learned how to use the physiotherapy equipment without any formal training, and was now graded as a junior doctor.

He was about to go back to his office when Rose called him on his personal communicator. 'Hi Rose, what can I do for you?' he asked.

'I'd like you to come to the chow house for lunch, and bring Pauline with you. I've booked you a table,' she told him with a smile.

'Is it lunchtime already? I do feel a little hungry. I'll call Pauline and we'll be there soon.'

'Good. I have something for you. It has some unusual properties. I'll tell you about it when you arrive,' Rose said, sounding a little quirky, and cut off.

Brian was puzzled. What did she have that couldn't wait until their next meeting? He called Pauline, told her they were going to lunch, and led her to his SCAT.

It wasn't long before they arrived at the MATCH and were shown where Rose was seated. Their table was close to hers and right next to

John's. As soon as Pauline saw Juliette, she made a beeline for her.

Juliette rose to her feet and hugged Pauline, who had to stoop a little, and said, 'You look so pale since your regeneration; we'll have to have some tanning sessions.'

'Don't remind me. I don't think I've been this colour since the day I was born. And then I was probably bright pink.' They both laughed.

John had been listening. 'On no you don't. I like you the way you are,' he said and gave Juliette a wink.

Juliette just poked her tongue out at him and replied, 'I'll keep one bit white for you.' And pointing her backside at him, gave it a pat.

Pauline and Juliette sat next to each other, chatting like old friends who'd been apart for a long time and paid no attention to the waitress.

'Can I have your order please,' the young lady said, with a slightly raised voice.

Pauline looked around and noticed everyone at the table was staring at them both. She looked at Juliette and, like flipping a switch, they both started laughing again. Through the laughter, the waitress eventually got their order and left.

John felt a bit out of it and crossed to where Brian was sitting on his own. 'Mind if I join you?' he asked.

'Please do. Those two are unbelievable. You'd think they were bosom buddies or something.'

John looked across at them cackling away like mad, and added, 'Well, if it makes her happy, I don't mind. I'm really glad she's found a friend.'

'Me too. I don't think Pauline has ever had a real friend before,' Brian said. Then he placed his order for lunch.

As they sat quietly eating their meal, Rose came to their table and sat down next to Brian. 'Hi, how are you coping at the hospital?' she asked.

'Just about coping. We're very short of staff, so I'm training Pauline to use the equipment. I'll have a chat about that when we have our next meeting.'

'This is our next meeting,' she remarked. 'I just want to let you know, that at four thirty this afternoon we will be entering the shuttle terminal to recover Simon. I've also been informed that the terminal manager is in there somewhere. We'll home in on his communicator to find his exact location.'

John stopped eating and looked at her. Realising he wasn't at all happy with having his lunch interrupted just to tell him that, Rose turned to Brian. 'Take a look at this,' she said, pulled out a small box, and handed it to Brian. Then she got up and left the table.

He looked a little puzzled when she left suddenly and looked at John. 'That's odd. She can't be used to giving people presents.'

'I don't think it's meant for you; I think you're meant to give it to Pauline, if it's what I think it is.'

Now Brian was really puzzled and opened the box. He looked rather surprised when he saw it was a ring, and just stared at it.

'Looks strange doesn't it?'

'What's it made of? It seems to be glowing slightly,' Brian asked John.

'Rose said it was Diamondium, a rare manmade gemstone.'

'Ah! I didn't know there were little bits of it. I've only seen it in the isolation dome.'

Now John looked puzzled. 'What do you mean?'

'The isolation dome is made out of this stuff. It's so beautiful in there, it takes your breath away,' he told John.

John handed Brian his laser pointer. 'Give the ring to Pauline and hit it with this laser. Don't do it in public, and prepare yourself for a nice surprise. She'll love it.'

'How do you know about it?' Brian enquired.

'I gave one to Juliette and Petal earlier, and they love them,' John blurted out.

Brian looked at him, feeling rather annoyed. 'So! Who else has one?' he demanded.

'Nobody. I think Rose has one, but if she has then that's it; there're no more left. You have the biggest gem in a ring, so ease up a bit.'

Brian sat back and his posture relaxed, 'Sorry. I don't know what I was thinking about. I should be grateful really. It's a truly remarkable gift.'

'Looks like those two have finished their lunch,' John said, looking towards Juliette and Pauline.

'Well I have to get back to the hospital. I'll see you at the shuttle terminal air lock at four thirty.' As he spoke, he followed John towards the girls.

Brian placed his hand on Pauline's shoulder to indicate they had to leave. After saying farewell to them all, she stood up, caught hold of his arm, and allowed herself to be pulled away. She just managed a quick wave before disappearing.

Juliette waved back. 'We're going shopping tomorrow if we have time,' she told John.

'Take me with you. Please!' begged Petal.

Juliette smiled and replied, 'We'll see.'

'I've got to get back to work. I'm not sure what time I'll be home though,' John told them all.

'I'll shine the light when you do,' Juliette said, winked, and followed it with a big kiss.

John stood still, like he was in a daze for a moment, then looked her straight in the eyes. 'I might be able to spare a few minutes now, if you want.'

Juliette saw the look on Petal's face and blushed. 'Go. You'll have to wait,' she whispered in his ear.

As soon as John left, Petal spoke. 'Can't you two keep your hands off each other for five minutes? What's so special anyway?'

Juliette looked at her, a little embarrassed at first. Then she smiled and said quietly so Fred couldn't hear, 'You'll find out soon enough what's so special.'

Then it was Petal's turn to feel embarrassed, only she didn't go pink, she went bright red.

'What did she say to you?' enquired Fred, a little confused about what was going on.

Petal just pushed him away, saying, 'Come on. Let's go.'

John left the chow house and quickly departed on his SCAT. It wasn't long before he could see Brian and Pauline just ahead of him and raced to catch up. He overtook them, made for the air lock out of Jumla City, and opened it ready for when they arrived.

Brian was shocked. 'How did you get that thing to move that fast?'

John just tapped his nose and didn't say a word. Instead he spoke quietly into his communicator and ushered them into the tube. He didn't enter, and as he was closing the door behind them, said, 'Take care. You can go that fast now. I've just removed the speed restriction from your SCAT. Drive safely.'

Brian just looked at him and smiled when he saw him pointing at his finger and giving the thumbs up sign.

Pauline noticed the movement and, sounding a little puzzled, asked, 'What was that pointing all about?'

'You'll have to wait to find that out,' he told her and opened the other end of the air lock to gain access to the main dome. 'I'll tell you when we get to the hospital, OK?'

Pauline nodded, snuggling into his back, and hugged him tightly as he sped off at high speed. She heard him say, 'Wow,' just as she felt the g-force of acceleration kick in. If it hadn't been for the quick reaction of the SCAT initiating its safety equipment, she'd have been left far behind. As it was, she was speechless, and just hugged Brian even more tightly.

Not long after, Brian parked the SCAT on the balcony of his office and, holding Pauline's hand, entered the room. He was hoping that he could have a few minutes alone with her, but a nurse was sitting in his chair, and jumped up when he entered.

He looked at her for a moment then asked, 'Is there anything for me?'

The nurse gave him the list of patients that had been treated earlier in the day, and after scrutinising the results, he turned to Pauline, and said, 'Looks like Juliette has a few customers. I'd better call her in.'

Juliette was surprised when Brian called. She wasn't expecting any work just yet. When he told her what needed doing, she realised there wasn't a lot to do and replied, 'I'll be over as soon as I get the children home. There seems to be a problem with spitter availability. It's becoming a regular thing at meal times.'

'OK. Get here as soon as you can. I'll leave all the information with the nurse I've assigned to your section. See you later. Bye.'

'Bye,' she said and cut him off.

Brian gave the nurse the information for Juliette and informed the nurse that she was now working directly under Juliette.

The nurse smiled and asked, 'That's a grade higher position than I had. Do I get an increase in status?'

Brian looked at her and replied, 'We'll see. It's a trial period for the next month. If nothing changes in that time you will be re-graded accordingly.'

The nurse nodded, turned, and left the room with a beaming smile.

'Right! I've got ninety minutes spare. Come with me,' he said, taking Pauline by the hand and pulling her out of the room.

'Where are we going?' she asked, trying to free her hand from his grip.

'To the soundproof room. I have something for you,' he told her, and she immediately stopped struggling.

After entering the room, Brian told her to close her eyes. When they were closed, he removed the ring from its box and, taking her left hand, placed the ring on her ring finger. She immediately opened her eyes and stared at it. Slowly a smile spread across her face, she leapt forward, embraced him tightly, and gave him a kiss.

'It's beautiful. What is it?' she asked quietly.

'It's called Diamondium, an extremely rare manmade gem. I've been told it's the biggest ring gem ever made,' he said smugly.

Pauline just stared at it. 'It's full of colours and radiating slightly,' she remarked.

Brian pulled the laser pointer from his pocket, switched it on, and turned the light in the room off. By the light of the pointer, he took hold of her hand and shone the laser at the ring. What happened next shocked them both.

The room was filled with bright light, and multicoloured rainbows danced everywhere within it. Brian looked at Pauline; the look on her face was full of wonderment and pleasure. He couldn't take his eyes off her. She looked so beautiful, and the light seemed to make her skin glow.

Pauline looked at him and smiled. 'It makes me feel so warm and relaxed,' she said sexily, and started stripping.

Brian watched, his face full of pleasure at the sight, and soon he was doing the same. 'It has a strange effect on me,' he told her, and pushed her back onto the bed.

He looked down at her and was surprised to see her remove her communicator. Now she really was naked; even the wig had gone.

'Let's enjoy the moment, who knows how long that light will last,' he told her as he lay next to her.

'You can use the laser again if it goes out,' she whispered in his ear, and stroked his chest lightly with the ring finger.

John arrived at the control room not long after Rose and walked straight into her office. She was busy reading information on her terminal screen. 'I wish someone would install a terminal in my head. There's so much information to take in and so little time to read it all.'

'What's it all about?' he asked, slightly puzzled. After all, she'd been at the research centre for many years and had never been idle.

'It's the isolation dome. Diamondium isn't to be messed with. So much energy was used to create it. It's reckoned that if someone tried to remove even one electron, it would turn into a mini sun. The nucleus of each atom is so close to the next, the electrons of one encircle the next. Looking at the atomic structure, it looks like a geometric work of art.'

John looked at the monitor and asked for it to be displayed in 3-D.

As the monitor created the image, he stood speechless. There was hardly any room for the electrons to fly round the nucleus. They were all intertwined so densely, if just one electron slowed or was even defected, it would start a catastrophic chain reaction.

Rose continued to explain about the properties of light they'd seen. 'When light hits it, the dense structure traps it, amplifies it, then lets it back out slowly in a pattern determined by the structure's size. It's amazing.'

'A light amplifier! Is that possible?'

'That's what it says, and I've no reason to doubt it. It is a remarkable substance.' She was quiet for a moment, then smiling, she turned to John. 'The gems I've given away have a nickname.'

'What's that? Sun stone!' he said jovially.

'No. They're called "Baby makers". The light makes the beholders randy.'

John didn't know where to look. Especially since Rose was giving him a look suggesting he already knew about that.

'I'll bear that in mind,' he said with a slight frog in his throat.

They continued to read information about other discoveries made over two hundred years earlier and were taken aback by some of it. Certain properties regarding the electron pulse displacement engines (EPD) had caused concern. They could be used to project force fields around objects and render them invisible. But after a terrible accident which destroyed a complete research centre, research into this had been abandoned due to a lack of atomic knowledge.

Juliette reached the hospital at four in the afternoon, just as Brian was about to leave for the opening of the shuttle terminal. As she walked through the building, she bumped into Pauline, scantily dressed and kissing Brian goodbye. She could see the glow around them both and realised they too had a Diamondium gemstone. As Brian left, he noticed her arriving and gave her a quick wave.

'See you later,' he said, and disappeared around the corner to his office.

As soon as Juliette reached Pauline, she was grabbed and pulled inside the soundproof room. 'Look what Brian gave me,' Pauline said, proudly holding her hand out with the ring still glowing, though not quite as brightly as earlier.

Juliette looked at the bed behind Pauline and remarked, 'I see you felt the power of the light.'

Pauline looked slightly embarrassed and replied, 'How do you know?'

Juliette pulled the gemstone out from under her top and showed it to Pauline. Pauline looked at it then at the ring, and, sounding a little annoyed, said, 'That's nearly twice the size of mine.'

Juliette looked at her for a moment before replying, 'Same effect though.' She giggled.

Pauline took her by the hand and told her exactly what happened when Brian shone the laser at it. And when Juliette told her exactly the same thing happened to her, they both started giggling.

'We've got the power to wrap our men round our little fingers,' Pauline told her. This idea amused both of them.

All of a sudden Juliette's face changed to a more serious look. 'Oh dear! I hope there isn't going to be any problems. Petal was given a ring with a small gem in it. I'll have to tell her about it.'

'Don't tell her she'll have control over men,' Pauline said jovially.

'Why not?' Juliette replied mischievously, and both giggled even more.

CHAPTER 8
UNFORESEEN PROBLEMS

John looked at the time and informed Rose they'd better leave for the opening of the shuttle terminal. As she stood up, he noticed her wobble slightly. 'Are you OK?' he asked, sounding concerned.

'Fine. Just a little tired. The lack of sleep last night didn't help,' she said as they left.

After entering the main dome, their journey across the grassy plain was in silence. As they approached the terminal air lock, they could see Brian waiting for them to arrive. There were also a number of engineering staff and labourers milling around waiting for them to arrive.

'Looks like everyone is ready,' said Rose, attempting a smile, trying to hide her true feelings.

John watched as she rode over to Rajinda Singh. After a few words with him, she called out, 'Standby everyone! I'm opening the air lock now.'

As the air lock started to open, there was a slight whoosh as the air pressure equalised, and everyone held his or her noses. The smell was horrible. It stank like boiled eggs and rotten vegetables, a mixture of rotten matter and sulphur.

'I'm putting on a mask before entering that place,' John shouted over to Rose.

'I only want you and Brian to go in. If it's safe, the rest can go in later to start repairing the place. But bring Simon out first,' Rose demanded.

But they didn't have to go and get Simon. As soon as the air lock opened, his SCAT immediately entered and made its own way out. When it appeared out of the blue, it took everyone by surprise; one or two even thought Simon had ridden it out himself, and cheered in response. They soon stopped when they noticed him slumped over the controls and covered in life-support jelly.

'Help me get him off that and onto the stretcher,' Brian told some labourers, and quickly set to work.

John started moving towards the air lock with his mask in place. He'd put on a light soil contamination suit, which made him highly visible as it was bright orange.

He'd started to pick up the signal from the terminal manager's communicator. 'As soon as I find the terminal manager, I'll call for a stretcher,' he shouted over to Rose.

She hurriedly rode over to him and placed a hand on his shoulder. 'Good luck in there. It's a bit of a mess. Wait for Brian; he can help you in there.'

John just nodded, and as he was about to enter the very long, descending air lock tube, he shouted back, 'I'll go alone. No need putting too many people at risk.'

He'd noticed the temperature inside was still quite high, and didn't want to be distracted by anyone else.

Brian went over to Simon's SCAT and asked it to lower the force field so he could remove Simon. As the field dropped, the smell hit him full-on, and it nearly made him sick. He quickly realised that Simon's body was in very poor condition, and care would be needed to remove him in one piece. Of the seven labourers sent to help him, only two had the stomach to remain, and even they felt sickened by the smell. It took twenty minutes to remove and place Simon on the stretcher. He was quickly covered and hidden from sight. He didn't look too pleasant and Brian didn't want Rose to see him that way.

'I'll take him to the hospital, and let you know when you can pay your last respects,' he told Rose.

She just looked at the stretcher and nodded in agreement. She didn't have a word to say, and her eyes were full of tears as he was taken away.

Just as he started descending, John received a message from Rose. 'Activate your force field. It should give you better protection.'

John looked at his instrument panel and frowned. 'I don't appear to have one fitted.'

'There is no force field fitted to the SCAT. It's an optional extra,' May told him.

'Just my luck. It's an optional extra and I don't have it,' he said to Rose, and started to move further in.

As he made his way down the long tube, he passed many air lock doors along the way; all of them were wide open. The air was becoming increasingly humid as he travelled further in, and his suit started glistening with the vapour collecting on its surface. He also noticed the haze, which was increasing as he moved forward, and this worried him; the visibility inside the terminal could prove to be a problem and hamper his task.

After descending the full length of the air lock, he was ready to enter the shuttle terminal and start looking for the missing manager. Slowly he crossed the lip of the doorway and took his first look inside. Visibility was limited and patchy in places, but he estimated he could see around twenty-five metres, and that was far enough. Everything was covered with a brown sludge, dripping in places where the moisture hit the cooling metal. At least he was moving forward, allowing the SCAT to automatically home in on his target. It was slow. There were many obstacles, both ahead and overhead, and occasionally he brushed against something soft, slimy, and slightly hot.

Visibility had dropped to almost zero. He tried using the SCAT's main lights switched to dipped beam, but the light reflected back off the vapour, and a yellowish glare blinded him. He had to rely on parking lights to see where he was going, and that, coupled with the mist on his visor, often left him driving blind.

After thirty minutes, he'd moved almost half a kilometre into the dome; but, according to his instruments, he still had quite a way to go. He could feel the heat coming through his suit. Even though the temperature had dropped to a safe level, it was bordering on uncomfortable. And without his mask he wouldn't survive long; the information being relayed from the engineers indicated the air was highly toxic, and it troubled him.

'How long will the mask remain functional?' he asked his machine.

'Your air supply will last for two hours and fifteen minutes at your current rate of use,' the SCAT replied emotionlessly.

John spoke into his communicator. 'May, set a countdown alarm for forty-five minutes from now.'

'Alarm set,' May replied.

John wanted to make sure he had enough time to get out of there before his air ran out. Breathing the air around him didn't look a viable option; it would be like breathing under water. There was so much sulphur in the air, the moisture would contain an extreme amount of acid.

He continued at a slow pace for another hundred metres before the SCAT picked up speed.

'We have clear space for the next three hundred metres,' May informed him.

John looked at his instrument panel and noted the lost communicator signal was just over two hundred metres off to the right. The SCAT automatically changed direction and headed for it. As he got closer, John could feel the temperature increasing and it made him really uncomfortable.

He reached the point where the communicator signal was originating from and looked at the ground beneath him. He couldn't see anything on the muddy, steaming surface, so he decided to dismount. As he lowered himself slowly to the ground, he sank up to his knees in the thick, sticky sludge. It was hot; he could feel it through his trousers, and it was extremely uncomfortable. He felt something under his foot and reached down to see what it was. His arm began to sting with the heat almost immediately, and as he touched the object, he instantly realised it was bare bones. With extreme difficulty and a lot of pain, he felt around and eventually found the communicator. By now his skin was suffering with the heat, and his breathing had become more rapid. Taking a good grip on the communicator, he tried to pull it free, and was surprised how difficult it was to move. The stickiness of the slime was holding it firm. Then, without warning, it gave way and he fell backward into the hot slime. As the communicator broke the surface, he realised there were still bones attached to it, and dropped it instantly. The mask had been pulled from his face as he'd fallen backwards and he couldn't reach it. He was desperately holding his breath. He felt the heat stinging his body and struggled to get to his feet. But the sludge stuck like glue and he could hardly move.

His face started to burn as the acid attacked his skin, and he gritted his teeth in pain

'May, help. I can't get up,' he called out with his last breath.

John looked on as his SCAT started to move closer. He could only just see now and held up his hand to catch hold of the footrest. With all his remaining strength, he pulled as hard as he could, and slowly started to emerge from the glue-like mud. Soon he was standing next to the machine and tried to find the mask by pulling on the airline. To his dismay, the mask and line parted. He took the tube, put it in his mouth, and sucked; there was nothing. With increasing pain, he used the last of his energy, and mounted the SCAT as quickly as he could. Once he'd got his leg over the seat, he activated the life-support system, and settled down. Within a few seconds, he was drifting off into an induced sleep.

As soon as John entered the tube, Brian accessed the medical system and set it to monitor John's vital signs. He was also monitoring the environmental conditions John was passing through, and they disturbed him.

'It's getting hot in there,' Brian told Rose as he saw the temperature around John rising.

'Get him out if it gets too hot,' Rose told him.

Brian looked at John's vitals, then replied, 'He's coping well at the moment. But I'll keep an eye on him.'

'Pull him out if he won't come voluntarily,' she insisted.

Brian looked to see what could and couldn't be done. 'I can't pull him out if he doesn't want to come. He's the only one who can control his SCAT,' he told Rose.

Rose looked at him, and he could see she looked really annoyed. 'I'll ensure we have control, if it's needed,' she told him.

Brian kept watching John's vital signs, and after awhile noticed his body temperature slowly increasing, which gave him cause for concern. Every few minutes he reported John's condition to Rose, and now even she started to look concerned.

'How much more can he take?' she asked, sounding really worried.

Engineers were monitoring the information being sent back by John's SCAT. They could see the temperature increasing as he went further in, and were also concerned. Analysis of the air inside the terminal indicated it was highly toxic; it contained too much sulphur and was slowly turning to acid. They were also monitoring his air supply closely.

Brian noticed that John's breathing rate had increased sharply and was about to call to see what was happening.

Then he noticed a sharp increase in John's body temperature and shouted to Rose, 'Something's up. His temperature just increased rapidly.' Before Rose could say a word he added, 'His air supply has gone.'

Two minutes passed before the engineers gave Rose more information. 'His SCAT has activated life support. John has been sedated.'

Brian had already seen it and continued examining the medical information from the SCAT in minute detail.

He received a message from May. *'John's vital statistics are stable, though he suffered mild scalding to most of his body and some acid burns to the face. The SCAT is now refusing to take my orders. Please advise on course of action.'*

'His companion is asking for instructions,' Brian shouted.

Rose rushed over and looked at the information. 'Tell his companion to get the SCAT out of there as quickly as possible. How long do we have?'

'Life support is good for two hours maximum, but with the conditions inside there, it could be much less. We must get him out quickly,' Brian told her.

Rose immediately contacted security. 'Access John Blight's SCAT profile and force it to universal control instantly,' she demanded.

A few minutes passed, which seemed like hours, before she had a reply. 'Universal control activated. Anyone can control it now,' security told her quickly, sensing the urgency of the request.

Shortly after, Rose received a message from the engineers. 'The SCAT is backtracking, and making its way out. It should be here in forty-five minutes at the latest.'

'I'll call the hospital and get a life-support stretcher over here to meet it. That will give us another two hours, which should be more than enough,' Brian told Rose.

Rose placed her hand on his shoulder, and said quietly, 'Thanks, I don't want to lose anyone else in there.'

On the way out, May relayed as much information as possible back to the engineers. They could now see it was too hot to venture inside without a hazardous environment suit, and they started making plans.

At least John had left the communicator behind, so they could locate the missing terminal manager's body later.

The amount of sludge was worrying the engineers; it would take quite some time to clean up that mess. And the amount of sulphur was even more worrying. That amount could only mean one thing—the thermal energy plant had ruptured the fragile crust of the earth, and urgent investigation was needed to find out the extent of the rift. The heat inside the terminal indicated there could be a large crack, possibly located between the pod store and Water Dome Number Two, where the problem had started.

Pauline showed Juliette where the patients had been taken and left her to it. As she walked along the corridor, a nurse came running towards her. 'Dr. James has requested a life-support stretcher to be taken to the entrance of the shuttle terminal immediately.'

Pauline's face went white, and she looked back over her shoulder, wondering whether to let Juliette know. She knew John was going into the terminal and wondered if it was for him. She decided not to say anything, just in case it was, and followed the nurse to the emergency equipment room. After making sure the stretcher was fully equipped, Pauline and the nurse left with the stretcher tied securely to the back of a spitter. When they reached the main dome access port, they untied the stretcher and floated it through the air lock to the other end. Another spitter was waiting for them and soon they were racing across the dome towards the shuttle terminal entrance. In the distance Pauline could see Brian and Rose sitting on their SCATs and called on her communicator.

'We're approaching now,' she told Brian, and watched him turn and wave.

Brian jumped off his machine and waited for her to arrive. As she stepped off the spitter, he walked briskly over and hugged her. The look on his face made her realise it was John who was in trouble.

'It's John, isn't it?' she asked, hoping he'd say no.

Brian just nodded, and watched as her eyes filled with tears. He pulled her close and said quietly, 'He's going to be fine. His SCAT activated life support and he's stable. We expect him out in around ten minutes or so.'

'I'll stay and help if you don't mind,' she said.

'That's fine. Does Juliette know anything?'

'Not yet, I didn't say a word just in case it was him,' she said with a quiet, shaky voice.

Everyone there was silent. Brian went back to his machine to monitor John's progress, and as he sat on the seat, Pauline jumped on behind, and hugged him tightly.

Brian was watching the air lock entrance and noticed flashing lights coming from within. 'Get ready,' he shouted, and everyone's eyes focused on access port.

Slowly the flashing lights got brighter and eventually the SCAT flew out of the opening. All its lights were brilliantly lit and flashed rapidly green, white, and red. The colour green indicated a medical emergency.

Pauline jumped to the ground and made straight for the stretcher, while Brian shot forward to meet John's SCAT. As he arrived, he noticed the condition of John's body and frowned.

'What a mess,' Brian said.

The life-support unit had only one function, to maintain the brain. All other bodily functions had been suspended, and were no longer of any use. Only the heart functioned, just to supply the brain with vital oxygen, and that was controlled by the pulsing, jelly-like object covering John's upper body. Brian knew that only a complete regeneration would restore him to full health.

Pauline came alongside with the stretcher and after taking one look, turned and was immediately sick.

'You'll have to get used to seeing people like this,' he told her calmly.

Pauline turned around and took another look. 'He'll need cleaning before we can regenerate him, otherwise it will take ages.'

'You have been busy. That's advanced theory,' he said, looking surprised by her remark.

Pauline set to work transferring John's limp and messy body over to the stretcher, and soon the new life-support "jellyfish" was active.

'He only just made it out in time, judging by the condition of the old life-support gel,' Brian told Rose, as she approached them.

'Juliette's going to enjoy giving him physio when he's been regenerated,' Brian said with a little smile and put his arm around Pauline's shoulders.

'You can be so insensitive at times,' she said sharply.

Brian didn't like being scolded, and slapped her behind. 'Off you go. I'll see you at the hospital when you arrive,' he said quickly, rushed to his SCAT, and shot off at high speed.

Pauline went red in the face with anger. That slap hurt her. She looked at the nurse, who had seen it all, and said, 'Come on, let's go. Someone needs a kick where it hurts.'

The nurse tried to hide her smile, but failed miserably. When she noticed Pauline scowling back at her, she quickly turned away.

Rose looked at the mess on John's SCAT and decided it needed decontamination.

'Get that over to engineering for a clean. When it's finished, send it over to my apartment. I'll give it back to John when he's fully recovered,' she told her staff, then continued to scan the information presented to her. 'Close the air lock. It's no good going inside until conditions improve. We have less demanding work to carry out first.'

When she'd finished speaking, she sped off towards the control centre at high speed, leaving the engineering staff to finish off.

Brian arrived at the hospital and headed straight for the regeneration room. A nurse met him and asked what all the fuss was about. Rumours were spreading that John Blight had been killed.

'What! He's not dead, he's just injured,' Brian barked back at her.

He was loud and a few nurses poked their heads around the door to see what was happening.

'You lot! In here now,' he demanded.

They all entered with their heads slightly lowered, trying not to make eye contact with him.

'I don't want Juliette Harper to know anything about what has happened until after he's inside this unit,' he said, sounding really annoyed. Then he thumped a full-body regeneration unit. 'Now get on with your work.'

Brian started to make adjustments to the unit's control terminal, opened the cover in readiness, then sat next to a nurse and waited.

Pauline arrived ten minutes later and pushed the stretcher over to a cleansing cubicle on the other side of the room. First though, she had to cover her hands with a protective film before removing John's clothing. A nurse came to help, and soon they were cutting John's disintegrating clothing away, most of which had been attacked by the acid in the sludge.

After twenty minutes of careful cutting, all the clothing had been removed and Brian came to see the extent of his injuries.

'Poor fellow. He must have been in agony,' Brian said quietly.

He'd noticed that the tips of John's fingers had been eaten away, as were his lips, which puzzled him. 'May, what suit was he wearing in there?' he asked.

John's communicator was now on a table next to the stretcher, nicely cleaned and ready for him when his treatment was complete.

'A basic soiled-environment suit and standard full-face air supply mask,' May answered.

'Who allowed him in there with just that on? It was obvious conditions were bad inside. Even I could smell the sulphur as soon as the air lock opened. Who issued his suit?' he asked again.

'Chief Markham told him to wear a protective suit, but not which type,' May replied.

Brian boiled inside. She should've known better than to send him in with so little protection. 'I'll be having a word with her,' he said loudly enough for everyone to hear.

Pauline pushed the stretcher into the cleansing cubicle and switched it on. After ten minutes, the unit stopped working and she pulled him out. She pushed the stretcher alongside the regeneration cubicle and helped Brian move him into it.

Brian closed the lid and started the process immediately. Turning to Pauline, he calmly said, 'I'm off to tell Juliette now. Be ready when she arrives.'

Pauline looked really sad when he said that, and just nodded. Turning, she went to the regeneration unit and looked at the settings. She instantly noticed that Brian hadn't defined any parameters for his genitalia, leaving the machine to work it out naturally. A wicked look appeared on her face and she looked around to see if anyone was watching. They weren't, so she entered some parameters and smiled. The regeneration unit not only restored body parts, it could also alter the shape and size of any part, within reason.

'That should make her smile,' Pauline said quietly to herself, and moved away from the unit to sit down.

Before she could sit, Juliette ran into the room crying. Pauline spun round, and rushed across the room to meet her. She placed herself in front of the unit and Juliette ran straight at her. Pauline only just managed to hold her back, and nearly fell backwards with the force of the impact. Juliette was crying uncontrollably, and as Pauline threw her arms around her, she too started to cry.

Brian entered the room, saw them both sobbing, snapped his fingers, and indicated to the nurse to leave the room. He walked across the room, and putting his arms around both of them, said to Juliette, 'He'll be in there for the next twenty-seven hours. Then he's all yours. So don't worry, OK?' Then he left them alone.

Pauline, still crying, managed a broken laugh, 'He'll be as bald as you when you see him again.'

Juliette couldn't help herself, and laughed with her.

Then Pauline, taking her hand, led her to the cubicle and showed her the information on the monitor. 'Study that,' she told her quietly.

Juliette stood there silently, looking carefully at the statistics. She looked really puzzled and just stared at them for a moment. Then she looked down at her hands, made some calculated measurements on her fingers, and turned towards Pauline, who was smiling back at her.

'Who put *that* figure in?' Juliette asked, pointing at the monitor.

Pauline saw the look on Juliette's face, and lowering her eyes, said ashamedly, 'I did. I thought it would be OK.'

Juliette looked at her, and realising she hadn't meant any harm, smiled and said quietly in her ear, 'That's not right.'

Pauline didn't know what to say, she just went bright red and quickly walked towards the monitor. 'What figure do I put in?' she asked, sounding a little embarrassed.

As Juliette whispered in her ear, Pauline looked at her and said. 'Are you sure?'

Juliette nodded, and Pauline's mouth dropped open with shock. 'I hope you're right. I could be in trouble if you're not,' she whispered.

'Don't worry, it's correct. You can ask him when he comes to.'

Pauline looked a bit shocked, and said out loud, 'I'm not asking him.'

Juliette was about to say something, but Pauline put her finger to her mouth and said, 'That's enough. I'm under oath not to talk about my patient.' Then pulling Juliette away from the unit, they made for Brian's office.

Rose was mulling over more information on the condition of the dome casings when she received a message from engineering. John's SCAT had been decontaminated and was on its way over to her apartment. She smiled and requested information on John's treatment. Realising he would be unable to work for at least the next two days, she started to organise the work schedules herself. She called home and told her son, Otho, to take Anne, her daughter, out for the evening meal, as she was too busy and couldn't make it until much later.

Anne, being seven years old, couldn't go out by herself. Otho was fifteen and a responsible young man whom his mum trusted to look after his sister. Otho didn't like going to the chow house with his sister; she always moaned about the food, and he wondered who he could go with for company.

He called Juliette. 'Hi, can Anne and I join you for supper please? Mum's working late again.'

Juliette wondered if he knew anything, and hesitated for a minute. Then Otho added, 'We won't be any trouble, honest.'

She smiled to herself and said, 'I won't be going to supper just yet. Call Petal. Take her and Fred with you, if you want company.'

Otho's face beamed. 'Thanks, I'll call her straight away,' he said and cut off.

Otho called the chow house to arrange a table for four, and was told he could have one straight away. The only trouble was all the spitters were occupied for the next forty-five minutes.

He called Petal. 'Hi, do you want to join me and Anne for supper? My mum and Juliette are busy.'

Petal went pink in the cheeks, and replied shyly, 'Yes. I'll get ready straight away.'

Otho's face was a picture of happiness, and he added, 'I'll be over as soon as I can. See you!'

Turning around he shouted, 'Yippee!' Then he noticed Anne staring at him, with her hands on her hips.

'Fancy her do you?' she asked mockingly.

'Shut up and get ready. We're going to supper with her and Fred,' he retorted.

She smiled, spun around, and rushed up stairs.

'Woo! Who likes Fred then?' he shouted after her.

She turned on the stairs and gave him a really nasty look before disappearing out of sight.

Otho walked to the front door to see if there was any sign of the spitter he'd ordered, and to his surprise, a SCAT stopped close to where he was standing.

Thinking his mum had sent it for them to travel on, he mounted it. 'Can you take us to the canteen?' he asked.

To his amazement, it replied, *'I can take you anywhere you wish to go.'*

'Wow! Thanks Mum,' he said to himself. And he rushed back inside to tell Anne to hurry up.

When Anne went outside, she was amazed to see him sitting on the SCAT waiting for her. 'Are we allowed to use that?' she asked, sounding a little hesitant.

'Sure. Mum must have sent it over. We can go anywhere on it. I asked,' he replied confidently.

Anne climbed on behind and held him around his waist. 'Drive carefully; you haven't used one before,' she warned him.

The SCAT heard what she said and replied, *'I will activate novice mode to protect you from harm.'*

Anne smiled and said, 'Thank you.'

Otho just laughed. 'You don't thank a machine.' He told it to go to Petal's apartment. He knew this would impress her.

Petal was waiting for Otho to arrive, pacing back and forth near the front door. Fred noticed she'd put on her best new dress and wondered what the occasion was, after all, they were only going for supper. Then the door bell rang and she ran towards it.

'Come in a minute,' she said to Fred. Then she noticed Anne standing just behind him. 'You too, if you want,' she added, sounding disappointed at seeing her.

As she passed, Anne whispered, 'I bet you wish it was just you and Otho going to supper.'

Petal blushed slightly and replied, 'Don't be silly, he's just a boy. Fred's over there; go and talk to him for a minute.'

Then it was Anne's turn to look embarrassed, and she looked away from Petal as quickly as she could.

Petal walked over to Otho, and catching hold of his hand, said quietly, 'Follow me. I want to show you the present John gave me earlier today. It's amazing.'

She led him into the kitchen and when standing next to the worktop, reached for a laser pointer she'd placed there ready for this moment. After switching the kitchen lights off, she turned the laser on and pointed it at her ring. The started to shine extremely brightly, and the whole room and everything in it was bathed in the amazing multicoloured light.

Otho was dumbstruck, and his mouth opened wide in awe. Petal seemed to radiate in the light, which made her look extremely beautiful, and he smiled.

'Wow! It's amazing. You look fantastic,' he said, and moved really close to her.

Before she could say a word, Otho kissed her on the lips, and she was slightly shocked. Then he kissed her again, only this time for longer, and put his arms around her, holding her close.

She liked it, having never been kissed like that before, and made no attempt to stop him.

Suddenly Petal froze. She'd heard a giggle behind her, then noticed the kitchen light was back on. Quickly pushing Otho away, she turned around and saw Fred and Anne staring at them. The look on their faces said it all; they'd seen everything.

'Wait till I tell everyone about this,' Anne taunted them.

Petal put her ring in her dress pocket as quickly as she could and walked over to Anne. Catching hold of Anne's dress, Petal almost picked her up off the floor, and through clenched teeth, said, 'I wouldn't say anything if I were you.' Then Petal dropped her instantly with a slight push backwards.

Anne fell back slightly, looked at Otho then at Fred, and ran into the lounge. Fred followed closely behind her.

Petal turned to Otho, placed her arms around his neck, and gave him a kiss. 'We'll have to be careful when we're not alone,' she said quietly to him.

'We have to meet away from here if we can,' he replied.

He gave her one last kiss, then led her out of the kitchen.

When Otho and Petal came into the lounge, they saw Fred with his arms around Anne. She was crying on his shoulder.

'Come on, let's go to supper,' said Otho, and led them all outside.

Anne watched Petal's face as she saw the SCAT, and saw Otho mounting it. The look was one of utter excitement. Anne waited until Petal jumped on behind Otho, then indicated for Fred to go next. As soon as they were settled, she jumped on behind Fred, and put her arms around his waist.

Otho looked back and shouted, 'Here we go!' And the SCAT moved off really slowly.

Petal giggled, and said, 'So fast! It almost took my breath away.' She lay her head against his back.

Otho heard what she'd said, and felt really embarrassed. 'Why so slow?'

he asked the SCAT.

'Saying "thank you" is polite. Even if I am a machine,' it replied.

Otho was speechless, and sat quietly as the SCAT slowly picked up speed. They were heading towards the MATCH on John's SCAT without permission.

Rose contacted Rajinda Singh and asked, 'How's the upgrade of the isolation dome progressing?'

'Almost finished. It was easier than we anticipated,' he replied cheerfully.

'Have you received my list of work priorities?' she asked.

'Yes I have. I see we're sealing the shuttle terminal. How do we make contact with the outside if that's closed off?' he enquired.

'We'll have to use the main tube access port to try and restore communications. When the shuttle terminal cools down, we'll start repairs to that.'

'If it cools down!' he remarked. 'I'm formulating a plan to seal off the crack Simon found in the terminal casing, but I think that's just the tip of the iceberg. I think the crack goes right through the pod store.'

Rose was quiet for a moment, then asked, 'Why do you think that?'

'I've examined the information in Simon's communicator and SCAT to see what data they collected before the incident and everything indicates the incident started well before they entered the area.'

Rose listened to all he had to say and looked extremely worried. 'I hope the crack isn't too big to seal.'

'It must go deep, possibly right down to the magma flow, judging by the amount of sulphur in there,' he said, frowning deeply.

Rose didn't want to hear anymore, and told Rajinda she was going to the chow house for a meal. After cutting him off, she crossed to the balcony, jumped on her SCAT, and sped off.

A short time later, she arrived at the entrance to the MATCH, and as she walked across the foyer, she noticed another SCAT. Wondering who was there, she approached the machine and asked, 'Who's your driver?'

'Otho Markham,' the machine replied.

Rose realised instantly it was John's machine, and losing her temper, demanded, 'Don't allow anyone to drive you without my or John Blight's permission. Go back to my apartment now.' And as it left, she stormed into the canteen.

Otho saw his mum coming towards him at speed and looked worried. He knew she must have seen the SCAT parked outside, and now wondered if he was supposed to have used it.

Petal noticed the change in his attitude and asked, 'What's up?'

He pointed to his mum, and she noted the look on Rose's face. It didn't take her long to work out that Otho must have taken the SCAT without permission. 'Whose SCAT is it?' she asked him quietly.

'Don't know. It just arrived when we were due to leave,' he said, trying not to show he was scared of his mum.

Rose arrived at the table and shouted, 'What do you think you are doing? That machine out there isn't to be used for joyriding. Why did you take it?'

'I thought you sent it for us to use because there weren't any spitters available,' he said, but didn't sound convincing.

'Well you'll have to use a spitter to get home. I've sent it away, and instructed it to only allow John Blight and me to use it,' she shouted out.

Then she realised what she'd said, and quickly glanced at Petal to see if she'd noticed anything.

Petal was quiet for a moment, then a serious look spread across her face. 'Is that John's SCAT out there?' she enquired, puzzled by Rose's behaviour.

After no answer from Rose, she called John's communicator. There was no reply; even May wasn't talking to her.

'What's happened to John?' she shouted at Rose.

Rose saw everyone in the canteen turn to look at them, and moved close to Petal. 'I'm afraid he's had an accident. He's at the hospital having treatment.'

Petal started to cry. 'He's going to be all right, isn't he? Is that why Juliette couldn't be here?' she asked impatiently.

Rose nodded and replied, 'John's going to be fine. Let me have a bite to eat and I'll take you over to the hospital.'

'Let Otho use John's SCAT and he can take me right now,' Petal said, sounding annoyed that she couldn't go immediately.

Rose gave her a nasty look. 'I will not allow Otho to ride it again. You'll have to wait for me or take a spitter,' she insisted.

Petal just slumped down on her chair, and fell silent.

Fred went white when he heard about John, and as soon as Petal finished talking, asked, 'Is Juliette OK?'

'Yes she's fine. I think she's looking after him right now,' Rose said, though she didn't really know if that was true or not.

Rose began to eat her meal while Petal fidgeted and stared at her. She was really annoying Rose. 'If you're trying to make me rush my food, you've got another thing coming, young lady,' Rose said, sounding really angry. 'How old are you?'

'Thirteen,' replied Petal. She turned her back on Rose, folded her arms, and let out a huff. There was nothing she could do except wait.

Otho, Anne, and Fred were leaving, but before Otho went, he whispered in Petal's ear, 'See you later?'

Petal didn't say a word. She just smiled and nodded. Standing up, she gave him a big kiss on the lips. She made sure Rose saw that.

Rose was looking at Petal's back, and frowned. She didn't say a word, and just carried on eating. She'd wait until John was on his feet, and tell him about it then.

Juliette sat opposite Pauline and Brian and felt uncomfortable. 'I'd better go home and check on Fred and Petal. I haven't seen them since this morning,' she told Pauline, and rose to leave.

Brian checked his console and informed her no spitter was available for the next hour. He looked at Pauline and said, 'Do you mind if I take her home? I shouldn't be long.'

Pauline looked at him, then at Juliette and smiled. 'Yeh. Go on then,' she said, and gave Juliette a hug. 'See you later, OK. If you feel lonely, give me a call and I'll be over.'

Juliette smiled, squeezed her hand, and followed Brian out onto the balcony. She gave a quick wave, and they were gone.

Pauline left to check on Danni and Fu. At least they weren't any problem now. She skipped down the corridor smiling at everyone she passed.

As she looked at Danni laying there, all wrinkled and old, she couldn't help feeling a bit sorry for her. Her treatment had been rather harsh after all. Then she felt a tap on her shoulder, and spun around. It was Brian. She gave him a puzzled look and asked, 'What are you doing back? I thought you were taking Juliette home.'

'Come on, we're all going to have something to eat. It's been quite some time since we had anything,' he told her, and pulled her back to his office.

Juliette was sitting on the SCAT waiting for them to arrive when Fred called her. 'Hi, Rose told us about John, when are you coming home?' he asked sounding slightly distraught.

'John is going to be fine, so don't worry. I'm going to have something to eat and be home straight after that,' she told him, holding back her emotions.

'I've just had food with Petal, Otho and Anne and on my way home now. Don't be too long. See you soon,' He replied, and cut her off.

Pauline jumped on in front of her and Brian squeezed in between her and the machine's console. 'Good job I'm not fat,' he told Pauline as he felt her pressing against him.

She just put her arms around him and said, 'Let's go, I'm starving.'

'So am I,' Juliette said instantly, and off they went.

Rajinda Singh contacted Rose. 'The isolation dome is ready. Do you want to make it habitable?' he asked.

Rose was silent for a moment. 'I'll get back to you shortly on that subject,' she replied, sounding slightly doubtful, and cut him off.

She sat thinking about how much effort would be needed to relocate everyone to the dome. Not only that, it would have to be stocked with everything they'd need to survive on. The more she thought about it, the less she felt like moving. 'Would it be worth it?' she kept asking herself, over and over again.

She was going to take Petal to the hospital but changed her mind. 'I'll have to take you home,' she told her.

'But I want to be with Juliette,' Petal said, and sounded quite cross with her.

Rose enquired on the whereabouts of Juliette and was informed she was going for supper, and then home.

'Juliette will be home as soon as she's had something to eat,' Rose told Petal sternly.

Petal didn't answer; she just made a sour-looking face and pouted.

Not long after, Rose dropped Petal off at home, and judging by the look on Fred's face, he was glad of Petal's company.

'Bye. Give my regards to Juliette and tell her I'm sorry for what happened to John,' Rose said, and left quickly.

After half an hour, Rose had made her mind up about what to do with the isolation dome. She called Rajinda back. 'Hi. I've decided to make it fully habitable as soon as possible. Can you crack on with that?' she asked him.

He knew by the tone of her voice there was something else, but replied, 'Sure, I'll get my staff and the farmers on to it straight away. Is there anything else?' he asked after noticing the worried look on her face.

'We won't be moving in straight away. I want to make sure everything is running smoothly first. I only hope the dome casings can withstand another round of banging tonight,' she said, sounding rather glum.

'If the banging is caused by a meteor storm, we should be out of it soon. Surely it can't cover the whole of our orbit, can it?' he pointed out.

'You're right; it should pass. Only we don't know the extent of it yet,' she replied.

'OK. I'll get started straight away, and call you in the morning. You look absolutely dreadful,' he said sympathetically.

'Thanks.' She told him bluntly, 'You don't look a pretty picture either.' She cut him off.

She looked in a mirror and was shocked. She'd never looked as tired as she did right now, and her frown wasn't helping either. Entering the control room, she walked up to the senior engineer and said, 'I'm off home.

If you need me don't hesitate to call, OK? I'll be back at nine in the morning if all is quiet.'

'OK ma'am,' he replied, and watched her quickly disappear.

The next morning Juliette didn't know what to do. She hadn't slept well all night, even though the banging had reduced to just a few small bangs every hour. She woke Petal and Fred early, and told them to get ready for breakfast. Petal wasn't pleased at being woken up and shouted at her. That upset Juliette, and tears started welling up in her eyes.

Fred noticed, and had a word with Petal. 'Don't be such a cow. Can't you see she's missing your brother?'

Petal got up, got dressed, and went to find Juliette. She was sitting by the communications console and talking to a nurse at the hospital. As she reached Juliette, the screen went blank and Juliette's head dropped.

'Sorry. I didn't mean to upset you. Is John OK?' Petal asked quietly and gave Juliette a hug.

'Yes, John's fine. I'll make sure he's home by midnight tonight,' she told Petal.

'That quickly?' asked Petal, sounding a little anxious.

'Is that a problem?' Juliette asked, noting her expression. She sounded a little annoyed.

'No. No problem. It's just that I wasn't expecting him to have recovered so quickly, that's all,' Petal said unconvincingly.

Juliette just looked at her, and knew there was more than what she was saying. 'Has something happened?' she asked.

'No! Why do you ask that?' Petal barked back.

Juliette just shook her head in disbelief and said, 'Come on, let's go for breakfast. The spitter has arrived.' She'd have a word with John when he was up and about. Petal was definitely up to something.

Juliette's companion told her transport had arrived and was waiting outside. When she opened the door and walked out, she had quite a surprise. There were two SCATs parked near by.

The nearest one greeted her. *'Good morning Juliette. I am your personal SCAT. I am ready to take you anywhere you want to go.'*

Juliette went white. The thought of being on that machine by herself scared her to death. 'You've got to be joking,' she screamed, and ran back inside.

Petal heard everything and ran after her. 'I'll drive if you want,' she told Juliette with excitement.

Juliette just looked at her and nodded. 'OK, but you'd better drive slowly.'

Petal yelped with joy and ran outside. Juliette followed and jumped on behind her. Fred climbed on and put his arms around her. They waited but nothing happened.

'It won't go,' Petal said, as she tried to get it moving.

Juliette remembered that the machine only obeyed one driver, and said, 'SCAT, let Petal drive you slowly to the chow house please.'

Before Petal could drive off, the SCAT automatically took over, moving slowly, just like Juliette had asked.

'I've been made aware of your fear of open spaces and high speed. I'll drive in full automatic mode until you tell me otherwise,' the machine said loudly enough for them all to hear.

Petal laughed. 'You can go everywhere with your eyes shut,' she told Juliette, and laughed even more.

'That doesn't sound too bad,' she replied, and managed a thin smile. 'At least I don't have to wait for a spitter now.'

Petal looked extremely jealous and asked, 'Do you think I can borrow it now and again, please?'

'You've got to be joking; you're far too young,' Juliette replied abruptly.

Petal's face dropped instantly and she sighed with disappointment. Then she blurted out, 'Well, Otho was allowed to drive one.'

'What did you say?' Juliette said worriedly.

Petal went quiet, and hesitated before replying, 'Nothing.'

'I'll be having a word with Rose about your "nothing" young lady,' Juliette said sharply, indicating she wasn't amused, and ordered her SCAT not to let anyone drive without her permission.

On the way to the canteen, Juliette asked Petal, 'Have you shown your ring to Otho yet? I bet he'd love it.'

'Yes. I did it last night and he thought it was wonderful,' she replied and giggled.

Juliette didn't say a word. She was extremely worried and wondered if she should wait until John was better before speaking to Petal. She decided to wait. Petal had quite a temper when riled, and she couldn't cope with that at the moment.

It was a long night for Rose. Although the bangs were less frequent than the previous night, she couldn't help worrying about them. She did manage to get some sleep, but it was only snatches now and again, and not really as much as she needed. She was going back to work just as tired as when she got home, and wasn't looking forward to it one little bit. After having breakfast with Otho and Anne in the canteen, she headed straight for engineering to see Rajinda.

When she arrived, the place looked deserted, with just a skeleton crew busily working away like bees.

'Where is everyone?' she asked, sounding a bit surprised at the situation.

'Senior Engineer Singh is at home sleeping, like half of our staff are. The other half are carrying out repairs to Farming Dome Number Six,' the nearest engineer replied.

She was just about to say something when a labourer asked, 'How is John Blight? Is he going to be out of action for long?'

She didn't know, and looked at him rather blankly. 'Sorry. I'm still very tired. I didn't sleep much last night. Again! I'll check on his progress and get back to you,' she told him.

Walking over to a communications terminal in quiet corner, she contacted the hospital. 'Can I speak to Dr. James please? I can't seem to get him on his communicator.'

'I'm afraid Dr. James hasn't checked in yet. He said he might be in late this morning when he finished work yesterday. I can get hold of him if you really need to speak to him,' said the receptionist.

'If he's sleeping, don't bother,' Rose said, sounding a bit annoyed. 'Is Juliette Harper about?'

'Negative. She informed us that she was taking the children to breakfast before she comes in. She should be here soon though.'

'At least someone is up and thinking properly. Can you tell me how John Blight's treatment is progressing, and when he's likely to be on his feet again?' she enquired, but it sounded more like a demand than a request.

'Our information indicates he will be out of regeneration at nine this evening. Dr. Harper will be taking over for physiotherapy treatment after that.'

Rose looked startled. She thought, 'Dr. Harper? Who changed Juliette's status? I didn't.'

She ended the call, contacted security, and asked who authorised Juliette's status change. She was shocked when told it was she; she'd authorised it at the last full meeting and had forgotten all about it. Then she remembered what Brian had told her at the meeting, and smiled. 'I wonder if she knows yet?' Rose said to herself, and called Juliette.

Juliette answered the call, and asked very pleasantly, 'Good morning Chief Markham. What can I do for you? You look happy. Good news!'

'I just wanted to know if you've been re-graded yet?'

'No, I haven't heard anything. But I'm not worried; as long as I can treat John this evening, that's what's important to me.'

'How long will it be before he'll be on his feet again?' Rose asked politely.

Juliette thought for a moment. She wondered if Rose wanted to put him to work straight away. She replied, 'My treatment will take about four hours to complete. Then he'll have to rest for at least twenty-four hours.' That last bit was over exaggerated, and she hoped Rose wouldn't realise it and be angry with her.

'That's fine. Let me know when he's ready for work,' Rose replied pleasantly.

'Will do,' Juliette replied, smiling at the positive response.

OK. That's all for now, Doctor Harper. Can you call in at the control room to see me on your way to the hospital please?' Rose had emphasized the words 'Doctor Harper' just to make sure she'd heard it.

Juliette just managed to say, 'OK,' before Rose cut her off.

Rose left engineering with a beaming smile on her face, and made her way to the control centre. 'Time to start work,' she said quietly to herself and chuckled, wondering what Juliette was thinking at that moment.

Juliette was talking to Rose on her communicator, and Petal was listening to every word. When she'd finished talking, Juliette turned to Fred and said, 'I'll be off to work once I drop you back home. Rose wants me to call in and see her.'

Petal looked at her, and Juliette noticed the strange look on her face. 'What's up?' Juliette asked.

'Did you hear what she called you?' Petal asked, sounding a bit excited.

'No! What did she call me?' she asked with a little laughter in her voice. 'Something nice I hope.'

Petal started laughing at her, and turning to Fred, said, 'She doesn't listen to what people say, and her being a doctor and all.'

Suddenly Juliette realised exactly what Rose had said and smiled back at her. 'From waste technician to doctor in one jump. Not bad, eh! I thought I'd have to wait until my dad gets here before being promoted.'

As she mentioned her dad, the three of them went quiet, and the smiles disappeared from their faces. They carried on eating in complete silence.

'Come on, let's leave. I don't feel like eating any more,' Fred said quietly, and they got up and left for home.

As soon as Juliette dropped Petal and Fred back at the apartment, she sat alone on the SCAT and said nervously, 'Take me to the control centre, and do it very slowly please.'

The SCAT moved off as gently as it could, and Juliette sighed with relief. 'Do you have a name?' she asked the machine.

'Small Civilian Airborne Transporter Number 0008AAA,' it replied.

'That's no good. Can I call you Stan?' she asked, trying to keep her mind off the journey.

'That is not possible. I am not designed to interact at a personal level. I can only obey orders, offer limited advice, record information, and carry out programmed tasks,' it replied without any emotion.

Juliette carried on asking questions. It kept her mind occupied while the SCAT flew smoothly through the air. Her SCAT was brand new, having been in storage for the past month. It had been built only two months ago, and was one of twelve delivered from the Canadian Research Centre, which itself was deep under the Rocky Mountain Range in North America.

Then she heard the machine say something that pleased her greatly. *'We are approaching the control room balcony. Please make ready to dismount.'*

Rose was looking out of the window opening onto the balcony. She noticed a SCAT coming closer, and was puzzled; it appeared to have no driver. As it glided to a stop on the balcony, a head suddenly appeared, and she burst out laughing. It was Juliette; she had ducked down behind the console and was hidden from sight.

Juliette heard laughing and looked oddly at Rose. When she entered the room, Juliette asked, 'What's so funny?'

'You are my dear. I thought you didn't want the SCAT and sent it back empty. Then up popped your head. Sorry, I couldn't help laughing,' Rose said, still smiling.

'I'm petrified. I hate open spaces, and it flies so high. I hope that thing doesn't mind me asking so many questions, it keeps my mind off flying,' Juliette said, and shuddered at the thought of doing it again soon.

'Thanks for coming. I have something to say that can't wait,' Rose told her in a more serious tone of voice.

'Is it me?' Juliette said inquisitively, trying to get some indication of what she'd done wrong this time.

'No! It's not you, silly girl. It's a serious problem concerning John's sister, Petal,' Rose said, sounding a bit snooty.

'What has she done?' Juliette asked, making as if she knew nothing, but she did know something was up. Petal said something earlier that caught her attention, only she didn't know what exactly it was. But Otho had seen the ring glowing, and that troubled her.

'I think she has a crush on Otho, and it has to stop before it goes too far,' Rose told Juliette in a slightly unfriendly manner.

'They're only young; that's what all teenagers do. It won't come to anything,' Juliette said, trying to appease her.

'It's not on. Otho has a bright future and any distractions at this time could jeopardise his career prospects,' Rose replied, sounding a little angry at Juliette's response.

Juliette thought for a moment, then replied, 'Let's get them together later this afternoon and have a chat with them both. I'm sure they'll see sense.'

Rose glared at her. 'I don't think they should see each other again. Inform Petal to keep away from him. I'll be having a talk with Otho myself, later.'

She was almost shouting at Juliette and had frightened her. Rose saw the scared look on her face, and said, 'I'm sorry. I'm really tired and a bit jumpy. Though I meant what I said; they should no longer see each other, got it?'

Juliette just nodded and started to leave. Then she turned around and stared at Rose. 'I think you are going about this the wrong way. It may cause more problems if we do it your way. I'll wait until John is well, and ask his advice before I speak to Petal.'

Rose just looked at her, then smiled. 'Fine. I'll still be having a word with Otho though.'

Juliette looked at her for a moment and relaxed her stance. She smiled at Rose and said, 'Come over to the hospital with me. I can take away your tiredness. It will only take fifteen minutes or so.'

Rose looked at her, and wondered why Juliette would try to help her after the way she'd just treated her. 'Why?' she asked, sounding rather shocked.

'I'm a doctor, and you need my services. Besides, I don't hold grudges against anyone, no matter who or how bad they are. You're only doing what a concerned mother would do after all.'

Rose looked at her with an open mouth. Here was a young woman who had just given her a lecture in how to be a good human being, and Juliette wasn't even annoyed with her. 'You are quite remarkable, young lady. I'll go along with your idea but we'll wait until John can be present as well. OK?'

Juliette nodded and smiled. She knew that approach would work; she'd often used similar techniques on her mother to get what she wanted.

Rose watched as Juliette mounted her SCAT, lay flat on the seat with her eyes closed, and ordered it to take her very slowly to Brian's office balcony. Rose couldn't help laughing to herself as she mounted her own machine and sped after Juliette, catching up with her in seconds.

On arriving at the hospital, Juliette headed straight for the regeneration section and checked on John's condition. As soon as she was satisfied all was going to plan, she led Rose to the physiotherapy section. On the way they passed the room where Danni and Fu were undergoing treatment and Rose couldn't help entering to see them lying there helplessly.

'If I had my way, I'd turn Danni's life support off,' she told the nurse quietly, so Juliette couldn't hear what she'd said.

The nurse looked shocked and placed herself in front of the unit's controls to prevent her doing it.

'Don't worry, I'm not going to do it. She's been punished enough,' Rose said to the still-shocked nurse.

'Come on. Let's go,' Juliette prompted Rose, and headed up the corridor.

As Rose passed a door, it opened and Brian suddenly appeared. Just before he closed the door, she caught a glimpse of Pauline sitting half naked on the bed inside. Looking back at Brian, she smiled and enquired, 'Good night's sleep?'

Realising she'd seen Pauline, he smiled and replied, 'Very pleasant thank you. And yourself?'

'Juliette is about to sort that out for me right now. I'll speak to you later,' she told him and followed Juliette into a treatment room.

Brian looked a little puzzled by that remark, but hurried off to his office without questioning her.

Juliette was standing next to a couch with a large therapy unit at one end. 'Can you lie on this and place your head next to this unit please,' she requested.

Rose lay on the flat surface and watched as Juliette placed the unit over her head. 'Close your eyes and relax,' Rose heard Juliette say, then felt a sting in her arm.

Juliette had given her a sedative just to make sure any side effects wouldn't cause problems. She sat next to the unit and set it for the revitalisation program. Within a few minutes it was glowing and performing its required task. Now she only had to wait for it to finish, give Rose the sedative antidote, help her to her feet, and it would be over with.

While she was waiting, she went to have a chat with Pauline. She hurried down the corridor, opened the door to the soundproof room, and entered.

Pauline was still in bed with her back to Juliette, and said, 'Back for more, you randy beast?'

'No thanks, I'm a one man girl,' Juliette replied.

Pauline jumped up, grabbed her dressing gown, and said, 'Oops! I thought you were Brian.'

'That's obvious. Anyway, I have a problem.'

Pauline started getting dressed and asked, 'What's up?'

'Petal made the ring glow for Otho Markham, Rose's son, last night. I don't know what happened yet, but something did.'

'Oops! Maybe we should have had a word with her about the ring. You'll have to find out, just in case it's serious.'

'It's serious. Rose is furious. She thinks that Otho and Petal are an item, and isn't at all happy,' Juliette said, sounding extremely worried.

'If she showed him the ring when it was glowing they are probably an item. And it's going to be difficult to keep them apart,' Pauline said, and a smile spread across her face.

'What's so funny?' Juliette enquired quietly.

'Wait till John finds out. Brothers are usually very protective towards little sisters. He'll probably go nuts when he finds out.'

Juliette went quiet for a minute then replied, 'It's Rose's fault. She gave John the ring to give to Petal. I just hope they didn't go too far.'

Pauline's face turned from a smile to a shocked expression. 'She's underage. I'm sure Otho wouldn't do anything stupid, after all he is fifteen and well educated.'

'I don't think they went that far, but she hasn't had a boyfriend before, and he's not bad looking.'

Once again, Pauline smiled. 'Fancy him do you?'

Juliette looked shocked by that remark and, picking up a pillow, hit

Pauline on the head. Pauline grabbed another one and hit back. The fight that followed left the room in a real state. The pillows had broken open and the filling was everywhere. When they stopped, they looked around and laughed uncontrollably.

Pauline stopped laughing and said, 'Brian will have a fit if he sees the place in this state.' Then she jovially added, 'As your senior, I order you to clean it up.'

'No, Dental Technician Pauline Mitchell. I, Doctor Juliette Harper, order you to clean it up.'

Pauline screamed, 'You've been promoted?'

'Yep! Found out this morning from Rose. It's official.'

Pauline hugged Juliette and kissed her cheek. 'Well done. Come on, let's go shopping to celebrate and take your mind off John for awhile.'

'Sounds good to me. I just have to finish with my patient, then we can go.'

Pauline looked puzzled, 'What patient? We treated everyone yesterday.'

'I'm treating Rose. She's tired, and I'm perking her up,' Juliette replied, and started to leave.

'What about this mess?' Pauline asked.

'Ask the auto cleaners to do it,' Juliette said, and closed the door behind her.

She walked into the treatment room and noticed the unit had finished. Taking an injector, she gave Rose the antidote and removed the cover from her head. Within a minute Rose was wide-awake and smiling. Juliette helped her to her feet and asked how she was.

'I can't remember when I felt this good last. All my tiredness has disappeared. Thank you. I'll speak to you later about you-know-what. I'll have to be going now.'

'OK. I'll let John know as soon as possible so we can arrange a meeting,' Juliette just managed to say before Rose disappeared out the room.

Shortly after, Pauline came into the room looking like someone had mauled her. 'You could have warned me about the auto cleaners. I was in the cleansing cubicle when one burst in. It started scrubbing me and I didn't know how to stop it. My bum is red and raw.'

Juliette had to sit down quickly; she was laughing so much her legs had gone weak. 'Look at the state of you. You look like you've been dragged through a thorn bush.'

Pauline looked in the mirror and started to laugh with her. Taking the wig off, she threw it across the room and looked back at the mirror. 'There, much better. I look as bald as you now,' she said, and started to giggle.

Juliette took Pauline to Brian's office and walked in on him at work. 'We're off to the shops,' Juliette told him.

Pauline gave him a kiss and asked, 'Can you take us to the shops please?'

'Its all right, I have my own transport,' Juliette told them, and walked out onto the balcony.

Pauline looked really surprised and followed her out. 'How did you get one of them?' she asked, sounding jealous.

'Don't know. It just turned up this morning. Must go with the job I suppose,' she said, shrugging her shoulders.

Brian came out, took one look at her machine, and exclaimed, 'Someone likes you. I couldn't get one for Pauline.' And with that he grabbed her, pulled her close, and as he gave her a kiss, squeezed her buttocks.

Juliette heard a loud moan and spun round. She saw Brian doubled up and the look on his reddened face suggested he was in great pain.

'That'll teach you for slapping my butt earlier,' Pauline said, as she caressed her backside.

Juliette smirked, caught her by the arm, and pulled her away from Brian. 'Leave him alone you bully.'

Pauline jumped onto the back of the SCAT, and tapped the seat in front of her. 'Get on. We're wasting time. Oh, and Brian. Make sure that's repaired before I get back, I may need it,' she sniggered.

Juliette's cheeks turned pink when Pauline said that. Juliette pushed her forward on the seat, and climbed on behind. 'You go in front. I still don't like flying. I'll hold on to you, OK?'

Pauline thought she would be allowed to drive it, and opened up the throttle. Instead, the SCAT gently lifted off and moved slowly forward.

'Can't this thing go any faster?' she asked.

'This is fast enough. We haven't got far to go, so don't ask to go any faster,' Juliette told her and shivered.

But when they arrived at the shops, they were all closed.

'Why are the shops closed?' Pauline asked Charles, her companion. Like Juliette, she never asked it for help, and treated it as something to be used.

'There is a holiday today. The staff are recovering from the sleepless nights they've had over the past few days,' it replied with an arrogant-sounding voice.

Juliette listened to it talking and couldn't help remarking, 'I couldn't put up with the attitude of that companion of yours. It's awful.'

'I know, but it stops people criticising me for not using it more often.'

Juliette smiled at that remark. 'I know. I'm the same. Though mine doesn't sound that bad.'

'What are we going to do now?' asked Pauline, sounding really dejected.

'Come on. Let's go to my place for a drink and see what's happening elsewhere. There has to be something going on somewhere,' Juliette told her.

When Juliette arrived home, she walked in and saw Fred and Anne sitting on the sofa watching some ancient movies. 'Where's Petal?' she asked.

Fred turned around and said, 'Hi, she's upstairs.'

Juliette looked up the stairs and noticed a bright glow coming from Petal's bedroom. 'Oh no!' she shouted, and ran up the stairs as fast as she could.

Rushing into Petal's bedroom, she noticed Petal was lying on the bed and her ring was glowing brightly. Juliette quickly looked around the room and shouted, 'Where is he?'

Petal hid the ring under her pillow and looked at Juliette strangely, 'Where's who?'

'Otho. I know he's here somewhere.' And Juliette started opening all the cupboard doors.

Petal didn't say anything and just watched her look everywhere. When she'd finished, Petal asked, 'Satisfied?'

Juliette stormed out of the bedroom and headed downstairs. 'I'm going to tell John to take that ring off her when he comes home. I don't trust her with it,' she told Pauline.

Anne heard Juliette and said, 'Otho just left. Mum called, and wanted to see him immediately.'

Juliette looked back upstairs and wondered how long they'd been together before he left. 'I'm going to have a word with her now,' she said to Pauline, and went back up.

She entered Petal's room and crossed to the bed. Petal sat up and waited for her to speak. 'I hope you and Otho aren't getting up to naughty things together. His mum doesn't want you to see him anymore. She thinks you will distract him from his studies.'

Petal's face went bright red. 'We only kissed. I wouldn't go any further. That's for my partner when I'm older,' she said, sounding really embarrassed.

Now Juliette blushed, and said, 'Good girl. Don't trust the ring. It will make any boy fall for you, even if they don't usually like you. It's dangerous. Keep it to yourself until you find the right man.'

Petal looked annoyed and replied, 'I'm too young for a man.'

Juliette laughed. 'I didn't mean now, I meant when you get older. You silly girl,' She said and hugged Petal.

As they both laughed, Pauline came into the room and looked puzzled, 'What's so funny?'

Petal replied, 'Just a little misunderstanding concerning men.'

'Ah! Men. Who needs them?' Pauline asked, sounding comical.

All three said in unison, 'We do.' And their laughter brought Anne and Fred up to see what was going on.

When they entered the room, all three were showing off their gems and Juliette was pointing a laser at hers. The light was blinding as all three gems started to glow brightly, forcing Anne and Fred to leave quickly.

To the three girls the light suddenly went out and they were plunged into total darkness.

'I'm blind,' screamed Petal, and started to cry.

Juliette was also blind, and felt around for her. As she pulled Petal close, she heard Pauline say with a very shaky voice, 'So am I.'

'Mister, I need help. Can you contact Brian James and tell him we've all gone blind and we need help, please?' Juliette asked, and even her voice was shaking.

A short time passed before Juliette's communicator chirped, indicating an incoming call. It was Brian.

'Juliette, what have you been up to?' he asked.

'We shone a laser at all three gems and the light was so bright we've all gone blind. Can you help please?'

'Exactly who's gone blind?' he enquired sympathetically.

'Me, Pauline, and John's sister, Petal,' she said quietly, and sounded really embarrassed about the situation she'd placed herself in.

They all heard Brian laughing, and Pauline, sounding a little annoyed with him, shouted, 'It's not funny. Are you going to help us or not?'

'No, I'm not going to help you. Your eyesight will recover within the hour, and until it does, keep out of brightly lit areas or it will take longer. And make sure the gems are put away until they dim,' he replied, still laughing as he spoke. 'Oh! And don't laser the gems when they're all exposed ever again, OK?' And with that, he cut them off.

Juliette suggested they all lay back and relax. Soon they were chatting about the experience they had when they first used the gems and giggled. Little did they know that Anne and Fred had sneaked into the room and were standing at the end of the bed.

Only when Juliette heard an almost-silent snigger did they stop chatting. 'Who's there?' she asked quickly.

There was no reply, just the sound of feet running across the floor and the door slamming shut. Juliette was fuming.

Rose was monitoring the progress of her engineers repairing Farming Dome Six. They were carrying out the repairs required, but were making poor use of the labourers. She was desperate to have John up and about again, and had only just realised how good he was at his job. She was amused to see labourers organising the engineers into work groups, while the labourers stood back and laughed at them when they screwed up, which was often. She'd been reading information on how engineers used to work many years ago, and was surprised to see they didn't only use computers, they also knew how to organise staff as well. She decided to try and overhaul the training of engineers to include management, and address the labour situation. She called to see if Rajinda had arrived in engineering and was put through to him.

'Rajinda. Hi. See what you can do to sort the workforce out. The labourers are running circles around the engineers out there.'

'I'll pop over and see how things are progressing. I'm not happy with the progress made so far. I'll get back to you,' he said, and cut her off.

Rose looked worried. Time was passing slowly at the moment, but she knew it would be different on the outside. She read the analysis report from when the tube access port was opened once again, and that, coupled with all the other information, seemed to paint a very gloomy picture. She called security and asked if the southern observation platform was safe to enter. After being told it was safe and being granted permission to enter if she wanted to go there, she decided to she would go immediately.

She called Rajinda back. 'Hi, I'm going to take a look outside before it gets dark. I'll be at the southern observation platform if I'm needed.'

'OK. Let me know what you see, if anything,' he replied.

Rose was wondering what he'd meant when he'd said 'if anything', but cut him off without questioning why he'd said it. She mounted her SCAT and headed to the main dome. Once inside, she took off at as steep an angle as she could manage and was soon at the observation platform entrance, popping her ears as she dismounted.

Crossing to the access panel, she placed her hand on the screen and was welcomed. *'Welcome to the southern observation platform, Chief Markham. Have a nice stay.'*

'I'll have to get that greeting changed; it's so annoying,' she said to herself as the access door opened with a whoosh.

Inside was dark. She asked for the lights to remain off as she entered and walked towards the outer wall. The only light in the room was coming through the open door and her eyes soon adjusted.

'Clear wall,' she demanded, and braced herself for the glow of daylight from outside. Nothing happened.

'Clear wall,' she demanded once again, and was shocked when an announcement stated, *'Wall is clear.'*

'Close the doors,' she said quietly, shocked at seeing nothing outside.

As the doors shut, she stood motionless, allowing her eyes to adjust to the darkness. Slowly she began to see beyond the wall, and what she saw frightened her. Looking around, she noticed how poor visibility was, but now and again it cleared, just enough to make out the outer casings of some domes. Without warning, an object smashed against the clear wall and she jumped backwards. There was only a small thud, but the object was massive and travelled so fast, it shattered against the casing. Rose was shaking from head to toe and wondering what it was when another object hit the wall. This time there was a slight clang, indicating it was metal, and again she jumped.

'Solid wall and lights on now,' she said with a shaky voice.

As the lights came on, she stood still while her eyes adjusted, then pulled herself together and made for the doorway.

'Open the door,' she demanded, and walked out onto the platform. As she mounted her SCAT, she contacted security once more. As they answered, she said, 'All observation platforms are off limits to everyone, unless they have my permission.'

The security centre noted her request and informed her all door access panels had been locked.

Not long after she was heading towards Farming Dome Six, where the engineering staff were working.

As she approached the dome entrance, she was greeted by Rajinda, who was puzzled to see her. 'Hi, I wasn't expecting you to come personally,' he said calmly. Then he noticed how pale she was and asked, 'Are you OK? You look like you've seen a ghost. What's up?'

'I've just come from the observation platform,' she said, pointing upwards. 'The mountains have gone. The domes are fully exposed, and being hit almost constantly,' she replied, still shaking.

'I think we'd better make plans to find out what exactly has happened out there, sooner rather than later.'

'I agree; the sooner the better. It doesn't bode well for those on the outside. They are more exposed than us,' she said quietly, so nobody else could hear her.

'I'll connect to the communications conduit in the tube through the access port and see if we can contact anyone on the outside,' he told her, though he wasn't hopeful that it would work.

'Good idea. Keep me informed of the situation. I'm off home to see if my children are OK,' Rose said, while turning her SCAT around, then left.

Rajinda also left. He was going back to engineering to get things organised over there. Opening the tube access port wasn't something he wanted to do, but it had to be done.

He called Rose. 'I'll make sure my engineers have better protection when they enter this time,' he told her.

'If you need to use another SCAT to complete the task, that's OK. But try not to lose it this time. We don't have that many,' she replied, then cut him off.

Petal was the first to start seeing again. At first it was just shadows, then shapes. 'My sight is returning,' she said excitedly.

'Thank goodness for that. I was worried for a moment. Brian said we'd only be blind for an hour and it's well over that now. Wait till I see him next,' said Pauline, and sounded rather cross.

Juliette checked the time with her companion. Although it had seemed like hours, it was nowhere near that long. 'I'm afraid it's only been forty-five minutes since we went blind. So it won't be long now; even I am starting to see something.' She managed a little laugh.

'I'm hungry,' Petal said, as they all heard her stomach rumble.

'We'll go for lunch as soon as we can see properly,' Pauline told her, and sighed. 'What are we going to do to keep ourselves occupied this afternoon?'

Petal spoke next, and what she said started them thinking. 'Why don't you volunteer to help with the refugees? They are asking for people to come forward.'

After a short period of silence, Juliette piped up. 'Good idea. We'll pop over to the relocation centre after we've eaten and see what we can do to help.'

'Can I come too?' asked Petal, sounding a little excited.

'No you can't,' Juliette rebuked. 'You will be going to school tomorrow if it's open.'

'That's not fair. I don't feel like going to school,' Petal said, sounding really dejected.

Well, you're going whether you like it or not, and I know John will agree with me on that.'

Petal let out another huff and sat quietly at the end of the bed.

Rajinda had been busy in the engineering dome and everything was in place, ready to open the tube access port. He'd brought deep-sea diving suites out of the archive store for the engineers to wear, and was checking them over. A SCAT had been fitted with a connector, and was trailing a flexible communication conduit ready to enter the port. At the front, a probe attached to a long pole would indicate if it was safe for the SCAT to go all the way in for the connection to be made. Now the only thing he needed was the go ahead from Rose, and then he would proceed.

'Rose. I'm ready to enter the tube. Do you want to be here when we go in?'

'I'm on my way over right now. I need something to take my mind off what I saw on the outside of the centre,' she told him. After cutting him off she rushed to the balcony and left.

When she arrived at engineering, she made her way over to Rajinda, who was next to the access port. 'How long will it take?' she asked, looking at the time.

'Not more than an hour, if all goes as planned,' he told her confidently.

'OK. Let's go for it,' she replied, but sounded a little cautious.

She watched as the engineers donned their cumbersome suits and stood waiting next to the port. They were wavering under the weight, as the suits weren't meant to be used on land. The clear shield was rolled into place, and secured around them and the access door. Just before it was sealed, all communications were checked and the OK given. Once sealed inside, the engineers started to unlock the access door and were soon ready to open it. With the pressure taken off the port seal, dirty water started to seep through into the enclosure, and the pressure slowly began to increase.

'Let the pressure equalise before you open the door,' shouted Rajinda. But it was too late. The door was opened. It flew around on its hinges and slammed against the dome wall. One engineer was in the way, but luckily for him, it only gave him a glancing blow. The force threw him backwards and he tumbled, over and over again, until he hit the clear shield. Everyone was shocked, and stared horrified at him for a moment, then felt relief as he sat up and put his arm in the air, indicating he was fine. His communicator had been smashed and wasn't functioning anymore, so the senior engineer inside pushed him back against the shield, and indicated for him to stay put.

The visibility inside the shield quickly changed and was just like before, zero. Rose heard an engineer tell everyone to brace themselves as the air inside tossed them about.

'The SCAT's entered the port and is moving slowly forward. We'll know shortly if it can enter the tube,' Rajinda told Rose, who looked extremely anxious.

It seemed like hours before the SCAT started sending back information on the conditions inside the tube, and it didn't look good.

'The wind in the tube is not as high as it was last time. It's down to 350 kilometres. The SCAT can just about handle that. Do you want to risk it?' Rajinda asked.

Rose was silent for a moment, deep in thought. She really did want to try and contact the outside world, but was there anything out there? She then replied, 'Send it in, but be prepared to pull it out if things don't go smoothly.'

Rajinda ordered the SCAT to enter and sat back. There was nothing they could do except wait. Ten minutes passed without incident, and as time passed, the stress they all felt started to diminish. 'How long will this take?' Rose asked Rajinda, worried about the lack of news.

'Shouldn't be too long. The communications conduit may take awhile to find and then the SCAT has to connect the flexible conduit to it. Don't worry, at least the SCAT is still fine.'

With the last word came the report they were waiting for. The connection had been made and the conduit had been energised and made ready for use. Rajinda looked at the information and frowned. 'It's drawing a terrific amount of energy. There must be a short circuit somewhere along the line. I'll get the SCAT to disconnect the conduit through to Coqen Junction in China and see if that cures the problem.'

Rose waited for him to program the machine and watched his face closely. He was still frowning when he sat back and stared at his monitor. 'That didn't do the trick. I'll reconnect that route and disconnect the Jumla Junction end.'

Again Rose watched as he carried out the operation, only this time his frown disappeared and he shouted, 'Presto! We have a link. Now to get the access port resealed and see whom we can talk to out there.'

Rose and Rajinda left the engineers to finish off clearing away the mess left after the access port had been resealed and headed back to the engineering control centre. When they arrived, Rose made straight the nearest communications terminal, and started to search for activity on the system. The strength of the signal was fluctuating and difficult to make sense of. After removing the noise from the data, they read what was being transmitted. It was a damage report from a tube air lock, just thirty kilometres from the centre. The air lock was unable to close due to damage, and the tube beyond it had ruptured. The conduit was dead beyond the air lock, which meant there were no communications in either direction.

Rajinda looked at Rose. He didn't need to say anything; her expression of utter disappointment said it all.

'How are we going to find out what's happened out there if we can't talk to anyone? There must be a way,' Rose said, and turned to leave.

Brian was getting ready to leave for lunch when he received a call from Pauline. 'Hi, how are your eyes. Can you see yet?' he asked before she had time to say anything.

'Yes. They're back to normal. Do you want to join us for lunch? We're starving and ready to go,' she replied.

'You won't kick me again will you?' he asked jovially, which made them both laugh. 'I was just about to leave myself, so I'll see you at the chow house soon,' he said, and cutting her off, quickly left the building.

When he arrived at the chow house, he noticed Juliette's SCAT parked near the entrance and looked inside to see where they were seated. But they had only just arrived and were looking out for him. Pauline sneaked up behind him and placed her hands over his eyes. 'Guess who?' she asked, and giggled as he turned and gave her a hug.

'Hi. Got a table yet?'

'Yep! We're over there somewhere. We'll be shown where in a moment when a waitress is available,' she told him quietly, while pointing to a windowed area deep inside.

When they were all sitting at the table waiting for their food to arrive, Brian dropped a bombshell. 'I'll have to check each of your eyes for damage. Regeneration may be required to ensure you don't go blind suddenly in the near future.'

Petal went white. 'I don't want to go bald,' she said, and started to cry.

As Juliette put her arm around her shoulder, Brian put Petal's mind at ease. 'It won't require that level of regeneration. Your eyebrows may thin slightly, but that's all. And it will take less than an hour to complete. So don't worry.'

Petal smiled and gave a little laugh. 'You had me worried for a minute. Well, let's get stuck in. I'm starving.' Lunch had arrived.

Rose went home to pick up Otho and Anne for lunch and was surprised to find Anne wasn't at home. After asking where she was, Rose was told she'd gone to lunch with Juliette and Fred. She decided to wait until they'd left the chow house before going herself, as she was also informed that Petal was there too.

She sat in front of the communications console and asked for a list of items held in the archive domes. Slowly she worked her way through the information, looking for anything that could be used to find out what was happening on the outside. It was taking time to read about each item so she asked for help from her companion, Pedro.

'Pedro, find me any item on this list that can be used to get information on what's happening on the outside, please,' she requested, sounding dejected.

Five minutes passed before Pedro came back to her. *'There is only one item that is capable of gathering information: a low-orbit mapping rocket. Here is the information on it.'*

Presented in front of her was a picture of a small rocket, almost three metres in length. As she read all about it, she started to smile. It could be programmed to do many different tasks and record enough information to give a reasonably good picture of what was going on outside. It could also communicate via simple pre-programmed messages, and receive data and voice messages. The only drawback was that after launch, it needed to be recovered if it was to be reused. It could orbit the whole planet twice, covering every square centimetre of the surface, and download the information as it passed overhead.

Rose was smiling once more. 'That'll do nicely,' she remarked and called Otho over. 'Come on, it's time for lunch,' she said, and they left.

On her way to the MATCH, she called security and asked them organise a staff meeting for Monday morning in the isolation dome.

Juliette was in the apartment watching a movie with Petal and Fred when her companion reminded her about John. 'I've got to go,' she shouted to Petal. 'John will be out of regeneration in an hour. I want to be there when he comes to.'

Petal looked excited and said, 'Can I come too, please?'

Juliette shook her head. 'Sorry. You'll have to wait until I bring him home later if you want to see him.'

'Don't mind if I stay up do you?' she asked hopefully.

'You can keep Fred company, OK?' Juliette said as she walked towards the door.

Soon she was flying through the air, as flat as a pancake on the seat, and talking incessantly. It wasn't until the SCAT landed on Brian's balcony that she sat up again. Jumping off, she walked in and found the place almost deserted. As she wandering down the corridor she bumped into a nurse coming out of the room where John was being treated. 'Where is everyone?' she asked, looking around the room.

'Dr. James is in the soundproof room with his partner,' the nurse replied as she walked away.

Juliette turned around and made her way up the corridor to where Brian and Pauline were, and when she arrived, opened the door slightly. 'Brian,' she called quietly.

'Is that you Juliette?' she heard Pauline say sleepily.

'Yes. Is Brian with you?'

Juliette heard what sounded like a slap, followed by, 'Hey! What was that for?' It was Brian; Pauline had woken him up with a slap.

'Juliette has arrived to get things ready for John,' Pauline told him, as she realised what time it was.

'You can deal with it if you want,' he said sleepily.

'I'll be out in a few minutes. You go to the physiotherapy section and I'll bring him to you when he's ready,' Pauline said quietly round the edge of the door.

'OK. But don't wake him up. I'd like to do that. I'll just pop into the physiotherapy section and make sure a unit is ready for him. Bring him to me as soon as the treatment is complete,' Juliette told her, then hurried away.

Pauline finished dressing and entered the cleansing cubicle. After a few minutes, she emerged fully awake and ready for work. Leaving Brian sleeping, she quietly closed the door behind her as she left and walked towards the treatment room. When she entered, there was nobody about and she made her way to the regeneration unit's control panel to see how long was left.

'Just ten minutes to go,' she said to herself, smiling. She sat down to wait.

Juliette was setting the controls on a full-body unit in a physiotherapy treatment room, smiling as she entered the data. She was reading the instruction manual but relying on the automatic settings to do most of the work. The only adjustment she made was to the section that related to the build of the person. She bit her lip as she entered that information. It was tricky, and setting the figures too high or too low could totally change the appearance of the patient. After checking the figures over and over again, she was eventually satisfied, and sat down to wait for Pauline to bring John to her. She couldn't help fidgeting, and rubbed her hands together to try and stop them from shaking too much.

Pauline wasn't watching the unit, she was chatting with a nurse who had come back into the room. A buzzer sounded and she turned to look where it was coming from. She instantly realised it was coming from the regeneration unit and crossed to see if it had finished. It had. She pressed the release button, and stood back as the lid opened wide. She watched as John slowly appeared naked in front of her, and stood gaping at him.

The nurse took one look at her, frowned, and reached for a folded sheet. Flicking it open, she quickly covered his body and said, 'There's no need to stare at him.'

Pauline turned a bright shade of pink, and replied with a slight stutter, 'I'll take him to the therapy section.'

'I'll help you,' the nurse said, sounding a bit annoyed at the way Pauline had acted.

'I was shocked,' Pauline quickly added. 'He was so muscular the last time I saw him, and just now he looked like someone else, totally different.'

With that the nurse's face changed to one of concern. 'You obviously haven't seen a full-body regeneration before, have you?'

'No this is my first,' Pauline said, still sounding a bit shaky.

As they entered the room where Juliette was waiting, Pauline quickly crossed to stop her from looking at him. 'I think you should complete the physiotherapy before you look at him. He doesn't look the same without muscles and hair,' she said quietly.

She looked across to the nurse and she nodded in agreement. Juliette looked back at Pauline and smiled. 'Had a good look did you?'

Pauline went bright red once again and lowering her eyes, said, 'He had to be removed from the unit, so it was impossible not to.'

'Ah well. I'm not worried. He's all mine and will soon be up and about.'

'When will he be ready?' Pauline asked, sounding a little surprised by her attitude.

'It will take about four hours. Then it's off home to rest for the next twenty-four hours. For both of us,' Juliette said, sounding confident.

'That quickly! Wow, you lucky thing. I'll leave you to it. et Brian know when he wakes up. If you need any help you know where we are, OK?'

'Fine, but I'll be OK. It's going to seem like a long wait though.'

Pauline was about to leave when she spun round and said, 'I'll keep you company. The time should pass more quickly if we're chatting.'

'Is that all you want? You don't want to see him naked again do you?' Juliette asked, and as Pauline's face turned red again, she laughed and said, 'Only kidding.'

Pauline laughed with her, but the nurse gave them a nasty look and left the room.

Brian couldn't sleep, so he got dressed and went in search of Pauline. When he found her chatting away with Juliette, he smiled. 'I was wondering where you were. I should have known you'd be here.' Then looking at Juliette, he asked, 'How are things going?'

Juliette stood up, crossed to the unit, and checked. 'Only five minutes left,' she said, sounding really excited.

Pauline walked over to Brian, caught hold of his arm, and turned to leave. 'We'll leave you to it,' she said, sounding a bit wicked.

Juliette just stared at her for a moment, then poked her tongue out. 'See you tomorrow. Have a nice night.'

'You too,' said Pauline, making a rude gesture with her fingers behind her back so Brian couldn't see it.

'I intend to,' said Juliette, sounding just like a child about to get a new toy.

It was time. The alarm sounded, indicating the process had finished. Nervously Juliette lifted the cover off the unit. The sight shocked her for a moment. There was John, looking just the same as he did before the accident, only totally different as well. He was completely bald, with not a hair anywhere on his body. His tan had disappeared and his skin looked so smooth, she couldn't help running her fingers over him. There was no reaction from him whatsoever, so she picked up the injector and gave him the sedative antidote.

She continued to stroke him and watched as his eyes started to open and goose bumps appeared on this stomach and arms.

His head turned towards her and he spoke. 'That really tickles.'

She hadn't noticed him move; her eyes were a little lower down, and the sound of his voice startled her. She stopped stroking him and smiled, but before she could say anything, he said, 'Don't stop; that's really nice.'

She did stop and replied, 'Oh no! You are coming home with me; it's time for bed.

She helped him to his feet and walked him around the room. 'I feel so full of energy,' he told her, and grabbed her around the waist. 'Let's go now,' he said, looking at the door.

'Not till you put those on,' she told him, pointing at his clothes.

As soon as he was dressed, he took Juliette by the hand and led her to Brian's office. It was empty, but he noticed the SCAT on the balcony and headed straight for it. He jumped on, and helped Juliette up behind him. He tried to get it moving but it refused to go. 'What's up with this thing?' he asked.

'Ugh. It's mine. Take us home please,' she said, and it slowly took off.

John couldn't help laughing. 'You've got one? I thought you said you'd never go on one by yourself.'

She watched him smiling and replied, 'It turned up out of the blue. Nobody knows who authorised it.'

'I requested one for you through security, though I wasn't sure if you'd get one or not,' he told her, and sounded really surprised. 'That was really quick. I only requested it this morning.'

Juliette looked at him oddly for a moment, then realised what was up. 'You've been undergoing treatment since yesterday evening.'

John looked shocked. 'I must have been in quite a state to be in for that long.'

'Not to worry. You are back again now. And just as bald as I was.'

He laughed and asked, 'Is my hair pink too?'

'You'll have to wait and see,' she told him, sounding mischievous.

The smile left his face for a moment, then he smiled again and said, 'No, you're not like that.'

As they approached the apartment, they could see Petal looking out the window. She rushed to open the door to let them in and brushed Juliette aside just to get at John. She didn't say a word. Instead she started crying and shaking with relief.

John picked her up and said, 'Either I've gotten stronger, or you have lost weight.'

Then he saw the look on Juliette's face, and realised why he felt so full of energy. Once inside, he took Petal up to her room, tucked her up in bed, gave her a kiss goodnight, and closed her door as he left. Walking over to Juliette, he whispered in her ear. 'What did you do to make me feel so good? You are going to feel the full force of my new energy in a just few minutes, you naughty girl.'

Juliette saw the look on his face, screeched with delight, and ran into the bedroom.

John followed her in, and slammed the door behind him.

CHAPTER 9
THE JOURNEY TO JUMLA JUNCTION

John was standing by his front door. He'd had his first good night's sleep since arriving at the research centre, thanks to Juliette, even if it was for only two hours. She was still in bed, having been kept awake most of the night, and showed no sign of rising before lunch. He tried to rouse her by pulling the bedclothes off her, but she moaned, 'No more, please,' as she turned over, and slipped back under the covers.

He'd been sitting at the communications terminal since then, trying to catch up with what had been happening over the past few days. He noticed there was a meeting that morning in the isolation dome, and that intrigued him. He'd never been there before and wanted to know all about it. After interrogating the system to find information, he became frustrated when told all avenues had been blocked by security, and decided to attend the meeting to find out why.

Juliette told him he had the day off to recover, but thanks to her therapy, he was full of energy and ready for anything. Now though he was really hungry and wanted something to eat. He'd already booked a table and was ready to leave for breakfast, so shouted upstairs, 'Anyone for breakfast?'

Two voices rang out in harmony, 'Wait for me.' And the patter of feet running down the stairs told him they were on their way.

'Juliette's not coming, is she?' Petal asked, with a wicked smile on her face.

John thought of something to say to stop her questioning him further. 'She didn't finish till late last night, and it was a long day for her. So she's having a lay in.'

Petal continued to smile, but said nothing, indicating she hadn't believed a word he'd said.

Breakfast was over quickly, and John was eager to get to work. He called a spitter to take Petal and Fred home. As there was one available immediately, he bundled them onto it and waved them goodbye. They weren't too happy, as they were expecting a ride home on the SCAT, which they loved.

John mounted his machine and asked it to go automatic to take him to the isolation dome. He'd read about how the main computer and communications had been linked to it, and wondered why.

He received a call from Pauline and answered it. 'Good morning. What can I do for you,' he asked cheerfully.

She hesitated for a moment, then asked, 'Is Juliette with you? I can't get through to her on her communicator.'

'Juliette is having a lay in. I kept her up most of the night.'

Pauline stuttered as she replied, 'Oh. I'll call in to get her up. We're supposed to be starting work this morning. Did she say anything to you?'

'Only that you'd stared at me last night. Don't worry, we're quits now. Remember the Bagman City balcony episode?'

'I—' she said, then there was silence for a few seconds before she cut him off.

He called Petal. 'Tell Juliette Pauline is on her way over to see her. She probably wants to organise a routine, now that they're working together.'

'OK. I'll see if I can get her up. Fred just tried and she kicked him out of the room,' she said with a laugh.

Having little to keep themselves occupied, Pauline and Juliette were taking on the task of welfare officers to try and sort out the refugee problem that now existed at the centre.

Smiling, he said, 'Tell Juliette I'll call her later,' just before Petal cut him off.

It had been just over a week since they'd arrived at the centre, and everything was far from normal. There was no contact with the outside, not a flicker from anywhere on the planet. Almost a week had passed since the tube access port in engineering had been opened in an attempt to obtain some information from outside. That was closed immediately, as there was a gale blowing through the tube, and the air was dank with a bad smell, like rotting compost. John didn't know the tube had been opened once again, and knew nothing about the very disappointing results they'd obtained.

As John moved along on his SCAT, he pondered over their situation for a moment, then heard an announcement, *'Standby. All dome access doors will be opening shortly.'*

Soon after, there was the loud sound of metal clanging on metal as each door opened, one after another. He'd read that the casing banging and aftershocks had subsided to an acceptable level and the night before was the first with no bangs at all. Still, everyday small tremors gave cause for concern, and the now-irregular shaking made everyone jumpy. But it wasn't enough to warrant keeping the main doors shut any longer.

He ordered his machine to go a bit faster and set off at high speed for the hospital complex. As he travelled, he accessed the latest engineering information ready for the meeting, and while scanning the information, was distracted by an alarm. He looked up to see two more SCATs coming in his direction and told his machine to link up with them. It was Brian and Rose; they were also going to the meeting he was heading for. Rose was in overall charge now that Simon had passed away in the terrible disaster, and on the whole she was doing a good job. The information he'd accessed told him that the shuttle terminal was sealed after he'd come out, and would remain so until conditions improved inside. He already knew Simon's body had been recovered, and there would be a state funeral later in the week due to his grade two status. John thought he deserved only the best, even though he'd only known him for a short time.

As Rose closed in on him, he raised his hand as a greeting, and held it there until Brian had also closed in. The three of them continued across the main dome and through the hospital complex in silence, and were soon at their destination: the isolation dome.

Rose entered first, followed by Brian, then John entered very slowly. The sight before him was wonderful; he'd never seen anything like it, and there was complete silence. John looked around in awe; his jaw dropped open, and he just stared at the glowing dome casing. 'It's just like the gem I gave to Juliette,' John remarked quietly.

The colour was brilliant, almost like bright sunlight, and at one point on the dome it was too bright to look at, almost like the sun on a summer's day. He looked around and noticed the city just below them, then exclaimed, 'Wow! Look at this place. What a place to live in.'

He followed Rose over to a section high up on one side of the city and watched as she settled on a balcony. He and Brian followed her, and were soon standing on a platform overlooking the whole city complex.

'Come on, follow me,' she said quickly, indicating she was in a hurry to get started.

They entered a large room fitted with a long table and walked to the nearest end. Rose sat down with a smile. 'Thank you. Take a seat.' She pointed to a couple of chairs stacked close by and they went for them.

'Anything to report from the hospital?' she enquired.

'Nothing that you don't know about already,' replied Brian quickly. He too had a smile on his face.

Rose looked at John and asked, 'What are you doing here? Juliette said you would be recuperating all day today.'

'I feel fine. She worked wonders, and I feel like a new man.'

'Eh! You are a new man,' Brian quickly pointed out.

Rose smiled. 'Well done,' she said praising Brian.

'Don't thank me. Pauline and Juliette did all the work. I just monitored in case something went wrong. It was the first time either of them operated at such a high level,' he replied happily.

John looked around. 'Is it only us at this meeting?' he asked.

'Almost. Rajinda is due soon; he's been delayed in engineering. I don't want too many people to know about this place yet,' She said, and quickly changed the subject. 'We need to find a way to regain contact with the outside.'

Rose went on to explain what was found when the tube access port had been opened, and watched John's face closely. She realised he wasn't taking in all she said, and asked, 'Is there anything up?'

'I've been thinking. If the tube is broken, let's fix it. We have a tube construction unit ready for use. We can use that to get through to Jumla Junction.'

Rose looked at him for a moment, then remarked, 'Why didn't some-one in my department think of that?'

'Does that include you?' Brian said, giving her a smug look.

Rose glared at him and retorted, 'I've had enough to think about. Unlike you.' Brian shifted his position on his seat, indicating he suddenly felt uncomfortable. She continued, 'If we do get through and take in refugees, how many injured can your hospital cope with?'

Brian thought for a minute, then, rather subdued, replied, 'We are equipped to handle fifty badly injured and two hundred minor casualties a day. The only trouble is we don't have enough doctors and nurses to treat more than ten people at a time.' Rose stopped him from speaking and suggested, 'If we can get through to Jumla Junction there may be more staff there. We can treat people faster if we can get those staff here.'

As Brian was about to comment on her suggestion, Rajinda walked through the door. He looked dazed and his skin ashen.

'Are you all right?' Brian asked, looking extremely worried.

'You could have warned me about that machine out there. I haven't used one before,' he said, looking angrily across the table to where Rose sat and pointing to where he'd parked his new SCAT.

'Sorry. I did tell it to take it easy until you got used to it.'

'Well if that was easy, I'd hate to have been on it when it was running normally,' he replied, still shocked.

'Did you see the dome out there?' John asked, trying to take his mind off his journey.

'I didn't see anything. I was petrified and closed my eyes,' Rajinda said, and sat down on a chair that Brian had brought for him.

'Follow me,' John said, and caught Rajinda by the arm, pulling him to his feet with ease.

Rose looked at John. 'How much energy did Juliette give you?'

John smile at her, and pulled Rajinda outside onto the platform. John watched his face as he started looking around. His jaw dropped and the colour quickly came back to his face as he started to smile.

'It's beautiful. What is it?'

'Rose said it's called Diamondium, a rare manmade substance,' John informed him.

When they re-entered the room, Rose told him, 'This place is still under wraps. Say nothing to no one about it. Any of you. OK?'

They all nodded, and looked at each other as if to ask, 'why not?'

'We will go for the tube option as soon as possible. John, I would like you to take the lead. When will you be ready to start work?' Rose asked.

'I'm ready now. We can start straight away if you want,' he told her.

She looked really surprised by his willingness to start, and replied, 'We'll have to do the planning first, and understand the risks involved before we go for it.'

'I can do that,' he said, and stunned everyone into silence. John had taken control of the meeting and there didn't seem to be any objections. 'Good,' he said, then started to outline his plans.

'I want to organise the tube repair team to find out what is going on outside. The equipment is available to carry out the task, and the sooner we start, the better. Any objections?'

Rose looked around the room and noted the attention everyone was paying John. 'I'm impressed,' she remarked. 'How long will it take you to get a team together, and when do you intend to start?'

'I will select the personnel required and I know the equipment is standing by. I could start within an hour, but I want to give the engineers time to gather all the information I need, so let's start at midday if that's OK with everyone?' John said with composure.

He looked around the table and there was a strange silence. Rose spoke with a smile on her face. 'If the engineers can get the information you require by then, you can go ahead with the repairs. Where do you intend to enter the tube?'

'We'll enter next to the tube access port, if conditions permit. I'll leave now and start issuing work orders if you don't mind,' John said with a smile.

Rose just waved him away with her hand. 'Off you go, boss.'

Once John had left the room, Rose started to explain what the scientists had found out so far.

'When we opened the tube access port last week, we noticed a foul-smelling sludge running through the tunnel. We analysed it, and were astonished by the results. It was made up of pulverised rock, earth, particles of Triron, and other manmade elements. There was also decomposing vegetable and animal matter. We also found a lot of human DNA mixed in with it. Whatever happened out there must be very serious indeed,' Rose said in a quiet, solemn voice.

'I have instructed the scientific and engineering section to prepare to launch our one and only probe into space. It will orbit the planet, sending back data about the surface and surrounding outer space. It's the only way of finding out if this is global or not. We also hope to find out what caused this disaster and if it has finished. Any questions?' she finished by looking around the table.

'I didn't know we had a space probe,' remarked Rajinda, with a surprised look on his face.

'You'd be surprised at what's been stored here over the past few hundred years,' Rose told him calmly. 'And it all works too.'

Brian spoke next. 'When will we have the information by?' he asked.

'We should have it by Wednesday afternoon, at the latest. Then we'll have to interpret it, especially if we don't see an immediate picture arising,' Rose replied.

'When do we expect some news from John Blight?' Rajinda asked.

Rose scanned the information on Jumla Junction John had left her, and replied, 'John should be back from Jumla Junction by Wednesday morning at the latest, if all goes as planned.'

Rose was satisfied that no more could be achieved at the meeting and arranged for another one for Wednesday at midday. She left and headed for engineering. She wanted to help John get ready for his journey.

When John left the meeting, he headed straight home, hoping to catch Juliette before she left for the day. As he approached his apartment, she was boarding her SCAT with Pauline, and he sped towards it. Just as it started to pull away, he ordered his SCAT to stop it, and was soon dismounting alongside. Juliette stepped off and met him. The look on his face told her that something was about to happen, and she bit her lip waiting for him to speak.

'I have to try to get through to Jumla Junction, and will be leaving at midday,' he told her, as he placed his arms around her.

''You are supposed to be resting today,' she said, sounding a little annoyed.

'Sorry, but I feel great and don't want to let anyone down,' he said, giving her a kiss.

OK, but don't do anything stupid,' she remarked, giving him a tight hug and a loving kiss back. 'I want you back safely. We need you.'

Pauline couldn't help overhearing what he'd said, and also stepped off the SCAT. 'Take care, and good luck,' she said, giving him a kiss on his cheek and squeezing his hand.

John looked at them and replied, 'I'll be back. I want to see your beautiful faces again.'

He turned, mounted his SCAT, and set off at speed for the engineering dome. He watched Juliette and Pauline waving farewell as he turned a corner.

Rose entered the engineering dome and headed for the space probe preparation team. It hadn't taken long to rig up a launch tube, and it was now ready for the probe to be inserted.

'Where are we going to launch it from?' she asked.

'We're going to take it to the southern observation platform. It will be launched from a hole cut through the outer wall as soon as it is ready.'

'How long before it's ready to be launched?' she asked the senior scientist in charge.

'About half an hour before we're ready to move it to the observation platform,' the scientist replied.

'Keep me informed please,' Rose said quickly and crossed to an engineering terminal. After checking on John's progress, she noticed he hadn't started yet and wondered why. She called security and asked politely, 'Can you tell me where John Blight is please?'

A few moments later she was told, 'He's with his partner and Pauline Mitchell. Do you want me to contact him for you?'

'No it's all right, I think I know what's going on,' she replied, sounding slightly sympathetic. She realised he'd gone to tell Juliette what he was going to do, and didn't want to sound too pushy by calling him. 'Just keep an eye on his movements please,' she said.

'He's just left his apartment and is heading for engineering,' she was informed, just before she cut off her link to security.

'Thank you. You can cancel the request to keep an eye on him. I'll meet up with him there. Thank you,' she said again and cut security off before they could reply.

On her way over to engineering, Rose was monitoring what was going on, and noticed a list of staff being assembled. As she read down the list, she realised it contained a cross section of every type of engineer at the centre. She was impressed by the variation of skills, and realised John knew what he was doing. She also realised she couldn't have done such a thing without a lot of thought, and over a much longer period of time. The list was complete and her SCAT console indicated her authority was needed to sanction the go-ahead. Without even questioning the request, she immediately sanctioned it. 'He's a one-man workforce,' she said to herself, and smiled.

As she entered engineering, she could see everyone was very busy and walked over to a senior engineer. 'Where is the tube construction unit being assembled?' she asked.

'Over on the far side, near the tube access port,' the engineer replied quickly.

Rose mounted her SCAT and headed in that direction without saying another word.

John arrived at the engineering dome and saw a group of scientists hovering over a small tube-like object. It was about three metres long, just over half a metre in diameter, and had a sharply pointed nose and a flattened ring around the slightly tapering end.

'What's that thing?' he asked.

'It's the space probe,' an elderly female scientist said. 'You must be John Blight.'

'That's right. Why? Is there anything wrong?'

'No nothing, just curious that's all. We've heard so much about you. Good luck on your journey to Jumla Junction,' she said, holding her hand out to shake his.

He took her hand as a goodwill gesture, then asked, 'Do you know where the tube construction unit is being assembled?'

'Over by the tube access port. Rose is on her way over there now. I think she wants to see how things are progressing.'

'Thanks, be seeing you around sometime,' John said jovially.

'Hope so,' she replied, smiling at how calm he was, given the situation he was about to get himself into. 'Tell Rose we are ready to launch at anytime now.'

John nodded, jumped back on his SCAT, and headed towards the access port.

Rose had never seen the construction unit before now, and was amazed how ancient it looked. It was made up of short sections coupled together to form a snake-like object. It was driven by caterpillar tracks not only at its base, but also up the sides and over the top. The front end was remarkably blunt considering it had been built to tunnel through solid rock.

She was watching the engineers connecting the whole unit together when John arrived next to her. 'Hi. Bit of a prehistoric beast, isn't it,' he remarked.

'You're telling me!' she exclaimed, with a puzzled look on her face.

'What's up? Don't you think it will do the job?' he asked, looking quizzically at her.

'Is the front section missing or something?' she asked.

John laughed at that remark. 'Call yourself an engineer? Haven't you noticed the laser cannons located at the front? It isn't designed to push things out of its way; it vaporises everything in its path and recycles the gaseous elements created. It's meant to tunnel, not just drive through.'

'Won't that slow things down?' Rose asked, feeling a little embarrassed; most of the engineers had heard what John said.

'Not at all. It doesn't have to tunnel through solid rock. It only has to deal with what's been deposited in the tube. So we should make very good progress,' he said, not even noticing her embarrassment.

Then he remembered the message he had for her, and said, 'The probe team asked me to inform you that they are ready to launch the probe.'

'Thanks. I'll go and see it off, and return before you go,' she said, relieved at the chance to leave the sniggering behind.

'OK, I'll call you when I'm ready to go,' he said.

Rose mounted her SCAT, raised her hand to acknowledge his remark, but didn't say a word. She just turned and departed as fast as she could.

John turned, looked the beast over before he walked forward, and then headed for the section second from the front. He boarded the command module, ducking his head as he entered. Once inside, he looked at the control console and was quite surprised. The unit looked ancient on the outside, but inside was a different story. Everything was state of the art, and he was quite pleased.

'Who's responsible for updating this unit?' he asked an engineer who was getting acquainted with the controls.

'Don't know. Whoever it was has left the research centre. I can find out if you wish,' the engineer replied.

'No, it's OK. I'm just happy that it's been kept up-to-date,' John said quietly.

'We engineers have little to do most of the time, so we potter around with the old equipment, just to keep ourselves amused,' the engineer told him.

'Well, keep up the good work! Who knows when, or if, any of the archived equipment will be required again? Look at what we're having to drag out now!' he said, holding his hand out to touch the beast's casing.

The engineer just smiled, said nothing, and carried on working at the controls.

John was taken by surprise when the machine suddenly lurched forward a short distance, then abruptly stopped.

'Someone should have updated the engines; they're a bit jerky when they start and stop,' the engineer said. 'But at least they are working.'

'Thank goodness for that!' exclaimed John, a little startled after being thrown against a cabinet at the rear of the command compartment. 'Wasn't it used a few days ago to repair Water Dome Two?' he asked, sounding a little puzzled

'Yes, but it was in automatic.'

'Ha! That's why nobody knew about the jerkiness,' John exclaimed, then asked, 'How long till we are ready to roll out?'

'We are ready. We just have to wait for Rose to come back and we can depart,' the engineer replied, with a smile on his face.

'Let her know we're ready,' John said, with a sense of urgency in his voice.

Rose reached the southern observation platform first. Calling security, she asked for the door to be opened, ready for the engineers when they arrived. As soon as it opened, she made her way over to the outer wall and requested, 'Clear wall and lights off.'

As the wall cleared, she once again looked out into the darkness. It wasn't as dark as it had been. Even so, she couldn't see anything, as visibility was almost zero. Every now and again she thought she could just make out the outer casing of a dome or two, but not for long. There was still the dull, smothered sound of things hitting the outer casing, but not as much as before and it was definitely a lot quieter. It worried her that objects were flying through the air. The probe could be hit on takeoff and damaged, or at worse, destroyed.

She received a call, telling her that the tube construction unit was ready to go, and she told them to wait.

'Turn the lights on,' she demanded, and was slightly dazzled for a moment until her eyes adjusted.

After what seemed like hours, the probe reached the observation platform. It was being carried on a floating pallet that arrived with the help of a large city hopper. It was the only craft capable of carrying such a heavy weight to the top of the main dome along with the all the engineers and their equipment. Slowly the pallet was manoeuvred through the door, past the rows of seats just inside the viewing area, and left standing close to the outer wall.

'Are you going to request a clear wall?' asked one of the engineers. He looked totally shocked when she replied, 'It is clear.'

An engineer approached Rose and gave her a list. On it was the order in which tasks had to be completed. It wasn't long; with only four steps the probe would be on its way.

'Right. Get the drill into place,' she demanded.

As the drill was positioned against the wall, an object hit close to where they were going to drill. The engineers closest to the wall saw the object shatter and heard the dull thud. It made them jump sideways and knock the drill out of place. Looking at Rose, one of them said with a shaky voice, 'What was that?'

'Storm debris,' she said calmly. 'Get that thing back into place quickly.'

As the engineers resited the drill, others brought forward the shield they were going to use to cover it. As everyone stood back, the shield, driven automatically, was placed over the drill and a seal made with the clear wall.

'Are we ready?' Rose asked.

'Yes, we are ready to drill,' came the reply.

'Everybody out, before we close the door,' she said.

The platform doors were closed just before a hole was cut through the outer wall, and she waited with her engineers for the all clear before entering. A few moments later, the doors opened and a strange smell greeted them as they entered. It was not pleasant; the odour of decomposing matter made them all hold their noses.

'Is the seal holding?' Rose enquired.

'Yes, just a small amount of outside air entered before the hole could be sealed properly. We entered before the air could be reconditioned,' an engineer replied quickly.

Rose looked at the hole in the outer wall and frowned. 'Is that large enough?' she asked the drilling engineer.

'It may look small, but it's a perfect fit. Too big and we wouldn't be able to attach the launch tube to it,' he replied, sounding proud of his achievement.

Rose watched as the drill unit was moved out of the way and the launch tube took its place. As the tube touched the outer wall, a green glow encircled the rim. 'There, it's sealed,' said someone at the back. 'Remove the shield.'

As the shield slid out of the way, everyone jumped when an alarm sounded, quickly followed by a very loud metallic voice from the stations safety monitor. It said, 'WARNING, AIR POLLUTION HAS BEEN DETECTED. EVACUATE THE AREA IMMEDIATELY. WARNING!' A countdown started from ten.

'Everyone out now!' Rose shouted. 'Quickly! We have to get out quickly.'

Within seconds the observation platform was cleared of personnel. The doors slammed shut, and a strange green glow appeared all around their edges.

'Well, that's it!' Rose said disappointedly, slapping her sides to show she was annoyed. 'I wanted to see the probe launch, but now it will have to be launched remotely.'

'What happened?' one of the scientists asked quietly.

'Not quite sure! It looks like the monitoring system detected a slight drop in pressure. Maybe the wall seal wasn't perfect. The only trouble is the monitoring system not only closed the doors, which are airtight, it welded them shut.' She paused for a moment before continuing, 'Now it'll stay shut, we haven't the time to repair it yet. Launch the probe now,' she said, looking at an engineer carrying the remote control unit.

The trigger was pressed, and everyone waited for a noise, or some sign, that the probe had gone. There was nothing.

'No good listening,' Rose remarked, amused by their reactions, 'the walls are soundproof. Anyway, the probe is silent until it reaches the sound barrier.'

One of the engineers looked at her and asked, 'What happens then?'

Rose looked at him silently for a moment, before replying, 'Why, nothing of course, just—nothing.' And she smiled. 'Lets get back to engineering; that thing will have sent us a pile of information already.'

Rose arrived back at the engineering dome long before the probe crew and made her way towards the scientists, who were receiving the probe's information. The look on their faces gave her cause of concern, and she rushed to see what had left them with their mouths agape.

'The probe—it's OK isn't it?' she asked, sounding extremely worried.

'Yes, the probe is fine. It's the information it's sending back that's worrying us,' a scientist with an ashen face told her.

Looking at the monitors, she made out the picture of the surface taken from directly above, only it wasn't an optical view, it was radar, and it shocked her. The dome complex they were in was supposed to be buried under the Himalayan Mountains; most of the domes were now exposed and clearly visible. There were only a few mountain peaks left; everything looked as if it had been smoothed over with sand paper, leaving no lumps and very few bumps. The atmosphere was heavy with moisture and particles—so thick, nothing was visible to the naked eye.

Storms were raging all around, with wind velocities in excess of 1500 kilometres per hour, strong enough to sandblast anything natural to dust. The upper atmosphere flashed with masses of lightning bolts, and with radiation levels so high, it could only mean the ozone layer was in trouble. The information just started to show the surface in their region as the probe lost touch. What they had glimpsed showed a completely different picture than what they were expecting.

Rose switched the monitor off. 'We can wait for a clearer picture before jumping to conclusions,' she said sternly.

'If the whole of earth's surface is like this, it could be the end of mankind,' one scientist remarked, and caused a bit of panic amongst her staff.

Suddenly all the staff started murmuring amongst themselves.

Rose replied quickly, 'We'll have to wait for its return in two days from now. Only then can we draw any conclusions. So no speculating, please.' She was looking straight at the scientist who made the remark with a grave, unforgiving stare.

John finished his preparations, and was ready to start the journey to Jumla Junction. Rose only needed to give the signal, and he would be off. He tried calling engineering but there was no reply, so he decided to nip over to see what was going on.

He arrived at the engineering dome, made his way to the level he'd been at earlier, and entered the room. There was Rose sitting at a console. Her face was in her hands and she looked worried. John looked at her and stopped to ask a scientist what happened. He was immediately taken and shown the information they'd received, and he frowned.

'When will we know the whole picture?' he asked.

Someone answered with a voice full of emotion, 'It will take forty-eight hours for the probe to scan the entire surface and download the information. Only then will we know the full extent of the destruction. We don't know what caused it and we're not even sure if we ever will.'

John made his way over to Rose and placed an arm around her shoulder. Giving her a gentle squeeze, he said quietly and calmly, 'It looks bad out there, but we're safe and well. So let's be strong and put on a brave face; we may be the last hope for mankind, and we shouldn't give up without a fight.'

Rose looked up at him and managed a thin smile. 'Thanks for that; I needed a tonic, and you are surely a strong one. Is it worth you going now?'

John noted her change, and added, 'We have to be certain about what's happened out there. Who knows how many people living below ground have survived. If any did, we need to find them.'

Rose looked up and nodded. 'You'd better be off then.'

John said nothing as Rose stood up and gave him a hug. It felt like a mother hugging her child, and it made him think of his mum. He left with a heavy heart, knowing that there was little chance of anyone living on or just below the surface bring alive. But he hadn't given up hope, and was about to go back to the tube access port when Rose caught his arm.

'Take your family to lunch before you go. But don't tell them anything of what you know,' she said quietly and calmly.

'Thanks, that's not a bad idea,' he said, and departed.

Juliette and Pauline had just signed up as councillors at the refugee centre when Juliette received a call from Petal. She didn't want to be disturbed, so cut her off before answering. Shortly after Fred tried, and she did the same.

'Don't you think you should answer them? It could be important,' Pauline told her, sounding concerned.

'Yeah. I suppose you're right. I'll call them back now,' Juliette said, feeling a bit guilty.

Before she had time to call, her communicator indicated another call. This time it was from John and she answered it immediately. 'Hi, what's up? Everyone is calling me,' she said calmly.

'We've all been trying to get hold of you. Do you want to come to lunch before I go away?' he asked, sounding a bit annoyed with her. She was silent for a minute and he had to speak again. 'Hi, you still there?' he asked.

'Sorry. When you said go away, it hit me what you were going to do. I'll be with you as soon as I can. I'll meet you at the chow house,' she said, running to her SCAT.

Pauline stood and watched, as she rushed off. 'Bye. See you later,' she shouted after her, but Juliette didn't hear a word.

Juliette jumped on her machine and said, 'To the chow house as quickly as you can.' She held on tightly, with closed eyes, and gritted her teeth as it took off at high speed.

John picked up Petal and Fred and booked a table on the way to the chow house. He had priority over everyone and always got a table immediately, even without booking. He landed at the entrance and waited for Juliette to arrive. He didn't have to wait long; a SCAT was approaching the MATCH at high speed, and it appeared to be without a rider. He was extremely anxious and wondered if Juliette had fallen off along the way. As it came to a sudden stop just a few metres away, he was surprised to see a head appear above the control console. It was Juliette, and her face was ashen. John took one look at her and burst out laughing. As she got off the machine, her legs seemed to give way slightly and he rushed forward to catch her. She instantly put her arms around his neck and hugged him tightly.

'Wow! That must have been some journey,' he said mockingly.

'It wasn't that,' she said with a slight whimper in her voice. 'It's the thought of you going away that worries me.'

'No need to worry. I'll be inside one of the strongest machines ever built by man. And I'll only be gone for two days at the most,' he said, trying to calm her down. 'Come on, our table awaits.'

They all entered and were shown to the best table in the chow house. The waitress said, 'This table is reserved for you and your guests, and will always be available for you.'

'Make it for my partner and these two as well and we've got a deal,' he replied.

The waitress made a note of his request and said, 'OK, that's fine.' Looking around at them all, she said, 'I hope you enjoy your meal. Please place your order using the panel there.'

She was pointing at a small panel at one end of the table and John remarked, 'That's new.'

'It's an upgrade to help staff get the right orders to the right table,' the waitress said with a smile, and left them to it.

Lunch felt really strange for John. He'd never know them all to be so quiet, so he asked them what was up.

Petal answered with so quiet a voice he could hardly heard her at all. 'There's a rumour going round. They say all the cities have been destroyed in this region. Is it true?'

John saw the look on Juliette's pale face. He realised that someone was feeding information out of engineering and had to think fast. 'As far as we know, the shuttle terminal has been seriously damaged and has to remain closed for the time being. The main intercontinental tube system runs alongside the engineering dome wall and we access the tube through an inspection port.' He paused for a moment for them to take in what he'd said, which didn't really mean that much to them.

Juliette butted in. 'Is there a problem on the outside?' she asked, shaking slightly.

John continued where he left off. 'There is damage to the tube in both directions and it's open to the atmosphere somewhere along the line. My mission is to carry out repairs and make the tube good through to Jumla Junction, which is the closest centre of activity. Once there, we can assess the state of the whole network, and hopefully regain contact around the world. As it stands at the moment, we do not know what has happened, or what caused us to be in this state.'

'Juliette said you'll be back in two days. Is that right?' Fred asked, sounding a little worried.

'At the most. It's only 150 kilometres away. By the time we get back, we should have a pretty good picture of what has happened, and will have restored communication links to the outside again.'

Juliette still looked worried and he could see tears appearing in her eyes. She came over to him, and taking his hand, led him over to a quiet corner away from Petal and Fred. 'I heard the mission you are going on is really dangerous. Do you have to go? Can't someone else go instead? I don't want to lose you,' she said, and started to cry.

John held her close. 'I already told you I'll be inside a machine that can withstand all nature can throw at it. So don't worry, I'll be back before you know it. Now please smile, the kids need you to look after them until I return and I don't want them worrying too much.'

Juliette wiped her tears on her sleeve and managed a forced smile.

'That's better. I hate seeing you cry. When I come back, I promise I will never go on another dangerous mission again.' Then he realised what he'd said. 'Even though this one isn't that dangerous.'

That last bit didn't quell her feelings, and tears rolled down her face once again. He held her close and hugged her tightly. 'I'll be back, so don't worry, OK'

She nodded her head. 'You'd better,' she said, trying to smile. She allowed him to kiss her teary eyes.

They went back to the table and Petal could see Juliette's reddened eyes. Her eyes welled with tears and Fred offered her a tissue. She took it without question, which was unusual, as she hated Fred doing nice things for her.

'Come on, let's get you lot back to the apartment. I have to get back to work,' he said calmly, trying not to sound like he was in a hurry.

Soon they were back at the apartment and Petal ran up to John and hugged him tightly. 'Take care. I love you,' she said, and stepped aside for Fred.

Fred took his hand and said, 'I hope to be as good as you when I grow up. Come back soon.'

John felt really proud of that remark and it brought a tear to his eyes. Juliette noticed and quickly rushed into his arms. She kissed his tears and remarked, 'Yuck! They're salty.' Then she kissed him on the lips.

When she finished, he said, 'So were your tears, but I liked it.' He licked his lips.

She kneed him gently in the groin and said, 'Kiss my tears of joy when you return and I'll believe you.'

He smiled at her, and as she turned away, he slapped her backside really hard. 'That will remind you of me,' he said, and quickly mounted his SCAT.

She leapt forward with the shock of his slap and, rubbing her cheek, said, 'You wait. I'll get you for that.'

The look on her face told him she'd forgotten everything for a moment, and he smiled. 'Look at your butt in a mirror every time you miss me. That will remind you I'll be back just to see what you'll do to me.' And with that he took off.

John quickly made his way back to the tube tunnelling machine to start the journey. It was well past midday, and everyone had been waiting impatiently for him to arrive. Everything was ready to go, so he made his way over to Rose, who was sitting on her SCAT chatting with Rajinda.

Rose saw him coming and, looking rather annoyed, said, 'At last. What kept you?'

'I've just said goodbye to my family. That took a lot longer than I'd anticipated.'

'OK. That's fine. They're all ready to go and just waiting for you,' she said, and her anger turned to sympathy. 'Is Juliette OK?'

'Yes. She's not taking it too well, but she'll be OK.' He was just about to go when he turned back to her and said, 'Oh! And just to let you know. Someone is leaking information about what we are finding. Rumours are spreading, and they're not good ones.'

'Thanks for that. I'll ensure all information is restricted from now on,' she said and gave him a pat on his back.

John walked over to the construction unit and entered the control cockpit. Once inside, he looked around, found a place to sit down, and apologised for his late arrival.

The outer door closed behind him with a slight click and it took a few seconds for his eyes to adjust to the dim lighting inside.

As soon as he'd strapped himself in, the machine started to move forward with a jerk as it made its way towards the dome wall. Screeching and grinding noises were made with every lurch, increasing in volume second by second.

'What's that noise?' he shouted, trying to be heard above the horrendous din that seemed to be coming from everywhere.

'It's the noise the machine makes when it's making a new tube section. We have to seal ourselves inside a tube before we crack open the dome casing. It'll only last about ten minutes then we should be through to the outside and heading for the tube,' an engineer shouted back, his voice almost indistinguishable above the noise.

Rose watched as the construction unit started up. A cloud of dust shot out from under it, almost obscuring the whole area, and made everyone move further away. Then the machine started screeching and grinding as it slowly moved forward. A ring of metal slightly larger than the outer shell of the unit started to appear just in front of the nose section, and quickly became a solid ring. It was getting longer with every forward jerk, increasing in length and becoming translucent as the unit entered into it. The longer it got, the more clear the tube became, and by the time the unit was half covered, it was completely clear.

Rose had put on a pair of ear defenders, given to her by Rajinda, and said, with amazement in her voice, 'It's making a Triron tube.'

He shouted a reply. 'It has to seal itself in before it can bore through the dome casing.'

Rose looked at him, startled. 'There's no need to shout. I can hear you well enough with these on,' she said, tapping her ear defenders.

They watched without saying another word while the machine jerked forward into the tube. As soon as it was completely covered, the noise changed slightly, and a wall of Triron sealed the end. The tube was now touching the dome wall, and the complete unit was enclosed within the protective shield of pure Triron. The noise level instantly dropped to zero as the seal was complete, and the machine started to cut through the dome wall in silence. The nose section disappeared in a haze as the lasers performed their function, but the seal around the construction unit stopped the haze from getting to the control section just behind, leaving the unit clearly visible as it drove forward.

It was fifteen minutes before the noise inside the tube construction unit subsided. Now there was just the occasional grind and groan, and the beast still lurched as it moved forward. Someone from the front section spoke over the intercom. 'We are picking up speed. We must be through the dome wall.'

Then the noise started again as the unit passed through the wall of the intercontinental tube. This time it didn't last for so long because the walls of the tube weren't as thick as the dome casing. Once again there was almost complete silence. The only difference was that now the construction unit was shaking and vibrating, making it uncomfortable to be inside.

John took off his ear defenders, and as his ears adjusted to the sounds around him, said, 'That's not too bad. I can live with that. For awhile, anyway.' He looked around the cab.

'We're not moving forward,' said the driver, sounding really concerned.

The senior engineer came over, looked at the information displayed on the control console, and frowned. 'Looks like we have a headwind, and it's holding us in position.' Then he looked a little more serious. 'Actually it's pushed us back five hundred metres from where we entered. Can you provide more power?' he asked.

'Not enough to make much of a difference. There's just enough left to hold us on station. The tube is much bigger than this unit, and half the traction wheels are not in use.'

The engineer went silent for a moment and watched as the unit engines increased in power, stopping them moving backwards. Then he shouted, 'Inform the rear section to seal the tube behind us. Immediately.'

John just managed to put his ear defenders on before the noise started up again, only this time it didn't sound quite so loud. Five minutes passed, and as time moved on, the engines onboard started reducing in power. When the noise stopped, the engines were just idling, indicating the tube was now sealed and the wind was no more.

'Right, let's start moving. Forward this time,' the senior engineer said, and went back to his seat.

John stood next to the driver and braced himself as the machine jerked forward once again. No one said a word; everyone was concentrating on what they were doing. He looked over the driver's shoulder and remarked, 'We're moving at twenty-five kilometres per hour. That's good.'

'It is a good speed, and as long as we don't bump into anything along the way, we should be there in about six hours. The tube is fairly clear at the moment, so let's hope it stays that way,' the driver replied.

John looked surprised by that announcement, and remarked with a hint of a smile, 'We may be back by morning at this rate!'

Within a few minutes of saying that, the beast shuddered to an abrupt halt, throwing everyone against the now-stationary equipment. It took a good few seconds for everyone to get back into their positions and hurriedly attach the as-yet-unused seatbelts. John came off the worse, but luckily for him, he only suffered a bump on the head.

'That hurt!' he said as he picked himself up off the floor, rubbing his forehead. He landed two metres from where he'd been standing. 'What happened?' he asked.

'We've hit something very hard. Looks like it could be Triron or something similar. We'll find out in a few seconds,' said the engineer in charge. 'Yep! It's Triron. And it's going to take awhile to get through. Scans indicate it's ten inches thick.'

Someone let out a gasp, and everybody turned towards the sudden outburst. 'Triron that thick is only used as support columns. They are used to support the very bottom of cities,' the crew member stated. Then he slumped down into his seat and sat, silently shaking his head.

The noise outside the beast dropped off suddenly for a moment before another, different sound, took its place. Everyone was speechless as the eerie noise increased in volume, and John looked slightly worried.

John looked around at their faces and remarked, 'Come on, keep yourselves busy. Let's check the equipment over!'

Without batting an eyelid, the crew started doing their checks. John didn't even notice their response; he was worried about what they would or wouldn't find out there, if they ever got to their destination.

Fifteen minutes passed, then another fifteen passed, and John was starting to get a little concerned about the slow progress. The crew had finished all their checks, and were sitting at their posts looking bored. Edging his way slowly over to the driver's console, he asked quietly, 'Why are we still going so slowly?'

'Element stripping,' The driver replied, slightly nervously. 'I'll carry out another scan. Then we should know how big the problem is.'

'Is there any way of seeing what's in the tunnel?' John asked enquiringly.

'We are equipped with forward and backward up-to-date visual scanners,' the driver said excitedly, as if he'd remembered a long-lost toy.

Within a minute they were looking ahead, trying to make out what was there. Every now and again the visibility would clear slightly as Triron particles, rushing past the monitor, took slightly different paths down the tube, heading towards the element storage banks which were just behind them.

The noise of metal being stripped and sent to storage sounded totally different after moving so quietly for the past half hour, and all the people inside the machine covered their ears. The noise's pitch seemed to increase and slowly rise in volume as the machine continued stripping the Triron blocking their path.

'How long is it going to take to remove this blockage?' John asked, sounding really annoyed that they'd been stopped.

'It will be about four hours at the current rate of stripping, and that's at maximum now,' came the reply he didn't really want to hear.

'Can't we go round it?'

'No, we need the Triron to carry out repairs further along the tube.'

John slumped down in his seat and went quiet. He was boiling inside, mainly because he had no control over the senior engineer. He was just going to have to wait like everyone else. Slowly he calmed down and thought about Juliette, Petal, and Fred. Then he smiled, looked at the driver, who seemed bored, and said, 'Two of the most beautiful women I know are as bald as I am.'

The driver looked oddly at him for a moment, then laughed. 'You need a lesson in how to attract good-looking women, young lad.' And he continued to laugh.

John felt really silly for a moment, then saw the funny side and laughed with him. 'I didn't put that across in the way it was meant, but never mind.'

He looked around the cab and noticed their laughter had put a smile on everyone's face.

'What's the joke?' asked the senior engineer.

The driver shouted over to him, 'John here fancies bald women.'

The next remark from the senior engineer wiped the smile off the driver's face, and made everybody laugh at him. 'John's partner is completely bald, and she's absolutely, stunningly, beautiful.' Then he looked at John and said, 'Sorry, I'm only speaking the truth.'

'I think she is too,' said John, and said no more about it.

The mood in the cab had changed from downhearted to light-hearted with those remarks, and John noticed the change. He smiled to himself, closed his eyes, and thought of Juliette waiting for him to return.

Time seemed to pass really slowly, and half the crew took turns resting. The noise was now a very loud, high-pitched whistle, and everyone kept their ear defenders on even while asleep. Four and one-half hours passed before the noise started to peter out, indicating the tube was almost clear. A few more minutes passed before the driver started the engines, and once again the unit jerked forward.

John looked at the forward scanner, noticed the thick layer of sludge at the base of the tube, and asked, 'What are we doing about that?'

'Removing useful elements and storing the rest for ejection when we come to a break in the tube, or we'll have to dump it sooner if we're full,' the driver told him.

He kept watching the monitor and noticed a haze. As they continued, the haze quickly obscured their vision.

'Standby. We're approaching a damaged section of tube. Ear defenders on now,' the senior engineer shouted out.

A few moments later, the unit shuddered as it came to a halt, and the noise increased as the section of tube was repaired. Slowly they moved forward, the pitch of the noise changing as the tube's hole changed shape and size. Then there was silence once again, and the construction unit moved slowly forward, then stopped.

John watched the hazy scenery on the monitors settle. He started to make out a large object sticking out of the sludge, and was alarmed. The scan result indicated the obstruction that had stopped them was another Triron pillar which had settled lengthwise along the tube in front of them. Instruments indicated it was forty-one meters long, and would take at least eighteen hours to clear. It would be quicker to go around, but the Triron would be needed for tube repairs further along, and couldn't be discarded. Once again John was fuming at the delay.

As they looked, a number could be made out on its side. The numbers were unique to every pillar ever made, and John made a note of it before switching the monitors off. 'Send that number back to engineering; they may have records indicating where it came from,' he said.

'We might as well get some more rest. Organise relief drivers for the next eighteen hours,' said the senior engineer.

It was just over an hour later that John got a message back telling him about the Triron pillar. He read it, and let out a gasp in disbelief. His eyes welled up, and he had to work hard to keep tears at bay. He rubbed his eyes, leaving dirt smeared over his face.

Written on the note handed to him by the duty driver were the words:

> "WE ARE SORRY TO SAY THE PILLAR COMES FROM
> INDORE CITY, THE INDIAN REGION OF EURASIA.
> IT'S A LONG WAY FROM HOME.
> GOOD LUCK WITH THE REST OF YOUR JOURNEY.
> LOOKS LIKE YOU 'LL NEED IT.
>
> ROSE"

John put the note in his pocket, and told the driver, who was now the senior engineer, not to say anything to anyone about the message. He nodded in agreement, and continued watching the machine's progress.

John slumped down in a corner at the rear of the command centre. He placed his head in his hands, thought about Bagman City, and wondered if his parents were safe. He still hoped to find some life at the end of the journey, but now knew there was only a minute chance of that. He sat back against the wall, thought of home, and drifted off to sleep.

The senior engineer woke John six hours later with a gentle tap on his shoulder. 'Some good news for us, but bad news for the people of Indore City,' he said quietly in his ear. 'We've absorbed the pillar; it wasn't as solid as it should have been. Looks like someone skimped on the building materials.'

John looked at the time and realised he'd been asleep a long time. 'Why didn't you wake me earlier? I could have relieved someone,' he asked.

'If you didn't need the sleep, you would've woken up earlier. At least you are fresh to make decisions from now on,' remarked the senior engineer. 'Take charge. I'm going to sleep now. Wake me if you need me, OK!'

John nodded and stood up. 'What's the situation?'

'We are travelling at thirty kilometres per hour and descending rapidly towards Jumla Junction. The tunnel is relatively clear, but visibility is not good. I suspect a tube breach somewhere ahead of us. Scans should pick it up shortly. OK?'

John nodded and turned towards the monitors. He didn't even notice the senior engineer slip into the corner he had just risen from.

The tube looked clear a few metres ahead; that was all the visibility they had, and it worried him. They were moving at speed, getting closer to the junction with every passing minute. Thirty minutes had passed when the scan monitor alarm sounded, and everyone braced themselves for an abrupt slowdown, which came quite quickly.

John was standing with his arms gripping the console in front of him. As the machine slowed rapidly, out of the corner of his eye he noticed something shoot past him. He looked, but couldn't see anything. A shout for help made him press the emergency stop button.

The machine stopped immediately and plunged them into almost complete silence. The only things he could hear were moans coming from the front of the control module. He dashed forward to see what was happening and tripped over the legs of someone lying prone on the floor.

Looking down, he could see the senior engineer slowly rising, holding his head, and groaning. His left arm hung limp by his side.

Looking up, he noticed the communications engineer sitting slumped in the corner of his console, staring directly at him. As he looked closer, he noticed the stare was unnerving, and realised the communications engineer was dead.

John helped the senior engineer to his feet and passed him to other crew members, who had a medical kit ready to use. He moved over to the slumped engineer and checked for a pulse with a probe he had just been given. Nothing. He stretched out his hand, placed it over the dead man's face and gently closed his staring eyes. John moved out of the way as crew members arrived with a stretcher and body bag.

Someone remarked, 'Poor fellow! This bag will preserve him for up to two weeks if necessary.'

John made his way back to the command console and sent a report back to the research centre. It stated:

"I am reporting a regrettable incident which happened at 2130.

The senior engineer was asleep in the control module and not secure. The tube construction unit slowed abruptly; he was catapulted forward and sustained some injury. He is concussed and has a broken left arm which we are tending too.

The communications engineer, David Johnstone, was not so lucky. The senior engineer hit him as he passed, the impact broke his neck, and he died instantly. Please inform his family of the situation, and offer our regret and condolences. His body will be returned when we arrive back.

We are taking measures to ensure this doesn't happen again.

John Blight.

End of message."

John started the machine; it moved forward slowly, and he scanned ahead to find out what was causing the problem. The scan showed a buckle in the tube wall and a large hole in the top. It extended twenty metres along the tube and estimates indicated it would take three hours to repair. There was nothing to do except sit back and wait.

John looked at the distance-travelled indicator and frowned. They'd only done fifty kilometres, and still had one hundred left before they reached the junction. At this rate, it would be many hours before they reached their goal.

They were now moving very slowly, and everyone sat back and tried to relax. Going slowly meant no sudden stops which could cause injury, but at the same time, they wanted to go fast to get the mission over and done with.

Everyone was awake. The machine was picking up speed. John watched the monitor closely. Visibility was very poor and, once again, he was relying on the forward scans for information. It wasn't long before they were travelling at maximum speed again, thirty kilometres per hour, and at this speed, it would take just under three hours to reach the junction.

Another ten kilometres passed without incident, then the scans began to indicate a problem with the tube just half a kilometre ahead. John slowed the machine down before they encountered the problem, much to the relief of the crew, and they slowly approached what was now shown as a break in the tube.

All indications showed there was a section of tube missing. John turned on the visual monitor and looked ahead. It was operating in night mode which made it look like day. He was surprised to see something. Visibility was at least two hundred metres at that moment, and he could clearly see the outline of a city tower, or part of one anyway. It was tilted at forty-five degrees and the rooftop was visible, showing the city hopper landing pad and wrecked rooftop buildings. The markings on the pad were unique to each tower, and with them they could tell what city it once belonged to. As he looked at it, his heart felt like stone and once again his eyes started to fill. Then the city tower was obscured as winds whipped up the sludge and turned the whole area as black as the night outside. He'd taken down the information, and immediately reported it back to the research centre.

As the wind dropped again, and visibility improved slightly, he could see the other end of the tube, and asked the engineers to set coordinates to meet up with it. Over 150 metres of tube had to be remade, almost all of it in free air. It would take time to complete. Two and one-half hours of deafening noise lay ahead, and he warned the crew what to expect.

The machine started forward at what seemed like a snail's pace. Everyone was wearing soundproof ear defenders but the noise could still be heard in the background, and someone was quietly singing to himself. Every word spoken could be heard by all, and care had to be taken when voicing an opinion. Jokes were the norm, and one member of the crew asked who else John knew who was bald, and if she had a partner. John didn't say anything about Pauline except that she too was beautiful, not as beautiful as his Juliette though.

John asked the crew, starting with the nose section, to say a bit about themselves. He found it interesting that most of the engineers and scientists had lived most of their lives at the research centre, and those with partners had children who would probably spend their lives there too.

By the time the last person had spoken, the noise stopped, indicating the tube reconstruction was complete. Before removing his ear defenders, John checked the scan and visual monitors. Apart from a layer of sludge in the bottom, the tube looked remarkably clear and he moved to set them going again at high speed. Soon they were travelling at twenty-five kilometres per hour, still descending towards Jumla Junction.

'Only thirty-nine kilometres left to go,' John told everyone. 'At this speed we'll be there in just over one and one-half hours.'

John had been driving for quite some time. He was looking at the forward monitors and started to slow the machine down. 'Scans indicate the end of the tube is just ahead,' He told everyone with a puzzled expression on his face.

The instruments indicated they had stopped, and John tried to make out what the scans were telling him. He waited for the computer to create a three-dimensional image that would give them a better picture.

It took almost a minute to display the result. He looked at the image and was shocked. Jumla Junction was missing. There was just a hole in the ground which was almost half filled with sludge. Powerful winds were whipping up earth and water into columns of mud, and the whole picture looked out of this world. The gaping hole stretched for many kilometres into the distance, too far to compute, and so wide the edges could only just be seen by the scanner. Trillions of tons of rock and earth had been removed, including the whole of the junction itself.

John couldn't believe what he was seeing. There was no sign of life, human, animal, or plant. He decided to try and look outside and see if the scans were really true. Forty metres of the tube in front of the unit was damaged, but only the top section was missing. After that there was nothing, just a long drop to the bottom of the pit. With his eyes on the monitor, he noticed a lull in the storm surrounding them and decided to pop his head out of the hatch.

'Move forward onto the broken section,' he told the engineer who'd just relieved him as the driver.

As the unit moved slowly forward, it started to repair the broken tube.

'Stop repairs. I want to look outside,' John said quickly.

The noise of repairs stopped seconds later and the machine ground its way forward, shaking as it rolled over debris left on the tube floor. Once it was out in the open, John moved back into the next section and ordered everyone out. He quickly entered an air lock and looked around for something to wear. He saw a safety suit and quickly checked the user instructions. When he'd finished, he put on the safety suit and checked his air supply. It smelled stale, but breathable, so he pressed the open button on the air lock operating panel. He stood waiting for the outside hatch to open, and shook slightly as he took his first glimpse of the outside.

What greeted him when it opened left him totally shocked. He could see about 150 metres clearly and a few kilometres further through an ever-thickening haze. All around were columns of water, mud, and rock, whipped up by powerful tornado-like winds, and lightning filled every part of the sky. It was the constant lightning that illuminated the early morning sky, as there was no sign of dawn, and probably wouldn't be for some time to come judging by the amount of debris in the atmosphere. The lightning was so bright he could see a column heading straight for them, and decided to get inside as quickly as possible. As the hatch slammed shut behind him, he could hear the rush of wind as the tornado hit. The whole unit shook and he ordered it back into the tube as fast as it could go. Within a minute, it was safely back inside and he ordered the tube to be sealed shut. Once it was closed off and they were completely underground, he ordered the driver to return to the research centre as quickly as possible. Soon they were travelling backwards at twenty kilometres per hour, the maximum possible reverse speed.

The picture of what he'd seen was imprinted on his mind: total desolation, nothing standing, not even a blade of grass. It was just brown, dirty, very wet, and extremely dark. It was completely inhospitable.

His hand brushed against the outside of his suit as he took it off; it was slimy and smelled like rotting seaweed.

'Do you want to stop?' the driver asked John.

After a short silence, he replied, 'What for? We have enough information, so just keep going till we get back, and don't slow down. If our return journey is without incident, we should be home in seven hours at the most.'

For the next two hours, the journey was smooth and without incident. Nobody said anything about what they'd all seen. It was totally unexpected. John was sitting in the corner trying to get comfortable when he felt a vibration. 'Did anyone feel that?' he asked, alarmed.

The senior engineer shouted over to him, 'Yes, I felt it right up my broken arm. Slow down.'

The vibration was steadily increasing as they slowed and everyone looked worried. Just before they came to a stop, an almighty explosion threw everyone around like rag dolls. The whole unit had been thrown onto its side and moans were coming from every section.

John banged his head, almost making him lose consciousness. He shook his head, trying to clear the stars he could see in front of his eyes, and slowly got to his feet. He checked himself over, and with only a small cut on one hand, realised there was no serious damage. He started to move through the cab to see who needed help.

As he walked around, he noticed a number of personnel unconscious and after checking them for injuries, moved them into the recovery position. With the unit at such an awkward angle, it was difficult moving about and it slowed him down considerably.

He noticed a few others were checking on staff in other parts of the unit and shouted across to one of them, 'Anyone seriously injured?'

'None yet. Most are just concussed, with only a few small cuts,' the staff member replied.

John made it to the senior engineer, who was wide-awake, and lifting him into a sitting position, asked, 'How are you?'

'No worse than before. Only a few more bruises. Help me to the system console. I need to find out what happened,' he said through clenched teeth.

John could see the senior engineer was in great pain and asked for the medical kit to be passed over to him. When he got hold of it, he fumbled around inside and found a painkiller injector. As he was about to press it against the engineer's arm the injector was pushed away. 'Don't give me that yet. I need to see what's happened first. Now help me up,' the senior engineer said, a little annoyed at John's action.

John helped him to reach the system console and propped him up against the nearest flat surface. The engineer started testing every section of the system, and as he progressed, the pained look on his face changed to a frown. 'Looks like one of the traction motors exploded. It toppled us over and wrecked the two end sections. I don't think it liked going so fast in reverse. Let's see if it still moves.'

John watched as he tried to get the unit moving. Then, suddenly, the unit lurched forward and slowly righted itself. Once stable, the engineer stopped the unit, sat on his seat, and carried out even more checks. 'Looks like we can only move forward, and then only very slow. The back two sections will be dragged along, as there's no drive units back there now.'

John looked worried, and asked, 'How far are we away from home?'

The engineer made a quick calculation and replied, 'Seventy-five kilometres. Just a little too far to walk, I'm afraid.'

'Well if we can't go backwards, we'll have to go forward, and do a complete circle,' John told him.

The engineer made a few calculations. 'This thing wasn't designed to do tight bends. It will take twenty hours to complete a circle. We'd better contact engineering and let them know we're going to be late for breakfast. At full speed it will take forty-five hours to get back,' he said, and watched the look on John's face.

'Well that's my promise broken. I said I'd be back in two days at the most.'

'I'll send all the data we've collected back with the message. They can analyse it fully by the time we get there,' he stated, and set to work.

John heard someone moan behind him and turned to see who was coming to, then helped a girl onto the driver's seat. 'How are you feeling?' he asked quietly.

'I've got a thumping headache and a few sore spots, but not too bad really. How long have I been out for?' she asked with a gruff voice.

'About fifteen minutes or so,' John replied.

'That long!' she said, and was suddenly sick.

John turned his head away. The smell was disgusting, and he knew it was going to be with them for the whole of the return journey. Then the senior engineer called him over.

'I can't get through to engineering. That explosion must have severed the communications conduit. Looks like we'll be out of contact till we complete the turn and reconnect to it,' he told John, and the look on his face said it all. They were on their own, and far from any help or safety.

John didn't say a word to the senior engineer, he just placed the injector against his arm and pressed the trigger. For a moment the engineer looked a little surprised, but soon relaxed, and fell asleep.

'Strong stuff!' John said to himself, then moved around the unit checking on staff.

He made his way to the rear of the unit and noted the number of injured and their injuries. It wasn't as bad as it could have been. The weight of the unit prevented it from moving too much in the explosion, and kept it from turning completely over. That would have been disastrous. He quickly made his way forward and entered the nose section. Here there was less of a mess, and the injuries were trivial compared to those at the rear.

He was about to talk to a member of staff when there was an even bigger explosion. He was thrown off his feet and thrown against the wall. Just before he lost consciousness, he caught sight of flames at the rear of the unit.

Rose received the message about the pillar from the tube construction unit, and frowned. She handed it to an engineer and asked her to find out where it came from. As she accessed archives, Rose took a look at the unit's progress. It wasn't going as fast as she'd hoped, and she shook her head. By the time she'd finished checking its progress, the information she'd requested had been found. Walking back to the engineer, she noted the look on her face. The engineer looked shocked. Glancing at the screen, she too looked shocked, and stared blankly at it for a moment.

'Are you sure that's right?' Rose said, hoping she was wrong.

'I double-checked it. If the number they gave us is correct, that pillar is many miles from home,' the engineer told her.

'Send the information, and tell them to check the number again. If it is right, I think we may be in trouble,' Rose said, then added, 'this goes no further. OK?'

The engineer nodded in agreement and sat down.

A short time later, the engineer came over to Rose and said quietly, 'We have another disturbing message ma'am.'

Rose quickly got to her feet and followed the engineer over to the console. She looked at the information and whispered, 'Find out what city that tower is from, and not a word to anyone.'

Rose sat next to the engineer as she accessed the archives once again. It took only a few seconds for the information they requested to appear on the screen and both read it instantly.

'I find that hard to believe. How can a city tower be so far from its origin? There must be some mistake with the information they've sent us.'

The engineer looked at Rose and calmly stated, 'The information must be correct. Each tower has a unique marking. Even the slightest mistake in the marking would come back as a negative. This one came back positive. It's from Shimoga, just north of the major city of Bangalore, in the Indian region of Eurasia.'

'I don't think we will tell them about it. Keep it quiet; I don't want to start a panic,' Rose told the engineer, who had started to cry.

Rose sat beside her, and placing her arm around the engineer's shoulder, tried to console her.

Ten hours passed and it was dawn. Rose was still awake and feeling really groggy. She remembered what Juliette had done for her the last time she felt like this and decided to have it done again. She called Juliette immediately.

Juliette was fast asleep when her communicator chirped. She woke up instantly and went to answer it. She hesitated when she saw it was Rose, just in case it was bad news. She thought for a moment before answering the call. 'Hi, how's it going over there?' she asked, trying to sound upbeat.

'Good morning Juliette, everything is going to plan. I've been up all night and feel really tired. Is there any chance of a quick tonic to keep me going? Like you did last time, please?'

Juliette looked at the time and realised it was almost time for breakfast. 'OK. Meet me at the hospital in twenty minutes and I'll give you enough energy to keep you going for the next three days if you want.'

'That's brilliant. I'll see you there. Bye.' Rose cut her off.

Rose went over to the young engineer she'd comforted earlier and told her to get some rest, then went over to the senior engineer and told him where she was going. 'Don't hesitate to call if anything happens, OK?'

He just nodded and carried on with his work.

Rose left immediately for the hospital to meet up with Juliette.

Juliette arrived at the hospital shortly before Rose and set the equipment ready for her treatment. When Rose did arrive, she was quickly placed on the treatment table and sedated. The physiotherapy unit was placed over her whole body. No words were spoken, and soon Rose was engulfed in the brightly glowing energy field. As the process was going to take awhile to complete, Juliette went to see if Pauline was up and about. She wasn't, so Juliette went back to the treatment room. As she entered, she heard Rose's communicator chirping away inside the unit. But there was no way to accept the call; the caller would have to wait. Thirty minutes passed before the unit finished treating Rose, and Juliette quickly administered the sedative antidote.

As Rose came to, Juliette told her that her communicator went off not long after entering the unit. Rose looked at it and walked away into a corner of the room.

Rose called the senior engineer and asked what he wanted.

'We've lost contact with the construction unit. Our information indicates there was an explosion just before communications were cut,' he said, sounding anxious.

Rose looked sideways at Juliette and noticed she was busy cleaning the equipment in preparation for the next use. Walking quickly past her, she said, 'I have to go. I'm needed in engineering. Thanks for the boost. I feel great.'

'That's OK. No problem is there?' Juliette said enquiringly.

'No problem. Just someone needing to be replaced. Everyone's tired,' Rose said, hoping her fib sounded convincing enough.

'Well don't send them all over here. I'll be taking the kids to breakfast soon. They are going to school this morning, whether they like it or not,' Juliette said, sounding bossy.

'Good girl. I've got to go. Bye,' Rose said, and disappeared quickly.

When Rose got back to engineering, she rushed over to the senior engineer and asked him for an update. She scanned the information and asked, 'Is that all we have? Didn't they send any data back?'

'Nothing. We've checked the conduit. It's broken seventy-five kilometres down the tube. There was a second explosion forty-five minutes after the first. Judging by its size, we don't expect anyone survived. If there were survivors, they would have been seriously injured, and are probably dead by now. A rescue would be too dangerous to undertake at this time,' she was told solemnly.

Rose walked away and sat at a console. She placed her head in her hands and hid the fact that she was crying. She really got to like John, and felt like he was one of her family. Now she was going to have to tell Juliette the sad news, and wasn't looking forward to doing it. There were also the twelve other engineers onboard, most of whom had partners, and they would also have to be told. She felt terrible, and tried to raise herself above the grief she now felt. 'I must get to work,' she said to herself, and crossed to a console next to the senior engineer.

'I'll take over for a few hours. Go and get some rest,' she told him calmly, as if nothing had happened.

She just sat and watched the other engineers working. They were busy carrying out repairs, along with other engineers all over the centre. Judging by the progress, it wouldn't be long before everything was back to normal again. Only she didn't have a clue what was normal now.

The space probe wasn't due to make its first report for at least another twelve hours, which seemed so far away. Time seemed to be passing slowly now and she was so full of energy she couldn't sit still.

Most of her staff noticed the way she was constantly getting to her feet and walking back and forth along an imaginary line, only to sit back down at the end of it. It made them feel very uncomfortable and they wondered what the problem was. They began to think something was seriously wrong, and tried to keep her from knowing about it.

Rose wasn't stupid; she noticed the change of mood in the room and walked to the front of the section. Looking at everyone, she raised her voice and said, 'The construction unit has made good progress and is currently seventy-five kilometres down the tube. It has made a few repairs and is maintaining a good seal. Some information has been sent back, but it's not enough for us to understand what's happened out there yet. We hope to get a better picture when we have all the data. The space probe is due to download data later this evening, and that information will keep us occupied for a few days while we analyse it. Try not to guess what has happened; rumours can spread rapidly, and they may not be true and cause undue stress. So take care about what you say to people. That includes your partners. All information is classified as top secret until further notice. That's all.'

She hoped that what she said would ease the situation, but it didn't. It only made everyone aware that bad news was coming at some time in the near future, and now an air of gloom descended on them all.

Rose bit her lip and sat down. 'I wish Simon were here now. He could calm a stormy sea if he spoke to it,' she said to herself. Then she realised she had to organise his funeral for later in the week, and started to jot down what would be required. At least that task kept her busy and her mind occupied.

Rose left engineering and made her way over to the hospital to find out where Simon was lying at rest. She entered the main entrance and was greeted by the receptionist. 'Good morning ma'am. What can we do for you today?'

Rose was taken aback by the polite young girl and said, 'Is Dr. James available please?'

The girl called him on the intercom, and shortly after, he appeared in the foyer. 'Hi Rose. What can I do for you?' he asked, sounding just as polite.

'I'd like to know where Simon is resting,' she said quietly.

'Follow me,' said Brian, in a slightly lowered tone of voice.

Rose followed him down a corridor, then down some steps, and ended up in the room marked "Mortuary". Brian walked over to a casket and lifted the lid. Inside was Simon. He looked as if he were just sleeping quietly, and the sight shocked Rose. After a sharp intake of breath, she walked up to him and looked closely.

'How come he's in such a good condition? He looked terrible the last time I saw him,' she asked, puzzled.

'I thought you might want an open coffin, so I regenerated his body to make him whole again.'

Rose looked shocked. 'That wouldn't have brought him back to life. Would it?'

Brian looked at her strangely before replying, 'You should know full well we can regenerate every cell in the body, including the brain. But we cannot program the brain to make the body function. Even if we could, it wouldn't be Simon; all the memories would have disappeared. So no, he wasn't brought back to life. It's just his body.'

The look on Rose's face changed as Brian spoke. It was like she wanted Simon to get up out of the casket and say hi or something, but now she looked completely drained of all emotion. 'Sorry I wasn't thinking straight. It was a shock to see him looking so well. If you know what I mean.'

'Don't worry about it. This is the first time I've ever done this, and I think it's going to be the last, judging by your reaction,' he told her.

I'll arrange his funeral for Thursday, if that's OK with you?'

'Whenever you want is fine by me. Just make sure everyone knows about it. OK?' he said sympathetically.

Rose just nodded and watched as Brian closed the casket lid. It was time for breakfast and Brian asked if she would like to dine with him and Pauline.

Rose thought for a moment. It would be a good time to tell them about the explosion in the tube and ask how to let Juliette know about the bad news. 'Yes, I'd like to have breakfast with you. I hope you don't mind my two little devils coming along as well.'

'Not at all, the more the merrier,' he said, sounding really cheerful.

She walked in front of him as they left; she was trying to hide the pained look on her face, knowing what she had to say to him later.

Rose, Brian, and Pauline arrived at the chow house for breakfast. As they were about to walk in, Pauline heard a familiar voice calling her. It was Juliette.

'Pauline. Over here!' said Juliette, calling from a few metres away.

As she turned, Juliette, Petal, and Fred came towards them. 'Come on, join us for breakfast. It'll be like a mini party,' Juliette told her, smiling as if she hadn't a worry in the world.

Pauline looked at Brian and asked, 'Do you mind?'

Brian nodded and smiled, indicating he didn't mind one bit.

Rose, on the other hand, looked at Petal and pointed a finger. 'Fine, as long as she doesn't sit near Otho.'

Petal's face dropped at hearing that. 'What have I done?' she asked, upset.

Rose just looked at Otho and back again. The action said it all and Petal stormed into the MATCH and sat at their reserved table. Juliette quickly followed and sat next to her. 'I'll have a word with Rose later. I'm sure she'll come round and let you see Otho.'

With that remark Petal, reddened slightly and went quiet.

Everyone took their places at the table and ordered breakfast. The atmosphere around the table was quite tense, but as they tucked into the meal, the tension eased and soon everyone was chatting. Only Otho and Petal said nothing, but they did catch each other's eyes now and again, managing some smiles and the odd blown kiss when no one was paying them much attention. Rose was the only one sitting at the table hardly saying a word, and Brian noticed her tense mood.

'What's up Rose?' he asked her quietly.

'I'll have a word with you and Pauline a bit later, if you don't mind.'

'Why, have we done something wrong?' he asked, puzzled by what she'd said.

'No nothing like that. I just need some advice. That's all,' she said quickly, trying to stop the impending interrogation.

'Is that all? You had me worried for a minute. OK, meet me at the hospital later, if you want,' he told her, then carried on eating his breakfast.

'Thanks,' she said quietly. She looked down at her plate and played with her food.

After breakfast, Rose headed straight back to engineering. Walking over to the duty engineers, she asked, 'Any news from the construction unit?'

The engineer shook his head and replied, 'Not a thing. They must be doing OK out there.' He carried on with his work.

She turned quickly and left for the hospital complex.

Brian and Pauline arrived at the hospital and entered his office. 'Ah. Home at last,' Pauline said sarcastically, and looked at Brian.

'I'll see about getting our place fit to live in this afternoon, OK?' he told her.

'I don't want to live there anymore. I want to live in the apartment next door to Juliette's. It is vacant,' she said with a pleading tone.

Brian looked at her and said, 'Rose will be over shortly to have a word with us. I'll ask her about it then, OK?'

Pauline looked at him and as she was about to ask why, Brian received a call from reception. He answered it and turned to Pauline. 'She's here. I must go and meet her. Back in a minute.' He rushed out of the room.

When he returned, he ushered Rose into his office and followed her in. She made for his chair behind the desk and sat down. 'Please take a seat,' she said quietly to them. And they sat down in front of her.

'I have some bad news. We lost contact with the tube construction unit yesterday evening. An explosion occurred about seventy-five kilometres from here and communications ceased. There has been no response since. Calculations indicate the explosion was big enough to kill or seriously injure everyone onboard, and it's too far away to attempt a rescue.' She paused for them to take it in, and watched as tears ran down Pauline's face. 'What I need to know is how to break the news to Juliette.'

Brian was by now holding Pauline tightly. She was shaking and crying uncontrollably. He just looked at Rose and said, 'You knew about this at breakfast this morning didn't you?'

'Yes, but I didn't think it was the right time to say anything,' she replied caringly.

There was silence; even Pauline had stopped crying, and she looked up at Rose. 'I don't think you had better say anything to Juliette. It would make things worse. And Petal, she hates you, so don't tell her. I'll do it.' And she looked at Brian. 'Will you come too please?'

'Sure. I wouldn't let you do this by yourself.' He pulled her head to him, holding it tightly against his shoulder.

'Leave it with us,' he said to Rose.

She looked at them both for a moment then stood up and walked out of the room. As she left, she heard Pauline crying once again, and felt sorry for her. The one thing she hated most was informing someone about the death of a loved one, especially when the people involved were well known to her.

She made her way back to engineering and quickly started work. She needed to keep her mind occupied.

Juliette had just come back from taking the kids to school when she received a call from Brian. Wondering what he wanted, she asked, 'Hi. What can I do for you?'

'Got time for a drink with Pauline and me? We hope to be moving in next door,' he said calmly, trying not to let his true emotions surface.

'Are you coming here?'

'Yes we'll be over in a few minutes, if that's all right,' he said quickly.

'Sure. No problem,' she said. And he cut off.

Juliette rushed upstairs to change into something a little nicer than her cleaning clothes. As she went back down, the doorbell sounded and she walked over to let her guests in. When she opened the door, she saw Brian first. Pauline was slightly behind him, and her face wasn't visible. 'Come in,' she said and turned to show them in. As Pauline passed her, Juliette wondered why she was looking away. When they were inside, Brian caught hold of Juliette's hand and led her to the sofa where Pauline had taken a seat.

'Sit down please,' he said quietly, then looked at Pauline.

Juliette noticed their strange behaviour and, getting worried, started to fidget. 'There's something's wrong, isn't there?' she asked with a shaky voice.

Brian knelt in front of her and, speaking quietly, started to explain what had happened. 'There has been an explosion in the tube and contact with the construction unit has been lost.' He stopped as Juliette was shaking so much Pauline had to put her arms around her quickly, just to stop her from falling off the sofa. Tears ran down Juliette's face and she started to whine.

He continued, 'We don't really know what has happened out there, but it doesn't look good. Engineering calculated there may not be any survivors. And it's too far to send a rescue party out.'

By now Juliette had become hysterical and Pauline had difficulty holding her. Both girls were crying, and Brian looked worried. He quickly ran outside to his SCAT and brought his medical kit inside. Opening the box, he removed an injector and placed it against Juliette's arm. He pressed the trigger and watched as she slowly relaxed and stopped shaking. Lifting her up, he carried her upstairs and laid her on her bed. Pauline followed closely behind and he said, 'Get her undressed and into bed. I'll go to the hospital and get a room ready, just in case it's needed. I'll leave the injector with you. Only use it if it's needed,' he said as he left.

It was almost an hour before Juliette came to. She sat bolt upright on the bed and stared at the wall in front of her. It scared Pauline, who was lying quietly beside her.

'That was a terrible nightmare,' Juliette said quietly to herself, and went to get up. She found her legs weren't working properly and looked really puzzled. 'What's up with me?' she said to herself again.

Pauline reached over and touched her shoulder. Juliette froze for a moment, turned, and shouted, 'John.'

Pauline saw the look on her face as soon as she realised it wasn't John, and quickly reached for the injector. Suddenly Juliette collapsed on her and started to cry loudly and uncontrollably. Pauline decided to let her carry on, and kept the injector just out of sight.

After what seemed like hours, Juliette started to quiet down and soon she was just sobbing. Every now and again, Juliette uttered just one word, 'Why.' She looked into Pauline's eyes as if looking for the answer, but there wasn't one, and she settled down on Pauline's lap. Pauline just stroked her shoulders and rocked slowly on the bed.

Juliette quietly, but clearly, said, 'He's not dead. I can still feel him. He's alive.' And she smiled at Pauline, who was now crying once again.

It was almost lunchtime, and Petal was due home. Pauline looked at Juliette and said quietly, 'Would you like me to tell Petal?'

Juliette looked at her and sat up instantly. 'Tell Petal what? What time is it? The kids will be home soon. They will need lunch.' She got dressed quickly.

Pauline was really worried and called Brian. 'Hi, Juliette is acting really strange. She keeps telling me that John isn't dead. And she's getting ready to take the children to lunch.'

'She's in denial. If she tries to leave, sedate her. I'm on my way over now,' he said, and cut her off. Pauline hid the injector behind her back and rushed after Juliette. She was downstairs, waiting by the front door for Petal and Fred to arrive home. She was fidgeting profusely and scraping her hands with her nails.

Pauline went up to her and asked, 'Will you help me make the bed before we go, please?'

'Sure,' she answered, and followed Pauline up the stairs. As she reached across the bed, to pull the sheets, Pauline placed the injector against her buttock and squeezed the trigger.

Juliette spun round and gave her a really nasty look. 'What was tha—' was all she managed to say before slumping onto the bed.

Pauline quickly undressed her again and tucked her up in bed just as the door bell rang.

It was Brian. He was followed closely behind by Petal and Fred.

Pauline must have looked terrible, because the first thing Petal said was, 'What's wrong?' She sounded really concerned.

Brian held her hand and led her over to the sofa. Slowly he said to her exactly what he'd told Juliette, and once again the injector had to be used; she too took it really badly.

He lifted her into his arms, and carried her upstairs. She was limp and breathing quietly, totally the opposite of what she'd been like just a few moments earlier. He entered her bedroom, placed her on the bed, left the room, and called for Pauline.

When she didn't come, he wandered downstairs and found her sitting next to Fred.

Fred sat silently through the whole thing, and when he eventually spoke, he asked, 'How is Juliette?'

Brian looked sympathetically at him, and said, 'She's sedated and sleeping quietly upstairs.'

With that, Fred ran quickly up the stairs and entered her bedroom.

Brian ran after him, and when he reached the room, he saw Fred lying next to his sister, sobbing quietly on her bosom.

Brian felt for them all, and as Pauline came to him, she too started to cry.

'I think we'll stay here tonight,' Brian told her. 'I'll get a bed sent over. We can take turn watching them. It's obvious John was quite a man for them to react like this.' He hugged her tightly, then added, 'Can you undress Petal and tuck her in too?'

Brian crossed the room and sat next to Juliette. He opened his medical box and took out some implements. Fred watched and asked what he was doing to her.

'I'm just checking her over,' he told him.

He took a sample of blood from her and ran a test to see if there were abnormal levels of enzymes. When finished, he crossed to Pauline and said, 'She and her foetus are healthy.'

'She's pregnant?' Pauline asked, and cried even more.

Fred quickly stood up when she started to cry, and demanded to know what Brian had found. 'What's wrong with my sister?'

Brian looked at Pauline for guidance, and once again heard Fred shout, 'Tell me what's up with my sister.'

Pauline looked at him, and with a soft voice, said, 'Your sister is pregnant. She's going to have a baby.'

Fred looked back at his sister and muttered, 'He'll never see it. He's gone.'

Brian felt terrible and wished he hadn't said anything about it. He went downstairs, sat on the sofa, put his head in his hands, and wept. Pauline followed him down, and seeing him in such a state, quickly crossed to comfort him. She knelt before him, placed his head on her chest, and stroked his hair.

Three hours passed, and Pauline was watching Juliette quietly sleeping on the bed. Juliette started to stir, and Pauline quickly crossed the room to sit next to her. As her eyes opened, the look in her eyes was one of complete emptiness, and Pauline felt her throat tighten.

'He hasn't gone, has he?' Juliette asked with a rough-sounding voice.

The roughness of her voice was a side effect of the sedative.

She turned over and saw Fred next to her. 'How long has he been there?' she asked.

'Since we told him at lunchtime. Petal is in her room; we had to sedate her too,' Pauline told her calmly.

Juliette lay back on the bed and quietly said, 'I don't believe it. My life can't be over before it's started.' And tears came to her eyes.

'Brian checked you over to see if you were OK.' Pauline paused for a moment, wondering whether to tell her.

'And!' said Juliette, sounding a little agitated by the abrupt end to her sentence.

Pauline looked at her, and with a thin smile, said, 'You're pregnant.'

Juliette looked at her for a moment, and started to cry. 'I wanted so much to have a baby with him. But how?' Then her mood changed, and sounding normal but puzzled, she said, 'I thought we couldn't.'

'The regeneration process removed his birth control implant. That's how it happened.'

Juliette looked up at her and said, 'He'll never see the baby now. But I'll make sure it knows how wonderful a father it had.'

Then both of them started to cry once more, and Pauline whispered in her ear, 'It! That doesn't sound right. You're having a baby boy.'

CHAPTER 10
IS THERE ANYONE OUT THERE?

Rose waited anxiously for the probe to make its first pass and download the information it was gathering. It had been almost twenty-seven hours since it was launched, and was now slightly overdue. She paced back and forth, looking repeatedly at the clock, which seemed to stop every time she looked, and constantly checked her monitor for signs of life.

She walked over to the senior engineer and said, 'I hope it hasn't been destroyed. We don't have another one. Any ideas why it's late?'

The engineer shrugged his shoulders and replied, 'I don't know much about the probe. I'll see if there's any information in the archives.'

'Never mind. It's too late for that. Either it's failed or been destroyed.'

'Don't be so disheartened; it might just be taking longer than anticipated,' the engineer told her, in a manner suggesting she was making everyone miserable.

Another hour passed before an engineer working at the back of the room shouted, 'There's a faint signal coming in, and it's getting stronger by the second.'

Rose rushed over to her console and quickly picked up the signal. 'That sounds like it,' she shouted back, pleased.

Then the probe registered its presence by sending bursts of data with a sound like a flock of chirping birds, and started sending a mass of information. The suddenness of data streaming onto their screens made them all excited, and they huddled around the monitors hoping to see something; but all they received was data, not pictures, or letters, just data. All the engineers and scientists in the room ran back to their console terminals and quickly set to work analysing what was being sent. The data was coming in fast, and just over an hour later, the download finished. Then there was silence once again and it sounded eerie. Now the data had to be analysed by the computer, and a preliminary report issued. Once that was done, they might have some idea of what happened on the outside. Everyone stood back and waited impatiently for the report to arrive.

When the report was finally issued, it only appeared on Rose's monitor. She quickly read the result, frowned, and thought about how to explain it to her staff. After what seemed like hours, she finally made up her mind about what to say to everyone, and walked to the front of the room. Looking around, she raised her arms in the air and clapped her hands together attracting everyone's attention.

With a dejected look, she said calmly, 'Our planet was nearly hit by a massive heavenly body. An asteroid, almost a quarter the size of our moon, and big enough to totally destroy earth, missed us by just over twenty-five thousand kilometres. It has caused planetwide destruction and completely destroyed the ozone layer. Storms, with winds in excess of fifteen hundred kilometres per hour now cover the whole planet, making it impossible to see the surface. The impacts on the outside of the domes happened every time fragments travelling with the asteroid struck the domes; some of those fragments were extremely large. They caused the damage we now have to repair. The fact that they did hit is testament to the ferocity of the meteor storm that followed the passing of the object. Some of our domes are no longer under the mountains; the Himalayan range as we knew it has been blown away. Deep radar scans show a surface totally different to what it was, but it's still too early to say much about that. A vast quantity of sea water has been displaced, and the whole surface of the planet appears to be in a terrible state.'

Rose paused before she continued, 'I will tell you more when all the data has been analysed. The probe is due to make another download twenty-six hours from now. It will take a few hours after that to completely analyse the data and we should have a complete picture then. Everyone here is under oath to say nothing, and I mean nothing, to anyone about this. That goes for your partners too. Anyone who disobeys this order will be severely punished.' Once again she paused for them to take it in.

She concluded her speech with, 'That's all. Those of you who have families can go home. Everyone else can rest here. We'll use only a skeleton crew tonight, but a full team is required for tomorrow morning. Good night.'

And with that Rose walked back to her terminal, shut it down, and went home herself.

When she reached her apartment, her partner, Frank Powell, was there to meet her. The look on Rose's face told him something was up. He put his arms around her, gave her a hug, and asked, 'What's up?'

'We've just had the first download from the probe, and it doesn't look good. I only hope the second pass will provide us with a more satisfying result. It's a mess out there,' she said really quietly, not knowing if Otho or Anne were awake and could hear her.

Otho heard something, and came down the stairs to see what it was. He saw Frank with his arms around his mother and asked, 'What's up?'

Rose, not wanting to tell him anything about what she'd just said, told him to sit on the sofa. When seated, she sat next to him and spoke softly, 'John Blight is missing. We think the tube construction unit exploded, and it probably killed everyone onboard. I've changed my mind about you seeing Petal. I think she could do with a friend at this time.'

Otho looked shocked, then replied angrily, 'So you will allow me to see Petal only because her brother has died. You're sick! It makes me feel as if you only want me as a trauma councillor for her. Well, just to let you know, we were still seeing each other, and intended to keep doing so. So keep out of our lives.' He stood up, turned his back on his mother, and went back to his room, slamming the door behind him.

Frank looked at Rose, and said, 'You could have handled that better. Now you'll never get him to leave her alone.'

Rose looked at him, embarrassed by his remark, and slumped backwards. 'It doesn't matter anymore,' she said, then got up and went upstairs to their bedroom.

Frank looked puzzled by her remark, followed her up, and quietly closed their door behind him.

Rose woke early, and headed for the chow house. On the way, she called Brian and asked how Juliette was taking the news. She felt downhearted when told how Juliette had reacted, and blamed herself for John's demise. He didn't have to go on the mission; it was, after all, a purely engineering task.

She entered the chow house, and was surprised to see Juliette sitting at her table with Pauline. They weren't saying anything and the looks on their faces said it all. They were still in shock. Then Brian turned up, and as he passed, said, 'Morning Rose. Any more news yet?'

'Not much. The probe downloaded data last night, but it's too early to tell what happened out there. A final download this evening should clarify everything. Can I join you please?'

'Yes, I'm sure nobody will mind you sitting with us. Otho and Anne are here already.'

Rose was shocked by that remark, but didn't say a word. She thought they were still at home in bed. As she approached the table, she saw Otho sitting at the far end of the table with his arm around Petal, holding her close. Otho gave his mother a nasty look, and she quickly averted her eyes. Once again, she said nothing, and sat down next to Brian.

Juliette looked over to Rose and smiled, 'Hi. I had some good news last night. I'm pregnant,' she said, and sounded really pleased.

It was too much for Rose. 'That's nice,' she said with a forced smile, then left the table quickly.

Brian ran after her and found her crying just outside in the foyer. When he caught up with her, he said, 'I'm afraid you're going to have to get used to hearing things that upset you. You are our leader now and need to be strong for everyone.' He sounded sympathetic up to that point, then changed his tone of voice, 'You may not like the way Danni Mitchell has acted in the past, but you must now take on some of her strong points and not let your emotions rule your head.'

Rose looked at him, straightened herself up, and said, 'You are right. I'm just being silly.' Then she walked back inside, and sat down for breakfast.

Brian smiled, followed her in, and sat next to her,

'How come Juliette is looking so happy?' she asked him quickly, as Juliette was preoccupied chatting with Petal.

'She's on a mild neurological sedative. It will be reduced throughout the day, and I'll reassess her condition when it wears off later this evening,' he told her, then started to eat his breakfast.

The day was going too slowly for Rose. She'd gone over every piece of information sent by the probe and asked the computer to prepare a presentation. There was just too much data for her to comprehend exactly what had transpired, and she had difficulty retaining some of the information in her head. The computer couldn't complete its task until the next download had been analysed, and she made no attempt to see what had been produced at this early stage.

She walked over to the senior engineer and said, 'When all the data has been analysed and the computer has produced a presentation, I want everyone to see it simultaneously. Any ideas on how we can do that?'

The senior engineer took hold of her arm and pulled her over to see a scientist who was sitting at the side of the room. 'This is Sam. She's the best when it comes to information presentation. Tell her what you want, and see what she can come up with.'

Sam looked at Rose, and wondered what was up. Rose had never spoken to her before, and didn't know anything about her.

Rose spoke quickly, 'The computer is preparing a presentation using the data collected from the space probe. When it's complete, I want everyone at this centre to see it. Everyone must see it at the same time. Have you any idea how we can achieve that?'

Sam thought for a moment. 'How long have I got?' she asked.

'Until midnight tonight, if that's OK. The computer presentation will be ready by then at the latest, and the sooner it's broadcast, the better.'

'Leave it with me,' Sam told her with a smile.

Rose turned and left her to it.

The day was also passing slowly for Brian. He was missing Pauline's company, and hadn't known how much he enjoyed her presence until now. He called her and waited for her to answer.

'Hi,' she said, sounding really cheerful.

'Hi, how are you and Juliette getting along?' he asked, wondering why she was so bubbly.

'We're fine. Just shopping at the moment. Only window though; we don't intend to spend anything. Juliette is looking at the latest pregnancy outfits on offer.'

'How is her treatment progressing?' he asked, sounding a little concerned.

'She's almost off the sedative now, and seems to be taking it in her stride,' Pauline replied quickly.

Brian heard Juliette in the background asking Pauline for some advice on a dress. The sound of her voice and what she said took him by surprise and he smiled. 'Looks like she's getting over the initial shock,' he said, and waited for her to reply.

A few minutes passed before she did. 'Juliette has just bought a black dress to wear for the funeral of Simon later this week. She's going to call Rose shortly and ask for a favour. So leave us to it, and I'll see you for supper at six this evening,' she said, and cut him off.

Brian was quite shocked. It was like nothing had happened and he wondered if Juliette had actually made any progress. It was still too early to know, so he decided to go along with Pauline. She knew Juliette better than he, and was confident she could handle the situation well.

It was late afternoon, and Rose was about to stop work to head for home. She was going to collect her children and go for something to eat before the rush. Everyone had been told there would be a presentation later that night, and the venue would be announced after supper had finished. She walked over to her SCAT, and was just about to mount it when she received a call. It was from Juliette, and puzzled, she answered it. 'Hi, Juliette. How are you?'

'I'm fine.' There was a slight paused before she continued, 'I've a favour to ask, if you don't mind.'

'Sure, if I can be of any assistance to you, just ask,' Rose said, trying not to show how worried she was.

'I was wondering if we can hold a memorial service for John and the tube construction crew. If we can, could it be just after Simon's funeral later this week, please?' she asked, her voice pleasant.

Rose went quiet. She hadn't been expecting that, and taken by surprise, felt really angry. She was just about to tell her off, when she realised how awful that would sound. She thought quickly and replied, 'I will see what we can do. We may have a separate event for John and the engineers once we establish if we can recover them or not. I'll let you know well before Simon's funeral, just to allow time for you to prepare. Is that OK?'

'Thanks Rose. I'll wait for you to call,' Juliette said, and cut off.

Rose was really unhappy. She thought the memorial service would overshadow Simon's funeral, and she couldn't accept that. She walked over to see the senior engineer and asked, 'How difficult will it be to recover the tube construction unit's crew?'

'I'll draw up some options. We can look at them later if you want,' he said, and looked at her with a frown. 'It's not going to be easy though.'

'I know, but we must go through the motions. Relatives will want to know why we haven't tried if we don't.'

The senior engineer agreed, and set to work.

Rose once again made for her SCAT, and before anyone else could stop her, she left for home.

A few hours had passed, and it was getting late. Rose left her apartment and rushed to get to engineering before the probe came back. Her communicator chirped, indicating an incoming message, and she took her eyes off her flight path to view it. Before she could finish reading it, she was suddenly thrown headfirst into the SCAT's console, banging her head. Sitting up quickly, she looked around and noticed her machine had stopped just in front of the main dome wall. She'd veered off course and almost crashed. Luckily for her, the machine made it impossible to crash. She quickly examined her head by looking in a wing mirror. She had a slight cut to her forehead and asked the onboard medical unit to provide a dressing. She watched as a robotic arm extended from the side of the console, and she took the small can of spray out of its grip. Using the supplied tissue, she cleaned the area, applied the spray immediately, and like magic, the cut disappeared behind an invisible layer of artificial skin. As the arm retracted, she looked at her communicator and finished reading the message.

'The probe has started to download data. What time will you be arriving in engineering?' The message was from Rajinda, who had taken over at the engineering control centre.

Rose looked annoyed because she wasn't there when it started. It wasn't due to start for another three hours. She adjusted her direction and shot forward as quickly as the machine would allow. When she arrived at engineering, she made her way over to Rajinda and punched his arm.

'What was that for?' he asked, rubbing his arm.

'I bumped my head when reading the message you sent me. Next time just call, OK!' she said sharply.

'The probe's hovering overhead at a height of thirty-nine kilometres. It started to download information just over twenty minutes ago, and will continue for the next six hours,' he told her.

She looked shocked. 'Six hours. How much data has it recorded? It will take many more hours to analyse it all if there's that much.'

'We estimate the presentation you requested will not be ready until after breakfast tomorrow morning at the earliest. Sam, our computer genius, is working to speed the process up,' he told her, and pointed towards where Sam was sitting.

Rose walked over to her, and asked, 'Are you still here?'

'I'm always here. I don't have a partner to go home to like most of the others,' she replied.

Rose looked at her and wondered what was up. She was very good looking and seemed to be quite a bubbly type of person. 'How come you don't have a partner yet? I'll see about getting you one for you. Life can be lonely in this place.'

The girl looked a little shocked by that remark and replied sharply, 'When I'm old enough, I'm sure I'll have no problem getting a partner. I don't intend doing so now; I'm only fifteen.'

Rose stared at her for a moment, then went red in the face. 'You're Zingansam, aren't you?'

'Yes,' replied the girl. 'Everyone calls me Sam for short though.'

Rose put her hand on the young girl's shoulder and said, 'I'm sorry. I haven't had a chance to meet you properly. So you are our special little genius, the youngest chief technologist ever. I'm pleased to meet you.'

'And me you,' she replied, smiling. 'I'll be working through the night on this, so please, make sure nobody disturbs me.'

Rose smiled back at her and nodded. 'I'll make sure you get anything you require, young lady,' she said and walked away.

Rose approached Rajinda and spoke quietly to him. 'Make sure she is looked after; she'll be working all night. Don't let anyone disturb her. We can't afford any more delays. I need to know what's happened out there; everyone does.'

Rajinda looked calmly at her and replied, 'Don't let anyone disturb her! You've got to be joking. The last person who disturbed her when she was busy ended up having to replace every electronic item he possessed. She bugged the lot. So don't worry about her being disturbed.'

Rose looked across at her and smiled. 'Some kid! Well, I'll leave you to it. Call me if you need me. I'm off home. My partner hasn't seen me much in the past few weeks.'

Rajinda looked a little annoyed. 'Neither has mine!' he stated, and turned away from her.

Rose realised she'd touched a raw nerve and left instantly.

Rose was fast asleep when her communicator chirped up. Looking at the time, she said quietly, 'What now!' and got straight up. When she was out of her bedroom, she called engineering to see what they wanted, and Rajinda said, 'Hi Rose. Some good news at last. The tube construction unit is boring its way into the tube access port. We expect it to be in engineering within the next ten minutes. Are you coming over?'

Rose went quiet for a moment, trying to take in what he'd said, then replied, 'Yes, I'll be over straight away.' And she cut him off.

Hurrying to get ready, she tripped over her own feet and cursed as she made for the front door. The noise woke Otho, and he rushed downstairs to see what was going on.

Rose told him what she'd been told, and Otho asked, 'Can I come too please?'

She thought for a moment, then, with a big smile, said, 'Sure, why not. You need to know what goes on in engineering at some time in your career.'

She mounted her SCAT and Otho jumped on behind. They were soon flying at high speed, and Otho whooped with glee; he loved going fast.

'Mum, can I borrow this now and again?' he asked hopefully.

'You might. It all depends what you want it for,' she said to his surprise.

'Yippee!' He shouted, and grinned all the way to engineering.

When they arrived, Rose headed straight to the tube access port. Otho stayed on the SCAT, pretending to drive it. He still didn't have permission to take it, but didn't care much; he was going to have permission soon enough.

Rose walked over to Rajinda, who was watching the clear shield being placed over the access port, and stood quietly beside him. He looked at her and said calmly, 'It looks like it wasn't destroyed after all. How do we explain that to everyone?'

Rose didn't say a word. She knew only too well there would be repercussions about it. Just now she was wondering if anyone had died in the explosions. She watched engineers opening the access door and waited with bated breath to see what state the unit was in. The air inside the shield fogged as the door swung open, obscuring all inside, and this made her feel very frustrated.

'How long till it's clear to open?' she asked impatiently.

'Not long. As soon as the port is resealed, we can start to remove the shield and extract the foul air inside. Then we'll know exactly what we are dealing with,' he told her, as calmly as before.

It was obvious there was no way they could go any faster.

Rose walked back to Otho and told her SCAT to let him ride around engineering slowly. She also pointed out Sam, the little genius, and told him to have a chat with her, just to pass the time.

Otho looked at her, and said, 'Isn't she a bit old for me?' He knew instantly what his mum was trying to do.

'She's the same age as you! So go on, have a chat with her.'

'She may be the same age in years, but not the same age mentally. She won't be any fun to be with. I know. Word spreads fast here. She fancies someone else anyway, someone older,' he told her, and drove away as quickly as he could.

Rose looked mad. She'd done it again. And walking back to Rajinda, she said, 'I'd better stop trying to interfere with Otho's life. I'm useless at communicating with people, especially him.'

Rajinda just looked at her and said nothing. He hadn't a clue what she was on about.

As the air inside the shield cleared, the construction unit came into view and everyone gasped. It was in a terrible mess. The whole rear section was crumpled and most of its drive units were in shreds from the explosions. Only five of the twelve drive units were left intact. As soon as the shield was removed, engineers moved forward to help get the personnel out.

The doors weren't opening, and Rose was extremely anxious. 'Is anyone alive in there?' she asked, her voice full of concern.

'If there was nobody alive, this thing wouldn't be here now,' Rajinda told her, then gave an order to his engineers, 'Get the doors open. It looks like they're jammed.'

Lasers started to cut around the doors, and soon two doors fell wide open. Not long after, all the unit's doors were open and slowly people started to emerge. Everyone was covered in black soot, making it difficult to see who was who, and some were helping others to walk.

Rose was waiting to one side, and as soon as she saw them coming out, called the hospital for help. As she closed in, she saw John. He was helping a female engineer to walk. Her leg was heavily bandaged, and he helped her over to a bench to sit down.

Rose looked at him and said, 'Nice to see you. We were extremely worried when the unit blew up, and we all thought we'd lost you.'

'It did blow up. Twice. And if it hadn't been for the onboard fire prevention system kicking in, we would all be dead,' he told her after clearing his throat.

Rose noticed John had a large lump on his forehead and tried to examine him. 'See to them first; they're worse off than me,' he told her, pointing to a number of staff sitting on the ground with bandages on various parts of their bodies.

'You smell awful. I suggest you find the nearest cleansing cubicle and freshen up before doing anything else,' she told him and, looking at the others, she said, 'I think they all need to freshen up.'

Rajinda was listening to what she'd said and called engineering control. 'Send over the mobile cleansing unit. We need it near the tube access port. Now.'

It was with them in under five minutes, and John was one of the first to enter. He stood still, feeling the tingling sensation as it cleansed his body, and inhaled the oxygen-rich, scented air. Soon he was relaxed and left the cubicle looking and feeling almost like a new man. He still had a large lump on his head which needed treatment. Before he did anything else, he called his SCAT and asked it to meet him in engineering.

He saw a number of staff in white uniforms, and realising they were hospital staff, walked over to a nurse to see about the lump. The hospital staff had arrived when he was freshening up, and quickly set to work helping the injured. After a quick examination, he was provided with a therapeutic cool pad and told to apply it to the wounded area. Within a few minutes, the lump was gone and he looked as if nothing had ever happened to him. Now there was just his slightly ripped clothing to see too.

'Where's Brian?' he asked a nurse attending the girl he'd helped earlier.

'He's with Pauline and Juliette tonight,' she replied.

Before he could enquire further he was interrupted. 'You'd better get changed into this,' said Rajinda, who was holding out a pale blue uniform.

John found a quiet corner and quickly donned the outfit. When he came back to where he'd been treated, he realised everyone was staring and smiling at him, especially the females. He looked down at himself, and realised why. The outfit he was wearing was skintight, leaving nothing to the imagination. He crossed to Rajinda and told him he was going straight home.

Just before he mounted his SCAT, he called a nurse over and asked, 'Can you handle these injuries?'

'These are only minor injuries. We nurses are trained to handle this type of trauma. The only person we can't do anything for is that chap over there. I'm afraid he's dead.'

'Well, as long as you know what you're doing.' John said to her.

'This is easy stuff,' she replied, staring at him and smiling.

He watched as she quickly organised the stretchers into a line. 'There, that will make them easier to transport.' She stopped smiling as they were towed away by a spitter.

Rajinda looked at John, and said quite sternly, 'That suit is a bit revealing, young lad. The sooner you get changed the better. So off you go.'

And with that John started his SCAT and shot off.

It was breakfast time, and Juliette was busy getting Petal and Fred ready to go to the chow house. Pauline was in the lounge trying to get Brian up, but he didn't feel like it. 'I'll have something later,' he told her and tried to go back to sleep.

'Oh no you don't,' she told him sternly, and pulling the sheet from under him, tossed him onto the floor.

Scratching his head, he sat, looked up at her, and laughed. 'Persistent little bitch, aren't you?'

She grabbed his pillow and started to hit him around the head. 'What did you call me?' she , shouted.

He caught hold of her and pulled her back onto the bed.

Petal entered the lounge just as he gave her a kiss, and shouted, 'Yuck. Get a room, will you!'

Brian slipped down behind Pauline. He didn't have a stitch of clothing on, and he was really embarrassed. He didn't say a word. He just pulled the sheet over himself and reached for his clothes.

'Thanks Petal, I couldn't get him up,' Pauline said, smiling at her.

Brian quickly got dressed and ran upstairs to Fred's room. 'Can I use your cleansing cubicle please?' he asked him.

'Sure help yourself,' Fred replied, wondering why Brian had such a strange look on his face.

Petal took Pauline upstairs to get ready, just as Juliette went down. 'Don't be long, you lot!' Juliette said, sounding cheerful.

As she walked towards the front door, it unexpectedly opened. She stopped dead in her tracks, let out a loud scream, and fell to the floor on her knees.

Petal, hearing the scream, ran downstairs as quickly as she could, and also stopped dead. There was John helping Juliette to her feet. Petal rushed forward and put her arms around them both, squeezing tightly. Juliette wasn't saying a word; she couldn't, John was kissing her. Petal felt Juliette's body trembling, and let go of them.

A few seconds later, John was holding Juliette even tighter; she had passed out and was limp in his arms.

Fred was standing at the bottom of the stairs and couldn't believe his eyes. 'John, you're not dead?'

'Who said I was?' he asked. 'No one told me I was dead.'

Brian came down to see what was going on, and seeing John with Juliette in his arms, rushed over to offer some assistance. 'Here put her on the sofa. I'll check her over,' Brian told John, then added, 'We were told you were dead.'

By now Pauline was with them and she was crying—not with anguish, but with joy. She ran over to John, and gave him a huge hug. 'We thought you were dead,' she told him through her sobs.

'So everyone is telling me,' he said, looking a bit bemused at their reaction to seeing him.

By now, Juliette was coming to, and Brian said, 'She's fine. It was just the shock of seeing you, that's all.'

John sat next to her, leaned over, and whispered in her ear, 'How could I die and leave such a beautiful girl behind. Eh!' Then he kissed her cheek.

Juliette smiled back and whispered in his ear, 'I knew you weren't dead. You couldn't be. I'm pregnant. We're going to have a baby boy.'

John was shocked and sat straight up. 'How?' he shouted.

Juliette's face dropped for a moment, then she burst out laughing.

John was running and dancing around the room, shouting into everyone's face, 'I'm going to be a father! I'm going to be a father!' He was kissing everyone, even Brian, who looked a little shocked.

John ran back to Juliette, lifted her up, and said, 'I'm starving. How about a celebration breakfast? Come on everyone, let's go.'

He rushed out, jumped on Juliette's SCAT, and looked back. He saw Petal standing next to him. 'Don't just stand there, jump on mine with Fred. You can have a go if you want.'

Petal didn't need to be told twice. The look on her face told him she wanted to. John ordered his SCAT to let her drive to the chow house. Looking at Juliette, he said, 'Come on, I can't get this thing going. You'll have to drive.

Smiling, she pulled his arms around her, and said, 'To the MATCH please.' And off it shot at a snail's pace.

Brian quickly caught up, and gave a wave as he passed. Pauline was hugging him. She winked at Juliette and blew John a kiss.

John thought it odd that everyone thought he was dead, and was determined to find out why. As far as he was concerned, they'd only lost communication. If engineering had carried out routine checks on the construction unit's engineering transmission, they would have seen the unit was still moving. After all, the engineering link hadn't been broken; it could transmit up to a distance of ten thousand kilometres through the tube. He felt anger building up inside him for a moment, then remembered he was to be a dad, and calmed down. He knew if Juliette felt the same way he did at that moment, she would be really excited too.

When they arrived at the chow house, Brian, Pauline, Petal, and Fred were waiting for them at their table. As they approached, everyone clapped, even others who were there joined in. John looked bemused and a little embarrassed by it and quickly sat down.

Soon after the clapping subsided, they were ordering food and chatting away like mad.

Juliette looked at John and said, 'I was so excited when I saw you walk though the door. I had a tingle in my belly and my knees went weak. Then, when you kissed me, I passed out, and I've had goose bumps all over ever since.'

John looked at her face, and sure enough, there they were. She was covered in goosebumps, and he couldn't help smiling into her eyes.

Otho went over to see what was so special about Sam. When he tapped her on the shoulder to attract her attention, she quickly responded. Before he knew what was happening, he was lying flat on his back on the floor.

Sam looked at him and, with a laugh, asked, 'What do you want little boy?'

Otho got to his feet, held his back, which was aching like mad, and said, 'I only wanted to know what you were doing.'

'Oh! Why didn't you say that instead of touching me? Only one person is allowed to touch me, and he doesn't know it yet,' she said with a wicked smile.

'Who's that?' he enquired politely.

'Never you mind! Now leave me alone; I'm really busy. When I see Chief Markham, I'm going to complain. I told her I wasn't to be disturbed.'

'Chief Markham told me to chat with you. She's my mum,' he said coyly.

'Well, run along little boy. I don't want you in my face ever again. Got it?' she said, sounding nasty.

Otho climbed back on his mother's SCAT and moved off. Behind him he could hear her laughing at his reaction, and he was fuming. 'I'll get her for that,' he said, thumping the palm of his hand with his fist.

Rajinda crossed to see how Sam was progressing. He walked up to her and asked quietly, 'How are you getting on?'

She looked at him and smiled. 'I've almost finished. Give me another twenty minutes and I'll explain what I've done. You'll like it, I'm sure,' she said confidently.

Rajinda nodded. 'Do you need anything?' he asked her just as quietly.

Sam looked like she was in deep thought for a moment, then replied, 'Yes there is. I'd like an apology from Chief Markham for sending that idiot of a son over to chat me up. If you don't mind.'

Rajinda just looked at her; he was really shocked. 'You can ask her for that. I won't do it.'

'Fine, tell her to get over here now,' she demanded.

'Don't push your luck, young lady. Chief Markham is the boss here at this research centre and it won't be wise to get on her bad side.'

'Ah! I didn't know she was that high. OK, I'll reconsider how I get my apology from her. Now let me get on with this,' she said, and turned her back on him.

Rajinda walked away, shaking his head, and spoke to Rose. 'That Sam is going to be a nightmare for someone. I wouldn't like to be her partner when she goes for one. I doubt anyone will have her.'

Rose looked at him, astonished by his remark, and said, 'Feisty is she?'

'A right cow, I'd say,' he told her bluntly.

After a further thirty minutes, Rajinda went back to see Sam. She was sitting with her feet up on her desk playing a computer game. Looking a little surprised, he asked, 'Finished?'

'Ten minutes ago. Where were you?' she said without looking at him.

'I'll get Rose and you can explain exactly what you've done, OK?'

Sam just shrugged her shoulder and carried on playing. Rajinda was fuming inside as he walked away.

Soon he was back with Rose and they pulled chairs close to Sam and sat waiting for her to speak. Sam turned off her monitor and started to explain what she'd been doing all night.

'I've created a three-dimensional presentation using all the data provided by the probe and the construction unit. It will show what has happened, how it happened, and what there is now. It's not a pretty picture and I expect many people will be greatly affected by what they will see. I intend to use the main dome to project the presentation on as large a scale as possible. So everyone must be inside the dome to see it. I suggest they all sit on one side to get the best view. It will look as if we will all be watching a film with distant and close-up images.'

She paused for a moment for them to take it in, and as they said nothing, she carried on. 'To many it will be a horror film and some will be traumatised by it. I suggest medical and security staff be issued with sedative injectors to prevent some people causing widespread hysteria. The security staff should be spread out to ensure any problem is dealt with quickly.

'The whole event has been sped up, but will still last for just over one hour.'

She turned to Rose and said, 'I want to give you a private showing first to give you time to prepare a speech. Everyone will need to know how we stand and what the future has in store from now on.'

She stopped speaking and there was complete silence. Eventually Rose said, 'We'll stop for breakfast before I view your interpretation of events.'

'It's not my interpretation; it's fact,' Sam replied sharply, annoyed by her remark.

Rose called all the engineers over and selected two to remain in engineering. The rest she sent for breakfast.

'We'll have the presentation at eleven, if that's OK,' she said to Sam and Rajinda.

They nodded in agreement and Rajinda left.

Sam walked up to Rose and said, 'I'd like you to keep that idiot son of yours out of my face from now on.'

Rose was speechless and just stood still as Sam walked briskly away.

'Rajinda was right, she really is a cow!' she said to herself, and called Otho to pick her up.

John was just finishing his breakfast when Rose entered the chow house with Otho and Anne. He was just about to have a word with her when there was a general broadcast. He stopped to listen and looked at Juliette, who had brushed up against him.

'There will be a presentation in the main dome at eleven hundred hours this morning. The meeting point will be against the main dome wall situated between the engineering dome entrance and the arrivals dome entrance.

'Everyone at the Himalayan Research Centre is ordered to attend. There will be no exceptions. Security will scan the entire centre to ensure compliance. Failure to comply will result in immediate arrest, and offenders will be dealt with severely.

'All personnel are advised to bring something to sit on; a blanket, cushion, or chair will suffice. The presentation will take approximately one hour and thirty minutes. There will also be time set aside to answer any questions arising from the presentation.

'Further advice can be obtained via your personal companions. That is all.'

Rose was now standing next to John and as soon as the broadcast finished, she said, 'We are finally going to find out what has happened out there.' Then she quickly went inside for breakfast.

Otho stayed back and, catching hold of Petal's hand, pulled her around a corner and out of sight. 'If you hear that I've been seen with another girl, it isn't true. My mum is trying to pair me off with a girl in engineering and I don't like her.'

Petal looked oddly at him and asked, 'Why would she do that?'

'She doesn't think you are good enough for me,' he told her bluntly.

Petal's eye's filled with tears as he said it and she turned her head away from him. He quickly turned it back and kissed her gently. She didn't resist, but when he pulled back, she said, 'Do you think she'll come round?'

'She'd better. I don't want to be with anyone else. I love you,' he said, and sounded like he meant every word.

Petal threw her arms around his neck and kissed him passionately. 'I love you too,' she replied when she'd finished.

Rose had been standing just behind Otho, and had heard and seen everything. She made her presence known by clearing her throat. Both of them jumped at the sound. Otho spun around, and looked startled at the sight of his mother just standing there.

After what seemed like hours, she spoke.

'Promise me one thing, young lady. Don't interfere with his studies and I'll allow him to see you.'

Petal looked at her, and still slightly shocked, could only manage a nod, followed by a strangled, high-pitched, 'Yes ma'am.'

Otho looked at her and asked, 'What's the catch?'

'There is no catch. If I can't keep you two apart, I want to be able to keep an eye on you. That's all.' Then she turned and left them alone.

Otho took Petal in his arms and swung her round and around.

When he put her down, she felt quite dizzy and giggled with delight. She caught hold of his hand and led him back to the table where everyone was now seated once again. They were too busy discussing what was going to happen later, and didn't notice her and Otho arrive.

'Hi everyone,' she shouted, and waited for them all to look at her before continuing. 'Otho and I are a couple. His mum has agreed to let us see each other.' And smiling, she turned to hug him.

'Not so fast young lady,' John said sternly, and instantly wiped the smile off her face. 'I haven't given you permission to see him, have I?'

Juliette looked down at the floor and said quietly, 'No, you haven't.'

A few moments passed before Juliette gave him a dig in the ribs. He looked at her and saw the expression on her face.

He walked around the table, took hold of Otho's hand, and said, 'If you harm her in any way, I'll be after you, OK?' Then looking at Petal, who was now smiling, he said, 'Remember what you said to Juliette. I expect you to live up to that.'

Petal went bright red, and glared at Juliette. Juliette was also red in the face, and averted her eyes.

'You really don't have any secrets between you, do you?' Petal said, sounding annoyed.

John looked at her and calmly said, 'Secrets cause problems. But don't worry. I won't repeat what she said.'

'You'd better not,' Petal retorted quickly.

After breakfast everyone went to John's apartment to wait for the presentation, and it was ten o'clock before John reminded them to get ready to go to the main dome. 'Come on everyone, and don't forget to take something to sit on.'

Juliette appeared with a large blanket. 'This should do for us four,' she said, giving it a pat.

Brian and Pauline each had cushions under their arms. 'Thanks for letting us borrow these,' Pauline said to Juliette.

'That's OK. Now let's go,' she said, and walked towards the door.

Not long after, they were all mounted on the SCAT's and ready to go. 'Drive carefully,' John told Petal, who was using his machine again.

She looked across at him and said, 'Race you there.' And she opened up the throttle.

What happened next left her slightly sore and everyone laughing. When she applied full throttle she wasn't holding on tightly, and as the machine shot off, it left her stationary and she tumbled to the floor. Luckily for Fred though, he landed on top of her and wasn't in the slightest bit harmed.

John dismounted and went to see if she was hurt. 'How are you?'

'I'm a bit sore, but nothing serious. That lump caused the most pain,' she said, sounding a little embarrassed.

'Hey! Watch who you're calling a lump,' Fred shouted back.

The SCAT had returned and was waiting to go once again, and Petal mounted it cautiously. Fred, on the other hand, refused to sit behind her.

John spoke to the SCAT. 'Drive in novice mode, and not at high speed.'

Only when he said that did Fred climb up behind Petal and hold on to her tightly. Petal looked around at him and shouted, 'Hey! Watch where you're putting your hands.' She pushed them down a bit.

As they entered the main dome, they were greeted by a multitude of people streaming across the grassy plane by any means possible. Every spitter was in use, as were some of the mobile corrals. The odd SCAT could be seen now and again, flitting about like a fly, and John wondered who was on it. As he approached the designated area, his communicator chirped, indicating an incoming call. He looked to see who it was and answered straight away.

'Hi Rose. How's it going?' he said, sounding like he hadn't a care in the world.

'Fine. We've marked out sections for people to sit in. It will keep everyone in groups of around a hundred. Security and medical staff have been allotted to each section as a precaution. You are in my section. It's section sixty-two, somewhere in the middle. If you can't find it, home in on my communicator. I'll send you my signature to use if required.'

'Why the security and medical staff?' he asked, sounding a little concerned.

'This presentation will cause a lot of distress to some people, and I want to avoid mass hysteria if possible,' she told him. And judging by the wobble in her voice, he knew it wasn't going to be good news.

As they got closer to the mass of people, it suddenly struck home what John had been missing—the masses. This was the first time since arriving he had seen so many people together at once, and it made him feel totally at ease. He could even sense Juliette relaxing at the sight of them. He quickly flew over their heads, looking for section sixty-two, and noticed the lineup of SCATs before seeing the number. He lined his up alongside the others and waited for Brian and Petal to arrive. When they did, they also lined up, and everyone dismounted. He walked over to where Rose was standing. She was busy giving instructions to security and other staff, and he asked, 'Can I be of any assistance?'

Rose looked at him and smiled. 'Yes, you can. I will have to leave Otho and Anne alone for awhile. Can you look after them for me, please? I have to address everybody before the presentation starts.'

John couldn't refuse and replied, 'I don't think that will be a problem. Where are they?'

Rose pointed to a group of engineers. 'They're with them at the moment.'

John settled everyone down on an open patch of grass and set off to find them. When he returned, he watched as Otho crept up behind Petal and gave her hair a gentle tug.

'Fred, I'll ki—' was all she managed to say before realising it was Otho. She smiled and patted the ground next to her. He sat down quickly and put his arm around her.

John smiled and sat next to Juliette. He looked at the time. 'Only ten minutes to go,' he said loudly enough for everyone to hear. Looking around, he noticed Rose had gone and couldn't help thinking about the task she now had to perform. He knew it wasn't going to be a pleasant experience; his trip to Jumla Junction told him that.

The minutes slipped slowly by. He didn't at first notice the lights start to dim; it was Juliette who noticed and said, 'It's starting.'

Within thirty seconds there was complete silence, not a murmur, not even a cough. The dome lights had dimmed so much, it was almost complete darkness. John heard a giggle come from where Petal sat. Otho, who was the closest, got a slap on his head.

'Enough of that,' John said.

Otho quickly moved further away, taking Petal with him. He didn't want another one of those off John.

Slowly an image started to appear towards the top and far side of the dome. As it became clearer, they recognised it as a massive 3-D projection of earth with the moon in the distance.

There was a murmur from the crowd; even Juliette whispered, 'That's beautiful.'

The next thing that happened took them all be surprise. Rose walked out from behind the planet and started to speak.

'People of the Himalayan Research Centre, what you are about to see is a computer-generated sequence of images depicting what has happened on the outside. It will start with what caused the problem, followed by what happened during, and finally what is going on now. After it has finished, I will be making a speech outlining certain points and talking about the future. Please remain calm throughout this presentation. It is not for the fainthearted. Staff are available to help you with any problem if you need them.'

And with that Rose faded into the night sky.

There was complete silence from everyone and everything. The earth looked perfect and the moon really bright. With the images floating high and set against the blackened dome walls, the audience felt as if they were floating in space.

From one side, an object could be seen getting closer, growing in size as it approached. Eventually it was recognised as an almost perfectly round asteroid.

John looked around quickly, and noticed everyone was watching it with their mouths wide open.

Just as he looked back, he saw the asteroid collide with the moon. And with it came the noise of just over five thousand people gasping in disbelief. It was just a glancing blow, but it caused the whole surface to shudder, throwing dust high above the moon's surface and making it look blurred.

The object was large—almost a quarter the size of the moon—and as it hit, a part of it smashed into small pieces. That coupled with a large amount of debris gouged out of the moon's surface was now seen heading towards earth. The large asteroid continued on its way, passing close to earth's surface. It passed so close to the surface, everyone could see it pulling at the atmosphere and distorting the land and sea under it.

The presentation then froze and an oral description of what was happening to earth followed.

'The asteroid hit the moon, shattering a large part into small fragments. It gouged even more fragments off the moon's surface, which added to the debris you can see heading towards earth. The asteroid passed earth, missing us by twenty-five thousand kilometres and causing massive destruction to the surface under its path. It also caused massive disruption to our atmosphere and destroyed the ozone layer. If the asteroid had not hit the moon, earth would have been totally annihilated. You will now see a computer-generated image depicting what probably happened next.'

The audio stopped and the whole dome was plunged into silence. Shortly after, the image started moving once again, and everyone looked up at it in shock.

John put both arms around Juliette and hugged her tightly. He could feel her shaking, and realised she was frightened by what they were all watching. He kissed her on her cheek but didn't say a word.

As they watched, showers of meteors started hitting the dark side of earth. Occasionally there was a glow as something exploded or erupted; they weren't sure what it was. The image sped up, and as the planet rotated, they began to see the extent of destruction. The surface was totally obscured by a layer of brown cloud so dense nothing else could be seen. The meteor shower persisted for two whole days before it petered out, after which the surface was no longer blue; it was now completely brown and devoid of any recognisable feature.

At this point the presentation froze once again, and the audio description continued.

'During the meteor storm almost all the cities on earth were destroyed. Any that survived, suffered great damage and cannot be expected to last long. The storms on the surface were so powerful that parts of the destroyed cities were thrown around like confetti. The amount of debris flying through the atmosphere caused just as much damage as the meteor storm. The storms threw so much debris about, the whole planet looked like it had been sandblasted and the terrain was totally transformed. The next images will show the extent of the damage. These images were sent back by the space probe and the tube construction unit. One image will be of our research centre, which is no longer

under the Himalayan Mountains. That range of mountains barely exists now. The images are quite disturbing and will shock many of you.

'We believe that showing you everything is for the best. It will dispel any rumours that may have unjustly given people hope.

'If anyone needs medical assistance, please see members of the medical or security staff for help.'

As the image started to move, the cloud covering the planet slowly disappeared. Now the surface could be clearly seen, and it was all the same colour, dirty brown. As earth revolved, the image started to zoom in on specific areas. It showed a landscape scarred with craters and holes from horizon to horizon. It passed over the Himalayan Research Centre and the domes could be clearly seen, white against the dirty brown surrounding them. It passed over Jumla Junction and stopped while another image was shown, one that John had seen for himself. It was the top of the city sticking out of the slime at an odd angle.

The image froze once again as an audio description broke the silence.

'The image you see was taken not far from here. Just over one hundred kilometres away the tube construction unit came across this object. For you who have never seen this sight before, it is the top of a city tower. All cities towers are similar to this one, but the markings you see are unique to each one. This city tower was originally sited above the city of Indore, in the Indian region of Eurasia. The force required to move such a heavy and large object so far provides us with some idea of the ferocity encountered at the height the storm. It also explains why there is so much devastation where meteors did not strike. The journey to Jumla Junction proves we are cut off from the outside; it no longer exists, as can be seen in the next image.'

The oration stopped, and John once again looked around. He could see many faces, all glistening with tears and all looking up at the image of where Jumla Junction should have been. He felt Juliette's fingers digging into his arm, and gently kissed her neck. Then he looked at Petal. Otho was holding her the same way he was holding Juliette, and he was glad she had someone with her. Fred was sitting next to him and was leaning heavily against his side. John took one arm from around Juliette and put it around him.

Fred looked up and John saw the frightened look in his eyes. 'Don't worry, we're safe here,' he said, just loudly enough for everyone within a few metres to hear what he'd said. John looked over to where Brian and Pauline were sitting. He noticed a member of the security staff speaking to them, after which Brian got to his feet and followed the man towards the temporary medical centre near the dome wall. Pauline stood up and looked around before spotting John looking at her. She walked quickly over to where he was sitting and sat down next to him and Juliette.

Juliette held out her hand. Pauline took it and squeezed it tightly, indicating she was in shock. Juliette managed a thin smile before looking back at the projected image.

John listened to the crowd; they weren't quiet anymore. There was a lot of murmuring and an occasional shout or scream pierced the darkness. He thought it sounded really eerie, and shivered.

The image started to move once again, only this time there was audio to accompany it.

'The next images will show what else the space probe found on its journey around the planet. You can see as we zoom out, there are a number of bright spots showing. There are six in all, and these represent cities that survived the meteor storm bombardment. They are totally isolated, and suffering as a result. All the cities were transmitting. Four were reporting widespread unrest and asking for assistance. The majority of their population were rioting due to a lack of food. The two remaining cities reported they have enough food to last for three more days, and are also requesting help. Sadly, there is no way we can offer help. Conditions beyond this centre are too hostile, and to venture out would be bordering on suicidal. Any help offered wouldn't get to those cities for many months, by which time it will be too late.'

John could see a city as the image zoomed back in, and wondered where it was. His thought was answered quickly but not completely.

'This is one of those cities. As you can see, it looks completely intact, but there is no way in and no way out. The atmosphere all over the globe is unbreathable and toxic. We can only assure you that no one here is from this city.'

There was a pause while the image moved on, and John was shocked how much noise the crowd was now making. It seemed the whole audience was crying, and now and again a scream cut through the air like a knife.

Fred managed a quiet few words that made Juliette start crying quietly in John's arms. He said, 'Bagman City's been destroyed hasn't it?'

John had to think fast, and made up a quick reply. 'It was destroyed by a massive meteor. Nobody would have suffered; it would have been over with instantly.'

Juliette turned and looked at him. 'You knew, and didn't say anything?' she said, angrily.

'I was ordered not to tell anyone anything. Even you,' he quickly replied, knowing at least that last bit was true.

The image continued moving, this time further north, and the oration started once more.

'As you can see from the images, the far north suffered the least from direct meteor strikes. But the cities still didn't escape the meteors' destructive power. The meteors just tore through city towers, exposing their populations to the storms now raging on the surface and filling them with the toxic atmosphere.'

The image stopped over the Canadian region of the North Americas and zoomed in.

'On its first orbit, the probe detected a signal and hovered over it to investigate. The signal was weak and came from the Canadian Research Centre. They were sending a distress signal. It was picked up by the probe, and it answered. They indicated they have 4,300 survivors, and would be able to give precise details of their predicament on the next run. They hoped to have a more powerful transmitter running by then. They also asked if we can give them all the information we collect, as they have no probe, and want to cooperate as much as possible.'

At hearing this there was a lull in the crowd, and John heard someone just behind him sobbing. The sobbing didn't sound sad; it was happy. He turned to see who was there and could just make out the young girl he'd see working in engineering earlier. He didn't know her name, but could clearly see she was smiling.

'This is the message we received on the second orbit.'

The image changed, and the face of an elderly man appeared before them.

John spun round quickly when he heard, 'Dad, you're still alive?' followed by uncontrolled crying and laughter. It was from the young girl, and he felt for her. He could see a member of the medical team approach and place an injector against her arm. Seconds later, two security staff gently lifted her onto a stretcher and took her away.

Her outburst had created quite a stir and made a lot of people angry. The anger stemmed from jealousy, brought on by her knowing her family had survived.

John turned back to listen to what the man was saying.

'This is the Canadian Research Centre, and I am Grade 3 Chief Technologist Qan Ni. I, being the most senior person, have been designated as leader. To put everyone at ease, we are in the same predicament as you. We are totally self-sufficient and can survive. We have enough food to last two years, by which time we hope to have found a solution to that one problem. This research centre's primary task was to improve and develop technology to enhance everyone's lives. Your centre concentrated on increasing food production. Our hope is that our two centres can join together and rebuild this shattered planet of ours.

'You will by now know the atmosphere is unbreathable and toxic to all forms of life. We have analysed the data recorded by your probe and obtained some disturbing results. The air is toxic and will take many decades to recover sufficiently to enable us venture out without breathing apparatus. Even more disturbing is the damage done to the ionosphere. That will take much longer to reestablish itself. The level of radiation reaching earth's surface is deadly to us. Due to this, we estimate the surface will be uninhabitable to humans and animals for the next two hundred years.'

At this point the speaker stopped. It was predicted that the audience would react to this news, and plans had been made for it.

John looked around, and many people were running about wildly, screaming and crying out loud. Every time they came close to medical or security staff they were injected. They then dropped to the floor like stones and were quickly carted away. It took twenty minutes to calm the crowd enough for the presentation to continue, by which time, hundreds of watchers had been sedated.

Brian returned and sat next to Pauline. 'I don't think I'm not required at the medical centre. We'll go to the hospital later,' he said quietly in Pauline's ear.

Pauline looked at him and with a smile on her face said, 'Looks like you are stuck with me forever now.'

John looked back at the image, and the oration started once more.

'There are just over ten thousand known survivors at our two centres, and this is enough to start over again. We can rebuild the cities and we will repopulate them. But we must take care how we do it. New guidelines on how people should live their lives will be drawn up and discussed when appropriate. At this moment in time, life goes on as normal for us.'

There was a pause, and this time when John listened, there was complete silence. He wondered how many had been sedated; it was so quiet. He looked around at everyone close by, and noticed Otho kissing Petal. He smiled, and wondered if they would be allowed to partner some time in the future. Things were going to be very different from now on.

The image of the man faded, and was replaced by Rose, who once again walked out from behind the planet. She stood still for a moment, and it looked as if she was looking at them all. Her eyes moved from one side to the other.

'As you have just heard, plans are being drawn up to replace our current way of life. These will not be to everyone's taste, but given time, they will be accepted. Your input will be of use in drafting the first changes we will be making.

'As for the future, we are not sure what lies ahead for us. The only thing we can be sure of is we will survive no matter what.

'Our first project is to establish a communication link to Canada. This will be done by bouncing radio signals off the surface of the moon. So the communication will not be continuous.

'Our second project is more complex and will take a lot longer to complete. We will be repairing the tube construction unit. It is hoped we can rebuild the intercontinental tube and link up with the Canadian Research Centre. That project is being planned at the moment and we hope to be starting the journey soon.'

Juliette turned and looked at John. She looked very frightened and said, 'They won't need you will they?'

'I shouldn't think so. The tube construction unit only needs engineers to operate it,' he said, trying to reassure her.

'We have a chance to make a better world for future generations. As for now, all that we knew has gone forever and we have to start over.

'Tomorrow will be known as "The Beginning" and this year has been re-designated "Year One". All facts relating to our previous life will be retained in the archive section forever and access made available to all.

'Any questions will be answered on receipt by one of my staff. Please go through your supervisors when requesting information, and any question that cannot be answered will have an explanation why. Please keep up-to-date with the current situation by accessing the information channel. This can be accessed via your personal communicators or any information console. There will be broadcasts when major changes or events occur.

'The next few months will be difficult for many of you, and help is at hand if needed. I hope we can establish a sound society quickly so that we can move forward and flourish. Thank you for your patience. I wish you all the best for the future.'

With the last remark, the image faded quickly, and slowly the dome lights came back up to full brightness. John stood up and looked around. There were many stunned faces, all with red eyes and tears streaming down their cheeks. He looked down at Juliette and pulled her to her feet. Fred stood up and caught hold of his sister's hand. Looking around, John saw Petal staring at him and flicked his head, indicating for her to come. She came and hit him hard as she ploughed into his side. She started to cry instantly, and he stroked her hair in sympathy. There was nothing else he could do.

John called everyone he knew to come closer. When they were all close enough to hear him talk, he spoke, 'It looks like everything has been destroyed out there. This is going to be our home from now on. We will be moving to a city here at the centre very soon and it will be our home for the rest of our lives. It's completely safe and won't be affected by what's happening on the outside. There is enough room for everyone who has survived and even room to expand the population.'

The last bit he said while looking straight at Juliette, and as he spoke, the look on her face changed.

'There's a city here?' she asked, irate that John knew about it and she didn't.

'No one is supposed to know about it yet so don't tell anyone else. It's still under wraps until Rose gives her approval for us to move in. I can't say any more about it right now,' he replied, a little worried that he'd already said too much.

'Tell me all about it later, OK,' Juliette said and hugged him tight.

Brian got to his feet and helped Pauline up off the floor. Looking over at Juliette, then back, he whispered slowly in Pauline's ear, 'Do you want a boy or a girl? Now will be a good time to start a family.'

Pauline smiled and replied, 'I'd like a child, but not right now and I'm not sure what sex I want. Let nature decide for us.'

Brian smiled, nodded in agreement, and as they made their way over to his SCAT, he looked back to see who else was leaving. He saw the devastated look on everyone's faces and decided to drive off immediately, heading straight for the hospital complex. There was enough work to keep him and Pauline very busy for the next few days.

John moved everyone towards the SCATs parked nearby and made sure they were properly mounted. He gave orders for them to be taken home in a group, as Petal was in no state to drive. He watched everyone dispersing and wondered how they had all taken it. If they felt like he did, they weren't going to be much use for the next few days. The shock of it all would take time to wear off, and for some the realisation of what happened hadn't yet struck home. It was going to affect everyone in different ways, and he hoped life would get back to normal (whatever normal was going to be) as quickly as possible.

There was complete silence. Juliette was sitting just in front of him as they rode quietly and slowly along.

He put his hand on her belly and whispered in her ear, 'Here's to the next generation. Our precious little responsibility.' And he kissed her neck.

'This is the first of many. We've a population to build,' she whispered back and held his hand firmly in place.

He could see the smile on her face reflected in the wing mirror he'd adjusted, and smiling back, he replied, 'I love you.'

She snuggled in even closer and quietly replied, 'I love you too.'

IN THE BEGINNING

THE END